# TOURMALINE

# TOURMALINE

## JON HENDERSON

Tyndale House Publishers, Inc.
Wheaton, Illinois

**Library of Congress Cataloging-in-Publication Data**

Henderson, Jon, date
    Tourmaline / Jon Henderson.
        p.   cm.
    ISBN 0-8423-7287-3
    I. Title.
  PS3558.E487T6      1992
813′ .54—dc20                                    92-13255

Printed in the United States of America
99   98   97   96   95   94   93   92
9     8    7    6    5    4    3    2    1

# PART I

# I

She had taken too long to get ready. Hurrying across the lobby, late for the tour, she was startled by a burst of laughter. She glanced over her shoulder through the cool shade of the foyer into the deeper gloom of the bar. Four figures were seated at a table.

Just as she was about to turn away, one of the men leaned forward. This brought his head into a dust-filled shaft of sunshine that angled down from a skylight in the smoke-blackened ceiling. She stopped, transfixed, her attention arrested by a man she had never seen before. She watched as he held court in the bar.

Even sprawled as he was in a broken-down rattan chair, he was in command of the party at the table, talking and laughing. He appeared to be in his early forties. His smile revealed white teeth in a rugged, browned face. One large, strong-fingered hand toyed idly with his glass. He said something more, then arched his eyebrows and thrust his head forward, the way men do when they're trying to con other men into believing something. After an instant's silence, the others burst into laughter, and he leaned back with a self-satisfied nod. He turned and held up four fingers to the bartender who waited impassively behind them.

"Annie, we're leaving! Are you coming or not?" Lee Parker had to shout to make herself heard over the insistent honking of the tour bus.

From the hotel doorway, Anne acknowledged the summons with a wave. She looked back once more toward the hotel bar then pulled her sunglasses down from their perch on her widow's peak and stepped out into the withering heat of midsummer Egypt.

Anne ignored the tour guide's icy stare as she boarded the bus. She walked down the narrow aisle and slipped into her seat. Lee welcomed her with an exasperated huff. "Honestly, Anne!" Lee exclaimed, shutting the bus window beside her.

Anne stuffed her large canvas carryall into the netting fastened to the seat in front of her.

"Our one day in Cairo to see King Tut," Lee said, "and you almost get left behind!"

When she received no response, Lee looked over at her.

Lost in her own thoughts, Anne still didn't reply.

*Nothing new in that*, Lee reminded herself. *Annie's been hard of listening since the day she was born.*

"Well, was he cute?" This time, Lee's question startled Anne out of her reverie.

Anne looked at Lee. "Huh?"

"I was asking you," Lee replied with pretended sweetness, "if you found out whether or not he has a cute friend for me."

"Who are you talking about?" Anne replied to her friend's old joke more sharply than she had intended. *Did Lee see me looking at him?* "What friend?"

Lee held up her hands. "Never mind! I was just kidding! You know," she went on, "when you didn't show up I thought that, just maybe, you'd been carried off on camelback by a sultan or something."

"It was nothing that exciting," Anne replied tolerantly. "I was just running late."

"As usual," Lee replied. She closed her eyes and smiled. "Imagine being kidnapped by a sultan! Living in his harem, eating dates . . . Now that's my idea of a dream date!"

Realizing that Lee hadn't seen anything, Anne relaxed and shook her head. "You are a hopeless romantic, as boy-crazy as a teenager."

"That's better," Lee retorted, "than being an old-maid schoolteacher like you."

"Old maid?" Anne retorted in feigned indignation. "I'm only twenty-five! You're older than I am!"

"I'm only six months older, and that's not the point."

Anne patted the top of Lee's head. "You're right," she said sweetly. "This is."

Lee laughed and shook her head. Anne settled back in her seat, her mind still filled with a pair of eyes and a smile.

Jake MacIntyre looked up, smiled, and then stood abruptly. "Boys, if I'm lucky I won't be right back." Those who could follow his gaze did so. Looking at one another, Jake's companions shook their heads as he arose and strode toward the lobby.

No effort was made to hide their amusement when he returned just a moment later.

"You're losin' it, Mac," someone said. "Whatsa matter? She bigger'n you are?"

Jake dropped into his chair and waited for silence. "Gentlemen," he began, "I have seen her."

Everyone groaned—they'd heard this before.

"Legs to here, boys, eyes to die for, and a headful of hair with the sheen of polished mahogany. Cool, tanned, and slender she was, with limbs as brown and supple as Moroccan cordovan."

*He's really on a roll this time,* Alex Stratton thought as he listened to his best friend and longtime partner. *Must've been some bird.*

"Seeing her in distress," Jake continued, "I instantly made my way over to her to offer her succor."

Eyes rolled as they grabbed their drinks and settled in.

Jake continued for some time, proclaiming the virtues of his latest potential conquest and his undoubted chances of success. "But when I arrived," he concluded, "she was gone—vanished in a swirl of white."

"Thank you, Casanova, for that update." Mort Steinmetz, Mideast bureau chief for Global Photo Syndicate, brought the proceedings back to earth. "Now can we get back to work?" Despite his five kids, eight grandkids, and thirty years of marriage to his lovely Rose, Mort still remembered the days when he'd had the same swagger.

Steinmetz laid out the details of the assignment that had lured them to Egypt. The secretary of state had arrived from Washington to act as the American observer of the signing of a new Pan-Arab treaty. *Time* had hired Global Photo to take pictures.

"Alex, you're gonna be down front, doing the close-up work," Mort explained. "Jake, I want you to take the long-range stuff. Do the crowd shots, and try out that new L-series 600mm AFD telephoto that Canon sent along."

The fourth man at the table, a photo editor for *Time*, opened his briefcase, pulling out layout sheets for the next week's edition. He began explaining the slant the magazine wanted to place on the article.

"We're playing up the U.S. involvement in organizing the treaty, so give me a tight three-quarters or full face of the secretary for the cover." The man checked his notes. "The article's laid out for eighteen columns in block-protect, with sidebars, so I'm going to need six to eight usable shots."

Jake nodded, asked a couple of questions about the kinds of photos they wanted, and then ordered another round. *Routine*, he thought with a mental sigh. It sometimes bothered Jake that after ten years as a photojournalist for GPS, and having taken some of the world's most-remembered photographs, no one knew who he was. He had never married. His parents had died in an auto accident while he was still in school. He had lost touch with his other relatives. In his darker moments it seemed to him that his life had shrunk to the six-point type size of the tiny "Photo by J. C. MacIntyre" credit that accompanied each of his photos.

Later that afternoon, Jake and Alex went to scout the site of the ceremony. Alex had learned from Jake years before that often the worst position for a photographer was the closest. The principle applied here: front-and-center would place Alex right in front of the dais. He'd be close to the treaty signing, but he'd have to work around the podium to get a clear picture. Instead, he found a spot at the far right. From there he could use a medium zoom to bridge the distance. He also knew that protocol would place the secretary of state on the left facing right; Alex would get photos that would play well to the audience back in the States.

After Alex had established his modus operandi, Jake searched for a spot for his shots. He didn't want an angle that would duplicate Alex's, so he searched the opposite side of the square for a rooftop. As always, this took time—it was important for Jake not only to find a good angle but a unique angle, his now-familiar signature.

Jake spotted a two-story building far to the left. The rear of the building fronted nicely on the square where the ceremony was to take place. He walked around to the storefront—it was a small rug shop—and, with the universal language of used tens and twenties, bribed the merchant into allowing him access to the building's rooftop.

Jake whistled contentedly as he walked out. The hard part of his job was already done.

After dinner that night three Israeli students sauntered into the bar.

"You are American?" one of them asked Jake.

Jake nodded.

"Do you know," they asked, "if this place carries King David beer?" Most of the hotels in Cairo that catered to foreigners served alcohol, and one of the more interesting fallouts of the Sadat-Begin accord was that the national brew of Israel had become immensely popular in Egypt.

"Sure does, men," Jake replied. "Have a seat." Catching the bartender's eye, Jake held up four fingers as the young men arranged themselves around the table.

"We are archeology students," one of them told Jake, "from Tel Aviv University, on loan for the summer to the Egyptian Department of Antiquities. We've been given a weekend's leave from the dig above Aswân, and we are very thirsty."

"First round's on me, boys." Jake grinned and pulled a pack of cards from his shirt pocket. "You guys ever heard of poker?"

The man across from Jake, who'd introduced himself as Nathan, snorted. "We play poker all the time in the dormitory. We're quite good."

A wary look crossed Jake's face. The three Israelis looked at one another and leaned closer. "Well," Jake said, "since there's three of you and only one of me, maybe you'll let me deal the first hand. . . . "

The next morning, just at sunrise, loudspeakers calling the faithful to prayer brayed into life. Jake stifled a curse and buried his head under his pillow. His fourth-floor room was level with the top of the minaret from which the call to prayer blared, and the harsh syllables seemed to bore into his aching head like a drill. The ancient summons died away, and Jake peered blearily from under the pillow. *You gotta cut this out, man*, Jake thought. *You're not twenty-five anymore.*

Despite the fact that he'd had a good breakfast and several cups of strong Ethiopian coffee, Jake's head still throbbed as he pushed past the nervous rug seller and trudged up the stairs to the roof of the dilapidated building. He opened the rooftop door cautiously, fully expecting to be confronted by a security detail from the Egyptian army, and was somewhat surprised when no one was in sight. A huge pigeon coop dominated the center of the roof.

Jake carefully closed the door behind him. He walked across the roof to the left edge of the building, which over-looked the vast square where the ceremony was to be held. *That rug seller's gonna pay big time for not telling me about this*, Jake thought as he knelt down in the thick layer of guano that covered the roof of the shop. Trying to ignore the pervading odor from the coop, Jake got to work unpacking his equipment.

An old, dented delivery van pulled up in front of the rug shop. The driver jumped out. He quickly but carefully looked around, then hurried to the back of the van and opened the doors. Two more men, their clothes as ragged and unkempt as the driver's, clambered out and pulled a rolled-up Persian carpet from the van. With the driver in the lead, the two men wrestled the carpet up to the door of the shop. The driver knocked on the door as passersby, forced to detour around the carpet, shouted curses at the three.

"Delivery! Open up!" The driver's Arabic was coarse and guttural. The rug shop door opened, and a sliver of a fat, sweating face peered out.

"Go away!" the face shouted through the crack in the door. "We're closed today!"

The driver planted his booted foot on the door and shoved, sending the fat man sprawling onto a pile of rugs. He stepped aside and allowed the two men carrying the rug to rush into the shop. The driver walked inside behind them and casually closed the door. The rug merchant, his face mottled with rage, hauled himself to his feet and faced the driver, who was the leader of the three. "Are your ears filled with dung?" the merchant shouted. "Do you not understand plain speech? I said that we're closed today! Now, in the name of Allah, get out!"

The merchant's blustering died the instant Hassan, the leader, motioned. One of the other men pulled a sawed-off shotgun from underneath his jacket and leveled it at him. "Quiet," Hassan said to the merchant, who was now ashen with fear. Hassan nodded to the third man, who knelt and unrolled the carpet. The rug seller's eyes grew wide as he saw a long, wicked-looking rifle that had been hidden in the rug.

"Be quick, Ali," Hassan said. The small man nodded. He assembled the rifle, attaching the steadying bipod and the powerful telescopic sight. Ali slammed home the magazine and stood, holding the rifle, the martyr-light shining in his eyes.

Hassan jerked his head, and Ali trotted up the stairs at the back of the shop that led to the roof. He turned to the other man. "Stay here. If this fat pig so much as belches, shoot him." The third terrorist acknowledged his commander's orders and glared at the merchant, who nodded mutely, the rolls of flesh beneath his chin quivering with the intensity of his terror.

Hassan ran up the stairs after his sharpshooter.

Crouched behind the camera, Jake watched as the group of emirs, sultans, and sheikhs paraded past the table. As each signed the leather-bound document, the dignitaries arrayed behind the procession applauded politely. Jake's practiced eye swept the viewfinder, watching everything, clicking off shots when the combination of action and composition suited him.

Jake noticed the crossed arms and identical scowls of the Libyan delegation. *That's a keeper,* he thought with satisfaction as he fired and wound. *Nobody likes the Libyans. . . .*

Concentrating on the ceremony, Jake didn't hear the stairwell door open. Ali kept low as he scooted straight across the roof to the other side of the pigeon coop. Hassan followed close behind, the coop blocking Jake from their sight.

The Egyptian minister in charge of the ceremony was the last to sign. Jake got his picture, the last he needed. *All right,* Jake thought as he relaxed, *that oughta keep them happy.*

Jake caught the glint of sunlight on metal out of the corner of his eye. He looked sharply to his right. What appeared to be the snout of another telephoto lens was sticking over the balustrade on the other side of the coop. Enraged, Jake vowed to thrash whoever had the nerve to sneak onto his turf.

Jake turned, then stopped short. He realized he was looking at the barrel of a rifle pointed toward the ceremony below. *Great. Just great,* he thought. *Now the cops show up. Probably a SWAT team. Here I am, definitely not where I'm supposed to be, and there's nothing but feathers between me and Dirty Harry over there.*

Carefully Jake picked up his camera and crept toward the staircase. As he rounded the back of the coop, Jake peeked around the corner. He froze. Instead of the uniforms and helmets he expected to see, Jake found himself looking at two men. At the sight of their black-and-red head coverings, Jake froze. It was the trademark of Shams Ahmar, a radical group of which little was known but its viciousness.

Jake swore silently. He instinctively reached for the small, lightweight camera that he wore on a short strap around his neck. Made in Germany by Leica, it was silent and virtually indestructible, and he always carried it with him on assignment.

Jake leaned around the back of the coop and braced himself against its edge. Pointing his camera toward Ali, who was steadying himself and aiming, Jake took one picture, wound, then refocused. Just then, Ali squeezed off three shots in quick succession. Jake snapped a second picture.

At the roar of the rifle, all the pigeons in the coop burst into frenzied flight. Jake was instantly enveloped in a cloud of feathers. The sound of frantic wings filled the air. Birds slammed against the bars beside his head. Startled and unbalanced by this new threat, Jake fell forward onto his knees, landing behind the terrorists.

Jake tensed for battle, then slowly realized that the frenzy of the birds had masked the sound of his fall. He still had a chance to sneak away. Jake inched backward, trying to regain his cover.

Ali peered through his telescopic sight for a moment, to ensure that he had done his job properly. *"Allah Ahkbar!"* he exclaimed to his commander. Hassan clapped Ali on the shoulder. They exulted in the sudden chaos that they had created below, feeling the rush of power in their veins.

Then both men swung around to leave.

Three pairs of eyes locked. The two assassins found themselves face to face with Jake.

For a frozen instant they stared at each other. Hassan's mouth became ugly as it twisted into a curse; Ali pointed the rifle at Jake.

Jake jumped, grabbed the barrel of the rifle, and pulled. His quickness threw Ali off balance, but the assassin swung the rifle around, and the buttstock slammed hard into the pit of Jake's stomach.

Jake doubled over. Ali backed off and began to aim. Breathless and desperate, Jake grabbed his first camera, the one with the heavy Canon lens, and heaved it at the assassins. It caught Hassan in the chest as he struggled to get his pistol out of the waistband of his pants, knocking him into his sharpshooter, spoiling Ali's aim.

Jake dove frantically to his right as a burst from the assault rifle blew open the staircase door.

He landed hard on his shoulder and swore as pain tore through him. Jake forced himself to roll toward the edge of the building and came to his feet beside the parapet that ringed the second floor. He saw the screaming Ali disentangle himself and hurl the camera over the side of the building. *Canon's not gonna be real happy about that*, Jake thought as he grabbed the edge of the parapet.

As a longtime veteran of more than a few rooftop escapes from outraged bosses and former gambling buddies, Jake swung himself over the edge with practiced ease and hung on with his fingertips. He winced as he put weight on his strained shoulder. Just as he got below the edge of the building, bullets slammed into the other side of the parapet. Jake dropped, landed easily, and rolled into the building's shadow.

*Three seconds until you're dog food, Mac*, Jake told himself as he looked for a hiding place. He had too far to run and nowhere to hide. Convinced that he was a dead man, Jake was almost ready to make a break for the nearer end of the alley when he spotted a recessed door: a side entrance into the rug shop. Jake threw himself into the doorway. He pressed flat against the rotting wood and hoped that he couldn't be seen by the pair above. As he tried to catch his breath, Jake heard angry voices raised in Arabic, then the thud of boots racing across the roof.

Jake sneaked a look upward to make sure they weren't waiting in ambush, then tore off down the alley.

Hassan and Ali thundered down the wooden stairs. The grin on the guard's face vanished the instant he saw his commander's expression. "This pig set us up!" Hassan screamed. "He sold us out!" The Palestinian's face purpled as his rage fed upon itself. "He's a traitor and the lackey of a CIA spy!"

"Effendi, please!" Hands raised, the terrified shopkeeper backed away.

Hassan's fury exploded as he pistol-whipped the rug merchant. *"The spy took our pictures!"* the commander shrieked at the rug seller. "Your partner has our faces, dung-eater, so I shall have yours!" Hassan grabbed the shotgun from the guard, aimed carefully at the gibbering merchant, and fired.

"We split up," Hassan said to the other two as he stepped over the dying man. "Meet at the safe house as planned." One by one, they slipped out, quickly adjusting their stride to the rhythm of the street, and disappeared unnoticed into the crowd.

The rug merchant died slowly, badly, and very much alone.

# 2

"Special for you, missy, only twenty dollah!" From behind the small table the jeweler grinned at the young woman. He figured her accurately for yet another of the rich Americans who parted so easily from their money, especially in the open-air markets surrounding the Pyramids. "Pure gold, missy, handmade, very best stuff!" He continued the litany, lifting his voice above a siren screaming several blocks away. He wondered if twenty was too much when he saw her reach for a carryall instead of a purse.

Anne looked at the earrings, noting with pleasure the detail on the small scarab beetles and the quality of the enameling. She smiled and nodded at the jeweler, then opened her carryall and rummaged about for her wallet. She absentmindedly took out the camera that her father had lent her and set it down on the tabletop without noticing that she had done so.

The jeweler relaxed when he saw the camera. He recognized the German brand name—Leica—and instantly realized that anyone so young who carried such an expensive camera would pay his price without question.

Just as Anne found her wallet, Lee pushed her way

through the welter of hawkers, all clamoring for her money. "Find something?" she asked.

Anne held out the earrings.

"Cute!" Lee exclaimed, holding them up in the sunlight. "How much?"

"Can you believe he's only asking twenty dollars for them?"

Anne opened her wallet, but Lee put her hand on her friend's arm. "Put the wallet away!" she hissed.

"But why? They're cute and I want them!" Anne insisted.

"How many times do I have to tell you never to pay their asking price? Now put them down, shake your head, and start to walk away!"

Annoyed, Anne did as she was told.

The instant Anne's back was turned, the jeweler signaled to a small boy who lounged indolently nearby. The jeweler nodded toward the table where Anne had left the Leica. At once the boy scuttled through the crowd. He grabbed the camera and darted away, keeping his eyes on the two women the whole time. The entire process took no more than two seconds, and the jeweler was very proud of his son for having learned so well. If the infidel woman noticed that her camera was missing, the jeweler would signal again, and his son would run up announcing proudly how he had rescued the camera from a thief. Usually the reward was very great. If not, then his brother-in-law knew many effendi who would buy such a fine camera for a handsome sum. *Surely Allah smiles on me today*, he thought contentedly. *May as well let the foolish woman have her trinkets.*

"Missy, wait!" he called.

Lee smiled. "See, I told you!" she said. "Now when we get back, let me do the talking."

The jeweler's head bobbed, and he smiled deferentially as they walked toward him. "Fifteen dollah, missy!"

"For this trash?" Lee seemed outraged, and it startled Anne. "Two dollars!"

"But missy, best work, top quality! Ten dollah!" *I don't like the look in this one's eye*, the jeweler thought, taken aback by the ferocity of Lee's bargaining. *Allah be praised that it's not her camera we stole.*

"Five dollars!" Lee snapped.

A hardness crept into the merchant's voice. "Eight!"

"Seven, and not a penny more!" Lee put her hands on her hips and glared at the man.

"Seven it is, missy," he agreed. He now very much wished her gone.

Anne paid the man. Happy, she and Lee walked away.

As he watched them leave, the jeweler wondered idly what it would be like to tame one like that. Then, content that the sale of the camera would garner him a month's earnings, he started looking for his next customer.

Stunned by what he had seen, Jake ducked into a doorway to collect both his breath and his wits. He heard the wail of sirens heading toward the ceremony site. Since he hadn't seen what had actually happened, he quickly generated several scenarios, all of them bad. He hoped Alex and the others were OK. *Hope they got it all on film.*

Jake remembered there was a police station a block over and immediately headed for it.

Halfway there, the honed instincts of a professional photojournalist kicked in. Jake paused. He palmed the camera that still hung around his neck, instinctively knowing that somehow, once again, he had gotten the unique angle on the news that day. Something big had happened. A regional story had just become an international event. That meant that the photos were worth a fortune to Global, and hence to himself. *The bigger the news, the more we can sell these for,* he thought. *An hour or two won't make any difference. We'll make sure that they're processed right.* Jake turned and began walking toward Global's Cairo office.

As soon as the last of the three assassins arrived at the safe house, Hassan picked up the walkie-talkie that lay on the table beneath the outlawed Shams Ahmar flag on the wall. The radio was small and of low wattage, with just enough power to reach several others like it nearby. It was almost impossible to intercept. After receiving the message, those in the next link of the chain would switch their radio to a different frequency and rebroadcast the transmission. This form of network was one of the many useful things the commander's extensive training at terrorist camps in Libya had taught him.

The word went out: Look for a camera-carrying infidel.

Hassan's precise, thoroughly detailed description isolated Jake from the hundreds of other camera-carrying infidels who each day walked the narrow streets of Cairo. Faces went to windows; eyes swept streets. Before the broadcast of the message was finished, the phone in the safe house rang. A location and direction were whispered; the phone went dead. Another terse message was sent; men began to converge.

In response to a gentle rub against his ankle, Hassan reached down and swept an Abyssinian kitten into his arms. "Too bad you are not a tiger, Salome," he said to the tiny, green-eyed face that he held in front of his own. "If you were, I could send you out to rend to pieces the infidel who has marred an otherwise glorious day." The kitten butted her head against the commander's chin. Hassan scratched Salome's ears until she purred contentedly. "It is just as well," Hassan told the kitten. "This way, I can deal with the interloper in my own fashion." Salome curled up in the crook of the commander's arm and went to sleep.

Anne and Lee headed back to the bus. They were to reunite with the tour group at the parking lot, then walk on with their tour guide to the Pyramids. On their way back, they were joined by a honeymooning couple from New Zealand who asked them to take their picture. Anne and Lee were more than happy to oblige, stopping in front of a two-story office building labeled with the letters GPS on a sign in front. The Pyramids rose majestically in the background. Lee snapped the picture.

"Weren't they sweet?" Anne said as the couple strolled off.

"And so happy," Lee added. "See, it's not so bad."

"I never said it was. Don't worry, I'll get married soon enough."

"No, you won't, teach," Lee replied, "if every time someone writes you a love letter you send it back with 'try harder' written across the top."

Anne made a face. "I only did that once, and only because he wouldn't stop pestering me. . . . Besides, he misspelled the word *infatuated.*"

Jack approached the huge parking lost on the outskirts of Cairo where tour buses parked. More than a few first-time visitors to Egypt were dismayed to find out that the Pyramids were not out in the trackless desert, but were actually no more than a thousand yards from the tenements of southwestern Cairo.

The Cairo branch of GPS was two blocks from the Pyramids, and Jake picked up his pace as the building that housed the office came into view. It had taken Jake much longer than he had intended to work his way out of the excited crowds that had thronged to the site of the shooting, and he was starting to worry about the prospect of being scooped.

Jake's hand again went to the Leica and the pictures it contained. *If someone else gets these on the wire first . . .*

Suddenly rough hands grabbed Jake from behind. They

clawed at the camera and jerked it away from his chest. A cruel-bladed knife flashed and began to saw at the Leica's strap. Jake swung a haymaking left. He hit the man just above the ear and sent him sprawling. Other hands reached for the camera. Jake took to his heels, racing for the parking lot in an attempt to lose his pursuers in the maze of buses. After a few quick turns, Jake found himself between the back of one bus and the front of another.

He crouched down, then leaned around the front of the bus against which he was propped and took a quick, careful look. With a sharp *whee*, a bullet caromed off the bumper of the bus, inches from Jake's head. Jake slid under the bus in front of him.

As he lay there, Jake saw a pair of boots, then another, race by. He now knew that if whoever was after him caught him with the camera, or even the film, he'd be killed without hesitation. Jake stared at the Leica. Too big to stick in a pocket. Jake looked to his left and saw that there were no more rows of buses between him and the crowds at the Pyramids.

*Well*, he decided, *if they're going to look for someone with a camera, let's give them lots of choices.*

He peeked out from under the bus. No sign of his assailants. Jake crawled from under the bus and quickly joined the crowd of tourists. To make himself less conspicuous, Jake took the Leica from around his neck. He wrapped the strap around his hand as he wove through the press of people, keeping his head down.

"Will you hurry up?" Lee shouted down at Anne from her precarious perch atop one of the grunting, verminous camels that lined the road leading up to the Pyramids. "I can't stay up here all day!"

"Got it!" Anne called back after she had taken the picture.

"Now let's switch, and you use my camera to take my picture." Anne left her bag by the side of the road. She walked toward the camel as the driver helped Lee down from the beast.

Jake was making his way to the far side of the Pyramids, where he hoped to slip unnoticed into the back streets of the city. He came abreast of two attractive young women, one being helped down from a camel. Just then, the heel of a hand flashed out of the crowd. It caught him just under the nose. Stunned, he felt the camera snatched from his loosened grip. Jake dove. He hit the thief in the back and sent him sprawling. The man staggered forward, tripping over a carryall resting on the road's edge.

Anne turned at the sound of the commotion behind her. She saw a man carrying something stumble across her bag and dart away. Anne screamed, *"My camera!"* and took off after him.

The thief had run only a half a block when a foot reached out and neatly tripped him. Anne stopped as the owner of the foot kicked the man in the ribs, then bent over and picked up the camera.

Jake shouldered his way to the edge of the excited crowd. The man who had retrieved the camera meticulously dusted the Leica on his kaftan and handed it to the woman. Jake stopped short, recognizing her as the woman he had seen at the hotel earlier. He watched helplessly as the man gave the Leica to her.

"I don't know how to begin to thank you, Mr. Bhargazi."

The short man stroked his mustache and flashed a smile at the two women. "No need to, Miss Dryden. All part of a tour guide's services. Part of the package price!"

"But the thief got away!" Lee exclaimed, still shaking with rage.

Mr. Bhargazi shrugged. "In Cairo, Miss Parker, cutpurses and pickpockets swarm like flies. Even if he had been caught. . . . " The tour guide smiled again. "Be grateful that we got Miss Dryden's camera back. Allah must be smiling upon you today."

Anne looked at the guide. "God, Mr. Bhargazi, not Allah, smiles down upon me."

"God it is then, missy. As you wish. Now, let's see about getting your picture taken." Bhargazi bustled off toward the camel driver.

"Miss Dryden," Lee commented in an official-sounding voice, "have you ever stopped to think about just how many legions of angels God must have to devote exclusively to the task of keeping you out of trouble?" She arched her eyebrows at Anne. "You lead a blessed life, indeed, my friend."

Anne bit her lip, looked at Lee, and nodded.

Jake started toward them, then restrained himself. *What're you gonna do*, he thought, *snatch it from her hands? There are more than a few men around here who'd love nothing better than to come to the rescue of a pretty girl being mugged. She gets the camera back, and you get beaten to a pulp and thrown in jail.* Jake shook his head. *Try again, Mac. . . . Wait until she gets back to the hotel. Maybe she'll take a closer look and see it's not hers.*

Jake backed away and melted into the mass of tourists.

From the other side of the dispersing crowd, an enraged Hassan watched, taking careful note of the infidel girl who now had the camera upon which his life depended. Cursing, he vowed vengeance on both the bungling operative and the fat tour guide who had tripped him up.

# 3

Cathy Hagura yawned and stretched her arms over her head. At thirty-one Cathy was the youngest senior agent the State Department's security division had ever had, a distinction earned in part by the seriousness with which she took her responsibilities. She knew that being D.O.—the duty officer—for the night shift was not the most demanding of posts, as most of the charges the division was assigned to protect were safely tucked away in their beds. She also knew that this assignment was a portion of the dues she had to pay on what she hoped was the fast track to the top. Consequently, she did this job as well as she did everything else.

Cathy yawned again, finished a cold cup of decaf, and peered at the digital clock on her desk. Built by her teenage, computer-nerd brother, it was ugly but kept better time than anything else in the office. Five fifty-two. Dawn was breaking over Washington, D.C.

*The division's "roadrunners" will be heading out about now,* she reflected idly. Each of the agents would be trying to hide how easily he or she kept pace with the cadre of older, less-fit ambassadorial joggers as they puffed their way around the Mall.

Jim Roberts, the day D.O., waved as he hung up his overcoat and headed toward the coffee stand. He grinned in anticipation as he reached for a paper cup. The quality of the office coffee had improved considerably since they had all started chipping in and buying their beans from a mail-order place in Seattle. Now, however, the topic of debate was just how strong the brew should be.

Cathy glanced at a picture in a brass frame. She smiled and reached for the phone. Her boyfriend, Greg, was hardly an early riser, and Cathy took fiendish delight in occasionally dragging him out of bed for breakfast at a place near Foggy Bottom, where the State Department buildings were located.

Cathy was five digits into Greg's number when the secure overseas teletype began clattering. "Hey, Jim," Cathy called, "what time is it in Cairo?"

Roberts checked his watch. "Noon," he replied. "The summit should be wrapping up just about now. Maybe that's our fearless leader."

Cathy hung up the phone and headed across the room, making a mental note to tell Greg how a machine had granted him a five-minute reprieve. She was halfway to the teletype when the red priority light over the machine began blinking. Cathy hurried. The message was complete by the time she got there. In a single motion she rolled the paper up and tore it off.

She read the terse communiqué. As she raced back to her desk, Cathy beckoned to Roberts, then reached for the red phone that was always at the duty officer's right hand.

Six thousand miles away, an exhausted Jake MacIntyre stumbled into a phone booth.

He wondered how it was that the woman—Miss Dryden, she'd been called—figured it was her camera, unless she somehow owned an identical Leica. *Well, could be*, Jake thought, *especially in an area saturated with tourists. Here everyone carries a camera.*

Jake dialed the number of the Cairo office of Global Photo. A high-pitched busy signal was his reward. Jake hung up and dialed again.

Busy. Still staggered from the blow to his face, Jake shook his head to clear it, then instantly wished he hadn't. He blinked to focus his eyes, then dialed Mort Steinmetz's private line.

"Steinmetz." Jake's boss answered the phone with his customary abruptness.

"Mort—"

"Jake, is that you? You sound terrible."

"I feel terrible. Look, Mort—"

"What in the world is going on?"

"I was hoping you'd tell me. Mort, for some reason people are out to get me."

"No kiddin'! Does that surprise you?"

"Huh? What do you—never mind. I need help."

"You better believe you do! Where are you? I'll come get you."

"In the snack bar by the Pyramids."

Jake had hardly hung up and found a table when Steinmetz burst through the doors of the snack bar. Jake painfully lifted his head and looked at his employer.

"Cripes, Jake," Steinmetz exclaimed.

"You're a mess! What happened?"

"Mort, you gotta get me outta here."

"You got that right. C'mon, let's get you to my house."

Steinmetz threaded his ancient, battered Citroën through the packed streets. A few minutes into the drive Mort looked at his star photographer. "So why did you do it?"

Jake looked back at his boss in defiance. "It's no big deal. I've done it dozens of times before."

Steinmetz was incredulous. "No big deal? You can sit there and call the murder of three diplomats no big deal?"

Jake did a long take, slowly swung his head toward Mort, then braced himself against the dashboard. "Murder?"

Mort looked over at Jake quizzically. "You haven't a clue, do you?" Mort pulled over quickly, sliding the car into a rare parking place, and hailed a street vendor. He threw the special edition of the *Cairo Times* in Jake's lap. The front page carried Jake's picture and the headline shrieked: "American Hunted in Summit Slaughter."

Steinmetz said, "This murder, my friend."

As Mort Steinmetz pulled away from the curb with Jake staring in disbelief at the headline, the street vendor glanced down at the stack of newspapers he was carrying, then looked again at the man sitting in the passenger seat of the Citroën driving away. He memorized the number on the Citroën's license plate, then ran into a brass merchant's shop. Without asking for permission, he picked up the merchant's phone and made a call.

Jake scanned the article in disbelief.

> **CAIRO—The atmosphere of goodwill and understanding that had enveloped the long-awaited Pan-Arab Conference was shattered today by a triple assassination that has left the conference in ruins and the diplomatic community shocked and saddened. Dead are Robert Moncrief, 68, the American secretary of state; Yousef Sharaz, 62, the Egyptian minister of foreign affairs; and Benyamin Shomron, 64, the Israeli foreign minister.**
>
> **Three shots rang out just as the signing ceremony, held outdoors in the courtyard of the For-**

tress of Babylon, was coming to a close. All three men were killed instantly by the shots that, in the words of an Egyptian Army captain, "were fired by a master sharpshooter." Sharaz was the host of the conference, while Moncrief and Shomron were in attendance as observers.

Sought in the slayings is Jeremiah C. "Jake" MacIntyre, an American photojournalist. Witnesses have placed MacIntyre on the rooftop from which the fatal shots were fired. Authorities report that while MacIntyre is still at large, he is not believed to have fled the Cairo area. Cairo police announced that they have recovered "irrefutable" evidence linking MacIntyre to the crime, but declined to specify the nature of the evidence.

Egyptian president Hoseni denounced the killings as "infamy of the blackest sort," and announced a national day of mourning for the slain diplomats. Hoseni also promised "the fullest cooperation" between the Egyptian authorities and the American and Israeli security agencies.

Still staring at the newsprint, Jake whispered, "I had nothing to do with this."

"I believe you," Steinmetz offered, "but. . ."

"But what?"

"But I'm about the only one around here who will."

Ed Mahoney regarded the faces turned toward him. A thirty-year State Department veteran, he had survived the debacle surrounding the assassination of Ambassador Cleo Noel in Khartoum and had risen to the command of consular operations, which was responsible for the protection of American diplomatic personnel overseas. *Great, just great,* Mahoney thought. *I'm supposed to retire next month, and this happens.*

All morning the telexes had poured in, augmented by satellite coverage from CNN. Cathy Hagura and Jim Roberts had sat in on a video conference between Mahoney and Lydia Doral, the American ambassador to Egypt. Doral reiterated the Egyptian president's commitment to cooperation in the investigation. Shaken and pale, her blouse stained with Robert Moncrief's blood, she told her longtime friend, "Ed, get someone over here now. This thing's liable to blow up at any minute."

Cathy and Jim looked expectantly at their boss. To them Mahoney was both friend and mentor: He freely imparted his experience and allowed them a certain amount of impatience with what seemed to them to be his conservative, old-fashioned ways. This was the first major incident of their careers, and the two quivered like racehorses. Mahoney looked back at them. He sensed their eagerness and decided to let them quiver a moment longer before he spoke. One of these two would take over for him when he retired. He hadn't yet decided which, and this could very well be the incident that would make up his mind.

"Hagura, you spent time in the Mideast, right?"

"Some," Cathy replied. "With the marines."

"OK, then it's your case. Jim will back you up from here." Cathy sensed Jim stiffen and avoided looking at him. She and Roberts were both great friends and fierce competitors, and she had a feeling that she was going to need his help with this one. Mahoney turned to Roberts. "Jim, call Allison Kirstoff and see what she can dig up for us about MacIntyre."

A British Air ticket folder landed on the table in front of Cathy. *Ninety minutes to get home, pack, and make the flight out of Dulles.*

Mahoney met her at the elevator. "Bob Moncrief was the best man at my wedding; I'm the godfather of his kids." Cathy looked up at the man who towered over her. She watched as his jaw muscles twitched with grief and rage. "Whatever it takes, nail MacIntyre. Hard."

Cathy nodded as the elevator doors closed between them.

*This day sure rolled over and died in a hurry,* Roberts thought with disgust as he reached for the phone. *First Moncrief gets snuffed, then I lose out to Cathy, and now I have to deal with the Lair.*

"The Lair" was the popular name for the office of Allison Kirstoff, the security division's resident analyst. Even to those accustomed to dealing with mysteries, Allison was something of an enigma. Since she was lean, tanned, and beautiful, it was inevitable that lunch and dinner invitations from the male members of the division had been offered from the moment she was hired.

Not for long, however. The uncompromising, withering disinterest with which she had spurned those advances had left her coworkers blinking and shaking their heads. That started the legend of the Lair. Since then it had been elevated by the men, out of pure self-consolation, into the great office joke.

Now, whenever a male agent was promoted to the division, within a few days one of the old-timers would point out Allison. If he was feeling particularly vicious, he would intimate to the newcomer that she had asked about him. The office would bristle with amusement as they watched the hapless young man groom and preen and then stride confidently into the Lair.

As always, a pool would have formed. For fifty cents you got to guess how long it would be, in minutes and seconds, before the victim slunk back to his desk, wrinkled and sweating, two holes bored into his ego by the twin lasers of Allison's sapphire eyes. Jim Roberts had been one such victim. He was unaccustomed to defeat, and the memory still burned.

"Allison, it's Jim Roberts," he said when Kirstoff had answered her phone.

"Expected to be hearing from you," she replied. "Looks like you're going to be kinda busy down there for a while. What can I do for you?"

Roberts grimaced at the too-familiar disdain in her voice. "We need a dossier on a Jake—"

"MacIntyre," Kirstoff finished. "Figured you would, so I pulled it up. It's coming out on the printer attached to your DN10000 now." Roberts looked over to the corner of the office. Paper was sliding silently out of the printer attached to the computer that sat there.

"Thanks, Allison," Roberts said. He took a deep breath. A faint heart never. . . . "How about dinner tonight?"

"Can't," Kirstoff told him. "I'm living with someone. Have been for some time."

"Y-y-you are?" Roberts stammered in confusion. "I didn't know. . . . Who?"

"Myself," Kirstoff replied sweetly. "And I couldn't go on doing that if I went out with you, now could I? 'Bye."

The line went dead. Roberts threw down the phone, grabbed the dossier, and stalked out of the office.

# 4

From his position to the side of the podium, Alex Stratton had had an excellent view of the assassinations. Despite his horror, the professional in him took over, and he snapped pictures furiously until he was out of film. Later he would wonder if that was the right thing to do.

It took two hours for Alex to make it through the crowd and the police cordons. He was searched twice, interrogated once. He showed his press card and his hotel confirmation slip and was finally let through.

Stratton strode into the Global office and set the film canister down on Steinmetz's desk. "We got it! It's all in here, Boss," Alex said, the satisfaction at having done a good job overriding his shock at what he had seen take place. "Is Jake back yet?"

Mort looked up and said, "He's at my place."

"Why is he there?"

Mort silently handed Alex the telex that he had been reading when Alex came in.

Alex stared at the telex in disbelief. "Jake? What? Aw,

c'mon!" He looked at Mort in confusion. "This only happened a few hours ago! How could they possibly be accusing Jake?"

Steinmetz looked up at the younger man. "The police have a bunch of witnesses, mostly guys doing long-range work like Jake was supposed to be doing. They saw Jake up on the roof that the shots were fired from." Mort scrubbed his face with his hands, wishing that the day had never happened. "How long were you and Jake together this morning?"

Alex hesitated, thinking, and then shook his head. "We didn't even leave the hotel together. Jake left before me. He said something about a special vantage point. You know Jake and his crazy angles."

"Yeah, the ones that always have the clearest shots." The phrase caused the two men to look at each other. Both saw it in the other's eyes: Jake MacIntyre? No way.

Immediately, both men had another thought. *Jake had seen something.*

The late afternoon light filtered cool and green through the shuttered windows of the room above Mort's house. It drifted across Jake's face and woke him up. Jake tensed, unsure of where he was. Then, without moving, he scanned the room through slitted eyes. He relaxed when he saw a table and chair familiar to him from previous stays. Jake propped himself up on one elbow and looked around. Seeing no one, he got up and shuffled over to the bathroom. Jake snapped on the light and surveyed his reflection in the mirror with distaste. His dusty face was streaked with dried sweat, his upper lip was caked with blood, and he needed a shave. Someone had set out soap, a razor, and a towel. The ancient plumbing groaned in protest when Jake twisted the faucet handle. Without waiting for the water to warm, Jake started lathering.

Alerted by the sound of running water, Mort came in just

as Jake finished shaving. Steinmetz pulled out the chair and sat down as Jake toweled himself dry. "So what's going on?"

"Mort, I honestly have no idea."

"Don't give me that. You were there!"

Jake combed his hair with his hands, then looked at his friend. "I'll tell you everything I know."

Jake sat on the edge of the bed. Still holding the towel, he told his boss everything that had happened since that morning. Steinmetz listened without expression until Jake finished.

"OK, let me see if I got this straight," Mort said. "You were somewhere you weren't supposed to be, and you got into a fight with two guys who weren't supposed to be there either. You say these guys are the assassins, and you have pictures to prove it, but you lost the pictures in another fight at the Pyramids. Now some tourist dame has them, only she doesn't know it."

"That's right," Jake replied quietly.

The older man gazed at Jake steadily. "Mac," he said quietly, "not even Hollywood would buy this yarn." Steinmetz became grim. "I've got only one question for you: Which country do you want to be executed in?"

Jake stiffened, then dropped his head into his hands. "I'm telling you the truth. I swear it. I've told you everything I know."

"I believe you," Mort replied, "but only because it's more impossible for me to believe that you'd do something like this than it is to believe your farfetched yarn. Now, let *me* tell you some things that *you* don't know." Steinmetz started holding up his fingers.

"Item one: You're being linked to every terrorist group in the Middle East, as well as the CIA."

"The *CIA?* Why would the CIA kill its own secretary of state?"

"Hey, a lot of people think they killed President Kennedy. Moncrief could simply be the means to an end. Besides that's not the point. The point is that the person they're pointing to is you. But it gets worse. Item two: Some Palestinian extremist factions are screaming bloody murder. They want to nuke Israel."

"They always say those things. And they don't have nuclear weapons."

"They don't," Mort said, "but a friend of theirs might."

"Saddam Hussein."

"He's called a press conference for this evening. I don't think it's to announce a food relief program."

"Right."

"Item three: The Israelis aren't making a sound. This scares me the most."

"They can deliver anything anywhere at any time."

"You got it."

"What I can't figure," Jake said, "is why everyone is pointing at me."

The afternoon light deepened as Mort responded. "That's item four. The really fun piece of news. When I read about that 'irrefutable,' unspecified piece of evidence the police had recovered, I called a friend over at police headquarters. Seems that they found, next to the body of a rug merchant with his face blown off, a high powered sniper's rifle. The rifle barrel had five, six good prints on it." Mort paused. "They're yours, Jake. My friend received the FBI report just before I called."

Jake paled as he remembered grabbing the rifle during the fight on the roof.

"The bullet that killed Moncrief is being tested by FBI ballistics experts," Mort told Jake. "They expect a match." Steinmetz waited until Jake's eyes met his. "And my friend had a message for you."

"For me?"

"Yeah. He said that, since you're a friend of mine, if you turn yourself in to him, he'll make sure you die quickly."

"Mort, I think you need some new friends—"

The sound of automatic gunfire and breaking glass downstairs brought both men to their feet. Mort beat Jake to the door and flung it open. The two men clattered down the rickety iron staircase and ran around to the front of the Steinmetz home. A large truck barrelled past, narrowly missing them. Jake caught a glimpse of the man in the back of the truck. He was holding a rifle, his face hidden by a black and red headcovering.

Gunpowder-scented smoke still hung in the air above the glass that littered the pavement. A spray-painted, coiled-snake-and-star design stenciled across the front of the house dripped crimson. Mort rushed through the blasted front door and into the living room. A line of bullet holes at eye level along the far wall neatly bisected a row of shattered pictures. In the corner a ruined television spat sparks.

Mort's anguished shout brought moans from the kitchen. Mort ran into the kitchen, nearly slipping on a pool of soup spilled from an overturned pot. Rose Steinmetz cowered in the far corner of the kitchen. Rachel, their oldest grandchild, was huddled in her lap.

"Thank God you're all right," Mort whispered as he gathered them up. He helped his wife and grandchild to a chair. "What happened?" Mort asked when his wife had calmed down. Rose took a deep breath. "I was getting dinner ready. Rachel was in the living room, watching cartoons. Just as I put the soup on Rachel came in and told me that there was a truck out front."

"A big truck, Grandpa!"

Steinmetz absently tousled his granddaughter's headful of black curls. Rose took a deep breath and pulled the child on her lap closer to her. "I was just about to go out and see who it was when it happened. Two men ran in. One of them stayed with us in here while the other searched all the rooms. They left, then the shooting started."

Mort stroked his wife's hair as she dissolved into a new spasm of crying. "I'm going to call the police," Mort said. "You OK?" Rose nodded without looking up.

Mort scooped up the soup pot, then stopped when something in it rattled. A large-caliber bullet lay in the bottom. He walked over and spotted a hole in the wall above the stove. When he set the pot on the stove and turned it so that the hole in its side pointed at the hole in the wall, it became apparent that the bullet had entered through the front window and had smashed through the kitchen wall with enough force to penetrate the pot and throw it from the stove. As he left the kitchen, Steinmetz started to shake.

On his way to the phone Mort thought about the symbol painted across the front of his home. In his line of work he thought he would have seen them all, but this one was new to him. Mort nodded encouragingly to Jake, who was carefully unplugging the television. At the sound of approaching sirens, Jake came abruptly to his feet.

"Jake, no!" Mort exclaimed.

"I can't stay here."

"We'll help you. Let's go to the embassy."

"The embassy? You've got to be kidding. Seems like the U.S. wants just as much a piece of me as Egypt and Israel. Gunfights would break out over who got to shoot me."

"Running away never helps."

"If I can get the film back, it will." Jake looked at his friend from across what had been a safe, warm place. "Sorry," Jake said, then ran out the door.

Steinmetz stared out the doorway as the sirens grew nearer. "God help you, Jake," he whispered.

Alex divided his time between processing his roll of film and explaining to the increasingly frantic photo editors at Global's headquarters that the sooner he got off the phone with them, the sooner they'd have the pictures.

"How about if I hold the film up to the phone," Alex told his counterpart at the Global Photo office in New York. "Then you yell a little louder, so the film dries faster." Alex examined the negatives, then nodded in satisfaction.

"Got one here of the U.S. ambassador cradling Moncrief's head in her arms. We'll put it out on the press wire as their page-one photo. Gotta go," Alex finished. "Wouldn't want to mess this up. Look for prints in twenty minutes."

After he had faxed the prints off to New York, Alex drove the short distance to Mort's house. Instead of getting to talk to Jake as he had planned, he spent the evening helping Steinmetz board up windows and sweep up glass.

# 5

Six hours east of where Cathy Hagura was boarding a 747, Anne Dryden sat staring out of her hotel window at the lights of Cairo. Still shaken by the incident at the Pyramids, she had passed up what the tour's itinerary touted as an "authentic Mideast feast, followed by an evening's shopping in the exotic, torchlit Khan el Khalili bazaar." *This just doesn't make sense*, Anne thought. *He was sitting in a bar, for heaven's sake, drinking beer and telling stories.*

As the only child of wealthy parents, pampered but not spoiled, she had been brought up in an environment where uncertainty was a rare and unwelcome intruder. Her parents had been raised in the social customs and traditions of Boston's Back Bay. While Pat and Joel Dryden had abandoned those customs whenever they came in conflict with their devotion to God or to each other, Anne herself had come to expect that she would fall in love and marry a doctor, attorney, or, at the very least, a fellow teacher.

Until now, Anne had remained aloof from the maelstrom of the opposite sex. Always immersed in studies or music or now in her teaching career, whatever awareness she had of men was vicarious at best. As Lee and Anne grew up together, Anne watched as Lee gaily plunged into the world of boys and dating. Anne had shared whispers and giggles and notes with her best friend. Later, Anne had held Lee as she cried herself to sleep after being used and deserted. Anne remembered how, over and over, Lee had sobbed, "He said he loved me, Annie. He said he loved me!"

Long, late talks with her mother in the safety of Anne's bedroom had helped to calm what adolescent turmoil and uncertainties there had been. Together they made their way through the Bible; Pat Dryden helping her daughter, just as her mother had helped her, uncover for herself what Scripture had to say about being a woman of God. After these talks, her mother had always bidden Anne good night with the same words: "Patience and faith, Love. Patience and faith."

Now that quiet certainty had been ambushed by a pair of eyes and a smile.

*You're being silly*, Anne told herself. *You don't even know his name or who he is, and you'll certainly never see him again.* Anne looked down and found that she had been toying unconsciously with one of the ribbons on the front of her nightgown. Exasperated with herself, she unwound the ribbon from her finger and threw her hands into her lap. *Get with it, woman*, she exhorted herself sternly. *Forget him. If you expect your first graders to calm down, then you'd better be able to do the same.*

As if to shut him out of her mind, Anne got up and closed the curtains with a tug. She went across the room to the chair by the light, where she picked up her Bible.

But as Anne began to read, Jake's laughter once more echoed in a corner of her mind.

By the time the 747 leveled out at 41,000 feet, Cathy was already engrossed in one of the two dossiers that lay on the tray table in front of her. Two agents—one FBI, one CIA—had been waiting for her by the gate at Dulles. Each had handed her a folder. The CIA dossier provided agency insight and speculation into the purpose and ramifications of the Pan-Arab Conference; the FBI folder contained all that was known about J. C. MacIntyre, which was mostly his army service record as well as the standard background information the Bureau had compiled when he had applied for a White House press pass.

Both agents had worn looks of disdain as they handed her the folders. Cathy grimaced as she remembered their annoyance that a small, Asian-American, female State Department employee had been assigned to a case of this importance. She was used to it, but that didn't make it any easier for her to shrug it off. Nonetheless she did so since it was, as she sternly reminded herself, her case.

In one of the folders was a photo of Jake on location in Australia. *Whee-ooh*, Cathy whistled to herself, *that's one good-looking man.* Cathy examined the photo more closely. *Well*, she thought with a mischievous smile, *at least if I get shot, it'll be a hunk who's doing the shooting. . . .*

The sound of a key in the lock of the hotel room door caused Anne to look up from her reading. Lee burst into the room, arms loaded with packages. She kicked the door shut with her foot. "You should've come along!" Lee said. She tossed the parcels onto her bed and began to tear them open and drag clothes out of them. "Lookit!"

Anne smiled, happy that her friend's insatiable passion for shopping had for the moment been appeased. She closed her Bible, unfolded her legs from beneath her nightgown, and shivered as her bare feet touched the tile floor. Anne padded over to where Lee was draping a brightly colored shirt over her chest. Across the room, the gauzy curtains stirred gently in the evening breeze.

"I'm glad I didn't go with you," Anne remarked as she surveyed the pile of clothes. "Doesn't look like there would have been anything left to buy." Anne viewed shopping as a necessary evil. The occasional phone call to Land's End, supplemented by an unending stream of Lee's castoffs, kept her in clothes. "How," she inquired, "are you planning to get all this stuff home?"

"Easy!" Lee exclaimed. She tore open another parcel, and a large lump of green canvas tumbled onto the bed.

"What is it?" Anne asked. "A skirt?"

"No, silly," Lee replied with a frown. She unrolled the lump. "See?" she asked proudly.

Anne peered at the green object. "It looks like a sleeping bag." She peered at Lee. "Why did you buy a sleeping bag?"

Lee huffed in exasperation and flipped her purchase over. "Don't you know a duffel when you see one?" She pointed to some stenciling. "Genuine U.S. Army surplus, and I got a great deal on it."

"And you expect to fill it with clothes?"

"Sure!"

"Well," Anne said firmly, "I'm not carrying it."

"Neither am I. I'll just give the porter a big smile. . . ."

A haunting smile flashed into Anne's mind. She closed her eyes and massaged her temples with her fingertips. *Go away!* Anne's brain screamed at the image. "Let's go to bed," Anne said suddenly.

Lee frowned. "You sure you're all right?"

"It's just a headache from too much sun today. A couple of aspirin and I'll be fine." Anne headed toward the bathroom.

Lee started to throw the duffel onto a chair, then stopped. Hanging from the back of the chair was the floppy sun hat Anne had worn all day. Lee picked up the hat and stood fingering it as she looked at the bathroom door. *Well,* Lee thought, *I guess she'll tell me when she's good and ready.* She hung the hat back up and started getting ready for bed.

Cathy finished the dossiers, then leaned back in her seat and stretched. *Doesn't make sense,* she thought as she took a sip of diet soft drink. *MacIntyre's record is spotless. The guy was an army ranger, and he's supposed to have done something like this?* Cathy frowned, and began rereading both folders.

It didn't make sense to Anne, either.

One of the things Lee had brought back from shopping was the evening edition of the *Cairo Times.* Seeing Jake's picture on the front page, Anne, with a sharp intake of breath, had grabbed the paper and read the article with growing disbelief. Now sleepless, she lay in bed, staring up at the ceiling in the middle of the night. It was inconceivable to her that the man who had sparked such a response within her could have done this.

Anne glanced idly at the window as the curtains billowed again, then, sensing someone in the room, sat bolt upright. A figure was crouched at the foot of her bed, rummaging through her carryall. Dark against the white plaster of the wall, the shape turned toward her and began to stand. Anne screamed.

Without realizing what she was doing, Anne grabbed the travel clock from the nightstand beside her and flung it at the intruder. It banged against the wall as the shape disappeared through the window with a clatter of roof tiles. Lee scrambled out of her bed and turned the light on. Footsteps pounded in the hall, and the doorknob began rattling. Lee put her arms around the shaking Anne as she started to cry.

Cathy tossed the folders onto the seat next to her and stowed the tray table. Wanting to make some notes while they were still fresh in her mind, she reached down and unzipped a compartment of the flight bag at her feet. The pocket into which she reached contained two items encased in leather: an organizer/notebook, which she pulled out, and her Browning Hi-Power.

Her hand brushed the pistol's smooth, hard case. She smiled as she remembered how the contemptuous grins had faded on those two agent's faces when she had breezed her way through the notoriously tough Dulles security with it by using an adroit combination of brusque authority and a winning smile. *Let 'em try that*, she thought.

Standing at her desk drawer, looking down at her weapons, she had contemplated which to take along. Like almost all discharged marines, Cathy had held onto her service-issue Colt .45. But, as a member of the elite consular operations detail, she had also been given a sleek, deadly Browning "brushed stainless" nine-millimeter Hi-Power. It had almost all of the striking power of the Colt, and its slimmer profile made it ideal for carrying in the small evening bags she had to use at the innumerable nighttime receptions that her charges so enjoyed attending. Cathy laughed to herself as she remembered one of the first rules taught to new female members of the consular detail: Memorize the dimensions of your weapon, as the ability to draw it quickly is the prime factor when selecting an evening clutch or handbag.

Since proficiency wasn't a consideration—Cathy was rated "Instructor" with both weapons—she chose the Browning primarily because it was smaller. Cathy also knew that the nine-millimeter ammunition would be more readily available where she was going. She stared at the top of the holster. Two clips. That gives me twenty-six rounds. Cathy closed the bag and leaned back, eager to get some sleep while she still could. *Dear God*, she thought as she closed her light-gray eyes, *please let that be twenty-six rounds too many.*

# 6

Hassan contemplated his operations officer over steepled fingers, drawing satisfaction from the uneasiness the man almost managed to hide. To demonstrate the depth of his displeasure, Hassan waited a moment longer before speaking.

"Well, Saiid," Hassan said calmly, "I can dismiss the incident at the Pyramids and the bungled attempt to recover the film from the woman's hotel room as *Insha Allah*—'the Will of God.' But the assault on the Israeli's house did not fail for that reason." If the commander had known that Mort Steinmetz was from Brooklyn and had never set foot in Israel, it would have made no difference. To Shams Ahmar, all Jews were Israelis.

Salome sat in the commander's lap and stretched out her paws languorously. She looked at Saiid. The young man shifted uncomfortably at the contempt with which the kitten's stare seemed to be filled. The Shams Ahmar commander stroked her idly. "Your analysis of the failed assault?" he asked Saiid.

Saiid Amash gathered every shred of his confidence, determined not to let his growing terror show. Three Amash brothers had died in the *intifadeh*—the Palestinian uprising— and his family's ancestral home had been first bricked up and then razed with a bulldozer. He was totally committed to the cause and ready to die for it. *Just not like this*, he thought as he returned his commander's stare. *In battle, in glorious battle. Not like this.* "Commander, the most recent operation failed due to faulty intelligence."

Hassan smiled. *It's the same everywhere*, he thought. *The Ops people in the field blame Intelligence and the Intel people blame Operations.*

"The residence specified as the objective in your orders was scouted," Saiid continued. "An approach plan was developed. The premises was entered and searched, but the targets specified in your orders were not found. At that point I declared the operation completed. The front of the building was subdued with machine-gun fire to neutralize potential pursuit, and we departed according to the specified procedure."

Hassan said nothing.

Saiid let his eyes slide over to the man who sat quietly in the corner of the room. Lithe and dark, he had eyes that stared coldly from beneath black hair. He never left the safe house, and he spoke a language that only Commander Hassan understood. This made Saiid nervous. The long, closed conferences between Hassan and the stranger made him nervous, too. Saiid saw the implacable finality in those black eyes and dropped his gaze.

"What about the back of the objective?" Hassan asked.

"No doors or windows."

"And the sides?"

"The same."

Hassan leaned back in his chair and folded his arms. "Who did the reconnaissance?"

"Bashat."

"And you, of course, verified it."

"No." Saiid paled as he saw his mistake.

The commander of Shams Ahmar leaned forward again. "Did Bashat report the presence of a staircase on the east side of the building?"

"No. . . . "

Hassan picked up Salome and stood, forcing Saiid to look up at him. "You are right, Saiid, the mission failed due to faulty intelligence. Yours!"

The young man flinched as the word was spat at him.

"You failed to verify the recon, and therefore you failed to search the second floor, and that is why you allowed our two primary targets to escape unscathed." The commander looked away for a moment as if thinking, then smiled at Saiid. "All this I can forgive," Hassan said expansively. "You are young, over-confident, and still learning. Now, outline for me your plan to recover the evidence."

Astounded at his good fortune, Saiid sweated profusely as he talked steadily for five minutes. At the end of Saiid's explanation, the commander glanced at the man in the corner. The man gave a barely perceptible nod. Hassan nodded in turn, then looked at Saiid. "Very good, Saiid. I see that you have learned from your errors and are back up to your usual standard." With grim satisfaction Hassan watched the young man wilt with relief, then snap to rigid attention when he said one more word: "Now. . . ."

Saiid began to tremble as Hassan went on. "What I cannot forgive is the inexcusable, unauthorized placement of our insignia on an operation—especially a failed one. An assault, led by our operations officer, which eliminated exactly seven photographs and a television set. All of which were, undoubtedly, archenemies of our cause."

Saiid closed his eyes as he remembered exulting in the roar of the gun, the crash of the glass as the bullets tore through it, and the screams from inside. At last he was able to exact vengeance—vengeance for his slain brothers, for the look in his mother's eyes when the hated Israelis leveled her home. Wild with joy and bloodlust he had taken the paint and emblazoned the front of one of their homes—now ruined just as his had been—with what he thought of as his signature. He wanted them to know that he had been there.

He opened his eyes, and there was a holstered pistol on the table in front of Hassan. The commander gave it a shove, and it slid across the table, a black-leather scorpion skittering toward the teenager.

"Too bad, Saiid. I had plans for you." The commander's voice was laced with neither pity nor contempt. It was expressionless and matter-of-fact, as if he was talking about shooting one of the adders that infest the Egyptian desert. "Good-bye, Saiid. Insha Allah." Hassan turned abruptly and left. The foreigner remained, motionless, in the corner.

Despite his exhaustion, Alex Stratton was awakened by the quiet but persistent knocking. It didn't surprise Alex that it was Jake at his hotel room door, nor did it surprise him that he had spent most of the night thinking about his old friend.

It still amazed Alex that, of all people, it had been Jake MacIntyre, high-school football star, who had befriended a scrawny little British kid when Alex's family had moved to the States. Jake protected him while he got adjusted, immediately nicknamed him "Brit," and had been one of the few who hadn't ridiculed or abandoned him when, a few years later, Alex had started going to church.

Through the rest of high school and on into college the unlikely pair lived, studied, ate, and—above all—indulged in their mutual, consuming passion for photography together. They augmented and complemented each other on very different levels—Alex reveling in the periphery of Jake's panache and daring; Jake's excesses and recklessness tempered by Alex's calm steadiness.

Alex remembered the late-night discussions, the half-eaten pizza they had ordered and forgotten when Jake challenged his friend's beliefs. "Hold it a second," Jake had said. "Explain something to me. You're telling me that 'God is love,' right?"

"That's what the Bible says."

"But the Bible also says that some people are 'prepared for destruction.' You read that to me yourself."

Alex had nodded as he saw what was coming.

"So, you're expecting me to believe that this God of yours loves the people he destroys?" Jake had shaken his head in exasperation. "It doesn't make any sense."

Alex remembered his reply. "I agree with you; it doesn't make sense. At least, not by our standards. I don't understand it, and I can't explain it. But I believe it to be true nonetheless."

Halfway through college Jake enlisted in the army to avoid being drafted. Always one to accept a challenge, to pursue the most difficult course available, Jake chose to forego a signal corps photographer's post in favor of volunteering for the elite, deadly rangers. "Take the high road!" Jake had taught his friend. "If there are two paths open to you, always choose the more challenging and, therefore, more potentially rewarding of the two."

Two years later Alex, a newly graduated rookie photojournalist, lay terrified in the stinking mud of Viet Nam, trying desperately to stop shaking enough so that he could take pictures. Machine gun bullets burrowed into the ground around him as he documented the successful attempt by an army platoon to rescue a squad of their mates trapped on the top of a nameless hill. That desperate charge had earned the platoon's commander, Lieutenant J. C. MacIntyre, the Silver Star. It had also earned Jake the Purple Heart and a medical discharge for wounds incurred in action.

After Jake's shoulder healed, it was Alex Stratton who introduced the jobless young veteran to his boss, Mort Steinmetz.

"What in creation's going on?" Alex asked. He fished a couple of Cokes out of the minibar and handed one to Jake.

Jake snapped open the small bottle and finished the contents in a single swallow. He grimaced at the now-empty bottle. "Never could understand how you can drink this sweet stuff."

Alex sat down across from Jake. The light from the room's single lamp glinted off his rimless glasses as he looked at his best friend. "Did you," Alex asked quietly, "have anything, anything at all, to do with this?"

Had any other man asked him that question, Jake's immediate response would have been a curse, a heated denial, and, a decade earlier, a challenge to fight. Instead, Alex got a slow shake of Jake's head.

The two men looked at each other intently.

"You think I'm lying?" Jake asked, an edge to his voice.

"No," Alex said. "I just have to ask."

"Why? Don't you trust me?"

"Of course I do. But you have to admit that you've been in trouble before. Nothing like this, but I have to ask the question. It's not what everyone is saying it is, but maybe it's something else. And maybe it's something you can't tell Mort."

Jake swore. "If I had something to tell you, I'd tell you!"

"Maybe." Alex leaned forward, elbows resting on his knees. "I know there are things you enjoy telling. To anybody. Even personal things." He paused, smiled, and continued. "Like the relish with which you recount your amorous adventures to anyone who'll listen."

Jake thought of the woman in the white sundress and how she had looked at him from the lobby of the hotel. He remembered how she made him feel, and then he remembered telling three other men his plans for her. Uncomfortable now for the first time in his life with the way he thought of women, Jake shrugged helplessly.

"But there's a lot you keep to yourself. You know that. I know that. If there were more to this whole thing, it would be just like you to try to shoulder it alone."

Jake sat impassively, stonelike.

"Jake, this is me, Alex."

Jake looked at his friend, and in that instant's glance were contained many years of shared secrets, hopes, triumphs, and fears.

"This is big," Alex said. "You're in real trouble."

"But—," Jake started to protest.

"But nothing, Jake. This is bigger than you realize. There are lives at stake besides your own."

Jake sat up, suddenly angry. The two men stared at each other, unwavering.

Unintimidated, Alex continued. "You're unwilling to turn to the only people who can get you out of this."

Jake looked up. "*I'm* the only one who can get me out of this."

"No, you're not. There are other, larger powers at work here."

"We've had this conversation before. You need *faith* for that. I can only put my faith in what I see. If I can take a picture of it, I'll believe in it."

Alex nodded, choosing not to force the issue. "The timing and brutality of these killings have really driven everyone over the edge. The longer you wait, the harder it's going to be to convince them that you didn't do it."

"I know. But the film in my camera has the evidence to clear me. I have to get it back. If I turn myself in, no one's going to believe that some woman tourist has pictures of the assassins." Jake shook his head, stood up, and walked over to the window. "For once, I don't know what to do."

"Mac," Alex said, "remember what you told me the time I was too scared to try out for the high hurdles on the track team?"

Jake frowned and shook his head.

"Well then, how about the time I wanted to ask Ellen Bradford out to the junior prom?"

Jake couldn't help but laugh. "You got so nervous you threw up in study hall."

"Well, that wasn't exactly the part I wanted you to remember. Anyway, what did you tell me that time?"

"I don't recall. What are you getting at?"

"OK. Remember what you said to me just before I had to tell my father that we had blown up his Buick?"

"See you later?" Jake said with a smile.

"No!"

"I remember. Something I haven't said in ages. Each time, I told you to take the high road!"

Alex nodded, now very serious. "Right. 'Take the high road.' The standard advice from the resident jock to his skinny, funny-talking British friend. Anytime you face a choice take the harder way, the more challenging way, the more rewarding way, the right way."

Jake's smile vanished as he realized what Alex was about to say.

"It's your turn now. Now the no-longer-skinny Brit gets to tell the aging jock that it's his turn to take the high road. That it's his turn to do what's right."

Jake fought with himself, torn between the instinct to

submit to his near-consuming fear and the desire to do what he
knew was both right and good.

Alex sat quietly before him, watching patiently.

Just as Jake turned toward Alex, ready to say something,
the phone rang. Jake closed his mouth. With a jerk of his head
he gestured to Alex to answer the phone.

Alex got up, wincing at the lost opportunity. He picked up
the receiver, spoke briefly, then hung up. "That's right, it was
the police," Alex said. "They want to talk to me."

Jake bolted out of his chair.

"Jake, this is your chance," Alex said. "Do what's right,
Mac, or it's just going to get worse."

"Brit, listen to me. I've got to fix this myself."

"I know how you feel. I used to think that I could 'fix this
myself' too."

Jake headed toward the door.

"When they get here," Alex told him, "I've got to tell them
the truth: that you were here, and that I don't know where you
are now. I'll tell them your side of it, and if they won't try to find
this tourist woman with me, then I'll try to find her myself. Call
me here tomorrow, and I'll let you know what I've found out."

Jake nodded.

"Just one more thing."

Jake paused with his hand on the doorknob.

"You're not in this alone."

Jake again started to speak, then stepped into the hall and
closed the door behind him.

The message light on her hotel room phone was blinking when
Cathy arrived. She tipped the porter, then dialed the operator.

"The message reads," the operator had told Cathy, "'Meet
us in the dining room at 8:00 A.M.'"

"Just like that, huh?" Cathy muttered, taken aback by the message's abruptness.

"Pardon, ma'am?"

"Nothing," Cathy assured the operator. "Is there anything else?"

"The message is signed, 'V. Petigura, Inspector, C.P.D.'"

Cathy thanked the operator and hung up. As she unpacked, she wondered who the rest of the "us" would be.

Cathy entered the hotel dining room precisely at eight. A tall, hawklike man rose from a table near the door and nodded to her.

"Vishnu Petigura, Cairo Police," he said as he shook Cathy's hand. Cathy looked up into dark, hooded eyes that watched her from deep within a gaunt face. Petigura motioned to a chair. "Please, have a seat."

A waiter deposited cups of coffee on the table.

"I realize that you are operating at a disadvantage, Miss Hagura," Petigura said with a friendly smile. "We know about you, and you know nothing of us."

*There's that "we" again*, Cathy thought.

"So," he continued, "let me tell you about who you'll be working with."

The policeman took a sip of coffee. "I head the antiterrorism division of Cairo Police. Mostly, we keep track of known dissidents and radical sympathizers. It's been a rather quiet assignment," Petigura said with a grimace, "until now. Before joining the Cairo police, I was in the government."

"Security?" Cathy asked, hoping to find some common ground.

The inspector nodded, and his eyes seemed to close even further. "Head of President Sadat's personal bodyguard."

Seeing Cathy's eyes widen, Petigura smiled. "Why, then, you are wondering," he said slowly, "am I not dead?" The smile vanished. "I was sick that day. A common cold." He answered the question he saw in Cathy's eyes. "No, I probably couldn't have prevented his death. But, I'll never know. So now I work to prevent the foundation he laid from crumbling away."

Petigura sat up. "Enough about me," he said briskly. "Working with us will be Lieutenant Dan Jeremias of the Mossad."

Cathy recognized the agency as Israel's version of the CIA.

"Dan and I have worked together before—" Petigura broke off and waved. "Ah, here he is now."

Cathy rose and shook the hand of the short, plump man who had arrived. Seeing him standing next to the tall, thin Egyptian caused Cathy to have to forcibly banish the near-irresistible desire to think of Laurel and Hardy.

When they were seated, Petigura continued. "I was telling Cathy," he told Jeremias, "that we had worked together before. What I didn't tell her was that it was during the Six-Day War." Both men smiled at the surprise that filled Cathy's eyes.

"The war went so badly so quickly for Egypt," Jeremias explained, "that, short as it was, even before the war was over, the Egyptians had dispatched a negotiating team to Jerusalem. The then-captain Petigura was chief of the Egyptian prisoner-exchange team. Having had some small experience in such matters—"

"Including being in on the Entebbe mission," Petigura interjected.

Cathy nodded her approving admiration. Israel's lightning rescue in 1976 of hostages held by hijackers at the airport in Entebbe, Uganda, had been an unqualified success.

Jeremias coughed modestly, then continued. "I was assigned as his counterpart." He took off his glasses and peered at the lenses, then polished them with his napkin. "I feel that we worked quite well together."

57

The waiter returned and handed Cathy a menu. As she studied it, she thought over her first impressions. Petigura was likable, but something about Jeremias's pedantic manner irritated her. *Oh, well,* she thought, *at least it'll make it easy not to think of them as Stan and Ollie.*

# 7

Taking advantage of a free morning to catch up on her journal writing, Anne basked in the midmorning sun. Lee had taken a disconsolate and homesick teenage girl from another tour under her wing, and the two had disappeared after breakfast in a swirl of shopping fever.

Anne had put on a short, sleeveless sundress and the wide-brimmed hat she had bought in Italy, then went out onto the tiny balcony at the end of the hall that ran the length of her floor. She arranged one chair so that it faced the sun and sat down, stretching her legs out on the seat of another. With her lap as her writing desk, Anne opened her journal and began to try to record all that had happened to her.

Some time later, when the sun-heated stone of the balcony had warmed her, Anne set down the pen and pushed her hat back on her head. She stretched, then dropped her arms onto the arms of the chair. Anne leaned her head back and felt her face and throat soak in the now-hot sun. *Greedy, aren't we?* she said to herself with a smile. *I know I've got to be careful, but I can't come back a complete paleface.*

The room on the fourth floor of Cairo Police Headquarters was spartan and windowless, the lighting harsh and the table and chairs a bleak battleship gray.

*Probably an interrogation room*, Cathy thought. She suppressed a shudder as she imagined what might have gone on in the spot where she was sitting. The Egyptian security forces were notorious for the ruthlessness of their interrogations, which was one reason why Cathy was determined to capture Jake before either of her colleagues did. Cathy slumped down in her chair. *I wouldn't have imagined that it was possible*, she thought, *but so far this meeting's been worse than the ones at State. Here three people are dead, and we're wrangling over seniority.*

Petigura had got the meeting off to a brisk start. But things had bogged down when Jeremias had promptly insisted on establishing seniority before continuing. Much of the morning had been wasted before Jeremias reluctantly admitted that he outranked neither an inspector nor a senior agent.

By the time they got around to exchanging the information they had brought with them, jetlag and frustration had combined to make Cathy exhausted and irritable. When Jeremias had turned to her and asked if "Senior Agent Hagura" would outline Jake's background, it was suddenly too much.

"Enough already!" Cathy shouted. Her fist hit the table with a bang that made the two men jump. "Every second we sit here and bicker puts the shooter one step closer to disappearing over the horizon."

Both men noticed that she had said "shooter" and not "MacIntyre."

"Now, first off, let's dump this title stuff. As of now, I'm Cathy." She pointed at Jeremias. "You're Dan. And you are," she continued, swinging around and stabbing a finger at Petigura, "Vinnie."

Petigura started, then grinned when he saw Cathy suppress a smile. From across the table, Jeremias snorted in disgust. Lines had just been drawn; alliances had just been made.

Since he made no sound, Anne felt, rather than heard, him come onto the balcony. As she dozed, a small spark of gentle awareness flickered into life within her. Accompanying the awareness was a restlessness, a resonating sense of longing that both excited and disquieted her. Anne opened one eye, slowly focusing on the alcove, which formed the balcony's entrance.

All indolence vanished when she saw him standing in the alcove, watching her. Anne, eyes now wide, swung her legs off the chair. She came to her feet, self-consciously smoothing the skirt of her sundress as she did so. The journal and pen dropped unnoticed to the balcony floor.

With an eye suddenly grown keen, she noticed everything about him: the sunlight on his hair, his half-opened shirt, the casual way he leaned against the arch of the alcove. She also noticed that he needed a haircut, hadn't shaved that morning, and generally looked as though he had spent the night in a particularly disreputable flophouse, which was exactly what he had done.

"Miss Dryden, I'm—," he began.

"I know who you are. What do you want?" Anne felt the blood rise to her face as she heard the harshness of her voice interrupting him.

Jake stepped toward her, and the balcony grew suddenly smaller as he effectively trapped her in its corner. Anne just watched as he approached. She felt no fear, and part of her was very surprised at that. Jake stopped near her. He reached down and picked up her journal and pen. Then Jake straightened up, and Anne tilted back her head to look at the man who towered over her.

*Those eyes*, she thought. *Kind eyes. Honest eyes. Worried eyes.*

Anne stood motionless as she returned his unblinking gaze. She realized that he was speaking again.

". . . if we could talk for a minute. You see, I need your help."

If Anne hadn't already been intrigued by this man, she was now—by how he made her feel and what he might want of her. She looked pointedly at her journal and pen, which had disappeared into the grasp of his massive hands.

Jake looked down and then back at Anne. "These yours?" he asked hesitantly and then grinned at just how unnecessary the question was.

Entranced once more by his smile, Anne smiled back and motioned Jake to a chair. She remained standing as Jake sat down.

"It's awfully warm out here," Anne said. "Would you like something to drink?" Anne's mother had taught her that one extends hospitality to guests, no matter how unexpected they may be.

Jake looked at Anne. His sharp glance deepened into a frown as he misread her intentions.

Anne bristled inwardly at the distrust she saw in the eyes of this man who had so suddenly encroached upon her life.

*Don't call the authorities*, his eyes said.

*I have no intention of doing anything of the sort*, hers replied.

His will held hers for a moment longer. Then, rather than surrender, she turned and left the balcony.

When the door to her room was safely shut behind her, Anne leaned against it. She trembled from more than the coolness of the smooth, painted surface on her back. She was both relieved and distraught to be away from him, and this unsettled her greatly. Head back, eyes closed, Anne cupped her hands over her mouth and nose. She breathed deeply, trying to slow her racing heartbeat. *What is going on here?*

# 8

*For a White House office, this is smaller that I thought it'd be,* Ed Mahoney observed as the chief of staff rose from behind his desk.

"Thanks for coming over at this ungodly hour, Ed," Mike O'Brian said as he shook Mahoney's hand. "I realize how busy you folks at State must be right now." O'Brian motioned for Mahoney to sit down.

Mahoney watched as the chief of staff collected some papers from his desk. *What'd you expect?* Mahoney asked himself, *Genghis Khan? The guy's survived as COS for almost two terms by being the master of both carrot and stick.* O'Brian reached into a desk drawer. *Wonder which one he's getting out?*

O'Brian sat down on the other end of the couch. "I need to have an update. A report has to be waiting for the president when he comes into the Oval Office this morning."

Mahoney reached for his briefcase. "Anything in particular that you'd like to know?"

"How about who did it, where they are, and when they're going to be captured?"

"How about," Mahoney replied, "we're pretty sure we

know, we don't know, and we have no idea. I haven't been in contact with Agent Hagura since she arrived in Egypt."

"She?" O'Brian said skeptically.

"She," Mahoney repeated. "I'm not any happier about it than you are, but she's the best I've got." Mahoney grimaced. "Considering what Congress has done to my budget . . ."

O'Brian quelled him with a look. "Tell me what I don't know, Ed. The president's due to confer with Israel's prime minister in an hour, and it'd really help if we had something concrete to report."

An aide brought in a tray of coffee and soda. O'Brian nodded to the man, who left.

"We've got a positive ID on the murder weapon," Mahoney offered. "FBI matched it up to the bullet that was dug out of Moncrief's head."

O'Brian winced.

"Sorry," Mahoney apologized. "When you're an ex-cop, you get used to these things."

"Do we know who owns the gun?" O'Brian asked.

"Nothing traceable," Mahoney replied. "Isn't who used it more important than who owns it?"

"Probably," O'Brian acknowledged with a shrug. "It was just a thought."

Something in the chief of staff's tone convinced Mahoney that it was anything but that.

O'Brian stood, indicating that the interview was over. "Be sure to keep me informed."

"Will do," Mahoney replied. He was halfway to the door when O'Brian's "One more thing, Ed," stopped him.

Mahoney turned. "You retire next month, don't you?" O'Brian asked.

Mahoney nodded.

"Better to go out with a bang than a whimper, don't you

think?" O'Brian asked affably. "Keep in touch." O'Brian turned his attention to his desk.

*So much for the carrot,* Mahoney thought bitterly as he walked through the anteroom.

Jake sat easily, leaning on the arm of the chair as Anne came back with the drinks. The image of Jake in the bar had rushed back into her mind and, after a moment's hesitation, she had opened the minibar in her room and taken out a bottle of beer. All uncertainty vanished when Jake's eyes lit up at the sight of the long-necked bottle. Jake finished half the bottle in a single swallow as Anne sat down across the table from him.

"Miss Dryden, you wouldn't believe how good this tastes." Jake grinned and took another pull at the bottle.

Anne found herself smiling at his enthusiasm. *I can't help but smile back at him when he smiles at me,* she thought as she watched him. *This is not a good thing,* she told herself. Anne took a sip of her Coke, and then looked at the man across from her. "Please call me Anne, Mr. MacIntyre. Only my first graders call me Miss Dryden."

Jake nodded.

"Now," Anne continued, "before you tell me how I may be able to help, I have a question for you: How do you know who I am?"

Much to Anne's surprise, Jake shifted uncomfortably in his chair and looked away from her before answering. "Well, Miss Dry—Anne—I saw you in the hotel lobby the other day."

Anne started slightly at the realization that Jake might have seen her watching him and found herself trying to remember what she had been wearing. Mentally scolding herself, she turned her attention back to him.

"I got up to, ah, introduce myself to you," Jake confessed, "but, by then, you were gone."

Anne's poorly hidden, amused smile served only to increase Jake's discomfort. Out of curiosity Anne asked, "How, then, did you find out who I was?"

"A few dollars in baksheesh to the bartender," Jake said with a shrug. "His cousin's the manager, and he got me your name and room number." Embarrassed, Jake surveyed the horizon for a minute before going on. "The next time I saw you," Jake said, very serious now, "was at the Pyramids."

Jake explained, talking rapidly, and Anne sensed that he spoke quickly out of urgency rather than fear. He detailed what had happened so far, and ended up with an earnest request. "So, you see, I need that roll of film."

Anne nodded. Then she closed her eyes and her shoulders sagged.

"What?" Jake asked with a sinking feeling.

"I used those mailer things," Anne explained. "You know, the prepaid kind. I mailed off a bunch of them yesterday."

Anne trailed off helplessly as Jake grimaced. "It was my father's idea!" Anne said defensively in response to Jake's anguished look.

Jake pounded the arms of the chair in frustration, and then brightened. "The camera! What's the serial number of your Leica?"

Anne looked at him and shook her head blankly. "I have no idea."

Jake's pent-up frustration erupted. "What do you mean you don't know?" he thundered.

Anne, near tears and furious with herself for it, worked hard to keep her voice level. "Look, Jake, you're the photographer, not me. It's my father's camera, not mine, and I barely know how to use it. So take it easy, OK?"

"Well, can I at least see the camera?" he inquired.

"Well, yes and no," Anne replied with a wince. "Lee's got

it right now. I'm meeting her for lunch, and then we're going out." Surprised at her strong response to Jake's exasperation, Anne said, "I'll meet you here, with the camera, at six. OK?"

Jake nodded. "Thanks," he said, his voice softer. He drained his beer and stood. "And thanks for the beer."

Jake's sudden grin caught her off guard, and she was at a loss for words. "I'll call my father," she finally offered. "He might be able to help."

"OK. I need all the help I can get right now."

Somehow, Anne sensed that that was a phrase Jake wasn't used to saying. "Remember," she said, "you're not in this alone."

Eyes the color of blue steel gazed down at eyes the color of emeralds.

"Funny," Jake said at last. "You sound just like a friend of mine."

Then he was gone.

# 9

Quiet lunchtime conversation and the sound of silverware on china vied with the whir of the brass-and-mahogany ceiling fan over Anne and Lee's table.

"Did you have a nice time with that girl?" Anne asked.

"Who?"

"The one you took shopping this morning."

"Oh, Beth." Lee shook her head. "Poor kid. Her boyfriend talked her into coming with him and then promptly dumped her for another girl on their tour. Now she faces seven weeks of being around the two of them all the time."

"That's hard. Will she be all right?" Anne asked.

"I think so," Lee replied with a laugh. "It's amazing what some new clothes, a couple of pastries, and a shoulder to cry on can do for a broken heart." Lee smiled. "We exchanged addresses and phone numbers. I'll call her after we get back." Lee dabbed her mouth with her napkin, then looked across the table at Anne. "Your fish must be a whole lot tougher than mine."

Anne looked up, startled, then followed Lee's gaze to her plate. She found that, without realizing it, she had meticulously dissected her fish fillet into small pieces. Anne gazed sheepishly across the table at her friend.

"OK, Annie, out with it. What's going on?"

"Nothing. I'm all right. Really." Anne didn't have to look at Lee to know that she wasn't believed. A waiter appeared and took Lee's plate. When he looked at Anne in inquiry, she motioned for her plate to be removed as well. The waiter cleared the table and left.

"Come off it," Lee said, frowning. "You didn't touch your breakfast, and now you just played around with your lunch. You and I both know," Lee added gently, "that it takes a lot to put you off your feed." The fact that Anne could eat anything without having to diet had rankled Lee for years.

Anne tried to smile. "I'm fine. I really am." *I can tell Lee anything*, Anne thought. *Why can't I tell her about Jake?*

Lee sighed. "Whatever you say."

A waiter pushed a copper-and-chrome cart up to the table. "Dessert, ladies?"

Lee pointed at the cart. "See those éclairlike things? You've just got to try one. Beth and I had two this morning . . . each," she added with a grin. "Anne?"

When no response was forthcoming, Lee gestured to the waiter, who served them each one of the pastries. "And coffee," Lee added.

The waiter left with the cart.

"You OK?" Lee asked solicitously.

Anne sat, hands folded, staring out the window next to the table.

"Anne!" Lee said insistently. Anne looked up, startled. "What's going on with you?"

"Nothing."

Lee's resentment of Anne's abruptness joined forces with

her so-far thwarted curiosity at her behavior. Suddenly, Lee had had enough. "Don't give me that!"

Anne flinched at Lee's tone. "Just leave me alone!" she replied, an angry edge to her own voice.

"I will not!" Lee threw her napkin down on the table. "Annie, talk to me."

Anne stood with an abruptness that rattled the silverware. "Go away!" she told Lee in a whisper that turned heads across the room.

"No!"

"Fine, just fine! Then if you won't, I will!" Breathing hard, her mouth set, Anne glared at Lee through her tears.

"Where are you going?" Lee asked quietly.

"Upstairs!" Anne turned away.

Lee blinked the tears out of her own eyes, then watched Anne hurry from the dining room.

The waiter returned with the coffee. "Something is unsatisfactory?" he asked when he saw the untouched pastries.

"The *food* was wonderful," Lee assured the man. "Check, please."

The hotel gift shop offered Lee no consolation, and she found herself leafing absently through a binder that lay on a table next to the concierge's desk. *I haven't felt like this since Brian died,* Lee thought as she flipped a page.

Brian Anthony Conner had been all that Lee was looking for in a man: handsome, charming, and with a confident authority that both encouraged and tamed her impetuosity.

Three things had arrived one late August day—an enormous thunderstorm, their engagement announcements, and the news that Brian had been killed in a motorcycle accident.

When Lee opened the door that night, Anne was there. A long time later Anne gently dislodged the sobbing Lee's arms from around her neck. She handed her friend a poncho. Lee, all sorrow and pain, looked at Anne, who led her out into the storm.

With Anne in the lead, they fought their way through the gale-driven rain up to the top of a promontory behind the Parker home. Far below, the storm-lashed surf boomed against the granite cliffs. When they reached the edge, Anne took Lee's hands in hers. She had to shout to make herself heard, her words punctuated by flashes of lightning. "God's listening, Lee. Talk to him."

And so Emily Parker threw back her head and poured forth her rage at Brian for having killed himself so foolishly, her fury at God for having allowed it to happen, and her despair at being consigned to a limitless, undying grief.

The remnants of the thunderclouds in the eastern sky were touched with red when Lee draped herself around Anne once more. Anne helped Lee down to her home and into her parents' arms.

A brochure in the concierge's binder caught Lee's eye. It offered the opportunity to charter for an afternoon's sailing one of the myriad small boats that fished the Nile. Lee, an avid sailor, thought for a moment, then went upstairs.

"Hey, Cleopatra, you want to go on a Nile cruise?" Lee asked as she entered the room. Anne turned from the window and looked at Lee, who abandoned her pretense of joviality and sat down next to her. "Annie, I'm sorry."

Anne nodded. "Me too. I shouldn't have walked out on you." Once again Anne debated about telling Lee more. She was confused. There were good reasons not to involve Lee in something as serious as what Jake MacIntyre was facing. At the same time, Anne had to admit that there were other things going on inside her, and she didn't want Lee to know what those things were. She felt that it was wrong to feel that way. It was a breach of their trust, after all these years.

"Then how about it?" Lee asked, breaking the silence. "We didn't come all the way to Egypt to stay cooped up in a gloomy old hotel room."

"Thanks, but you go ahead. I don't feel like crowds just now."

Lee persevered. "No, not one of those. Just us. A little sailboat." Lee affected helplessness. "C'mon, Annie. Please? You know how I am about sailing, and I haven't gotten to go in weeks."

Anne smiled, shook her head, and turned back to the window. "Why don't you take Beth? She needs you more than I do right now."

"Somehow, I don't think so." Lee hesitated, then pulled up a chair and sat down facing Anne. "Annie Laurel," she said firmly, "I'm going to try this one more time. You can get mad at me. You can walk out on me. You can hate me if you must. But something is terribly wrong with you, and I'm your best friend, and I want to know what I can do to help you. So you talk. I listen."

*Those magic words.* Anne turned eyes awash with turmoil, uncertainty, and a touch of fear toward her friend's level gaze. Years ago, as childhood friends, the two had made a solemn promise to each other: whenever one saw the other withdrawing into herself because of some failure, disappointment, or uncertainty she would not fail to invoke this command and the other, no matter how deep the hurt, would not fail to respond. While they had come to know their covenant as accountability, it remained for them what it was: the refusal of two joined spirits to allow the other to slip away in the slightest degree. *You talk. I listen.* Over the years the phrase had been used sparingly, seriously, and always with the greatest of love.

Anne smiled. A rueful smile, laced with just a tinge of grateful annoyance, which amplified the trouble in her eyes. As they always did during these talks, Anne interlaced her long, slender fingers with Lee's shorter, stronger ones and turned to face her inquisitor and counselor. The unspoken rules were always the same: one talked, and the other listened without judgment, comment, or unsolicited advice.

Anne paused, took a deep breath, and said in a rush, "I've met someone."

Mindful of their rules, Lee fought hard to keep her face expressionless.

"It makes no sense," Anne confessed. "I've barely met the man. I know almost nothing about him." She frowned. "It's nuts. I feel so foolish."

Lee suppressed her smile at Anne's puzzlement.

"He's not my type at all. He's raffish, abrupt, impatient, and thoroughly disreputable." Anne paused. Then she said quietly, "Without saying a word, he makes me blush."

*God in heaven,* Lee muttered to herself. *Annie's saying this?* Lee's eyes widened in silent acknowledgment; only twice in her life had she seen Anne Dryden blush. *Who is he?* Lee's mind shrieked.

Seeing Lee's eyes narrow, Anne rushed on. "No, he didn't do or say anything offensive. He was polite, gentle, and kind."

*Make up your mind, woman!* Lee thought admonishingly. *Which is he, Frankenstein or Fred Astaire?*

Anne turned again toward the window. "I just wish," she said more to herself than to Lee, "that I could stop thinking about him." Then she smiled. "He's got the biggest and bluest eyes I've ever seen! Eyes I can get lost in." Anne's smile turned thoughtful. "I'm not too sure I like that. . . . "

She took a breath as if to continue and laughed when she felt Lee's grip on her fingers tighten in anguish.

Anne retrieved her hands from Lee's grasp. This was their time-honored signal that it was all right for the other to speak.

Lee burst forth like a breached dam. "Who is it? Someone on the tour?"

Anne wrinkled her nose at the thought. This was an expensive tour, paid for by Anne's parents, and hence all the males on the tour were either balding fathers or adolescent sons. "No, silly! Of course not! Anyway," she said with a dismissive wave of her hand, "it's not important. We're off to Kenya tomorrow, and I'll never see him again."

*You're not getting off that easy, Annie Dryden,* Lee thought. "Oh, I get it!" she said knowingly. "You're the one who stole Beth's boyfriend!"

"Oh, please!"

"Well, then, who? Where did you meet him?"

"I first saw him down in the bar the day we went to the Pyramids," Anne said. "Then he came here this morning, and we talked." Anne saw Lee's expression and hastily added, "Out on the balcony, of course."

All of Lee's alarm bells were starting to go off. For Annie to be in love was a truly great thing, but it was sounding like this guy wasn't the right kind for her. Protecting the lovely, innocent Anne from just this type was a longtime calling of Lee's. *And now,* she thought, aghast, *Annie's fallen for some Arab gigolo!*

"Annie, what's his name?" Lee asked. Outwardly all innocence, her heart seemed to pause as she awaited Anne's reply.

Anne gazed steadily at her friend and confidante. "His name is MacIntyre."

Lee's eyes grew wide. "That's the name of the guy on the news, who—"

"Yes."

"It's not the same—"

"Afraid so," Anne said. "Jake MacIntyre."

*Sweet Jesus, give me wisdom,* Lee asked as the dilapidated cab they had hired made its way southward along the Corniche el Nil, the boulevard that paralleled the east bank of the Nile. Lee watched Anne, noting with concern how she gazed fixedly out of the cab window, looking at the luxury hotels on Gezira Island without seeing them. *I'd be worried, too, if I'd fallen for an alleged assassin,* Lee thought.

It explained everything. It wasn't just that Anne had fallen for some guy with great eyes. He was being hunted by nearly everyone in the world, and he had found refuge for a few brief minutes in Anne's life. What should she do? What should she feel? Lee's heart went out to her friend.

"Annie," Lee asked, "does he know how you feel? About him?"

Anne turned her eyes from the Nile, looking past Lee across the cab out the other window into the depths of the Islamic portion of Cairo. "Of course not! I didn't tell him anything." As if realizing something, Anne went on. "He's the first man I've ever met whom I didn't understand at first sight. All the others have been so obvious."

Lee nodded, understanding perfectly.

"It's not me he's interested in." Anne paused, frowning at what she had said. "I haven't quite figured it out yet, but I'm attracted to him because he's not attracted to me. . . . " She trailed off, and looked at Lee helplessly. "I'm not making much sense, am I?"

Lee peered over her sunglasses at Anne. "Perfect sense." *Just like you always do,* Lee thought as Anne shrugged. *God, if Annie's guardian angel has a twin, how about assigning her to me? Just for a while, maybe?*

"I want you to meet him when he comes tonight," Anne said.

Just then the cabdriver spoke up. "You ladies American,

no?" he asked, looking at Anne and Lee in the rearview mirror. "What you think a that photo fellah that shoot up the conference? They go catch him, they hang him one time, no?" the cabbie asked with a nasty laugh and a grin.

Anne stiffened.

Lee looked savagely at the cabdriver. "You just mind your own business!" she snapped. *So much for your tip, buster.*

The cabbie shrugged and turned back to his driving.

"Annie," Lee said, hoping to soothe her worried friend, "When he comes back tonight, we'll get this all straightened out. He knows what he needs, and whatever it is, we'll see that he gets it. Maybe it'll all work out." Lee added privately, *Somehow.*

The two women exchanged smiles. "Thanks," Anne said.

"Trust him?" Lee offered, nodding heavenward.

Closing her eyes and taking a deep breath, Anne nodded as the taxi squealed to a stop.

# 10

Cathy had decided that if she hated the room in which she now sat then it must hate her too. That was, she figured, as good a reason as any for why no progress had been made. Between the stubbornness of Dan Jeremias and the high-level bureaucratic wrangling and finger pointing, she was surprised that they had accomplished anything at all. *This afternoon had better be different from yesterday,* Cathy thought as Vinnie, who had been on the phone when the other two arrived, entered the room.

Vinnie sat down at the head of the table full of smiles and energy, as usual. Joint authority for the investigation had at last been hammered out, effectively silencing Jeremias and allowing them to proceed. Since it was within his jurisdiction, the Egyptian had been named to lead the investigation, so he opened the day's discussion.

"I presume that we've all had a chance to read the suspect's dossier that Cathy passed out yesterday. Any ideas?"

Dan Jeremias came to life immediately. "Anyone can see from this that MacIntyre did it."

"OK, Dan," Cathy said coolly. "Tell us why we can see that."

Jeremias began ticking points off on his fingers. "First off, opportunity. Even you," Jeremias said, smiling condescendingly at the bristling Cathy, "cannot deny that he was placed by reliable witnesses at the murder scene. Next, capability." Jeremias flipped open the dossier in front of him. "MacIntyre, J. C.," Jeremias continued, reading now. "Rated 'Marksman' while in the U.S. Army; served as a sniper with the rangers in Viet Nam before his field commission; regularly hunts. Your Wyoming State Police records show that he holds no fewer than seven different gun permits."

"You gotta admit," Vinnie interjected, "that MacIntyre could've made shots like those."

Cathy nodded in agreement, then asked, "But what about motive? Why in the world would he do such a thing? We have no case without motive."

Jeremias smiled, raising his hand for attention. "Over lunch I called a friend who works in the Tel Aviv branch of Global Photo, MacIntyre's employer." The Mossad agent gazed smugly at the nods of approval. "I asked her," he continued, "to find out for me where MacIntyre had been sent on assignment since joining Global." The plump, little man took out a sheet of paper from his briefcase. "Among the cities that MacIntyre, in his years with Global, has visited are—" He paused for effect.

*Dramatic little sucker, isn't he?* Cathy thought disgustedly.

Jeremias, assured of their attention, continued. "Rome, Istanbul, Baghdad, East and West Berlin, Bogota, and . . . " Jeremias looked up, smiling at no one in particular. "Last, but certainly not least, Beirut." Jeremias stood. "Now, if you'll excuse me for a minute. I have to use the rest room. I'll be right back."

Cathy wondered if he really had to leave or had simply planned a dramatic exit.

Vinnie glanced at Cathy, realizing how furious she might be for not thinking of doing what Jeremias had done. "Can't deny it, Cathy. He's sharp," Petigura said. His admission broke the silence that had engulfed the room. "Annoying, but sharp nonetheless."

Cathy nodded in bleak concurrence, then looked at her colleague. "But," she objected, "all those cities are perfectly reasonable places for a photojournalist to go! Where he's been doesn't provide a motive."

"True," Vinnie agreed. "But you must admit that that list sounds like some sort of Cook's tour for terrorists."

Jeremias rejoined them. "So," he asked, "are we in agreement?"

"Cathy," Vinnie asked, "does the FBI have a make on the rifle yet?"

The rifle and the dead rug seller had been discovered soon after the killings. As the suspected murder weapon it had been sent, along with the bullets removed from the victims' bodies, to the FBI ballistics lab for matchup.

Cathy nodded. "No problem there." She retrieved a fax from her notebook. None of them had seen the rifle before it had been shipped off; the men leaned forward in eager anticipation. *Boys will be boys*, Cathy thought.

"Weapon in question," she read, "is a 7.62 millimeter Heckler & Koch G3SG/1."

Jeremias whistled.

"The serial number," Cathy continued, "indicates that it was manufactured by the H&K facility at Oberndorf-Neckar, Federal Republic of Germany, in August 1975." She held up the faxed photo. "This particular piece is equipped with an accuracy-enhancing, roller-delayed, blow-back action and a Zeiss 1.5-6x light-gathering scope. The weapon has been recently fired, in both its semiautomatic and automatic modes. The twenty-round box magazine has six rounds left in it. Ballistics tests are underway."

"You heard of these, Dan?" Vinnie asked.

Jeremias nodded. "The H&Ks are the Rolls-Royce of sniper rifles. Very accurate, very expensive. At seven thousand U.S. dollars apiece, even we don't buy very many."

"No way the PLO could get one of those by themselves," Vinnie muttered. "Unless it belonged to MacIntyre. . . . "

Vinnie and Jeremias looked at each other. Technology was one of the few advantages that they had over the forces of terror. Now, thanks to Western dealers, that bulwark was being eroded.

"Do they have the range?" Cathy wondered.

"In the hands of a marksman," Jeremias said, stressing the word slightly, "they have an effective range of up to 600 meters."

"Third of a mile?" Cathy asked. Metric distances were not her strong point. Vinnie nodded confirmation. "The rug seller's roof is 515 meters from the podium. Long shot," Cathy stated.

"True," Jeremias agreed. "But the weather was good, and it was windless." The Israeli looked at his colleagues. "All in all, a lovely day for killing."

"One more thing," Cathy added. "FBI found prints on the rifle's barrel."

"MacIntyre's?" Jeremias asked hopefully.

Cathy nodded, then closed her eyes to avoid seeing the smug expression on the Mossad agent's face.

"Sounds like MacIntyre's our man," Vinnie said.

"But it still doesn't feel right," Cathy protested.

"Objection noted," Vinnie said.

"Never mind, Cathy," Jeremias said. "When we catch him, if we just turn him over to the Mossad, I promise you he'll confess."

Motioning to the furious Cathy to stay in her seat, Vinnie whirled on the Mossad agent. "We'll do nothing of the sort, Dan! When MacIntyre is apprehended, the interrogation will be conducted by all of us! Do I make myself clear?"

"Of course, Lieutenant," Jeremias replied. "Of course."

Vinnie handed out photos of the insignia that had been stenciled on the wall of Mort Steinmetz's house. "Either of you seen this before?" Vinnie inquired.

"It's kind of hard to make out," Cathy said.

"You're right," Vinnie replied. "So I went over and eye-balled it myself. Really weird. In the center is a snake coiled around a star, with a double circle forming a border around the whole thing."

"Is that writing in the border?" Jeremias asked as he squinted at the photo.

"You tell me," Vinnie replied. "The word in the top half of the border is *PUKA*, the word in the bottom half is *INTI*." The Egyptian looked at his partners. "*PUKA INTI*. That mean anything to either of you?"

Cathy and Jeremias shook their heads. "Could it be Hebrew?" Cathy asked.

The Israeli intelligence man shook his head. "And even if it was," he said scornfully, "what Arab terrorist group is going to scrawl a Hebrew slogan on their victim's house?"

"Good point," Cathy said.

"That's it for today, then," Vinnie said. "Be sure to query your agencies about that insignia."

As the trio rose to leave, Vinnie snapped his fingers. "Oh, yeah. Cathy, any word from Interpol on a code name for this case?"

At the request of the investigating nations, the international police organization had agreed to take the case under its auspices.

"Got it right here," Cathy replied. "Just in from Division II of Interpol's General Secretariat." She rooted around in her notebook and pulled out another fax. "Code name: TOURMA-LINE."

# II

Anne and Lee got out of the cab at the foot of the Giza Bridge and walked down the path from the road to the ancient stone jetties that lay in the bridge's shadow. Vociferous entreaties by each boat's owner as to the special worthiness of his particular craft welled up around them as they made their way along the quay.

As they surveyed the boats and their beckoning owners, each endeavoring to outshout all the others, Anne grabbed Lee's arm. "Look!" Anne exclaimed, pointing at one of the boats. "Isn't it cute?"

The object of Anne's attention was one of the small sail-boats—*dhows*—that have sailed the Nile for three thousand years. This one was square-sterned and had a triangular, brilliantly-colored sail that seemed to consist mostly of patches. The well-kept, little vessel creaked pleasantly in the afternoon breeze.

Seeing Anne and Lee's attention directed his way, the dhow's owner bustled up to them. "Afternoon, missies!" The short, corpulent man beamed, displaying an amazing array of gold teeth. "You want Nile cruise? I'm Achmed, give best cruises here! All the tour guides know me, everyone refers their friends to me! Take care of you, missies, you betcha! Achmed can't be beat!" The small man, wearing a battered captain's hat pushed back on his head, grinned disarmingly at the two women.

Lee cast an appraising eye over the boat. Convinced of its seaworthiness, she turned to Anne. "Well, how about it?"

Anne looked at Achmed. "What's its name?" she asked.

The skipper winced, then gestured dramatically toward his craft. "It, missy? *It?* This boat is not an 'it'; she's a 'she'!"

Achmed waggled his finger at Anne, his good-natured grin glittering in the sunlight. "I'll have you know, missy, that the *Queen Nefertiti* is just as slender and graceful as you are! She's a queen, all right: the queen of all the Nile!"

Anne and Lee exchanged glances as they whispered to each other, "The *Queen Nefertiti?*"

Lee struggled to keep her composure and suggested that Anne buy some fruit. "I'll talk to Achmed here, OK?" Anne, knowing which of them was by far the better haggler, nodded agreement and strolled off toward the fruit vendors who were sprawled in the shade of the Giza Bridge.

In time Anne returned, laden with dates and bottles of soda, to find Lee reclined on the cushions that littered the stern of the *Queen Nefertiti*. "You took your time, slave!" Lee said. She gestured imperiously at Anne. "Now hop aboard smartly so that we may be off!"

"A thousand pardons, Highness!" Anne replied, curtsying low in mock deference. "Please do not have your slave thrown to the crocodiles!" Without rising from her curtsy, Anne threw a date at Lee, whose ancient Egyptian elegance was disrupted by the sticky fruit thumping squarely against her chest.

Laughing, Achmed flamboyantly helped Anne aboard.

Once under way, the sail billowing like a rainbow over

their heads, Achmed began pointing out the sights. "Don't worry, missies!" Achmed exclaimed as they sailed northward along the narrow finger of river that separated Roda Island from mainland Cairo. "With Achmed, you see it all!" Standing behind them, one calloused hand resting lightly on the tiller, the captain of the *Queen Nefertiti* gestured to the west. "See, there's the Manyal Palace!"

Anne and Lee admired the intricate window screens and the lush gardens that spilled down the hill atop which the palace rested. "Soon," Achmed continued, slipping the dhow into the center of the current as the channel turned westward, "we see the Salah el Din Mosque, and the Cairo Tower, too. Don't worry! With Achmed, you see it all!"

As they enjoyed the view, Anne's thoughts drifted back to recent events. "Lee," Anne wondered aloud, "do you think that Jake's telling the truth?" Certain doubts had begun to creep into her mind.

"If his story wasn't so incredibly farfetched," Lee replied, "I'd figure that it was just an exceptionally clever opening line. But there's one easy way to find out." Lee rummaged around in her large rattan carryall and pulled out the camera.

Lee turned over the Leica in her hands. "This isn't your camera. Yours wasn't as beat up as this." Lee fingered the Leica's strap. "And besides," she went on, "if you look close, you can see this strap is a dark blue. Your father's strap was black, right?"

Anne nodded.

"And your camera strap didn't have this gash in it."

Anne frowned as she remembered Jake telling her of how he had been attacked.

Lee watched her. She was very glad for Anne that Jake was a truthful man and very worried for both Anne and Jake because of the nature of that truth.

Anne sighed. "Daddy's going to be furious at me when he finds out that I've lost his camera."

"Well, there's not much we can do about that right now," Lee said. "I can't wait," she added, "to get back and meet this superspy of yours."

Anne cast an exasperated look in Lee's direction. "He's not a superspy, Emily Elizabeth, and he's not *my* anything."

"Right," Lee replied. "So, anyway, do you think that this total stranger for whom you have no feelings whatsoever would mind if we used his camera?"

"See, I knew you'd tease me this way if I told you."

"You love it."

"I do not," Anne said, ignoring the comment but not quite suppressing a smile, "and anyhow I can't see it would do any harm to take a picture or two. Let's find out. If worse comes to worse, well, maybe I can make it right by giving him a—" Anne stopped intentionally in midsentence.

"Yes?"

"—nother roll of film," she finished quickly, sticking her tongue out at Lee.

Lee shook her head. "Really, Anne, I'm glad you don't meet guys like this more often. It makes you kind of—"

"Fun?"

"More like *funny*."

"You're just jealous."

"Hey, I have an idea!" Lee suddenly stood up in the dhow. "Achmed! Take our picture, will you?"

Achmed cheerfully obliged. He took the Leica, quickly adjusting the lens and f-stop, then snapped the picture of Lee and Anne. He'd done this before. Then Anne and Lee took each other's picture with their newfound friend.

As they drifted along in silence, Anne relaxed against a large, overstuffed pillow. Warm in the sun, soothed by the swaying of the dhow, she found that Jake's face had again drifted unbidden into her daydreaming mind. His eyes sparkled as he laughed. They talked easily together. Jake had one strong hand on the tiller, and his other hand was reaching out to her. . . . Then it was night, and it was just she and Jake, stars and pillows and the dhow's gentle rocking. . . .

Anne shook herself awake. She could feel herself trembling, filled with feelings she didn't understand, a mixture of joy and uncertainty.

"Dreaming?" Lee asked from the other side of the dhow.

"Sort of." Anne shook her hair out of her eyes and reached for her hairbrush in her carryall. "Seems like we've been sailing for quite a while."

"It's great, isn't it?" Lee said.

"Just how much is this costing us, anyway?"

Lee told her.

"You're kidding!" Anne exclaimed. "Why so little?"

Lee looked superior. "Easy! I found out that if you're willing to bargain, then they won't ask much, just to get you aboard. Then, if you like the cruise, you stuff money under the cushions. Like this," Lee said. She demonstrated by shoving a dollar under one of the cushions.

"How fun!" Anne exclaimed. She rooted around in her carryall and came up with a five. Achmed watched the two out of the corner of his eye and grinned.

They were in the main channel of the Nile now, and other dhows surrounded them like butterflies. Powerboats zoomed past, their wakes setting the *Queen Nefertiti* to rocking.

As they drifted past the gardens that dominated the southern end of Gezira Island, Lee barked regally, "A date, slave!" and reached her hand out to Anne.

"Yes, Highness! At once, Highness!" Anne replied, the

very picture of deference. Bowing humbly over Lee's out-stretched hand, Anne delicately spat the pit from the date she had just finished into Lee's palm .

"Oh, how gross!" Lee screamed. She threw the pit over the side and plunged her hand into the Nile as Anne and Achmed laughed uproariously.

"Achmed!" Lee commanded. "Fling this impertinent wench to the crocodiles!" Lee frowned. "And, while you're at it, fling yourself to them, too!"

"Your wish is my command, Highness!" Achmed replied, bowing low. "But, there be no crocs hereabouts."

"Darn!" Lee pouted. "Oh, well . . . "

"Lee," Anne laughed, "remember your Lewis Carroll?"

> *"How doth the little crocodile*
> *Improve his shining tail,*
> *And pour the waters of the Nile*
> *On every golden scale!"*

"Now, missies," Achmed went on, "You come with me up to Aswan. You come with me three, four days upriver, and I show you some real crocodiles! Up there, missies, the crocs get five, maybe six meters long."

The two women looked at the little dhow, all of four meters in length, and then, wide-eyed, at each other.

"One o' them gets ahold o' you, he go down to the bottom 'n stay there till you stop kicking. Then he stick you under a log—four, maybe five days, till you soften up."

"Good Lord!" Lee exclaimed.

"Yes, missies. Nile crocs best there is!" Achmed smiled at the shaken pair, his solemn demeanor betrayed by the twinkling in his eyes.

Assuming an orator's pose, Achmed continued the recitation, changing Carroll's words slightly to suit the occasion.

> *"How cheerfully he seems to grin,*
> *How neatly spreads his claws,*
> *And welcomes little missies in,*
> *With gently smiling jaws!*

"Yes, young ladies. I've read it, too."

Their laughter was soon drowned out by the roar of a boat's motor.

The sound grew louder, and Lee, Anne, and Achmed turned around to see a speedboat headed straight for them. The driver seemed oblivious to the danger he was creating. Achmed yelled, furiously gesturing toward the driver to change course.

At the last instant the powerboat veered sharply away, nearly swamping the dhow with its wake. Achmed, purple with rage, shook his fist at the departing boat. "Sons of trollops!" he raged. "Gutterborn, illegitimate, hellspawned—"

"They're coming back!" Lee shouted.

The powerboat roared up, then swerved and came to rest a few feet from them. Its wake washed over the side of the dhow. Two men sat in the cockpit, watching them impassively.

Achmed leaped up onto the dhow's gunwale. He shook both fists and hurled abuse in Arabic at the pair. Suddenly, a third man popped up from the open area in the back of the speedboat. Sunlight glinted off the submachine gun he held. Flame spouted from the gun's snout, and a row of jagged holes appeared in the sail.

Achmed looked up at the sail. He frowned as puzzlement supplanted his rage.

Just as he looked back at the powerboat, a burst from the

machine gun caught him in the chest. It hurled him off the dhow's stern and into the Nile.

Both women screamed. They jumped up.

"Kill this one?" the man with the gun asked his partners. He swung the machine gun toward Anne.

"No!" the man behind the wheel barked. "The dark-haired one, she is the one commander wants!"

A gust of wind caught the *Queen Nefertiti*. Without a hand on the tiller, the dhow jibed sharply. The boom lashed across the deck, catching Anne in the small of her back, throwing her over the side.

She disappeared for a moment, then surfaced near the speedboat. The other man sitting in the powerboat's cockpit got up and reached over the side. He grabbed Anne by her hair and one arm and hauled the frantically struggling woman into the powerboat.

"Annie!" Lee screamed.

"Kill that one!" the driver of the powerboat ordered. The gunman, who had been watching Anne, brought up the gun and swung it around at Lee.

Lee threw herself backwards into the water and dove deep. Muffled *thunks* reached her ears as a volley of bullets tore through the dhow, which now shielded her from the gunman. Lee tried desperately to stay below the surface. She watched as the already-swamped *Queen Nefertiti*, her bottom torn out by the large-caliber bullets, started sinking lower into the water.

Her lungs frantic for air, Lee knew that she had to surface. She looked up, saw the black bulk of the powerboat, and realized that they were waiting for her. She angled toward the far side of the dhow, hoping it would shield her from their view long enough for her to catch a breath of air. Closing her eyes, she began to pray as she floated toward the surface.

Just as her head broke the water, the speedboat's engine

came to life. Lee shook the water out of her eyes. The speedboat already was powering away.

Lee turned and looked up at the flashing blue light of a Cairo Harbor Patrol boat and its crew approaching.

Two crew members in khaki uniforms reached out to Lee and hauled her aboard. She collapsed onto the deck, gasping. A pair of gleaming boots came into her field of view. She pulled herself to her hands and knees and looked up at the boat's commanding officer.

"Are you OK?" he asked, kneeling down beside her.

"We have to catch that boat," she cried, gasping.

"It's already too late. It's so much faster than we are. By now they're around the far side of Gezira Island."

Lee flung her hair out of her face, showering droplets, and looked out over the patrol boat's gunwale at the smoky, crowded Cairo skyline. "No!" she screamed. Lee beat her fists on the teak decking. "No, God, no! Annie! *Annie!*"

# 12

"I'm not cleared for this sort of thing," Ed Mahoney protested. He kept his hands away from the folder in front of him, as if it were trying to bite him.

Mike O'Brian smiled at Mahoney from behind his desk. "Took most of the morning to pull off," he said as he slid a piece of paper across the desk, "but you are now."

Mahoney blinked at the White House seal at the top of the page. He scanned the letter, which informed him that he had just been given a security clearance that he hadn't even known existed.

"The downside," O'Brian said soberly, "is right there in front of you." He pointed at the folder. "Read it and weep—we've decided that your inquiring mind needs to know." The chief of staff stood up. "I'll be back in a minute."

Mahoney picked up the folder and unfastened the clasp that held it shut. He opened the cardboard cover and looked at the first page:

**OPERATION EHUD**

was centered at the top of the page. In the lower right-hand corner was

**DeltaBravoSeven**
**Eyes Only—Michael R. O'Brian**
**Copy 2 of 5**

The two and the five were handwritten. O'Brian's signature was scrawled on a line beneath his name. Mahoney looked at the notations, then picked up the letter on the White House stationery. His new security clearance, it reminded him, was DeltaBravoSeven.

Wondering what he had gotten into and wishing he hadn't, Mahoney turned the page and started to read.

> **Operation Ehud was proposed by Israel after the Yom Kippur War and ratified by the United States after the takeover of the U.S. embassy in Tehran. It calls for the intermingling of U.S. and Israeli technology to enable the localized delivery of a single, tactical offensive strike in such a fashion that blame could be assigned positively to neither country.**

Mahoney blinked several times in disbelief, then turned the page.

> **Ehud takes advantage of a series of circumstances to create a smoke-and-mirrors scenario. In 1985 a defecting Soviet pilot flew his YAK-36 Forger fighter/bomber from its base at Yerevan in the Soviet province of Georgia 750 miles to the airstrip at Safad in the northwest corner of Israel. At the extreme limit of the Forger's range, the aircraft ran**

out of fuel on final approach, and its pilot fought the YAK to a dead-stick landing. The aircraft was delivered intact to Israeli Intelligence.

That same year the U.S. Air Force acquired a number of Israeli "Popeye" TV-guided, medium-range missiles in an effort to improve its standoff strike capability.

Mahoney looked up. He remembered an article in *Aviation Week* describing how the new standoff technology allowed ordnance to be delivered from outside the range of enemy search radar. He frowned, then went back to reading.

One of the U.S. modifications to the Popeye, renamed the AGM-142A Have Nap, was to permit it to be loaded with a specially designed, 350-kilo, high-explosive warhead. The shaped-charge/en-hanced-yield warhead is effective against a wide variety of hardened targets.

The Have Nap is "smart" ordnance in the sense that its inertial guidance computer may be preprogrammed through the delivery platform's OAS (Offensive Avionics System), or target selec-tion and ordnance delivery may be achieved after launching via the AGM-142A's internal TV-based homing capabilities. To this end, a specially modi-fied AN/ASQ-172 STV (Steerable low-light Tele-vision) Fire Control System was installed in the YAK.

Under the provisions of Ehud, one of the modified Have Naps was delivered to Israel and mounted on the YAK-36, which had been retrofit-ted to accept it. If both countries invoke Ehud and agree upon a target, the Forger will be used to deliver it.

The tactical beauty of Ehud is that it renders culpability essentially unassignable. A Soviet aircraft delivers a strike via a missile of either American or Israeli manufacture.

*If this is beautiful,* Mahoney thought, *I'd hate to know what they think is gorgeous.* He went back to the report.

Advantages:

The YAK's transponder is intact. This will allow it to reply to IFF interrogations as a Soviet aircraft.

The standoff capability of the AGM-142A allows the aircraft to launch from outside the airspace of the target country (and hence from international or, ideally, third-country airspace).

The Have Nap's "fire and forget" mode provides maximum time after launch for the pilot to escape, and its heat signature cannot be traced to a particular nation.

Contraindications and Limitations:

For optimal effectiveness, a pilot who is neither Israeli nor American should pilot the Forger.

The Have Nap requires a heat-generating target.

The relatively restricted range of the AGM-142A (roughly 80 kilometers) limits the available targets.

Target lists are attached.

Mahoney wanted to pinch himself and wake up from this nightmare. He thumbed through the lists of targets until he found the one labeled EGYPT.

"A semicircle," it read, "centered on the coastal city of Baltim and ranging from Alexandria on the west to Zifta on the south to Port Said on the east." *And somewhere in that semicircle,* Mahoney thought, *is Cathy Hagura.*

O'Brian came back into the room.

"You've got to be kidding," Mahoney said. "Is this some kind of joke?"

"If it is," O'Brian said quietly, "then Israel is waiting to deliver the punch line."

He sat down behind his desk. "The Israelis are fed up. They're champing at the bit to try out their toys." O'Brian held Mahoney's gaze. "Don't forget how they sat on their hands for us during the last war—we owe them this one." The chief of staff shrugged. "They know it, too, and they're calling in their markers. Yatzhin invoked their half of Ehud on the phone this morning. He wants our choice of target within forty-eight hours."

"And we're going to tell him to take a flying leap, right?"

O'Brian just smiled. "That depends on you."

Mahoney came out of his chair. "I'll have nothing to do with this!"

The chief of staff put his feet up on his desk. "Sure about that, Ed? What if I told you that you were the only one who could prevent Ehud from happening?"

Mahoney frowned. "I don't follow you."

"The president pointed out to the prime minister that an American was allegedly involved in this little atrocity, and that his country was also participating in the manhunt. He asked for, and got, forty-eight hours to track MacIntyre down." O'Brian looked at Mahoney. "If we don't hear from your agent within that time, with either MacIntyre or some really fine evidence clutched in her hot little hands . . . " O'Brian held his hands up, his spread fingers making a ball in front of his face, *"Ka-boom!"*

*Welcome to Wonderland,* Mahoney thought. *Off with their heads.*

"Who, or what, is an 'Ehud'?" Mahoney asked as he rose to leave.

"Ehud," O'Brian explained, "was one of the great covert-ops men in the Old Testament." The chief of staff grinned. "Terrific name, isn't it?" O'Brian looked pointedly at his watch. "Only forty hours left. Better get to work, Ed. Keep in touch."

"I am Lieutenant Karanis of the Cairo Harbor Patrol. And you are?" The question trailed off expectantly.

Lee looked up, startled out of her anguish. "What? Oh, I'm Lee—Emily Parker."

The man who addressed her was short and portly. Kind eyes regarded her from above a mustache shot with gray. "This is a terrible thing that has happened, Miss Parker," Karanis said. The gold braid on his peaked cap glinted as he shook his head in sympathy. "We will have to make a full report, of course."

Karanis offered his hand to Lee. "Until we dock, perhaps we would be more comfortable in the wheelhouse." The lieutenant helped Lee to her feet and escorted her to the boat's small cabin. Once inside, he radioed Harbor Patrol headquarters and reported Anne's kidnapping. The patrol boat captain then came back to where Lee sat, hands over her mouth, staring blindly at the passing shoreline. Seeing Lee shiver, Karanis took off his uniform jacket and offered it to her.

The lieutenant ordered that coffee be sent up. Karanis then picked up a clipboard and sat down next to Lee. "Now, then, Miss Parker. What is your friend's name?"

"Anne Dryden."

"Her nationality?"

"We're American."

"Age?"

"Annie's twenty-five."

Karanis shook his head. "The same age as my daughter Fatmeh." *And not too old*, he thought, *for the slave trade.* Karanis suppressed a shudder. "And how did you happen to be out sailing today?"

In a dazed, detached fashion, Lee told the lieutenant about how she and Anne had chartered Achmed and the *Queen Nefertiti* for an afternoon of sight-seeing. "I know them both," Karanis said. "A good man and a good dhow." His knuckles whitened with rage at the loss of an old friend. "Do you know anyone in Cairo?"

"No."

"Do you know of any reason why anyone would want to kidnap your friend?"

Lee shook her head bleakly.

As the questions continued, the wheelhouse door opened, and a seaman brought in two mugs of coffee. Lee accepted the proffered mug without realizing she had done so. Only a fraction of her mind was answering the lieutenant's questions; the rest of her was consumed with her worry for Anne. Preoccupied, she took too big a sip of the steaming coffee; a scalded tongue jolted her out of her reverie. She looked at Karanis, who was filling out a form. "Lieutenant, could this wait a little while? Please?"

Karanis smiled compassionately. "Of course, Miss Parker. My apologies." The lieutenant said something in Arabic to the helmsman and then left the wheelhouse.

Lee clutched the mug as if trying to draw Anne back through the thick, white porcelain. Frightened and afraid, Lee bowed her head, her prayer little more than a mental whisper.

*Father God, Annie needs you. She always needs someone to take care of her, and now she's alone and very scared. Watch over her, Jesus. Bring her back to us. Please, please don't let them hurt her.* Lee swallowed hard and took a deep breath. *And God, if Annie's guardian angel does have a twin, send her to Annie. She needs her more right now than I do.*

The last thought of her prayer started tears falling.

A car was waiting for them at the Harbor Patrol dock. Lee looked at Karanis as they disembarked. "We must finish taking your statement, Miss Parker," he explained. "And then, of course, your embassy must be notified."

Karanis was mercifully silent on the drive to headquarters. He helped Lee out of the car and into the building. After a short elevator ride, Lee found herself in a harshly lit room. A tall, thin man with a neatly groomed mustache rose as Lee and Karanis came in. "Miss Parker, I am Lieutenant Rahab of the Cairo Police. Please, do sit down."

Two other uniformed officers stood silently in the corners of the room. "I am very sorry that this has happened, and every effort is being made to locate—," Rahab glanced at a clipboard he was holding and finished, "Miss Dryden." Rahab sat down next to Lee. "But first, just a few more questions."

The air-conditioning came on, and Lee shivered in the resulting draft. Rivulets of tears trickled down her cheeks. *I can't believe this is happening,* Lee thought as fear and disbelief fought within her for supremacy. Images paraded through her mind: the glitter of Achmed's teeth became the glint of a gun barrel, Anne's relaxed laughter modulated into her frantic screams.

Lee shivered and then sneezed. "I'm cold," she said.

"I quite understand, but we need more information."

The questions seemed endless. Where were they staying in Cairo? How long had they been in the country? Any contacts with Egyptians? On and on. Lee answered them by rote as she huddled on the chair, alone, wet, and miserable.

"Did Miss Dryden have any visitors?" Rahab asked.

Lee looked up, blinking. "One. This morning."

"Do you know who it was?"

Lee scrubbed her face with her hands. "Yes."

"We need to know who that might have been."

Lee hesitated, then spoke. "Jake MacIntyre."

The lieutenant's eyes grew very wide.

Two floors above where Lee sat, Vinnie Petigura slammed down the phone. Cathy and Jeremias looked at him inquiringly.

"Harbor Patrol," he explained. "Someone was kidnapped off of a boat out on the Nile a little while ago. Witness downstairs says that MacIntyre visited the missing woman this morning." Vinnie stood. "Let's go."

All three headed toward the door.

Vinnie, closely pursued by Cathy and Jeremias, burst through the door of the interrogation room downstairs. Rahab introduced himself and began running down the details of the case. Cathy pushed her way past the two men to where Lee sat, forlorn and shoeless. Her sodden sundress clung to her, and wet curls clustered around her face.

Cathy took one look at Lee, and a small volcano erupted in the interrogation room. "Just what's going on here?" Cathy shouted.

Rahab, his report interrupted, looked up.

"And you—," Cathy thundered, stabbing a finger at the aghast Rahab, "don't you know anything about procedure? Where's the policewoman who's supposed to be here when a woman is being questioned?"

Rahab looked helplessly at Vinnie.

Cathy helped Lee to her feet and started toward the door.

"Vinnie!" Cathy commanded. "I want a car and driver waiting at the front door by the time we get there." She glared at the assembled men as she escorted the dazed Lee to the door. Once safely beyond them, Cathy turned around. *"After* this woman gets a hot shower, and *after* she gets a change of clothes, and *after* she gets some rest, then I'll bring her back! Not before, got it?"

Vinnie nodded, not trying to hide his admiration, and picked up the phone.

Dan Jeremias made a move as if to block the doorway. "But—," he blurted.

"Move it, Jeremias!" Cathy snarled. *"Now!"*

Jeremias moved.

Cathy led Lee downstairs and into the waiting car.

While Lee showered, Cathy called the American embassy. Cathy knew that Lee would want to tell someone about Anne's disappearance. She also knew that the Egyptian phone service varied between cantankerous and nonexistent, so she called the embassy's communications section to arrange the connection.

"Commo," a cheerful voice said from the other end of the line.

"Cathy Hagura. Can I get a good phone line between here," she said, reading off the phone number of the hotel, "and the States?"

"No problem, Cathy. When do you want it?" Everyone on the embassy staff had been briefed that whatever Agent Hagura wanted, Agent Hagura got.

Cathy looked at her watch. *Let's see. Enough time for something to eat and to talk for a while.* "How about at nine?" Cathy frowned as she tried to remember the time difference between Cairo and the U.S. "What time is that in the States?"

PART I

"Let's see, 9:00 P.M. here is 3:00 P.M. eastern time," the voice replied. "Will a four-wire do?"

"A what?"

"A four-wire. It's a straight, dedicated satellite linkup." The voice paused. "You don't need encryption, or anything, do you?"

Cathy blinked, then smiled as she got an idea. "No. A four-wire will do. So long as it works."

"Guaranteed. Just call back at nine."

The bathroom door opened. Cathy looked up from her notes. Lee, hair wrapped in a towel, came out of the bathroom. The places she had missed while drying herself off blotched the oversized red T-shirt she had pulled on. Cathy wrote in her notebook as Lee pulled clothes out of the closet.

Once dressed, Lee sank down into the chair across the table from Cathy. "I don't know how to thank you," Lee stammered, not knowing what to say to this stranger who had rescued her.

"It's OK, Miss Parker. Those men should've known better than to let you freeze in that horrible room." Cathy paused, looking sheepish. "I guess I should introduce myself," she continued. "There wasn't time on the ride over here." Cathy pulled out the folder containing her badge and ID card and held it up. "Cathy Hagura, U.S. State Department."

Lee, taken aback by the badge, blinked several times. "What can I possibly do for you . . . Agent Hagura?"

Cathy stuck the folder back in a pocket. "First off, call me Cathy, OK? That 'agent' sounds too much like spy shows on TV."

"Fine," Lee replied. She relaxed a little. "Call me Lee." Slowly realizing what had just happened, Lee looked admiringly at the woman who sat across from her. Here was someone forceful enough to cow a roomful of policemen, yet sensitive

105

enough to realize that she had needed help. *You're quite something, Agent Hagura,* Lee thought. *A velvet fist in an iron glove.*

But Cathy knew that her action was done only partly to protect Lee. Sequestering Lee was the best way to get a chance to talk to her first, before Vinnie and Jeremias. As the investigation progressed, Cathy had become increasingly convinced of Jake's innocence, a feeling shared by neither of her fellow investigators. She knew that both the Egyptian and Israeli governments had been leaning heavily on their agents for a breakthrough in a case that was inflaming old antipathies in both countries. Cathy felt that this pressure was responsible for the overzealous desire by Vinnie and Jeremias to see Jake caught and convicted. Out of this feeling had come the need to protect both MacIntyre and his right to due process.

And in Lee, Cathy saw a crime victim, a woman being treated insensitively by a bunch of blundering men. She had seen enough of it in the States, and it infuriated her. She responded immediately and forcefully to another woman's needs.

The two women emerged from their thoughts at the same time. The short, stocky Hawaiian looked at the tall, blonde New Englander she had just rescued.

"Feel like some dinner?" Cathy asked.

Lee was surprised to find herself nodding. Throughout all of this, a part of her had been thinking of Anne, and that part was worried, confused, and not hungry at all.

"Up to talking while we eat?" Cathy asked, reaching for the phone. Lee nodded again as Cathy dialed room service.

The starched, liveried waiter set the table and then motioned to them. Each woman's chair was held for her, and her napkin was swished into her lap with a flourish. Both Cathy and Lee managed to refrain from laughing until the door closed behind the waiter and his cart.

"Wow!" Cathy said as she surveyed the table. "Pretty fancy service for a dump in downtown Cairo." She looked up quickly at her dinner partner. "Sorry. That didn't come out the way I meant it."

Lee shrugged. "That's OK. This *is* a dump. If I'd had my way, we would've stayed with the rest of the tour at the Semiramis InterContinental. But," she continued, gesturing at the small, plain room, "this is how Annie likes it. More authentic. Says that it helps her get a feel for a place."

Cathy started to reply, then stopped when she saw that Lee's hands were folded and her head was bowed. She waited quietly until Lee looked up. "Do you always pray before meals?" Cathy asked.

"Always," Lee replied firmly. "Except," she added with a sheepish grin, "when I'm rushed, busy, mad, or I just plain forget."

"You didn't forget tonight," Cathy said.

"That was for Annie," Lee said quietly.

As they ate, Cathy looked at the woman who sat across the table from her. "Tell me about Anne," she said in response to the need that was plain on Lee's face.

"Where do I start?" Lee pulled a breadstick from the basket in the center of the table and toyed with it as she talked. "Well, for one thing, Anne Dryden's like no one else you've ever met."

"How so?" Cathy asked.

"Things that are important to most women don't interest her at all. She doesn't care much about clothes, or makeup, or anything like that. I can't remember the last time we went shopping together.

"She gets up in the morning, puts on whatever's handy,

runs her hands through her hair, and off she goes. Of course, with her face and hair and figure, that's all she really needs to do. . . .

"It's typical of her that she prefers a hotel like this. It's a place unconcerned with outward appearances, but inwardly it's graceful and elegant." Lee gestured at the linen tablecloth and at the silverware that gleamed in the candlelight. "Who would've thought that some place that looked so unassuming from the outside would serve up a meal like this? Annie's like that. It's the inward things that are important to her."

"Like what?" Cathy asked.

"She cares for people." Lee's face tightened at the thought of her friend. "I'm not sure who loves the other more—Annie or her first graders. Every year she becomes a part of each one of their lives. Like everything else she does, being the best possible teacher is all that matters."

"What else does she do?"

"Annie reads more books in a month than I do in a year, and she plays the violin like you wouldn't believe."

Cathy took a sip of coffee, then asked, "Does Anne have a boyfriend?"

"Boyfriend?" Lee laughed. "Believe me, I've tried." Lee warmed to her favorite topic. "For years I've introduced guys to her. At most one date, and then nothing."

Cathy grinned. "Any idea why?"

"I'll ask how it went, and she'll shrug and say, 'Oh, he's nice enough, but he just doesn't have that certain something.' When I ask her what that 'certain something' is, she shrugs again and says, 'I don't know, but I'll know it when I see it.'" Lee made a face. "Really!"

Cathy laughed. She understood both points of view.

"Actually," Lee continued, "Annie has a lot of trouble making friends."

"With the looks and brains that you say she has, I find that hard to believe," Cathy said. *I should be so cursed*, she thought.

"That's just it," Lee replied. "Men who go after her for her looks are put off by her brains, and women who admire her for her brains are put off by her looks."

All Cathy could do was shake her head in amazement. She glanced at her watch—9:03. "Lee," Cathy said, "someone in the family should be notified of Anne's disappearance. Would you be able to do that?"

Lee took a deep breath and nodded. "Annie and I have been trying the whole time we've been here to get a line to call home. No luck."

"That's what I figured," Cathy said as she picked up the phone and dialed. "We'll go through the embassy." A minute passed, then Cathy handed Lee the phone. "That dial tone is in the States. Who're you going to call?"

"Annie's parents."

# 13

At the shout of "Hi, Professor!" Joel Dryden looked up from the bed of irises he was tending. Dryden, a lean, compact man in his late fifties, settled back on his haunches and wiped his brow on his sleeve. He waved to Dave Wilkins as he made his way up the long drive to the rambling farmhouse that was the Dryden family home. Usually Dave just put the mail in the roadside box, but his making the trek up the drive meant that there was news to share.

As Dave puffed his way up the driveway, Joel looked out over the stands of red cedar and white pine that lined Somes Sound. Through breaks in the lowering, rain-heavy clouds, shafts of sunlight traced lines of jade-green in the slate-gray waters. Across the sound, forested hills rose sharply toward Sargent Mountain inside Acadia National Park.

The house in Trenton, Maine, had been the Dryden summer home for a hundred years. Many a soft June evening had been spent rocking together on the porch as they watched little Annie and her friends, wild with glee, shriek in delight as they chased fireflies through the long Maine twilight. Joel and his wife, Pat, had decided to move there after Anne had entered college and Joel had retired. Now they waited hopefully and none-too-patiently for the next generation of toddlers to come along and again fill the lawn with laughter.

Although the Drydens were from "away," as the natives of Trenton described anyone not from their immediate vicinity, Joel and Pat, as longtime summer residents in good standing, had been welcomed and accepted when they moved in to stay. When asked what he had done for a living, Joel merely smiled and replied, "Government service." This had caused some concern among the residents of Trenton until he assured them that he had not worked for the IRS.

Upon retirement, Joel had accepted an adjunct professorship in international relations at nearby Bowdoin College, where he taught the occasional course. The townspeople, after finding this out, insisted on calling him "Professor," and Joel had given up on trying to dissuade them from doing so.

Dave completed his trudge up the driveway. Joel rose and shook the man's hand, giving the postman time to catch his breath. "So, what brings you all the way up here?" Dave smiled. Joel's chiding of him over the alleged arduousness of the quarter-mile, gentle climb from the road was an old joke between them. "Postcard from Annie?" Joel asked hopefully.

"'Fraid not, Professor. How long has it been since you heard from her?"

Joel grinned. "A week, as you well know."

Dave grinned back. Anne had been the summertime sweetheart of Trenton since she was born, and all the Drydens knew and appreciated the fact that Anne's postcards were read by most of the townsfolk before Dave delivered them. "I wouldn't worry if'n I were you, Professor," Dave said encouragingly. "You know how girls that age are. And," he continued, throwing up his hands, "you know them foreign postal services. . . . " Dave riffled through the sheaf of mail and pulled out an envelope. "Got one here I'd like the stamp off'n, if'n you don't mind."

Dave's son, Marshall, was an avid stamp collector. Joel had long ago started giving Marshall the stamps from the letters he received from around the world.

Joel took the proffered envelope and examined the stamp on it. "Interesting," he said. Joel peered at the stamp more closely. "I don't believe I recognize it." He took out a small pocketknife, slit the envelope open, then carefully cut out the stamp and handed it to Dave. The postman slid the stamp into a shirt pocket.

"Thanks, Professor!"

"No problem. When Marsh identifies it, you have him come by and tell me, OK?"

"Sure thing."

Dave paused, then rummaged around in his bag. "Oh, yeah. Almost forgot the latest batch of Annie's pictures." He handed Joel a bulky envelope. "See ya." Dave strode off, whistling.

As he walked around to the back of the house, Joel pulled the pictures from their mailing envelope and began leafing through them. When he reached the back porch, he kicked off his green gum boots and entered the kitchen.

Pat Dryden looked up from the piecrust she was rolling out and smiled when Joel held up the now-familiar, yellow packet as he sat down at the kitchen table. She dusted her floury hands on her apron and leaned over her husband's shoulder to look at the pictures.

"Oh, look!" Pat exclaimed. "Seems like they're having a wonderful time! . . . Annie looks tanned and happy. . . . Wonder where she got that *darling* hat?"

Joel handed her a picture of the two girls sitting at an outdoor café. Across a narrow, cobblestoned street from their table was a river spanned by a succession of stone bridges.

Pat, not recognizing the locale, nudged her husband.

"Where's this?" she asked, holding up the picture. "Look at those little streets, and that river, and those wonderful buildings. It looks terribly romantic."

"Huh?" Joel exclaimed. He peered at the picture. "Oh, that's the Via Vecchio in Florence. That little shop they're sitting in front of makes great ice cream, and just behind them is the Goldsmith's Bridge. Beautiful city."

Pat Dryden pulled up a chair next to her husband's, sat down, and leaned against his shoulder. "Then how come you've never taken me there?"

Joel beamed innocently at his wife. "Because, just like you said, my dear, it's terribly romantic. Much too romantic for someone as down-to-earth as you—"

"Well!" Pat turned away in mock anger, then nestled back against Joel as he handed her the next picture.

During her tenure as chief pediatric psychiatrist at the teaching hospital of the University of California at San Francisco, Dr. Pat Sewell had been known to her residents as "the Razor." They had bestowed the nickname upon her out of respect for the sharpness and keen edge she had demanded both of them and of herself. They looked upon her with an awe bordering on fear and fought for the privilege of accompanying her on her rounds. In her early thirties, at a time when all her friends had married in their early twenties, she was labeled a career woman, and a husband and family were things she had tried to stop thinking about.

One night at a party, a friend had introduced her to a man she thought Dr. Pat Sewell ought to get to know. Thirteen months later Dr. Pat Dryden found herself the guest of honor at a baby shower given by her nurses and residents. In the ensuing months, as her child grew within her, Pat had wrestled with what she should do with her life.

The war within Pat was fought daily: A patient of hers, a toddler whose little life was already a shattered jumble of abused and neglected shards, had at last responded to Pat's gentle ministrations and lifted her chubby arms to be held. She had swept the baby girl up into her arms, both of them crying, and Pat Dryden the physician had thanked God for using her as a tool in the miracle of a little girl, knowing that she was safe at last. Then the life enwombed within her would kick, or stir, or make its presence known, and Pat Dryden the mother-to-be would identify with Sarah, Hannah, Elizabeth, and all biblical mothers who had waited so long to be so blessed.

Talks with her pastor, her mother, and her friends provided a multitude of opinions but no solution; prayer provided solace and encouragement but no answers; long wintry nights holding Joel's hand under the mound of quilts that covered their bed provided comfort but no resolution.

Then, in the early hours of what would be a very fine spring day, Pat Dryden, now both physician and mother, red-faced with the strain of labor and sodden with its sweat, first looked into the eyes of her seconds-old daughter. She resigned from the university the next day and had never thought of the decision again. Pat had kept her medical license current while Anne was growing up, and when Anne went off to college, Pat resumed a part-time practice. Days tending her garden were interspersed with days tending the local children at the Trenton clinic; trips to consult at the hospitals in Augusta and Portland alternated with long weekends with Joel in Vermont.

She was content.

Just as they finished looking at the pictures from Italy, the phone rang. Joel handed the packet of photos to Pat, then reached out and snagged the phone from its cradle on the kitchen wall.

Isobel Wilkins, Dave the postman's wife, ran Trenton's switchboard. As the unofficial town criers, she and Dave saw to it that any interesting or exotic piece of news was broadcast throughout the village. But respected even more than their efficiency was their discretion; if the news was in any way embarrassing or confidential, it never left their lips.

"Professor, I've got a person-to-person for you or Doctor Dryden. It's from Miss Parker." Isobel paused. "I think she's upset about something."

"Go ahead, Isobel. Put Lee on." Joel pointed toward the extension in the family room. Pat, her face a mixture of surprise and concern, headed toward it.

"Hi, honey, how're you—" The anticipatory smile vanished from Joel's face. "Lee, I can't understand you. . . . Calm down, honey, and tell me what's wrong. . . . Annie? . . . What about Annie?" Joel heard his wife's sharp intake of breath.

"Auntie Pat, are you there?" Lee inquired on the other end.

"Yes, dear, I'm right here." Pat laid the photos on her writing desk and sat down in the desk chair.

"Oh, Auntie Pat, I'm so sorry. . . . " Lee dissolved into sobs.

"*Emily Elizabeth Parker, you stop it right now and tell me what's wrong!*" It was Pat's "doctor" voice, and involuntarily Joel winced at her tone. He had heard it before: when Pat was reprimanding an unruly resident; when she was telling a father that if she had her way he would never see his daughter again, much less lay his hands on her; and, a very few times over the years when it had been directed at him. Pat's voice carried the commanding tone of someone in unquestioned authority and who demanded instant obedience. Pat had never demanded obedience from her husband; but she had demanded his undivided attention, and with that voice she had always received it.

Joel was somewhat surprised at hearing it, as he had never before heard his wife use that tone on a child. But, the thought flashed through his head, *neither Lee nor Annie's a child anymore.*

"That's better, dear." Doctor Dryden was now again Auntie Pat: soothing, calming, nurturing. Lee's frantic sobbing subsided, and she began explaining what had happened to Anne.

Joel listened, stunned, to the news of his daughter's abduction. "Lee," he interjected, "are you sure that Annie's been kidnapped?"

"The police here think so." Lee paused. "They had guns, Uncle Joel."

"Is there someone there I can talk to?" Joel asked.

"Yes. Her name's Cathy, she's a government agent, and she needs to talk to you, too."

Just as much as Pat, Joel wanted to know what had happened to Anne. But Lee was at hand and needed caring for, too. Joel spoke firmly but gently to the only daughter of his oldest friend, Jack Parker. "Lee, honey, now you listen to me. Whatever's happened to Annie, it's not your fault. You got that? It's not your fault, honey. We know that you love her just as much as we do and that you've done everything you can to take care of her."

"You listen to your Uncle Joel, now. OK?" Pat added. "And Lee, sweetheart, you remember something else: We love you just as much as we love Annie."

"Thanks, Auntie Pat."

"Lee," Joel said, "you call your folks—we'll call them too. Now let me talk to whoever's in charge there. And you come right home."

"But, what about—"

"Annie's in God's hands now. All you can do is love her, think of her, and pray for her."

"I am, Uncle Joel, I am."

As Joel waited for the government agent to come on the line, he turned, and his wife's arms were around him. Juggling the phone with one hand, Joel put his other arm around Pat and gathered her to him. He felt her warm tears dampen his shirt as he held her shaking shoulders. Joel then realized that someone was saying "Hello?" into the phone, and he tore his attention away from his wife.

"Yes, this is Joel Dryden. Who is this?" Hunching his shoulder to hold the phone against his ear, Joel groped for a pencil and some paper as he listened. "Senior Agent Cathy Hagura of the State Department Security Division," Joel repeated as he wrote. "Yes, Agent Hagura, go ahead."

He scribbled for a few seconds, trying to get it all down. "Agent Hagura," Joel asked, "is there someone there, a woman, to take care of Miss Parker? . . . You will? Thanks very much . . . . Yes, I'll contact the embassy." Joel shook his head and held Pat a little more tightly as he tried to catch up with the onslaught of events. "Isn't there anything more you can tell me? . . . Yes, I'm sure you're doing everything possible. Let us know if there's anything we can do. . . . Thank you. Good-bye."

Joel straightened. The phone fell to the floor as he wrapped his arms around his wife and stroked her hair.

The kitchen door opened. Through tear-blurred eyes Joel saw Meredith Llewellyn framed in the doorway. Not wishing to intrude, she stood there silently, anguish plain on her face. Joel motioned with his head for her to come in. Meredith walked across the kitchen, arms outstretched in comfort. As Pat turned and was encircled by those arms Joel realized that, through Isobel, the word had gone out: *The Drydens need help. Something's happened to Anne.* Since Meredith lived next door to the Drydens, Isobel had called her first, knowing that she could arrive quickly.

And arrive they did. Friends, neighbors, anyone who knew Anne headed toward the Dryden family home. The kitchen counters disappeared under cakes, pies, and casseroles. The women clustered around Pat, touching her shoulder or holding her hand, as their husbands listened to Joel with stern faces and clenched fists.

Henry French, the gnarled old lobsterman who had taken Anne for her first boat ride, came in, still in his foul-weather gear. Henry approached the Drydens, twisting his oilskin hat into a shapeless knot, his face working. "I'm not much of a prayin' man, as you know," Henry said as he stared hard at the floor, "but I'll be a prayin' for Annie, I will."

"Bless you Henry," Pat said. "Thank you very much."

Then Christopher Andersen and his wife, Kay, were there. The pastor of the Dryden's church, who had baptized Anne and who looked forward to presiding at her wedding, put his hands on her parents' shoulders and looked at each of them in turn. "Come on," Andersen said at last. "There's someplace we need to be."

With the Andersens and the Drydens leading the way, those present streamed out of the Dryden kitchen and down the hill to the road. In the clear spring twilight they walked, hand in hand, Joel's face grim, Pat still wearing her blueberry-stained apron. Walking northward in silence, their numbers growing as houses along the way emptied. The cluster of people rounded the bend in the road that led to the Trenton Evangelical Church. The small building stood before them, built by a sea captain long ago, warm light surging forth from its windows and open door. They entered, walking to the front as those behind them found seats. Pat and Joel sat with Kay Andersen in the first pew.

Christopher Andersen continued to the altar. He turned to face those gathered together and raised his arms in supplication. "Let us pray," he said. A silence punctuated only by the cries of the feeding ospreys soaring in the evening sky overhead fell upon the church as heads bowed together.

"Heavenly Father, blessed Lord God Almighty, we call upon you now to send the Holy Spirit of your Son, the Lord Jesus Christ, to watch over, protect, comfort, and keep from all harm Anne Laurel Dryden. . . . "

# 14

"We'll find her. I promise," Cathy assured Lee as they stood the next morning in Terminal 2 of Cairo International Airport. Lee smiled and nodded gratefully down at her new friend. Cathy had helped Lee deal with the American embassy, kept the rabid press away from her, and ran interference for her with Jeremias and Vinnie. In the time since Anne's abduction Lee had grown very fond of her short, tough guardian angel.

Anne and Lee's tour had left that morning for Nairobi. Cathy had arranged through the embassy for Lee's passage back to the U.S. The final departure call for her flight sounded, and Lee scooped up her bags. Anne's luggage was already on its way home and would be delivered to the Drydens.

"Don't forget this," Cathy said. She handed Lee her passport.

"Cathy, I—," she began.

"*You*," Cathy interrupted, "take care of you and the Drydens." Cathy looked up at this most unlikely of friends. "Like you told me last night: God will take care of Anne. And," she continued, "if I have anything to say about it, he'll let me help."

"What about Jake?" Lee managed to ask.

"I'll do the best I can for Jake, but no promises."

Lee nodded. "Bye, Cathy."

The airline's desk agent rushed toward them, waving.

"It'll be all right. Here." She handed Lee a travel packet of Kleenex. "Try not to use them all up before you get on board."

They exchanged smiles and a quick, baggage-encumbered hug. The agent hustled Lee onto the plane.

Lee stuffed her flight bag into the overhead compartment and sat down. She unzipped her purse and slipped her passport into its compartment. The hard corner of a small cardboard box pressed into the back of her hand. Frowning, Lee pulled the unfamiliar box from her purse. As the plane lifted off, she opened it. Inside was a pair of small, scarab-beetle earrings.

# 15

Cathy saw Lee off, then went to the embassy. There she waited as a uniformed marine guard unlocked a door on the embassy's top floor. Cathy followed the embassy's communications officer into the room. Shadowless fluorescent lighting caused the table in the center of the room to stand out in sharp relief. It also glinted off the fine copper mesh that lined the floor, ceiling, and walls. The shiny mesh reminded Cathy of the decor in some of the Washington clubs that she and her boyfriend, Greg, frequented.

"Welcome to the clean room!" the officer said proudly. "We've got one in every embassy now."

"What's the copper wiring for?" Cathy asked. "An antenna?"

The communications man smiled. "Just the opposite. We call that our mosquito netting 'cause it keeps out bugs."

"Bugs?"

"Yeah. You know. Listening devices."

"Oh, those kind of bugs."

"Every clean room is carefully shielded against and regularly inspected for foreign information-gathering devices. This copper mesh ensures that any signals generated by all this computer equipment don't leave the room." The man waved at one of the walls. "Just across the street over there is the Russian embassy. You can bet your socks that they've got everything above a tin can on a string pointed at this place."

Life in an electronic fishbowl was an accepted part of a diplomatic career. For just this reason Lydia Doral had used the teleconferencing equipment in the room to make the report that Cathy had watched the morning of the assassination.

The officer waved Cathy toward the sole chair at the table in the center of the room. Cathy sat at the table, which was featureless except for what looked like a computer screen and keyboard recessed into its surface. A push-button telephone was embedded in the desk next to the keyboard. Above an outlined area on the desk a red LED shone menacingly.

"Used one of these before?" the communications man inquired.

Cathy shook her head.

"OK, Agent Hagura," the officer began. "Check this out." He opened a panel on the front of the desk. Inside were rows of circuit boards, cables, and colored lights. "There's two million dollars' worth of computer in here." The man looked fondly at the desk and caressed it. "This baby," he said, "has got the newest BiCMOS-based, RISC chip set there is. Parallel processors with full pipelining and a Translation Lookaside Buffer, too." He smiled not at Cathy, but at the computer's console. *Really* sharp."

Cathy stared up blankly at the man. To her, anything electronic that worked was a blessing; anything that didn't was a curse. She had met Greg when he had volunteered to come over and set up her stereo for her.

"The software's something else, too," the commo man continued. "Really elegant." He ran his fingers over the keyboard. "I get to use the newest ANSI-standard C++ compiler." He looked archly at Cathy. "It cost us, but it's worth it." The technician's face lit up. "It does register coloring, with both peephole and level-two interprocedural optimization!"

"Yeah," Cathy said, "but can you work a VCR?"

"What?"

"Never mind."

The officer mistook Cathy's enforced patience for interest. "You up on one-way encryption algorithms?" he asked. "Coded the ones for this little honey myself."

The man smiled a condescending, acne-ridden smile. With a forefinger he pushed his glasses back up on his nose, then he leaned over and winked at Cathy. "Have dinner with me, and I might tell you how they work."

"Sure!" Cathy said brightly.

"Really?" the commo officer replied.

"You will bring your weapon, won't you?"

"Weapon?" The communications man gulped.

"Uh-huh. You see, I'm here hunting someone. If I find him, there might be a gunfight." Cathy smiled her best innocent-little-girl smile. "You will," she asked sweetly, "help me kill him, won't you?"

The man backed away a step, flustered. "OK, then. You got your key card?"

Cathy nodded. Like all security division officers, she had been issued a key card. It was the size of a credit card and devoid of any identifying marks. To lose the card was to commit a cardinal State Department sin, and Cathy always kept hers close to her.

The officer walked over to one of the glowing computer terminals that lined one wall of the room. Carefully shielding the keyboard from Cathy's sight, he typed briefly, paused, and typed again. The light in front of Cathy changed from red to amber. "Here's how it works. When I leave, you press your key card against that plate." He pointed to the outlined area on the desk. "The magnetic field in the plate activates a radio transmitter in the key card. The card transmits your access code to the computer. If it likes you, the computer will make the connection."

"And what if it doesn't like me?" Cathy asked, annoyed by the man's pedantic manner.

"Then, in five seconds the room'll be full of very upset people." He looked at Cathy. "Leave the card there until you hang up, OK?" Cathy nodded, now all business.

Next he pointed at the terminal's screen. "Answer the questions it asks you. Get them right, and this light will turn green." He gestured at the amber light.

Cathy didn't bother to ask what would happen if she didn't answer the questions correctly.

"*After* the light turns green," he cautioned, "*then* you pick up the handset, OK?"

Cathy nodded again. "How do I dial?"

"You don't," the officer replied. He pointed at the terminal against the wall. "I entered it for you. All set up. Any more questions?" Cathy shook her head.

"OK," the man said again. "Then I'm outta here."

"Oh, by the way," Cathy added. "Were you the one who set up that four-wire for me last night?"

The man shook his head. "Nope. Must've been Mark, the night commo."

"Well," Cathy said with a charming smile, "be sure to thank him for me, will you?"

"Sure," the man muttered jealously. He looked at Cathy out of the corner of his eye. "You really carry a gun?"

Cathy opened the left side of her jacket.

The man stared. "Right. OK."

Cathy fought hard to retain her studious demeanor.

"Sorry," he apologized, "for asking you out and all that. . . ."

"No problem." Cathy smiled. "See you around."

"Sure," he muttered and quickly left, shutting the door behind him.

Cathy took out her key card and pressed it against the pad. Nothing happened. She turned the card over and tried again. Still nothing. *Great*, Cathy thought. *Now I have to go find Romeo and ask him for help.*

As she started to get up, she noticed that something had appeared on the formerly blank screen. "ENTER SSN:" was followed by an insistently blinking cursor. *Huh?* Cathy frowned. *What's an SSN?* All that came to mind that SSN might stand for was Social Security Number, so she tried that. The screen rewarded her with "ENTER G.M.'S DATE OF BIRTH:" That was easy—G.M. was her boyfriend, Greg Miahara.

As the questions continued, Cathy saw the pattern. The access authorization was based on personal facts, information unknowable to anyone not very close to her. Even if someone managed to steal her card and gain access to this room, it was highly unlikely that they would know her parents' address or the name of her childhood pet. Cathy dimly recalled filling out a personal information questionnaire when she had joined consular operations. Now she knew why.

Satisfied, the computer displayed "CONNECTING." Cathy reached for the handset, then checked herself just in time. A few seconds later, the light changed to green. Cathy picked up the handset, unsure what to expect.

"Mahoney," a familiar voice said.

Cathy looked at the handset in disbelief, and then at the computers along the wall.

"Hello?" Mahoney repeated.

"Hi, boss!" Cathy replied.

"Hagura? That you? What're you doing on this line?"
Cathy hesitated. Suddenly, the wonderful idea that she'd had last night didn't seem quite so brilliant. *May as well take my medicine.*

"Well, boss," she said diffidently, "I've always wanted to try one of these secure phones, and this seemed like a great opportunity." Cathy winced in anticipation. *Here it comes.*

"Right," Mahoney replied. "I'll wait until you get back to chew you out about how much this is costing."

Cathy stared at the phone in amazement. *Yow,* she thought. *If he's passing up a chance to yell at me, then he's really worried about this case.*

"Listen up," Mahoney was saying. "New orders: If you don't find MacIntyre by this time tomorrow, you're to be on the next El Al flight to Tel Aviv. Got it?"

"Huh?" Cathy blurted. "We're just beginning to make some headway—"

"Don't buck me on this," Mahoney said firmly, annoyed at having to be arbitrary. "Just do it. Clear?"

"Oh, and what should I tell Petigura and Jeremias?" she asked irritably. "That I'm going to powder my nose?"

"You tell them *nothing.* Got it? Just pack up and go."
Mahoney paused. "Now," he continued in a lighter tone.
"What's new?"

Cathy suppressed her seething irritation and forced herself to report. "The investigation is picking up speed," she told Mahoney. "Now that the procedural matters are sorted out, the evidence is coming together." Both she and Mahoney knew that by "procedural matters" Cathy meant Jeremias. "Looks like MacIntyre's our shooter." *Lord, how I hate to have to say that.*
"Thanks for the help, boss," Cathy said. A phone call from

Mahoney to his counterpart in the Mossad had caused things to quiet down considerably.

"Anytime, Cathy." Mahoney smiled. It was nice to know that he was still needed.

"Got anything new for me on that insignia that I faxed you?" Cathy asked.

"We're passing it around over here," Mahoney told her, "but nothing yet. By the way," he added as an afterthought, "where was the security detail that was supposed to be guarding that roof?"

"In an alley near the rug seller's shop," Cathy responded.

"Why weren't they at their post?"

"Because they'd had their throats cut and were busy bleeding to death."

"Wonderful. Anything else?" he asked. "At these rates, there'd better be."

"Yeah. One other thing. Yesterday afternoon an American was abducted. A female civilian tourist." Cathy paused. "It's weird. They grabbed her off a little, rented boat out in the middle of the Nile. Shot up the captain and sank the boat. Right in broad daylight."

"So what?" Mahoney asked.

"According to her roommate, it seems that MacIntyre visited her yesterday morning."

"Interesting. Got an ID?"

"Right here." Cathy riffled through her notes. "Victim's name is Dryden, Anne L. U.S. passport num—"

"*What?*"

"Boss?"

"Did you say 'Dryden'?"

"Yes."

"Anne Laurel? Hometown listed as Trenton, Maine?"

"Yes. Boss, how did you know that she—"

"Cathy, listen to me." Mahoney's voice was strained. "Who else knows about this?"

"Petigura and Jeremias, the Harbor Patrol captain who took the report, and some Cairo police lieutenant." Cathy could hear the sound of Mahoney writing.

"OK," Mahoney said tersely. "Listen up. No one else, and I mean *no one*, gets to know about this. Understand? I'll see to it that Jeremias and the Egyptians are ordered to forget that they ever heard the victim's name."

"Boss, how did you know who the victim was?"

"Never mind. You don't need to know."

*Terrific*, Cathy thought. *Just great. Some report this is turning out to be.*

"Let me know immediately of any developments," Mahoney ordered. "But," he stressed, "only on this line. Got it?"

"Right," Cathy replied. *Who is this woman? Why twenty-four hours?* "Boss, what's going on?"

"Tell you when you get back. Maybe."

The line went dead, and the computer screen blanked. Cathy retrieved her card and stood up. She headed toward the door, feeling unhappy. Everything was very wrong.

Mahoney took off his glasses and pinched the bridge of his nose. *Well*, he thought sourly, *at least I've got something to report.* He picked up his phone. "Get me Mike O'Brian at the White House."

# 16

The man who hauled Anne out of the water dumped her unceremoniously onto the deck of the speedboat.

"Harbor Patrol!" the gunman yelled, pointing to the south. The boat's sudden acceleration caused Anne to topple from her hands and knees onto her side. A tarpaulin was thrown over her. It rippled as someone crawled underneath it. A man's face came into a beam of light that streamed through a hole in the tarp. "You keep quiet," he said with a wicked, broken-toothed smile. "You talk, you move, I stick you." The thin blade of a dagger glinted in the shaft of light. Dazed, the bedraggled Anne nodded compliance. Her captor's face illuminated in the beam of light made her think of Jake in the hotel bar, and Anne cried quietly.

The boat slowed and stopped. The tarp was swept away, and Anne had a glimpse of sky before a filthy rag was tied over her eyes. Fingers dug into her arms, jerking them behind her. Her involuntary gasp of pain sparked a chorus of guttural laughter. Hands tied, Anne was led up a flight of steps and into a car. After a short drive, Anne and her captors got out and went into a building. An elevator ride was followed by a walk down a hall. A door slammed behind her. Anne's hands were untied, but before she had a chance to rub her wrists she was shoved into a chair. A new set of fetters bound her arms to the arms of the chair.

Since he happened to be facing eastward, Jake missed the spectacular sight of the sunset-washed Pyramids glowing golden against the darkening sky. Not that Jake, lost in thought as he was, would've cared if he had known. He had spent a restless and impatient afternoon waiting for the time to return to Anne's hotel to retrieve his camera.

Jake leaned on the parapet of the tiny rotunda that encircled the top of the minaret that dominated the El Azhar Mosque. The mosque, set deep within the twisted labyrinth of alleyways that is Old Cairo, had become his refuge since the assassinations. Jake had met the mosque's muezzin, its religious leader and proprietor, years ago. He had been traveling along the Suez-Cairo road when he came across Jidra Mukaba and his family. They had been standing beside an ancient Plymouth with steam pouring from beneath its hood.

Jake had pulled over and, with the assistance of the water and duct tape he always carried while driving in the desert, soon had the Plymouth patched up. The Mukaba family's thanks had been profuse, and they had insisted that he follow them back to Cairo for dinner. Ever since, Jake had made a point of visiting them whenever he was in Cairo.

This time, however, Mukaba's smile had faltered for an instant when Jake had appeared at the rear door of the mosque that led to the muezzin's quarters.

"Jake, effendi, how are you? Come in, come in!" Mukaba beckoned Jake inside and quickly closed the door behind him. The two men stood in the narrow, dimly lit hallway, regarding each other. It was Mukaba who broke the silence. "What can I do for you, my friend?" The look on the muezzin's face was easy for Jake to read.

"Jidra, my friend, I need your help."

"First," Mukaba said, "I must know something. Did you do this terrible thing I read about in the papers?" Mukaba regarded Jake, searching his face with the insight every clergyman develops after a lifetime of immersing himself in the problems of others.

"No, I did not," Jake replied. "By the Prophet, I did not." To emphasize his innocence, Jake invoked the name most holy to Islam.

Mukaba sighed. *It is God's will that this infidel should come here at this time and under these circumstances,* he thought as he pondered what to do. Mukaba knew that, under the strict code of laws laid down in the Koran, Jake had a right both to hospitality and to refuge as one wrongly accused. He also knew what would happen to him and his family should it be discovered that he had harbored this most-wanted of fugitives. Nonetheless, Mukaba realized, *my duty is clear.* "Come in, my old friend, and tell me all about it." Jake followed the muezzin into his tiny living room.


Jake noticed how low the sun was in the sky and glanced at his watch. In a few minutes he'd leave the mosque and walk to the hotel. For the first time in days, Jake felt that he had a glimmer of hope to which he could cling. Even if Anne had sent the film off, he'd be able to get his camera back. Armed with the fact that it was registered to him, he'd be able to face the authorities. At least, he hoped, that would hold them at bay until the film could be recovered.

As lights flickered on in the teeming mass of hovels below

him, Jake's thoughts drifted to the intriguing subject of Anne Dryden. Intriguing because, as he thought about the woman who had so suddenly come into his life, he realized something. And he wasn't sure that he liked it.

What disturbed Jake was that he was attracted to Anne. What he had tried to shrug off as mere necessity, as no more than requiring her assistance to recover his property, now had to be faced for what it really was. It was a feeling both new and foreign to Jake, and it made him uneasy.

*Is it simple desire that I feel?* Jake wondered. He knew all about desire, and he knew that Anne's slender figure and brilliant smile had been creeping into his restless dreams these past few nights. But, he realized, it wasn't those things that he looked at when she was near.

*It's those eyes*, he thought.

In his mind she again tilted her head to look up at him, her eyes turning in the sunlight to emerald fire as they emerged from the shade of her hat. Gorgeous green eyes. He knew that he most certainly desired her. He also knew that there was something else about her that he wanted too. Something that left him both wary and eager, and very uncomfortable.

It was time to go. Jake turned and entered the minaret. As he made his way down the spiral staircase inside the hollow shaft of the tower, something Anne had said began to nag at him. Something he had heard somewhere before. Jake paused as he tried to remember. His hand rested on a marble banister worn smooth over the centuries. *Got it!* As he had left the balcony, she had said, "You're not in this alone."

*Why say that?* Jake wondered as he continued his descent. Obviously, she was offering to help. But it seemed to Jake that both she and the other person who had said that, the person whose name remained tantalizingly just out of reach, had meant more than a mere offer of their aid. But, if they hadn't meant themselves, who had they meant?

The more Jake thought about it, the more the notion that he needed help grated and chafed, rubbing raw his pride. It was bad enough that he, Jake MacIntyre, the lone wolf, the consummate system-bucker, had found himself in circumstances that he couldn't master and control.

But it was even worse that he needed Anne Dryden's help to extricate himself. *It's supposed to be the other way around,* Jake thought with an exasperated shake of his head. *I'm the one who's supposed to come to her rescue.*

Still shaking his head, Jake walked across the landing at the base of the minaret to the door that opened onto the mosque's courtyard.

As the last sliver of sun disappeared below the horizon, the sleepy Mukaba shuffled across the floor of the mosque to a battered table. He flicked the on switch of the ancient amplifier and waited for the glow from inside the dented case that told him the tubes were warm. After a moment he pressed the play button on the old Tandy cassette player, and the call of the faithful to evening prayer blared across the slums of Cairo. Picking up his worn prayer mat, the muezzin went into the courtyard to lead the throng in worship.

Jake picked his way through the crowd of forms prostrate on their prayer rugs. He waved to Mukaba as he did so. *I'll show 'em,* Jake thought. His confidence grew as he passed through the arched entrance to the mosque and made his way through the Cairo throngs. *I'll get my camera back. With it and the pictures, I'll prove to them that I didn't do it.*

Jake turned right and walked along a street that ran alongside the hotel. *I'll show them who's in control of my life!*

Jake turned right again.

The street in front of the hotel was a sea of flashing blue lights and police uniforms.

Faces turned toward him. Fingers pointed. Shouts went up.

Still firmly in control of his life, Jake MacIntyre turned and ran.

# 17

In the same instant that the blindfold was stripped from her eyes, something smashed into the side of Anne's face. That something, Anne saw after she had shaken the tears from her eyes, turned out to be the gloved hand of a man who was standing in front of her. Anne noted with grim satisfaction that the blow must have hurt him, too, as he was unconsciously rubbing the knuckles of the hand with which he had struck her. The man said nothing. Behind and slightly to the right of her tormentor stood another man, taller and darker, watching her without expression.

"I hope, Miss Dryden," Hassan said in a voice far more pleasant than Anne thought it had any right to be, "that I won't have to do that again."

Anne stared at him without speaking.

Hassan shrugged. "It's really quite simple: Give me the roll of film, and you may walk out of here."

"Which roll of film?" Anne asked. "I've quite a few." Anne could see Hassan's eyes harden as he struggled to control his temper.

"You have a roll of film that belongs to me. I want it back."

Anne looked up at the man, her face guileless. "I have no idea what you're talking about."

The blow caught her on the point of the chin this time, nearly dislocating her jaw. Anne's head snapped to the side, crashing against her shoulder. "It is the roll of film that you used at the Pyramids. Give it to me, or you will die."

"I don't have your film!" Anne gasped between sobs. "I don't have any exposed film!"

"Where is it, then?" Hassan snapped.

"I sent all my film home to be processed."

"You lie!" he snarled. Clenching his fists, he turned his attention to Anne's body. Then, abruptly, Hassan whirled and walked across the room.

Anne grimaced at the taste of blood in her mouth and winced again at the pain that shot through her jaw when she swallowed. She watched as her kidnapper reached into a glass case that sat on a table. After doing something that she couldn't see, Hassan returned and stopped just in front of her. The muscles of Anne's jaw tightened as she saw just how and where his eyes lingered as they wandered over her.

"Now," he said quietly, "for the last time. Where is the film?"

"I've already told you." Desperation crept into her voice. "I sent it—" Anne bit off her reply as she saw Hassan step toward her.

The Shams Ahmar commander grabbed a handful of Anne's hair. Savagely he jerked her head backward. Anne screamed as the high-backed chair cut into her neck. "That's better," Hassan told her. "Tell me, now, or I shall break your neck." He tugged on her hair, and Anne screamed again.

Almost unable to breathe, Anne struggled to tell him that she needed air. Her "I can't—" was silenced by a brutal blow to her exposed throat.

"You can," Hassan assured her. "And, I promise you, you will."

The commander's hand came into Anne's field of vision. He held a glass vial. Anne gasped as something within it moved. Hassan pushed the cork out of the bottle's mouth. "Since I seem to be unable to convince you, perhaps my small friend here will be more persuasive." Slowly, he upended the vial.

Anne went rigid with terror as the small, black scorpion landed on her face. She could feel the sharp points of its feet on her cheek, just below her eye. Hassan's hand moved. His gloved finger flicked the spiderlike animal. Its venomous tail, quivering with rage, loomed over Anne's eye like a malignant shadow.

Anne felt hysteria begin to consume her. "When I touch him again," Hassan told her, "he strikes."

"No, please."

Her interrogator chuckled. "It will be most interesting to watch you after he has buried his barb in your eye." Hassan paused. "Once you have recovered, we will begin again. I hope that by then you will have decided if you wish to be cooperative or blind."

He prodded the animal, and its tail flickered forward.

"You've got to give yourself up."

Alex stood face to face with Jake in the middle of the hotel room. "If you're too scared to do it for yourself," Alex snapped, now truly angry, "then how about for her?" Alex threw into Jake's lap the edition of the *Cairo Times* that told of Anne's kidnapping.

For the second time, Jake stared openmouthed at a headline.

Alex strode across the room. He whirled on his friend. "Where's it going to stop, Jake? Mort's family was almost wiped out. Now a woman you claim to be interested in has disappeared. Her best friend nearly drowned, and they haven't found the body of the guy sailing the boat." Alex spread his hands. "If you're out to impress her with your popularity, you've done so in a big way."

Jake lifted his eyes to his friend's. As a ranger in Viet Nam he had faced danger and death before, but then the danger always had taken the form of a defined, declared enemy, and death had always been a calculated and accepted risk. Never before had he been stalked by an unknown enemy who struck out not only at him but at those he viewed as noncombatants. He was a man who considered himself to be firmly in charge of his life, and his first taste of terrorism had both undermined that belief and unnerved him.

"I know you're scared," Alex told him. "I'd be scared, too, if I were you."

Jake's reply was interrupted by the sound of the hotel room door splintering open. Four masked men burst into the room. The oiled metal of their automatic weapons glistened in the lamplight.

For Anne, time had ceased to exist. Fire spread slowly outward from her eye and across her face, blending into a haze of pain and terror that slowly enveloped her. *I can't see!* her mind shrieked. *I'm blind!* The horrifying thought began to lay claim to her reason.

As the darkness gathered around her, Anne clung to her Protector. She felt him there with her. She knew that each blow hurt him far more than it did her. She knew also that he had endured infinitely more agony than she ever would, and he had come through it triumphant. Because he had already endured such pain, she could, too; because he had already overcome evil, she would be able to overcome as well.

The door to the interrogation room burst open. Hassan released his grip on Anne's hair as he whirled toward the door, his pistol already out of its holster and aimed at the intruder.

Anne's head slumped to one side, and she felt the scorpion slide off her face. Pain racked her neck and shoulders, then unconsciousness enveloped her.

"Commander!" The man who had come in gasped as he fought for breath. "We've captured the American!"

"Where did you find him?" Hassan demanded.

"At the hotel on the Shabat al Aram," the messenger explained. "Room 206."

Hassan gestured toward the door. "Bring him in."

Suddenly the other man in the room—the taller, darker one—spoke. "Wait to bring him in until I tell you." The foreigner's English was smooth and unaccented. The messenger looked at his commander for confirmation, then disappeared.

Furious, Hassan whirled on the foreigner. "You will not give orders!" he screamed. "I am in command here!"

"You," the foreigner replied calmly, "are in command, not to mention alive, only as long as I wish it."

Hassan's rage was replaced by fear, and he backed away a step.

"Now," the foreigner commanded with a gesture at Anne, "wake her up. I'll take over the interrogation from here."

"What?" Hassan said irritably.

The foreigner glared back at him. "I said *wake her up!*"

A thumb pressed into the nerve behind her ear brought Anne shuddering back to consciousness. Nausea filled her as her head twitched.

"Who did you send the film to?" the foreigner demanded to know.

Wanting only for the pain to go away, Anne answered the question through bruised and puffy lips. "My parents."

"Who are they, and where do they live?" he demanded.

"Joel and Pat Dryden. They live in Maine," Anne whispered as consciousness fled from her again.

The foreigner stiffened. He beckoned Hassan over to him. "What did she say?" he asked, wanting to make sure that he had heard correctly.

"Joel and Pat Dryden," Hassan said, repeating the unfamiliar names with difficulty.

The foreigner smacked a fist into his palm. "This makes it absolutely imperative that we recover that film!" He waved Hassan aside and stepped in front of Anne. "You are," he asked, "the daughter of Joel Dryden?"

Eyes still closed, drifting in and out of consciousness, Anne nodded.

"Dr. Joel Dryden?"

"Nobody calls Daddy 'Doctor,'" Anne mumbled. "He doesn't like it."

"Where were your father's postings?"

"Postings?" Anne murmured. "We don't have a post office. Dave brings the mail."

Anne's head lolled to one side as she passed out. "Put her in the storeroom," the foreigner ordered Hassan. "I'll finish with her when she's conscious."

Hassan looked at Anne, his eyes feasting on her as he untied her. He grabbed Anne's wrists and yanked her to her feet, pressing her against him. The motion brought Anne to agonizing consciousness. Her eyes opened to the sight of Hassan's face, only inches from hers. "I had planned on enjoying you," he told her. "But now, I find you too ugly."

Anne closed her eyes and turned her face away. Hassan shoved her into the arms of a guard. "Get her out of here."

"After you're done with her, she's mine!" Hassan told the foreigner.

The foreigner barely smiled. "Perhaps, Commander, perhaps." He turned to a guard. "Bring the American in."

# 18

Rough hands hurled MacIntyre into the darkened room and slammed the door behind him. Slamming hard against the far wall, Jake whirled and flung himself back across the room. In his blind, adrenaline-charged fury, Jake slammed his bad shoulder against the door. He staggered back, gasping with pain. Breathing hard, Jake groped his way around the perimeter of the room as his eyes adjusted to the dim light that leaked in around the badly hung door.

Without warning, Jake tripped over something in his path. He fell forward, off balance, and cracked his head against the wall. Jake sprang toward the form huddled in the corner. He grabbed a handful of hair and pulled the object's head backwards, his other hand clenched into a hard fist, cocked and ready to strike. As he did so, his face came into the sliver of light that shone from around the door.

"No. Please!"

Though little more than a choked gasp, Jake recognized the voice and stopped dead.

"Anne?" The fingers entangled in her hair loosened their grip, the clenched fist opened. "What are you doing—"

His question was never finished, muffled as it was by her hair, as Anne threw herself against his chest. At the sight of a familiar face, *his* face, and with his arms around her, Anne cried.

They sat for a long time in silence, Jake stroking her hair, letting her cry herself to sleep. Eventually Anne's breathing slowed and evened, and Jake lowered her head into his lap. Anne's face moved into the shaft of light from the door. Her face was so swollen as to be almost unrecognizable, and ugly bruises stood livid even against the tan of Anne's skin. Jake stared at her, and then slowly looked up; not at the door, but through it at those who were beyond it. Picking Anne up, Jake slowly backed up against the far wall, opposite the door. He sat, cradling Anne, facing the door, his eyes never leaving it. Jake MacIntyre, ex-commando, had just made a vow. He had just promised himself that whoever had done that to her would die. Slowly and by his own bare hands.

Anne awoke. She stretched, then sat up suddenly when she realized what she was using for a pillow. It was day outside, and enough light filtered in through the badly maintained roof that they could see one another. The fire in her face had subsided, but she could see out of only one eye. She turned that side of her face away from Jake, not only so she could see him, but also to hide her ugliness.

"What did they do to you?" he asked. Jake's face hardened into a mask of hatred as Anne recounted her interrogation.

Anne touched her face lightly. "It doesn't hurt as much as last night." Anguish filled her voice. "But I can't see out of one eye." She suddenly had an awful thought. *Will they let me teach anymore?*

Jake sat quietly beside her until she looked up again. *Let's take her mind off of it*, he decided. "Sleep well?" he asked with a grin, looking down at his lap.

Anne tucked her legs beneath her and demurely smoothed her skirt over her knees. She was infuriated with herself because her attempt to ignore his remark was belied by the blush that now suffused her cheeks.

"Not at all well, thank you," Anne replied. She didn't dare look at the challenging smile in those eyes of his. Anne ran her hands through her hair. She grimaced as her fingers caught in a mass of snarls. "I must look simply awful," she said softly to herself.

"Well," Jake began. He waited until she looked up, startled, before he finished. "You did look better the other day on the balcony—"

The slap caught him completely by surprise. The flat of her hand hit the hollow of his cheek with a ringing smack. Jake didn't flinch, didn't move. But as Anne, enraged equally by both this man and by how he made her feel, raised her hand again Jake enveloped it in his.

Anne paused. Hassan had been filled with lust; the foreigner with simple, implacable hatred. She fully expected to see one or all of those in Jake's eyes. Instead, she was surprised to see something that she considered all too rare. Where she had expected to see totally justified anger, Anne saw the quiet confidence of a completely self-assured man. She knew that she was teetering on the edge of incurring his wrath and without question he would act unhesitatingly if she crossed that boundary.

Anne also realized that she was teetering on the edge of a precipice of an entirely different sort: that of falling in love with Jake MacIntyre. Startled and disturbed by the thought, Anne realized that Jake was still holding her hand. She looked at their hands, and Jake let go. Anne snatched her hand back into the safe haven of her lap.

Jake grinned again, and the tension between them dissolved. "Nice shot," he said, rubbing the red mark on the side of his face. "I guess I deserved that."

"You most certainly did," Anne said, her anger softening. She tucked her hands into a fold in the skirt of her sundress. "I guess I'm more scared than I thought I was." Anne glanced away, and then back at Jake. "This all has to do with those pictures of yours, doesn't it?"

Jake shrugged helplessly. "It must. I really have no idea who those people are."

Anne felt his helplessness.

"How did they get you here?" Jake asked.

Jake listened. Hatred kindled in his eyes as Anne told him about the shooting of Achmed and the sinking of the *Queen Nefertiti*. The anguish on Anne's face caused him to bite back his expletive-laden comment.

"Do you know what happened to Lee?" Anne asked anxiously.

"She's all right," he told her, recalling what he'd briefly read in the newspaper article.

Anne breathed a silent prayer of thanks. Without thinking, Anne bit her bruised lip, and her eyes filled with tears. "Oh, Jake, they're so horrible!"

Unbidden, Jake extended one arm in an offering of shelter and comfort. Anne curled up into that refuge, knees against his leg, her head resting on Jake's shoulder. Jake ran his fingers over the bruises on her cheek. He didn't notice that Anne trembled as he did so.

"Who did this to you?" Jake asked, trying to keep his fury out of his voice.

Without looking up, Anne said, "The leader did; the one with the gloves." Jake etched the image of Hassan into his mind, incising it forever into the stone of his hatred for a man who would do this.

"Did they . . . ," Jake asked, pausing, searching for a way to ask the question he needed answered, "hurt you?"

Anne hesitated, not sure of what he was trying to ask. Then she understood. Anne turned her face toward his. "No. They didn't," she said, giving her head a small shake to further reassure him. "Not really."

Anne watched Jake closely. She sensed that this was immensely important to Jake. She also knew that its being important to him was somehow equally important to her. Anne watched as the berserk rage that had been on the verge of igniting within him was muted into something else, a quieter something that she couldn't quite discern.

A bell from a church began its slow, sonorous peal.

"Ever been to Edinburgh?" Jake asked. Anne's head came up and turned toward him, the stiffness in her muscles protesting.

"Once. Why?"

Jake leaned his head toward the sound of the bell. "That bell reminded me. Best church bells I've ever heard were in Edinburgh one Sunday morning, from a little church up on a cliff."

Anne brightened. "I know which one you mean! Saint Giles Cathedral. Daddy's friends with the vicar. When were you there?"

"Few years ago. Global sent me over to do a photo essay on the Tattoo. You know what that is?"

Anne sat fully up and swung around, facing him. "Yes!" she exclaimed. "All those military bands, and the flags, and the horses!"

Jake folded his arms across his chest and grinned. "When were you there?" he asked.

"When I was twelve. Momma and I flew over to meet Daddy after he had finished some business in London." As she remembered, Anne tilted her head to one side. "It was so exciting! We got to see the Tower of London, and the Changing of the Guard, and Piccadilly Circus, and—" Jake's blank look interrupted her tour. "Well," she continued, "we went to St. Giles Sunday morning, and then we walked up the Royal Mile to breakfast. Just as we passed the Flower Clock they started ringing the changes."

"Ringing the changes?" Jake asked. His eyebrows arched in inquiry.

"That's what you heard. Ringing the changes: Ringing all the church bells in a set pattern of repetitions." Anne made the motion of pulling a bell rope.

"Great food in Scotland," Jake mused. "Bangers, and pasties, and sausage rolls—"

"Oh, don't mention food! I'm starving!" Anne protested. She made a face then winced, her hand cradling her throbbing cheek. " But now that you mention it," she went on, "how about high tea: scones dripping with butter, and cakes with clotted cream and jam—"

"Tea?" Jake snorted. "In the land of a thousand whiskeys? Not to mention truly great beers: bitters, ales, and stouts. . . . "

Relaxing against him, Anne felt happy and safe. "Beer?" She wrinkled her nose in distaste. "Ugh! Can't stand the stuff!"

Jake remained silent. Anne watched him closely. She waited for a response until she began to worry that she had somehow offended him.

Anne's apprehension vanished as she saw Jake smile slowly. A smile that reached into her and claimed a part of her as his own. Anne felt the precipice on which she stood begin to disappear beneath her.

*This is not to be!* Felt, not heard, the warning slashed its way through her. Anne turned away from Jake, as the choice she faced and the futility of trying to further avoid it were made plain to her. Instilled into the very heart of her being by years of sermons, lessons, talks with her mother, and time spent in reading the Bible was the immutable truth that he, whoever he may be, first and foremost must be a Christian. If he wasn't, then nothing else about him could make any difference. Not to be? *But it must be!* her innermost self screamed in response. Nonetheless, the echo of that warning resonated through her.

Anne returned her eyes to his. The fire in her gaze was now muted to an anguished, confused despair. Shaken and hurt, she tore herself away from him. Anne drew her knees up to her chin and wrapped her arms around them.

Mystified, Jake reached out to her.

This time she avoided his touch. "Why can't you be what you're supposed to be?" she snapped. Anne pounded her fists on her knees in frustration. She turned her back on him.

Jake stared at her back for a long time and then threw up his hands. *If I live to be a hundred and fifty,* he thought in amazement, *I still won't understand women.* Jake sighed. He leaned his head against the wall and went to sleep.

Jake's sudden, sharp snore made Anne jump. She turned around, and her exasperation with him increased when she saw him sleeping peacefully. Eventually her exhaustion overcame her annoyance, and Anne curled up next to him.

The Psalms of David whispered through her mind as she rested her head on his shoulder. Emotional and spiritual comfort thus assured, Anne slept as well.

# 19

"Six hours, Ed," O'Brian reminded him. "Any news?"

"Nothing." Mahoney shook his head. Then he remembered Cathy's report of Anne's abduction. "But, what about the girl who was kidnapped?" he asked.

"Thanks for telling us about her," O'Brian replied. He smiled at Mahoney.

"You do know who she is, don't you?" Mahoney asked.

"Yes, we do. Sorry, can't talk about that. You know how it is."

Mahoney thought of his new security clearance. He began to protest, then he remembered that "secret" and "covert" were not the same thing.

"Good timing on your call," O'Brian said. "The president was on the phone to Prime Minister Yatzhin. I was able to slip him a note about the kidnapping just before Yatzhin tried to blindside him with the news." He smiled. "Smooth move, Ed. The president doesn't forget good work like that."

"What about Ambassador Doral?" Mahoney asked.

"Why do you want to know?"

"She's an old friend, and protecting ambassadors is my job. *Was* my job."

"We notified her to leave, and she refused."

"Doesn't surprise me." Mahoney heard the chief of staff mutter something uncomplimentary about Doral.

O'Brian got up and walked across his office. He pulled down one of the maps that hung from the ceiling, and northeast Africa appeared behind him. "Ehud's ready to go," he reported. "The Israelis picked the target and have come up with a humdinger of a plan." He looked over his shoulder at Mahoney and grinned. "You're gonna love this. Lord knows where, but they've dug up a renegade Libyan fighter pilot who trained in the Soviet Union. He's willing to fly the YAK into Libyan airspace—he knows all the transponder codes—and come into Egypt from the west." O'Brian traced an arc on the map. "Gives us a whole new set of targets, and the heat will end up being put on our friend Colonel Qaddafi."

"What's the target?" Mahoney asked in spite of himself.

"Some dump just inside the Libyan border. The Egyptians have a nuclear power plant there, so that'll raise the question of was it blown up, or did it blow?"

O'Brian tugged on the map, which zipped back up into the ceiling. "The cooling towers give off more than enough heat to make the Have Nap happy, and Israel gets nuclear results with conventional ordnance. Place is called Siwa."

In a room across from the safe house where Jake and Anne were being held, the foreigner turned cold eyes on the infuriated Shams Ahmar commander. Each disliked the other intensely, and the fruitless questioning of Alex had set both men on edge. Hassan's father had died at the hands of the British in the 1952 revolution, and that hated occupation still burned bright in his family's memory. Alex's lack of knowledge as to the whereabouts of the film had made his questioning brief; his Dorchester accent, faint but still discernible, had made it savage.

Now the question of what to do with their captives caused that antipathy to explode.

"*No!*" Hassan bellowed. "The woman is mine!" Fists clenched, he whirled to face the foreigner. "The men are more than enough for us to buy our way out of this!"

The foreigner shook his head. "Even before she revealed her identity," he said quietly, "she was much too valuable to be relegated to your petty, carnal desires." The foreigner flicked his fingers in dismissal of the notion. "Now," he continued, "the situation is just the opposite of what you so foolishly perceive it to be. Our success or failure depends solely on the proper use of the Dryden woman; the men are completely expendable."

"But why?" Hassan interrupted, annoyed at being unable to follow the foreigner's thinking.

The foreigner shook his head, a pitying smile on his face. "The fact that you need to ask proves that you don't deserve to know. Don't worry about it," the foreigner said, an edge of steel creeping into his voice. "I'll manage the operation from here on." He paused to smile at the furious commander. "From here on I'll manage it *openly.*"

The foreigner's condescension was too much for Hassan. "*Farouz!*" he shouted, and seven armed men burst into the room. "Now," he said triumphantly, "we'll see who's openly managing this operation."

The foreigner didn't move. "Perhaps," he said evenly, ignoring Hassan's confident smile, "I underestimated you."

Then the foreigner jerked his head. Four of the men clustered around Hassan slowly walked over to the foreigner's side of the room. "But," he continued as Hassan looked on aghast, "I don't think so."

The two groups, guns bristling, faced each other. "What do you want?" Hassan asked from between clenched teeth.

The foreigner offered him a conciliatory smile. "Since we seem to have achieved something of a standoff, I suggest the following: It seems time for a parting of ways. I take the Dryden woman and leave you the men."

"Never! The woman is mine!"

"Your problem, Hassan, is that you never learned that one thinks with one's brain."

The foreigner jerked his head again, and the man standing behind Hassan pressed the muzzle of his rifle against the base of the commander's skull. "Are we agreed then, Commander?" the foreigner asked amiably, turning the title into a slur.

Hassan nodded numbly.

"Good. Now take your hostages and get out." He gestured to one of his men to accompany them. "See them away."

Those men still loyal to Hassan followed him as he stormed out of the room.

"Muhammad!" he barked. "Get the truck ready!" One man trotted away. The rest continued down a hall to the room where Alex lay unconscious.

"Bring the Britisher," Hassan commanded. "We leave at once."

Two men dragged Alex out of the room.

Jake came instantly awake when Hassan threw the door open. His attempt to get to his feet was hampered by Anne's head, which was again resting in his lap as she slept. The Shams Ahmar commander stared at Jake as he lifted Anne from his lap. Consumed by his craving for Anne and berserk with the knowledge that he'd never have her, Hassan drew his pistol and fired blindly.

Reflexively, Jake threw himself to the right. The bullet missed by inches, cratering the plaster of the wall. Anne sat up, shocked into wakefulness. Jake dove in front of Anne and came to his feet, shielding her from the pistol. As he did so, the edge of his hand slammed against the commander's wrist, knocking the pistol out of his grasp and across the room.

Jake froze as one of the guards shoved the muzzle of his rifle into his ribs. Breathing hard, he looked down at the swarthy, wild-eyed Hassan. Jake flexed his fingers unconsciously, as he realized how much he wanted to break the little man's back over his knee like rotten matchwood.

As Hassan met Jake's level gaze, the commander's bravado ebbed away, leaving only the stinking mudflats of fear. "We leave," Hassan shouted. "Now!"

He backed toward the door, where the foreigner's guard watched silently. One of Hassan's men handed him his pistol.

Jake reached behind him. Anne took his hand, and he pulled her to her feet. Jake felt Anne press close to him as they started toward the door.

"*No!*" Hassan screamed. "She stays!" The knuckles of the hand that gripped the pistol whitened as he spat each word.

"She leaves with me," Jake said evenly, "or we don't go anywhere."

Hassan motioned with the pistol. A man ran around to Anne's side and leveled his rifle at her head.

"*We leave!*"

Slowly and deliberately, Jake turned his back on Hassan. Anne, her face pale and taut, looked up at him. "Go," she said. "I'll be all right."

Jake shook his head.

"Go!" she insisted.

Anne looked over Jake's shoulder as Hassan started toward them. The man with the rifle shifted his stance. His finger tightened on the trigger.

"I won't let them get away with this," Jake said. "I'll be back for you."

"I know you will," Anne whispered. "Now go. I'll be taken care of, and watched over, and kept safe."

Deep within Jake something stirred into life, and he knew without question that what she said was true.

Hassan grabbed Jake's shoulder and pulled. Jake stood immobile as he held Anne's hands in his and looked into her eyes.

Unable to budge Jake, Hassan pressed his pistol against the small of his back. Jake saw fear tear through Anne's eyes.

Anne looked away, her eyelashes laden with tears. "Go! Now!" she gasped.

Jake could see that she was near the breaking point. He lifted her hands and gently kissed the tips of her forefingers. Their eyes met once more. Jake released her hands, turned, and walked through the door.

Hassan motioned for his men to follow Jake. He swept Anne with one last, lecherous gaze and slammed the door behind him.

In the sudden ringing silence, Anne sank to her knees. The far-off church bell continued its slow tolling as Anne prayed for Jake's safekeeping.

# 20

The phone in the interrogation room rang. Vinnie Petigura answered it casually. He listened for a few seconds, then he sat up with a start. With a forefinger he jabbed a button, and the spindles of a cassette player hooked to the phone began to turn. Cathy and Jeremias listened to the stream of Arabic. The speaker made the caller's voice harsh and raspy. Vinnie took notes as he listened. He asked several questions, some of which were answered. Then, with a click, the line went dead.

Vinnie walked over to a map of Egypt that covered one wall. He studied the map as the other two grew increasingly impatient. Finally, he turned to them. "That was Dokki, one of my most trusted informants," Vinnie explained. "He reported that those responsible for the assassinations have left Cairo and are headed by road for Siwa."

Petigura pointed at a small town on the extreme western edge of the country. "From there, he said, the assassins intend to escape by night over the border and into Libya. They left an hour ago. Five men: three Arabs, an Englishman, and," Vinnie said, now looking at Cathy, "an American." The inclusion of an

American in the group caused a chill to go through Cathy. She could feel Jeremias's stare.

Vinnie picked up the phone and dialed an extension. "Petigura here. The assassins are reported to be headed toward Siwa. Call the Bawiti and Farafra police departments. Tell them to establish roadblocks. All cars are to be stopped. The passports of all foreigners are to be checked. Take all precautions— the suspects are to be considered armed and dangerous." Vinnie turned to his colleagues. "That should be sufficient. As you can see from the map, to get onto the only road to Siwa they must first pass through either Bawiti or Farafra."

"Could they be past the roadblocks already?" Cathy wondered.

"No," Vinnie replied. "It takes three hours to get to either town." Vinnie leaned on the scarred table and smiled. "Looks like this is our break."

"Should we go after them?" Jeremias asked.

"I don't think so," Vinnie said as he sat down. "The forces of both towns are most efficient. There shouldn't be any problem."

At the safe house, the foreigner replaced the phone in its cradle. He smiled briefly as he said a mental farewell to Dokki. He complimented himself on having created the mysterious informant and on having learned Arabic so well that the gullible police were all too willing to believe that a gang member had turned renegade. *Good-bye, Dokki*, the foreigner thought. *You were a most useful fiction in eradicating those competitors who got in my way.* He walked to the room in which Anne was a prisoner.

Anne looked up from her prayers as the door opened. Having prepared herself for Hassan, she was strangely relieved to see the foreigner standing there instead. "Come," he said curtly. "We leave."

The lights sweeping across the face of the modern multiband scanner mounted on the Land Rover's dashboard stopped suddenly. Hassan adjusted the volume as he and the driver listened to the broadcast that ordered the establishment of the roadblocks. Hassan consulted the map spread out across his knees. He spoke to the driver, who nodded concurrence.

A small pothole stirred Jake out of his doze, then a larger one jarred him awake. His captors had herded him and the now conscious Alex out of the house and into the back of the new, expensive-looking Land Rover. After an endless time in the canvas-enclosed truck, both Jake and Alex had fallen asleep.

Alex groaned. Their guard watched them closely. "How're you doing?" Jake asked.

Alex sat up. The swaying of the truck caused him to bury his head in his hands. "Been better," he admitted. "Is this what it's like when you drink too much of the cheap stuff?"

Jake smiled at his teetotalling friend. "Kind of," he replied. "But usually the bruises don't show so quickly."

Alex raised his head and licked dry, broken lips. "What I'd do for a drink of water right now."

The guard stirred, gaining both men's attention. He snapped open a pouch on his web belt and took out a canteen. "You. Water," he said.

Alex took the proffered canteen. "Shukran," he said as he looked hard at the young man who sat across from him. "Shukran gazlian." *Thank you. Thank you very much.*

As Alex drank, the man bobbed his head and smiled. "Afwan," he replied. *You're welcome.*

Alex handed the canteen to Jake. Jake looked at the guard, who again nodded. He drank eagerly. Jake wiped his mouth on the back of his hand and gave the canteen back to the guard.

Alex nudged Jake. "Thank him."

"For what?" Jake asked. "For dragging us out into this

godforsaken desert? For beating you senseless? For touching Anne?"

Alex smiled to himself. *So it's happened at last*, he thought. *I was right. She is some bird.*

"Mac," Alex replied, "this guy isn't driving this truck. And I don't know about Anne's, but he wasn't present at my interrogation. He may not be innocent, but he doesn't deserve your hatred."

Alex and Jake held a hard stare for a long time. Finally, Jake turned to the guard. "Shukran gazlian."

The Land Rover slowed to a stop as a policeman, hand raised, stepped into the middle of the road. Beyond him, a car blocked the southbound lane. The policeman stepped up to the truck. "Your documents, please." He glanced incuriously at Hassan, who ignored him. In the back of the Land Rover, all three men listened tensely. The guard drew his pistol and gestured for silence.

The driver handed the policeman his license and the Land Rover's registration. "Your destination?" the policeman asked as he inspected the papers.

"Rashda," the driver replied casually. "What's all this about?"

"Fugitives from Cairo," the policeman explained. "What's in the back?"

"Machine parts. Can we go, now?" the driver asked. "We're running late."

The policeman returned the driver's papers. "I'll just look in the back, and then you'll be on your way." He smiled. "Since both my partner and I are stuck here, there's no one to give you a speeding ticket. You'll get to Rashda on time." He waved to his partner to get the car out of the road.

The policeman stopped suddenly as he rounded the back of the Land Rover.

Hassan stood there, smiling. A burst from his Uzi caught the policeman in the stomach.

Hassan jumped into the cab as the driver swung the Land Rover off the road. The other policeman, trying to start the car, looked up at the burst of gunfire. His partner lay sprawled on the asphalt, and the Land Rover was speeding westward.

The man stared for a moment then grabbed the car's radio.

Jeremias looked at his watch. "It's been too long," he declared. "They must've evaded the roadblocks."

Vinnie shook his head. "Impossible."

The phone rang again. Vinnie grabbed it, listened, then paled. "Good God," he whispered.

Anne and the foreigner were the only occupants of the aircraft's cabin. The cabin walls were paneled, and heavy velvet curtains covered the windows. She sat in one of the overstuffed leather chairs that surrounded a teakwood table. Anne slipped her sandals off. The plush carpet on the floor felt wonderful to her bare feet.

Anne had been hustled into an enclosed van. When she emerged, she found a jet waiting on the tarmac. The guards who had accompanied them stopped at the bottom of the stairs that led up into the aircraft. The foreigner had motioned her aboard, then followed her up the stairs.

Moments later, engines screaming, they were airborne.

# 21

At 130 knots, the desert below the Bell 206L LongRanger blurred into a stream of colors. Cathy, Vinnie, and Jeremias had been driven to the airport. They hustled into the helicopter, which had then hurtled westward.

Every gully had been overflown, every potential hiding place circled. Cathy, sitting in back, tried to convince her stomach to ignore the sudden changes in direction and altitude. Jeremias sat across from her. His grim, gray-faced expression convinced her that he, too, was not enjoying the ride. Vinnie, from his copilot's seat, provided them with a running travelogue. *I wish he didn't sound so cheerful,* Cathy thought as she listened to him through the headset. *If he's enjoying this, I'll kill him myself.*

Jeremias spoke up during a break in Vinnie's monologue. "Still convinced of MacIntyre's innocence, Cathy?"

Cathy looked at Jeremias, expecting to see the smug self-confidence that she had come to know and hate. Instead, she was greeted by a look of honest inquiry. *Maybe he's not as bad a sort as I thought.* Cathy shrugged noncommittally in reply. Although she had refused to allow her colleagues to see it, the revelation that an American was among the fugitives had shaken her. All her experience and instincts told her that Jake wasn't a killer and kidnapper; all the evidence said that he was.

"Vehicle sighted," the pilot reported. The helicopter swung to the left.

"Well," Jeremias said cheerfully, "we'll soon find out, won't we?"

Cathy remembered Ed Mahoney's orders. *Nail MacIntyre. Hard.* If he was involved, and if he was fleeing, then she was going to be the one to do so. The Browning was in its holster under her jacket. She patted it, then settled into her seat.

The helicopter approached the Land Rover from the rear, closing rapidly as it skimmed along just above the ground. Standard engagement procedure called for the pilot to pass over the truck and come down just in front of it. This usually panicked the driver into braking and swerving.

Hassan noticed the helicopter's approach in the oversized, side-view mirror attached to his door. "They've found us!" he shouted as he pointed at the mirror. The driver glanced at his mirror and nodded. He slammed the accelerator to the floor. The Land Rover shot ahead, bumping its way across the rutted desert road.

"They've seen us," the pilot reported calmly. He looked at Vinnie, who nodded and motioned "up and over" with his hand.

"*Brake!*" Hassan screamed at the driver as the helicopter swept up over them. The truck fishtailed wildly as it slowed. Dust and the sound of the helicopter's engines filled the cab. Hassan, cursing, grabbed the wheel and cranked it, the violent swerve nearly overturning the Land Rover. It slammed back down onto its wheels outside the cloud of dust, broadside to the helicopter. Hassan grabbed his submachine gun, leaned out of his window, and fired a burst at his pursuers.

Caught by surprise, the pilot swore as he pivoted the

helicopter around. They ended up about fifty feet in front of the Land Rover just as flame erupted from the Uzi's muzzle. "Shots fired!" the pilot reported. He yanked up on the controls, and the helicopter darted straight up, then banked steeply to the left as the pilot evaded another burst of gunfire. Circle left, Vinnie motioned.

The pilot swung the helicopter around. It came up just behind the truck and slightly to its left. The helicopter easily paced the Land Rover as its driver swerved back and forth in a futile attempt to dodge the aircraft. Vinnie took out his pistol. He opened the window and, bracing himself against the door frame, fired at the truck's left rear tire. A miss. Vinnie fired again, and the tire disintegrated.

Inside the back of the Land Rover, all three men flattened themselves against the truck bed as a bullet tore through the canvas siding. They felt the truck skid sharply and come to a shuddering stop.

"OK," Vinnie said as the helicopter came around again. "Here's the plan: Izzy'll put us down hard, then it's everybody out. Izzy then takes off to keep out of range." Vinnie grinned at Cathy through the small window in the bulkhead behind him. "Keep low, folks. It's kind of nasty out there."

*He is enjoying himself,* Cathy realized. She flinched as a bullet shattered the window next to her head. *Well, I did leave the marines because they wouldn't put me on hazardous duty.*

"Ready?" Vinnie asked as the helicopter dropped suddenly.

Cathy's Browning was in her hand.

Jeremias pulled back the slide on his Walther P5 and nodded.

"Ready!" they replied together.

The helicopter slammed into the ground. Cathy winced

as the impact seemed to compress her spine. *I'm short enough as it is.*

Jeremias threw the door open and disappeared through it. Sand whipped up by the rotor blades stung Cathy's face as she hurled herself out of the door and flat onto the ground. The wind around her became a brief tornado as Izzy flung the helicopter up and out of danger.

Izzy had put them down thirty feet behind and slightly to the passenger's side of the Land Rover. A small rise between them and the truck provided them some scant protection, and they hugged it as they surveyed the situation. For a seconds-long eternity nothing happened.

Then, everything happened at once.

The driver, crouched low, peered around the corner of the truck. Unable to see the three figures hidden behind the rise, he stood and stepped into full view.

"Halt!" Vinnie shouted. "You're under arrest!"

The driver jumped, turned toward them, and fired. Three shots were fired in return. Killed instantly, the driver collapsed. The three agents came to their feet and ran toward the truck.

When the shooting started, Jake, Alex, and the guard had flattened themselves against the floor of the truck. Now they heard the whine of bullets ricocheting off metal, a horrifying sound Jake remembered from Viet Nam. The three men looked at one another.

"Time to go," Jake exclaimed.

The terrified guard tore the canvas from the back of the Land Rover and jumped out. A single shot from Jeremias cut him down.

Alex slowly and carefully raised his hands and stepped down out of the truck.

At the sound of gunfire, Hassan jumped out of the cab and ran toward the back of the Land Rover. Three figures were running toward him. Hassan aimed at the one who wore the uniform of the hated Cairo Police and fired.

Vinnie ducked as the bullet whistled past his ear.

Alex and Hassan met at the corner of the truck and stopped a few feet from one another.

Hassan looked at Alex. Betrayed, his operation destroyed, he blamed this man, one of the hated British, for his being stopped so very few miles from a haven in Libya. The terrorist commander looked at Alex and saw in his face the reflection of a lifetime of oppressions both real and imagined.

Jake saw the gun come up.

He dove, knocking the gun out of Hassan's hand an instant too late.

Vinnie fired. His shot shattered the commander's leg an instant too late.

Cathy's bullet tore through the Land Rover's gas tank, engulfing both it and the body of the driver in flames.

Alex looked down at the round, red hole that had appeared in his chest. He sank to his knees.

Jake was there before his head hit the ground. "It's going to be OK, man," Jake said, just like he had in Viet Nam. "We'll get you out of here and to a hospital. It's gonna be OK." Ever so slightly, Alex shook his head just like, Jake remembered, they had in Viet Nam.

With dying fingers, Alex fumbled in his shirt pocket. He pulled out a worn, dog-eared Bible. The one, Jake knew, that he always carried with him. A wet, dark-crimson stain was spreading across its lower edge.

"Take it," Alex whispered. "Read it." He coughed. His breathing shallowed.

Jake nodded. His eyes never left Alex's as he put the Bible in his own shirt pocket. The torch of faith had once again been passed.

Alex looked up at his best friend and longtime protector. "Kiss her, just once, for me. OK?" The spark within him began to flicker and dim.

"You got it, Brit. You got it." Two old friends exchanged one last smile.

Jake felt the breathing stop. He saw Alex's eyes lose focus. Then Jake realized that Alex was no longer looking at him, but beyond him—looking at something that Jake now knew was really there. Still and quiet, cradled in his best friend's arms, Alex Stratton continued to smile.

Jake lowered Alex's body to the stony ground. He knelt beside him for a long time, only distantly aware of those clustered around them. *Well, God,* Jake thought. *I guess somebody's supposed to say something to you now. I don't know what it's supposed to be. But I do know that Brit was a good man, and that he believed in you.*

A moan from Hassan brought Jake back. He looked at the man who had killed his best friend, who had abused Anne, who had so disrupted his life. Jake looked at the bloodstained man writhing on the ground and something inside him came apart.

*"You bastard!"* Jake roared. It was an animal roar, a roar of unstoppable bloodlust.

Blindingly fast, Jake grabbed the dead guard's pistol and came to his feet. He kicked Hassan's wounded leg to get his attention. Hassan screamed and then screamed again when he saw the gun pointed at him.

"You're going to die," Jake said calmly. "Three shots, so it'll be slow. One bullet for me, one for Anne, and one for Brit."

Terror shone through the pain in Hassan's eyes as Jake's finger tightened on the trigger.

# 22

"Jake. No."

Cathy was surprised at how calmly she had said it. She was surprised that she could say it at all. Now absolutely convinced of Jake's innocence, she also knew what she had to do. If he killed the murderer, then she would have to kill him. If the innocent killed the guilty, then the innocent would die, too. She didn't want to have to be a part of that.

Out of the corner of his eye, Jake saw the barrel of a Browning pointed unwaveringly at his head. The former ranger subconsciously noted with approval the woman's military, two-handed stance. He also saw two men standing quietly on either side of her as they watched. Vinnie and Jeremias had agreed with a glance that this was between the two Americans.

"Don't do it, Jake." Cathy used her best hostage-negotiation voice, the one that always worked. "You kill him—I kill you."

Jake ignored her.

*So much for Plan A,* she thought. *Not surprising—ex-commandos aren't afraid to die.*

Jake kicked Hassan in the leg again.

*OK then, my friend,* Cathy decided. *It's time to play hardball.*

*Step 1: Get them to listen.* "Is this what they teach the rangers? To shoot the wounded? I may be just an ex-grunt—" *That got his attention!* "But even I know better than that." Cathy kept going. She didn't dare stop and think.

*Step 2: Get them to talk.* "Is this what you want? Look at this scum. He's so scared he's wet his pants. What does killing him prove? Who're you out to impress? Anne?"

Jake slowly turned toward Cathy. "How do you know Anne?" he snarled.

*Bingo!*

"I met Lee Parker, her best friend."

Jake's gun wavered ever so slightly.

Cathy softened her tone. "Jake, do you want me to have to tell Anne that I had to shoot you and leave you for the vultures?"

Cathy sensed the imperceptible change in Jake's stance. The faintest of relaxations. The sweat that plastered her bangs to her forehead stung as it dripped into her eyes.

*Step 3: Give them a reason to give up.* "Go ahead, Jake. You shoot the scum, and he loses. Then I shoot you, and both you and Anne lose. But you know what, Jake? If you end up in a body bag next to Alex, then he loses, too."

Jake glanced at Cathy. In a land where the sun had once stood still, time seemed again to have stopped.

"Jake!" Cathy was now yelling, her intensity almost touchable. "I watched Alex die, and he didn't lose. He died, but he didn't lose! You shoot, and Anne and Alex both lose. One scum in exchange for two who love you. Doesn't sound like much of a bargain to me." Cathy paused and took a deep breath. *This is it.* "Your choice, Jake."

Jake heard his own breathing, and he watched Hassan's. His heartbeat was pounding in his ears, and it seemed as if Anne's heartbeat was again warm and soft against him.

"We'll prove that you're innocent." Cathy's words were echoing across the windswept desert. "Jake, you're not in this alone."

The phrase tore like wildfire through Jake's mind.

That was it! Now he remembered! Both Anne and Alex had told him that. *You're not in this alone.* Two people who believed in the same God had been trying to tell him the same thing.

Anne and Alex. Believing the same thing. Telling him the same thing. Promising him the same thing.

*Could it be true?* Jake wondered.

*Where two or three come together in my name . . .*

*Remember that you're not in this alone*, Anne had said.

*. . . there I am with them . . .*

*You're not in this alone. I'll be praying for you*, Alex whispered one last time.

*I'll be taken care of, and watched over, and kept safe*, she had said.

*You're not in this alone.*

His Bible pressed against his heart as Jake MacIntyre snapped on the pistol's safety and raised his hands.

# PART II

# 23

At the sound of the visiting-room door slamming, a bundle of rags in one corner of the room stirred. Lydia Doral, who had just entered the room with Cathy, stared at the bundle. A moment later, a small head popped out of the rags and peered sleepily at them.

"What a sweetheart," Doral said with a smile at the sight of Salome. "An Abyssinian." The ambassador bent down and stroked the kitten's nose with a fingertip. "Wonder who it belongs to?"

"It's a she," Cathy explained, "and she's evidence."

Doral straightened up and looked at Cathy. "Evidence?"

"I found her out in the desert, where we captured MacIntyre." Cathy picked up Salome, who purred happily. "She must have jumped out of the truck before it exploded. I certainly couldn't leave her behind, so I brought her back." Cathy smiled at the cat. "As evidence." Cathy put Salome down on her pile of rags, and the kitten promptly settled back to sleep.

"The reason I wanted to talk to you before you left," Doral said as she perched on a corner of the visiting-room table, "is to congratulate you on the success of your mission. I'll see that a commendation is placed in your personnel file." When no response was forthcoming, the ambassador leaned forward. Her intelligent, experienced eyes regarded Cathy for a long moment.

"Most agents I know," Doral remarked quietly, "would be dancing in the streets at having solved a case like this. You, however, look as if you'd just been handed an extended tour at the consulate in Timbuktu."

Cathy smiled thinly. "I'm sorry, Mrs. Ambassador. The praise is appreciated. It's just that I don't think it's deserved."

"Why not? Your colleagues, as well as the helicopter pilot, have reported on your actions in the desert. Most commendable."

"However commendable those actions were," Cathy said frankly, "I think that they resulted in the capture of the wrong man."

The ambassador leaned back in her chair, cupping her chin in her hand. One of her long, slender fingers tapped slowly against her cheek. Then Doral smiled slowly. "I imagine that you're expecting me to ask you why, aren't you?"

Taken aback, Cathy only nodded.

"You're on the consular side of things, Cathy. The side that, I must admit," Doral added with a smile, "makes things happen. Embassies and ambassadors are guarded, visas and passports issued, schedules are kept." Doral brushed away an errant wisp of hair. "On the ambassadorial side, things are a bit different. In our case, appearances are everything." The thin, elegant woman smiled drolly at her younger counterpart. "Our job, quite unlike yours, is to, through negotiation, keep things from happening that we don't want to happen—to ensure that words speak louder than actions."

"You sound," Cathy said, "just like my boss."

"Doesn't surprise me," Doral replied with a smile. "Ed

Mahoney was my *chargé d'affaires* when I was stationed in Kuwait."

Cathy took a deep breath. "I don't think that Jake MacIntyre killed those men."

"It's possible that he didn't," the ambassador agreed. "The evidence is, at best, circumstantial. But," Doral said sharply, "it *appears* that he did."

"And," Cathy replied sourly, "appearances are everything."

"Have you thought about what's happened in the past few days, Cathy?" She waved Cathy into silence and answered her own question. "Of course you haven't. You've been too busy getting shot at."

Doral sat up. "Words—the Pan-Arab Treaty—were obliterated by an action—no, two actions—with worldwide ramifications. And, in some ways, the Dryden kidnapping is the worse of the two." She paused to let that sink in. "Why? Because, justifiably or not, the American public views this not as a kidnapping, but as the taking of another hostage." Doral's voice became intense. "A *female* hostage."

The ambassador placed her hands on the table. "Think about it, Cathy. Think about the American credo: the men provide for and protect the women. While less true than it used to be, the nasty, dangerous tasks are still deemed 'a man's job.' No self-respecting man, the credo says, would willingly place a woman in harm's way." Doral smiled at the exasperation that flickered across Cathy's face. "So," she went on, "right about now, in every barroom, beauty shop, and cafeteria in America it's being decided that," Doral affected a drawl, "this time the A-rabs have gone too far."

Doral got up and began to pace. "And that consensus, however ill-informed, is transforming itself into telegrams and phone calls to congressmen, senators, and," the ambassador said as she spun around, "to the White House. Have you met the president?"

"Once, at a reception for State Department personnel."

"Did he seem timid to you?"

"You mean, like he was portrayed during the election?" Cathy shook her head. "No, not at all."

"He isn't," Doral agreed. "The president is a competent, levelheaded man. Which is more than I can say for some of his advisers." She leaned against the wall and folded her arms across her chest. "His one failing is that he sometimes allows those advisers to overrule his natural good judgment."

"Like how?"

"Like allowing those advisers to prey on his fear of appearing timid. Like allowing them to use that fear to convince him that this kidnapping is sufficient justification for another 'incursion.'"

"Incursion?"

Doral smiled wryly. "War."

The ambassador resumed her pacing. "The president has a few of these little incursions under his belt. And, as you know, one big one. By and large they've been successful, at least by modern America's definition of success: quick and spectacular, with few American casualties and lots of enemy territory overrun. So he can afford to feel expansive. It wouldn't be hard for certain of his advisers to persuade him that the time is now ripe for another one."

"But we were just over here!" Cathy protested.

"So we were," Doral agreed. "And the pervading feeling in America is that we left with the job only half done." She perched on a corner of the table. "So we draw another line in the sand and come marching back. But, this time there'll be a difference." Doral waited.

Cathy frowned at the ambassador, then her eyes went wide. "We wouldn't!"

"We most certainly would," Doral responded, "if certain elements of the administration and military have their way."

She looked past Cathy, at the far wall. "One bomb and one bomber. And we've got plenty of both."

"But what about the Russians?"

"They're too busy coping with the fact that democracy means more than fast-food franchises and imported porno magazines." Doral looked at Cathy. "The Chinese don't have enough CSS-9 ICBMs to retaliate effectively, and the rest of the world would probably cheer."

There was a discreet tap at the door, and a large man stepped inside.

"That's why," Doral continued after a nod at the man, "I said before that appearances are everything. If we appear to be doing something, that buys the president time. And if the prime suspect appears to be an American, not to mention an American man, all that public outrage is turned away from the Gulf."

"And onto Jake MacIntyre."

Doral nodded. She motioned to the large man at the door. "Let's go."

Flanked by Cathy on one side and the attaché on the other, Doral stared at Jake through the bars of the holding cell. A long, silent flight back to Cairo with Alex's blanket-wrapped body at his feet had culminated with the echoing clang of a cell door slamming shut.

"As America's ambassador to Egypt I shall see to it, Mr. MacIntyre," Doral said, "that you are accorded all of the—," she said, hesitating for a fractional pause that was not missed by either Cathy or Jake, "rights to which you are entitled as an American citizen."

"Thank you, your—" Jake stopped, unable to recall the honorific title due an ambassador. "Thank you, ma'am. I appreciate it." He glanced at the large, quiet attaché. He was obviously Doral's muscle, despite the briefcase that he carried like a taxi-squad fullback. "When will I get to talk to a lawyer?"

Doral frowned. "That won't be necessary quite yet, Mr. MacIntyre. Under the provisions of the accord governing this investigation, each affected nation is entitled to remand its nationals for arraignment in their home country. This will be effected by Agent Hagura tomorrow. Counsel will be arranged for you then."

"Whatever you say, ma'am," Jake replied with a shrug. The ambassador turned to leave. "Mrs. Doral!" Jake called.

Doral paused.

"I just wanted to tell you how sorry I am about the secretary. I know that the two of you were friends."

Doral looked over her shoulder, displaying her famous profile.

"I also wanted to tell you," Jake continued, "how well I remember your eulogy at the funeral of Anwar Sadat. Especially the part about the 'new dynasty of hope.'"

Doral turned around. "You were there?"

"Yes, ma'am. I photographed it for my agency."

"Would I have seen your work?" The ambassador was now interested.

"Did you see the following week's *Time?*"

"Yes, I did." Doral tilted her head as she remembered. "I very much liked the cover."

"Thank you," Jake admitted.

"You took that?"

"Yes, ma'am. And the picture on page forty-two."

"That's my favorite picture of me!" the ambassador exclaimed.

"Well, then," Jake replied, "when I get out of this, I'll have a print made for you."

Doral smiled. "That, Mr. MacIntyre," Doral said, trying unsuccessfully to regain her regal demeanor, "is entirely up to the federal courts of the United States of America."

"Of course," Jake said humbly as he tried not to smile. "Thank you for all your help."

Doral left, shaking her head, with her bodyguard in tow.

Cathy trailed a few steps behind them. She stopped just long enough to give Jake a big wink and an OK sign.

The Saudi Air Force E-3A AWACS surveillance aircraft turned onto the last leg of its triangular course. It was on a training mission over the Red Sea, and all aboard were tired, thirsty, and bored.

"Target, bearing two-four-five," the intercept officer reported. The radar officer, a reservist on her annual training tour, acknowledged the acquisition. *Probably another 747 full of people going someplace exciting,* she thought with a mental sigh. She stabbed the button labeled inquiry that glowed blue on her instrument panel. The antenna that rotated just over her head fed data on the target into the onboard computer. Almost instantly the target on her screen changed from blinking green to blinking amber. A message appeared on the screen below the target: "UNIDENTIFIED CONFIGURATION."

The air force captain sat up in her seat and motioned to the duty officer. "Sir," she said, pointing at the blinking image, "no ID on target."

"Is it in one of the standard air corridors?" the D.O. asked.

"No, Colonel, it is not."

"Very well, then," the colonel said with a nod. "Let's find out who's out there." He grinned at the captain. "Care to make a small bet as to the outcome?"

The captain declined. She had dated the colonel several times and knew full well what the terms of the bet would be.

"You're missing your big chance, Captain."

*Like fun I am*, the captain thought. The colonel looked over at the radar screen and gave the order to identify the target.

The radar officer flipped up a small plastic cover and punched a red button marked IFF. The E-3A broadcast an IDENTIFY: FRIEND OR FOE signal to the target aircraft. This was not something done lightly, as it caused the AWACS to light up the radar sky like a beacon.

The target's transponder replied instantly to the interrogation. "Humph," the captain groused, "civilian."

"What type?" the colonel asked, annoyed that he couldn't read the string of numbers and letters that had appeared on the screen.

"Care to make a small bet?" the captain asked with a grin.

The colonel shook his head.

"Target shows as civilian," she reported. "An extended-range Grumman Gulfstream IV." The captain read off the jet's flight plan, altitude, and destination. She smiled at the D.O. "Nice plane, Colonel. Take me out in one of those someday, and you might get somewhere."

Chuckling, the colonel turned back to his desk. "Log it. Then let's head for home."

# 24

"MacIntyre's in custody," Mahoney told O'Brian on the phone.

"So I heard," O'Brian replied, stifling an early afternoon yawn. "Good thing, too."

"Why?"

"The Israelis scrambled the YAK ahead of schedule."

"*What?*" Mahoney sat up in his desk chair.

"Guess they got a little too itchy. But, it seems that Lybian pilot was somewhat less than trustworthy. Apparently he decided that a U.S.-armed, Soviet-built fighter was just the ticket to get back into Qaddafi's good graces."

"He didn't make it, did he?"

O'Brian chuckled. "No. When he didn't turn south as expected, the Israelis yelled for help."

"And?"

"We sent an F-14 up from the *Constellation*. One Sidewinder later, poof, no defector."

Mahoney took a deep breath and whooshed it out in relief. "We dodged a bullet on this one."

"Yeah. I guess we did. Hey, I've got a meeting. Good news about MacIntyre."

Mahoney heard the click on the other end, then hung up the phone. *Hmm*, he thought. *He sounded disappointed.*

Anne awoke. She shifted uncomfortably, and the foreigner looked up.

"Do you speak English?" Anne asked.

No reply.

"May I go to the bathroom?" She inclined her head toward the rear of the cabin. *I have no idea what I'll do if he says no*, Anne thought. The foreigner merely returned to his writing.

Taking this as an assent, Anne hurried back to the tiny washroom. When she was finished, she washed her hands and face with wonderfully hot water and lots of soap, then buried her face in a thick towel that she pulled from a gold rack.

The face that greeted her from the mirror as Anne emerged from the towel was barely recognizable. Blackened eyes and cracked lips caulked with dried blood were framed by greasy strands of matted hair. She could see nothing out of her injured eye. Anne trailed her fingers over the bruises that mottled her cheek, her hand unconsciously following the path that Jake's had taken. She felt dirty and defiled. Every place that Hassan had touched cried out to be bathed and cleansed.

Her elbow bumped one of the small compartments that lined the washroom wall. It opened to reveal a supply of moist towelettes. Their cold, perfumed wetness was a blessing to her dry, chafed skin. Further poking about uncovered some small packets of hand lotion. Anne tore open one of the packets. She smoothed the cream into the skin of her neck, which itched fiercely. *See, you did get burned that day out on the balcony*, she chided herself. All at once she was back on that balcony, staring up at Jake from underneath the brim of her hat. She looked at her fingertips, pink and moist with lotion, and again felt them pressed against Jake's lips. Suddenly it was all too much to bear, and inner blackness engulfed her.

*Why are you doing this to me?* Anne flung her anguished mental cry heavenward as she sagged against the washroom door. *Is this how you show me that you love me?*

Turmoil of a sort that she had never before experienced roiled within her. How could her Protector, her Friend and Comforter, allow this to happen to her? Had she angered God, and was this his way of showing his displeasure? Wonder became uncertainty, which then cascaded into doubt and fear.

For the first time in her life, Anne Dryden was truly scared. Like the surfaces of a diamond being examined under a jeweler's loupe, the facets of Anne's spirit came under scrutiny. On the one marked Faith a small, almost unnoticeable imperfection was found. This tiny flaw was a small pit of unbelief that marred an otherwise shiny surface. And, like a depression in the desert sand when the winds sweep across it, tumbleweeds of doubt began to collect in it. *Don't believe God. Give up. It's hopeless.*

Anne reeled before the enemy's assault. Her faith, an untried sword not yet tempered by adversity, nearly shattered when the first blow slammed into its edge. *Give up!* the enemy demanded. *Give in!* The evil wind, now a full gale, shrieked within her. *You are all alone!*

Then the roar of the hell-born tempest overwhelmed her and she could no longer bear the anguish. Anne staggered out of the washroom and down the aisle. She flung herself onto one of the couches that lined the cabin walls and sought refuge in a welcome but fitful sleep.

# 25

Catlike, Jake paced back and forth across the front of the cell. He was unaccustomed to confinement of any kind, and the small cell made him feel trapped and caged.

The very real fact that he might spend the rest of his life in one of these cells gnawed at him as he paced. Inside him, a small something scrabbled frantically. It was desperate to get out, to regain its freedom. As fear ate away the barriers surrounding this desperation, its scratchings grew louder in Jake's mind.

Jake looked around him as he paced. Everything was chipped. The paint, the fixtures, the concrete floor. Even the steel frame of the cell door had several big chunks taken out of it. *Don't want to know what did that,* Jake thought grimly. It seemed to Jake that recently a lot of chunks had been taken out of his life, too. His career, his future, even his life was now in jeopardy.

As Jake paced, he thought of the missing chunk that disturbed him the most. It was the one most recently added. The one named Anne. Her absence bothered him. Very much. That worried him since, by his usual standards, he had gotten exactly nowhere with her. In the past, always, those who had resisted his advances were dumped unceremoniously. *Love 'em and leave 'em*, Jake reminded himself. *That's how to deal with women. But why*, he asked himself, *don't I feel that way about this one?*

Confusion welled up in him as unfamiliar feelings burst forth. The instant he had met Anne Dryden the rules had changed. Moreover, those rules that he had so thoroughly mastered no longer even applied. One look at her and, he now realized, it had never even occurred to him to try to play the old game at which he was so good: figure out what she wanted from him so as to get what he wanted from her. *What do I want from her?* he wondered.

Until now, *wanted* had meant that she, whoever she was, was to be available to him on his terms, at his convenience, and for his purposes. Now Jake considered a new definition of *want* that had suddenly appeared in his mind. While his physical desire had in no way abated, to that desire had been added the ideas of respect and permanence.

Jake started at these sudden, unexpected thoughts that invaded his mind. *Where did that come from?* Jake turned the terms over in his mind. *Forget this*, he told himself sternly. *Any babe I shack up with had better be able to fend for herself.* He shook his head, trying to dislodge the unwelcome intruders, but try as he might, he couldn't.

*But now what?* Jake wanted to know. *How long is this one going to last?* It was important for Jake to find this out, since preserving his sense of freedom by delimiting the relationship was a MacIntyre specialty. He had always carefully reminded himself that at the end of the night, or weekend, or vacation he'd be free to go. Love 'em and leave 'em. A part of him still insisted on knowing when he could break it off.

He tried to imagine leaving someone like Anne after she had been his for a night, or weekend, or vacation. But he failed.

Confused, he cast about to determine why and found that much-traveled road closed—bricked up, blocked off, now forevermore forbidden to him. Startled, Jake searched for another path. He found a path that until now had been cobwebbed and barricaded with doubt, selfishness, and disbelief. That path was now open. Light shone forth from the entrance, and in that light was the promise of a new way of life.

Jake frowned in uncertainty. *A life with someone? But that'd mean marriage.* The notion stopped Jake dead in his tracks. Until now he had managed to avoid the two kinds of prison: jail and marriage. Now he was locked up in one and contemplating the notion of the other. *Marriage means bills and houses and lawn mowers and station wagons. It means kids. . . .*

Jake handled the ideas gingerly, as if afraid that they would latch onto and burrow into him like some sort of domestic leech. *Still,* he mused with a grin as he considered the prospect, *it would mean waking up every morning to a smile.* Jake scratched his head. *And you know, if I lived in a house, then I could have a dog. I always have wanted a dog.*

A distant shout caused the bars just before his eyes to snap into focus. Confusion and insight both vanished in the same instant, to be replaced by the possibilities of lingering imprisonment or imminent execution. Enraged at the turmoil and uncertainty inside him, furious that the events in his life were now beyond his control, Jake grabbed the bars and pulled. His muscles knotted and sweat beaded his forehead as he tried to remove the barrier that prevented him from fleeing this place and these equally incarcerating ideas. Berserk with fury, Jake threw back his head and roared.

Something in his bad shoulder went *pop.*

Jake roared again, this time as he fell to the floor in pain. When his vision cleared, he used his good arm to get up off his knees and onto the filthy bunk. Jake looked around him at the bare, cracked walls of the cell. *I can't take this*, he thought bleakly. *A lifetime of this? No way.*

Exhausted, Jake stretched out on the mattress.

Jake awoke and instinctively looked to see what time it was.

He frowned at the bare wrist that he brought up in front of his face. *Where's my watch?* Then he remembered that his jailers had taken it, and the cell walls closed in once more.

Jake stretched. Life had returned to his numbed arm, and he winced as he flexed it experimentally. A twinge of pain caused him to straighten up, and as he did so the Bible in his shirt pocket, forgotten until now, pressed against his chest.

Books had always been an important part of Jake's life. Reading was a great diversion on long plane trips and during lonely hotel-room nights. He always had a book or two with him; they were easily obtainable and transportable, and Jake had not yet found anywhere that they weren't accepted in barter. One paperback for one meal was a universal constant. Grateful, Jake fumbled the small book out of his pocket.

Jake couldn't open the Bible, and it took him a moment to figure out why. He riffled through the pages, separating them. Jake watched as Alex's dried blood, which had glued the pages together, drifted downward in small, black flakes and settled onto his pants.

The cell was very quiet. Too quiet. In all their years together, he and Alex had been anything but quiet. *I wish you were here, Brit. I could use a little good advice right now.*

Jake opened the Bible. *What was it that you were always after me to read? Oh, yeah.*

A flea jumped from one of Jake's knees to the other as he turned to the Gospel of John.

# 26

"It's time to go."

Jake looked up from his reading.

Cathy stood outside the cell. A small flight bag sat beside her. Nearby were Vinnie Petigura and two Cairo policemen.

Jake tried to stretch and grimaced as his stiff muscles protested. He was suddenly very tired. "What time is it?" he asked through a yawn.

Cathy looked at her watch. "Five-thirty."

"P.M.?"

"O-five-thirty, soldier," Cathy replied. "Our flight leaves in an hour."

Jake yawned again.

"Trouble sleeping?" Cathy asked.

"Like you wouldn't believe," Jake replied.

Cathy nodded.

*No wonder I'm tired,* Jake thought as Vinnie unlocked the door. *I've been reading for hours. He looked at the small Bible.*

The cell door opened, and Cathy waved him through.

As they started down the corridor, Vinnie said, "Cathy, did you forget these?"

Jake and Cathy both turned and looked at what he was holding. "Vinnie, I really don't think that those are necessary."

"As long as he is within my jurisdiction," Vinnie said coolly, "I must insist."

Cathy looked at Jake. She could see the anger kindled in his eyes. "Jake," she said quietly, "any resistance will only prejudice your case."

Jake stared at Vinnie. Before him was the man who had incarcerated him and who now wanted to place upon him, for all to see, a badge declaring him suspected and accused. Again the part of Jake that clung stubbornly to self-determination fought to be allowed to lash out and escape.

He had spent the night reading of another man. He had read how that man, also unjustly accused, had voluntarily surrendered. He had read of the power in that man's words and deeds. He had read how that power was changing the world, one life at a time.

Jake stretched forth his arms. As, he had read, that man had done. The handcuffs snapped into place.

# 27

Pat and Joel Dryden, along with Lee's parents, Debby and Jack Parker, met Lee's commuter flight at Portland International Airport. Upon seeing them, Lee dropped her bags, raced across the tarmac, and tried to fling herself into the arms of both women at once. Joel and Jack fetched Lee's bags, then Lee was enveloped in the massive, bearlike embrace of her father. Finally, she looked up at Joel.

"Thanks, Uncle Joel," she said as she returned the shapeless, now-sodden handkerchief he had given her before retrieving her bags.

"We're glad you're home, honey," Joel responded. He brushed her bangs out of her eyes, just as he had done since she was three, and gave her a hug.

Pat and Joel looked at their oldest friends. They saw how hard the Parkers, out of respect and concern, were trying to conceal their joy that their daughter was home safe and unharmed. Pat looked at her college roommate and maid of honor. From her eyes shone her thanks and appreciation for their consideration.

"When Lee's rested," Pat said, "would you come stay with

us for a while? It'd be so nice to have you there when—" A sudden wave of anguish swept over her, and she reached for Joel's hand.

"When we find out that Annie's safe and sound," Debby finished smoothly. "Of course we'll come visit for a while."

Jake and Cathy were the last passengers to board the commercial flight. Their seats were well forward, and this spared Jake from a long walk down the aisle past rows of wondering, accusing eyes. As soon as they were airborne, Cathy reached over and unlocked the handcuffs. Jake looked at her.

"Well," Cathy said, "my boss'd kill me if he knew, but I figure that you're not planning on hijacking the plane. Right?"

"Now that you mention it," Jake said sarcastically, "I had been planning to overpower you, steal your gun, and commandeer the aircraft."

Cathy shifted slightly and slid her hand under the edge of her jacket. "Care to try it?" Her tone was soft and casual, but dangerous.

"But," Jake continued with an exaggerated frown, "there's one slight problem."

"What's that?" Cathy asked warily.

"Where do I tell the pilot to go? Every Arab in the world is out for my blood, so the usual destinations like Libya and Iraq are out." He looked at Cathy ingenuously. "Got any suggestions?"

Cathy wilted with relief. "Sheesh, Jake, don't do that to me." To her surprise, she found herself laughing at the *Gotcha!* in his eyes. "I know!" she said brightly. "How about Cuba?"

Jake shook his head. "I've been to Cuba, and even I'm not desperate enough to go back there."

Cathy acted like she was thinking, then snapped her fingers. "I've got the perfect place!"

"Where?"

"The British Virgin Islands!" She looked at him archly. "I'd be a lot easier to overpower if I knew that you were going to force me to go with you to someplace like that."

Jake frowned. "No good."

"Why not?" Cathy asked, vaguely offended by the rebuff.

"My visa's not current."

"Rats!" Cathy feigned disappointment. "Well," she said as she settled into her seat, "I'll think about it and let you know."

As a veteran of many long flights, Jake was used to the sense of timelessness that accompanies the cabin's unchanging illumination and the monotonous roar of the engines. He had long ago developed a method to break up the routine of eating, sleeping, and reading or watching a movie, and he put it into effect now.

Jake put on his headphones and switched to the jazz channel. He was a big fan of Wynton Marsalis, so when Marsalis's hot rendition of "Cherokee" came on, he made a mental note. Since the channels repeated themselves every hour, the next time he heard "Cherokee," he'd know that another hour had passed.

"You know what I can't figure out about you?" Cathy said over lunch.

Jake looked at her inquiringly and took another bite of airline sandwich.

"You're so calm. I don't understand it." She looked up at him. "If I were in your shoes, I'd be out of my mind."

Jake looked past her, through the scratched window and into the cloud-filled sky.

"I don't exactly know why, either," he said at last. "I should be scared, but I'm not." Jake leaned back and looked at the ceiling. "I've been scared. First time in Nam that my platoon was ordered out on night patrol—never been so scared in my life. I knew that the Cong were out there, just waiting to get me.

Jake turned toward Cathy. "You were a marine—remember your first battalion sergeant?"

Cathy nodded. She suppressed an involuntary shudder at the memories of boot camp and of her drill instructor, Staff Sergeant Carol "Amazon" Kahn.

"I had," Jake went on, "a former D.I. for my platoon sergeant. Scrawny little guy named Maitz. He got me through that first patrol. As we left, he told me that he'd stick right with me, and he did. He was always there, right beside me, whispering what to do in my ear. Whenever I froze up, he whispered, 'Keep goin', kid, you're doin' just fine.' He took care of me, so that I could take care of my men."

A flight attendant came by and collected their lunch trays.

Jake fished his Bible out of his pocket and held it up. "Have you read this?" he asked Cathy.

"Not really."

"Moses sounds a lot like me. He got scared and ran away. So God told him to go back to where he was wanted for murder. Some people there needed help, and God wanted Moses to be the one to help them."

"What did Moses do?" Cathy asked, now caught up in the story.

Jake shrugged. "Moses, not unreasonably, said 'Who, me? Go back there?' But, then, you know what God said?" Jake riffled through the pages of Exodus. "And God said, 'I will be with you.' Now, personally, I like that. I really do. 'I will be with you.' Period. Just like that. All you need, right by your side. . . . Just like Maitz was."

"Sounds great, if it could be for real," Cathy said.

"This is what's so strange right now," Jake said. "I kind of believe it is for real. Something about it is. I'm feeling something through all this. Like I'm being taken care of . . . so that I can take care of other people."

The cabin lights dimmed, and the movie screens came down. Cathy put on her headphones, and Jake switched on his overhead light, returning to the story of the Israelites and their Deliverer.

# 28

The white wicker chair on the Dryden's screen porch creaked in protest as Lee shifted her weight. She plucked from the bowl one of the pea pods she had picked earlier that morning, shelled it deftly, and threw the pod into the wastebasket. Across from her, Pat Dryden sat with her feet propped on an ottoman, totally absorbed in the acrostic in the latest issue of *National Review*.

"Aunt Pat?" Lee asked diffidently. Pat looked up from her word puzzle.

"Yes, dear?"

"It's nothing," Lee fibbed. "Never mind."

Pat closed the magazine. She set it and her pen down, looked at her goddaughter, and waited.

Lee managed to shell another two pea pods before wilting under that gaze. "I was just thinking about Annie," she admitted.

Pat smiled. "So was I." Knowing there was more, she continued to wait.

"And I was just wondering if . . . ," Lee began methodically shredding a pea pod.

"If what, dear?"

"If, in any of her postcards, she had mentioned meeting—," Lee hesitated for a fraction of a second, "anyone."

"Annie mentioned quite a few people that you met," Pat told Lee. "Anyone in particular?" She hadn't missed Lee's prevarication.

"It wasn't someone *we* met," Lee hedged, torn between the need to unburden herself and the equally urgent need to protect Anne. "It was someone she met."

*Why can't I come out and tell Pat about Jake?* Lee asked herself. *It's not as if Annie's raided the cookie jar or something. She hasn't done anything wrong; she's fallen in love. Then why*, Lee wondered, *do I feel like such a snitch?*

Lee looked so worried that Pat frowned. Her frown deepened as she wondered whether Lee needed her advice as a confidante or as a physician.

Outside in the yard two squirrels bickered briefly, then bird-song-laced silence reigned again.

"Emily, tell me. If it concerns Anne, I have a right to know."

Lee's head bobbed up involuntarily at Pat's quiet demand. She saw that her godmother's gaze hadn't cooled, but was even more penetrating.

"Annie met a man on the tour, Aunt Pat, and I was just wondering if she had written to you about him because, because. . . ." The colander full of pea pods clattered to the floor as Lee threw up her hands. "Because I think that Annie's fallen in love. I don't think she realizes that she has, and we only had a chance to talk about it a little bit. I didn't get to meet him, and anyway I'm not absolutely sure if she really feels about him the way that it seems she does." Lee paused for a deep breath.

"And?" Pat asked.

"And not knowing is driving me crazy!"

Pat used every iota of the imperturbability acquired during her thirty years as a practicing psychiatrist to mold her face into an expression of mild interest tinged with surprise. "She didn't mention anyone, dear. Who is he?"

Lee gave her godmother an I-hope-you're-ready-for-this look.

"It's Jake MacIntyre, Auntie Pat."

Pat's calm veneer slowly splintered as she recognized the name. "Emily Elizabeth, if this is some kind of joke. . . ."

The aircraft came to rest on the tarmac at Dulles. Jake grimaced as the handcuffs snapped back into place.

"Sorry," Cathy said in apology. "But I've got my orders." Jake nodded, and they sat quietly as the rest of the passengers filed off.

As soon as the plane was empty, two men in dark suits came in through the cabin door. They strode over to where Jake and Cathy were waiting. "Hagura?" one man asked as he flashed a badge. When Cathy nodded, he said, "We'll take it from here."

The other man grabbed Jake's arm. Jake pulled away reflexively, and the first man slammed him against the galley door. "Look, you," the agent said, his forearm hard against Jake's throat. "Just how do you want to do this?" Jake fought for breath as the man leaned against him. "You can walk, or you can crawl." Jake sagged against the door as the man abruptly took the pressure off him.

"Jake, go with them," Cathy said.

Jake glanced at her.

"He won't be any trouble," Cathy said to the agents. Cathy's lips tightened with anger as one man looked at her contemptuously and the other ignored her.

"Thanks for the offer, but I'll walk," Jake told the agent.

With Jake sandwiched between the two men, they left the airplane. Cathy followed, then halfway down the jet way called out, "Wait!" The trio stopped. Cathy hurried up with the overcoat she was carrying. She tucked it between Jake's arms, hiding the handcuffs.

Jake looked at the overcoat, then at Cathy. "Wondered why you were carrying that. Thanks."

Even with the police cordon, the exit from the jet way was chaos. At the sight of Jake, lights flared into blinding brilliance, punctuated by the popping of flashes. Through the security detail that hemmed him in Jake saw faces familiar to him in the jostling, shouting throng. "Jake! This way, Jake!" old friends called out to him.

Anger flared briefly within him at the sight of some of those who had identified him as having been on the rug seller's rooftop. Almost instantly that anger was replaced with the recognition that these men and women were only doing the job that he had done a thousand times before. To give them what they needed, Jake paused, facing them silently, making sure that they got their footage and their pictures.

Cathy watched as Jake's eyes searched them and measured them, his quiet calm set against the noisy melee of the crowd. One of the agents pushed Jake in the back, and they moved on.

They went out a side door, then down a flight of stairs to where a nondescript government sedan and driver waited. One agent opened the rear door and motioned to Jake. Jake got in, and the man slid in beside him. As the other agent opened the front door, Cathy moved to get in.

"You're all through, little lady," the man said. He barred the way with his arm. "You're not needed anymore. You can go home now and do the dishes." He surveyed Cathy speculatively and added, "Or something."

Cathy looked the man over, then smiled. "I doubt," she

told him with mock sweetness, "that you'd be 'something' enough for me."

The man swore, then got in and signaled to the driver.

Cathy shook with fury as she watched the sedan pull away.

Long after they had gone to bed, Pat lay awake in the still darkness. As the crickets outside chatted among themselves, she thought about everything Lee had told her and Joel. Since the moment her daughter had been knit together in her womb, Pat had always found it easiest to talk about Anne while resting her head on her husband's shoulder. Tonight was no exception, and as they lay nestled together under the covers, they wondered what to do.

"I must admit," Joel said into the darkness, "that of all the advice I've planned to give someone courting my daughter, 'Throw yourself on the mercy of the court' has not been among it."

"Joel!" Pat snapped. "How dare you be frivolous when Annie's fallen in love with someone like that!"

"Like what?" Joel chided in response. "Look at what we know: We know that Annie apparently had some encounter with Jake MacIntyre that was important enough to tell Lee about, and we know that Lee believes it enough to bring it to our attention."

"But look at what he's done!"

"What he's allegedly done," Joel reminded her.

Joel turned to face his wife. As he always did, he cradled her head in his hand. Joel felt her shiver as his fingers traced the edge of her ear. "Do you, my love," he said more softly, "trust Lee's belief that Anne's feelings for Jake are genuine?"

Joel felt Pat nod.

"And do you trust our daughter?"

"Of course."

"Then, might it be reasonable to assume that Annie, as a grown woman of God, could have seen something in Jake MacIntyre that we don't know about? That there might be something about him that would cause her to be attracted to him?"

A smaller nod.

"Then, if we trust Lee, and if we trust Annie, and we trust God, how about if we at least start out trusting this guy? Or, if you're not up to trust, perhaps we at least give him the benefit of the doubt?"

After a long, silent struggle, Pat whispered, "What do we do?"

"Tomorrow, I'll make arrangements for us to meet Mr. MacIntyre." Pat sensed him smile. "During visiting hours, of course."

"Joel Elijah Dryden, you are incorrigible!"

"Thanks, my love. I do try."

# 29

"He's not guilty!" Cathy shouted.

Although it made her shorter than she already was, Cathy slumped down in her chair and glared at the two men in the room.

Ed Mahoney took off his glasses and scrubbed his face with his hand. "I know how you feel. I'm not happy about it either. If this was any other case, I'd insist that the evidence wasn't near conclusive enough. But Tourmaline isn't any other case. Egypt and Israel are foaming at the mouth. They both need someone to trot out for a show trial, but so far Egypt's got a charred corpse and some flunkies, and Israel's got nothing. You remember the old Mideast philosophy of 'You hit me, I hit you back twice as hard.' Their citizens are angry, frustrated, and screaming for blood."

Mahoney leaned back in his chair and spread his arms. "Do you have any idea what we had to do to get Israel and Egypt to agree to let us extradite MacIntyre? The president—the president mind you, had to publicly promise that, and I quote, 'Those involved in this atrocity will be indicted and speedily prosecuted to the fullest extent of applicable law. Their trials shall be both thorough and quick.' And even at that, the rest of the Arab community is starting to talk of Egyptian-Israeli-American collusion."

"A 'thorough' trial is fine," Cathy snapped. "A 'quick' trial is fine. But what about a fair trial?" The young woman pounded her fist on the table. "I didn't almost get my rear shot off just to bring MacIntyre back here for a lynching! If due process is going out the window, then why didn't we just leave him in Egypt?"

Mahoney stood and glanced uneasily at Jim Roberts, who had remained silent throughout the exchange. "I think," Mahoney said quietly, "that you're too involved in Tourmaline."

"You'd better believe I'm involved."

"Which is exactly why," Mahoney continued, "I've decided to have Jim file the indictment and be State's man on the prosecution team."

"What?"

"Look, Cathy, you did a great job on the field part of the case. The evidence is impeccable. . . ."

Cathy snorted in disgust.

"And MacIntyre is back in one piece. It's just that you're not right for the courtroom phase."

"Why not?" Cathy demanded to know. "What difference does it make who assists the U.S. Attorney?" She threw up her hands. "Security's no different than the FBI: we're all just a bunch of lawyers or accountants who happen to be able to handle a gun."

Mahoney listened impassively.

"What is it?" Cathy demanded. "Is it that I got my degree in the marines while Jim went to a big-name Ivy League school?"

Mahoney shook his head.

"Well, then, what?"

"It's just," Mahoney said slowly, "that you don't present the kind of image that needs to be displayed at this trial."

Suddenly, Cathy understood. Silence hung in the room as she stared at her colleagues. *So that's it*, she thought. *Six men are dead so far, two countries are in chaos, a girl is abducted in broad daylight, and it all boils down to 'image.'*

Cathy nodded to herself as the pieces fell into place. A small, minority female unconvinced of the suspect's guilt would definitely not be what they would want to help prosecute this case. From their point of view a big, blond, country-boy cannibal like Jim would be just perfect. While most of the world watched, he'd strut, posture, and eloquently call for the already-trussed defendant to be stuffed and slowly roasted. Cathy looked up. Neither man met her gaze. *Did they work this out while I was off getting shot at? Or was it imposed from above? Doesn't make much difference. Hagura*, Cathy thought bitterly, *you really blew it. If you had just stayed in the marines, you'd be a major by now.*

In a calm, quiet voice that disturbed the men more than any scream, Cathy said, "Fine." She left the room. Neither of them looked up from his desk as she made her way through the office and out the door. She was inside the women's room down the hall before she burst into tears of frustrated rage, and she was very proud of herself for having made it that far.

# 30

Anne awoke to the ongoing nightmare. Dragged from the depths of sleep back to the stark reality of her abduction, both Anne's battered muscles and bruised emotions cried out in protest as she swung her feet off the aircraft's couch. She was no less tired than before, and now her head throbbed dully.

Anne looked down the aisle. Her captor's head wasn't visible above the seat back, but she could see his left hand as it held a book. Anne wondered briefly if he ever slept, then she clutched her stomach as it growled insistently. Suddenly she was both very hungry and thirsty. After another furtive glance, she made her way to the back of the plane, where she remembered having seen a small galley opposite the washroom.

Her inspection of the galley revealed three bottles of mineral water, some tins of corned beef from Argentina, and two paper bags. Urged on by her ravening hunger, Anne eagerly opened one of the bags and peered into its depths. She averted her head in disgust as she was enveloped in the sickly sweet aroma of rotting fruit. Anne dropped the bag in the tiny sink, and wrinkled her nose as she waved away the cloud of tiny, white flies that had accompanied the odor.

She opened the other bag somewhat more cautiously, then smiled as she dumped a half-dozen hard rolls onto the galley counter. Most were hopelessly moldy, but Anne selected the best two and was able to pick the spots of mold off them with her fingernails.

Anne picked up a tin of corned beef. As a child of the age of the aluminum pop-top, she frowned at the lack of a ring on the top of the tin. A careful inspection of the sides of the tin revealed no ring, nor was her removal of the label any help. Anne shook her head in exasperation as her contemplation of the meat inside the tin caused her stomach to growl with increasing distress.

*Well, isn't this stupid,* Anne thought irritably as she tried unsuccessfully to suppress her hunger pangs. As a last resort Anne turned the tin upside down. The small key soldered to the bottom of the tin was greeted with another frown. A few flicks of her fingernail broke the key off. Anne held the key in one hand and the tin in the other. She looked back and forth between them as she pondered how to use the key to open the tin.

A few moments of additional examination and a silent hallelujah later, Anne managed to open the tin by using the key to peel off the metal strip that encircled its top. She had also managed to cut her finger on the razorlike edge of the strip, and she sucked her wound vigorously as she backed into the washroom.

With her washed finger bound in toilet paper, Anne returned to the galley. *The pilot can probably hear this stomach of mine,* she thought as it rumbled even louder. A search of the galley drawers revealed no knives, so Anne tore the rolls open. After another glance down the aisle, she discreetly broke the meat in two and folded the rolls over the halves.

*No plates. Now what?* she wondered. *Just hand it to him?*

Her mother had trained Anne well in table manners, and even in this situation she couldn't bring herself to just hand the man his food. Without realizing that she did so, Anne grimaced at the thought of his hand touching hers.

With a small, satisfied nod at her ingenuity, Anne entered the washroom again. This time, she emerged with two unused washcloths. With a washcloth-wrapped sandwich in one hand and a bottle of water in the other, she walked down the aisle to where her kidnapper sat reading.

"Excuse me," she said quietly, "but I thought you might like something to eat." The man jumped, and Anne flinched in reaction to his sudden movement. He looked up at her, then dropped his eyes to the proffered food and water. When he returned his gaze to hers, she saw in the formerly expressionless eyes the briefest flash of reaction. She couldn't bring herself to label it gratitude, but something had been there.

The silence between them grew awkward as Anne stood holding out the meal. Finally, she offered them to him again. Her captor frowned, as if offended. With lips pursed in anger, he lowered the tray table next to him, then looked pointedly at Anne.

*Well, of all the nerve!* Anne thought, incensed at the realization that he wanted her to serve him. Reluctantly discarding the notion of flinging the food at him, she glared at her abductor. Desiring to keep as far away from him as possible, Anne pressed herself against the seat in front of the man as she leaned over him, putting the sandwich on the tray. The bottle clattered against the tray table as, out of pure spite, Anne dropped it the last quarter-inch. Without a backward glance, she turned and marched down the aisle to retrieve her own meal.

Two bites into her meal, Anne stopped and set the sandwich down. The words for her belated grace came hard. She sharpened her will and forced her spirit heavenward. Determined to keep the smothering darkness that was all around her at bay, Anne concentrated on interceding for her parents and Lee, and she bit her lip with worry as she prayed for Jake. When she was able to be genuinely grateful for the blessing of a moldy sandwich and a stale bottle of water, Anne resumed her dinner.

All the window shades on the plane were drawn, so Anne treated herself to a risky dessert by sliding up the one nearest to her. It was night, and silvery overcast extended to the horizon. Anne had been counting on seeing the sun, and depression clawed at her as she watched the plane's moon shadow in its flickering dance over the cloud tops that raced by just below the plane.

*One of your psalms talks about the moon by night, God. Which one?* Anne slumped back into her seat, stiff and exhausted. *It's one of my favorites.* She was still shaken by her exchange with her captor. She was also cold. There were no overhead compartments that might hold a blanket, and she was unable to force herself to walk past the man to check the front of the plane. She curled up, trying to warm her feet by tucking them underneath her. *Tell me about the moon, Jesus. Please tell me about the moon.*

Cathy rested her chin on the back of her couch. Through her living room window, she watched as the lights of the Washington Monument came on. Greg put another CD into Cathy's player and then settled into a corner of the couch. "Can't talk about it, or don't want to?" he asked her as she snuggled up against him.

Cathy had called him from the phone booth after her confrontation with Mahoney and Roberts. On his way over to her apartment after work, Greg had made three purchases. The remains of two of the three—a pizza and a bottle of white zinfandel—were scattered across Cathy's coffee table.

Greg worked at CIA headquarters in Langley, Virginia.

Part of his job was to update the State Department on matters that the "Company" thought might be of interest to Foggy Bottom. It had been at the end of one such official consultation that he had first asked Cathy out, and he claimed that he knew of no other man who had needed an encrypted phone line to ask for a date.

Now they found themselves in the surreal position of many Washington couples: that which they could talk about together over the phone in the afternoon was strictly off-limits after 5:00 P.M. It was a source of endless amusement to them both, and they had developed their own code to circumvent it.

"Do I know about this?" Greg asked. *Is this official business?* Cathy shook her head. *No. Personal.*

Greg switched from work-code to couple-code. He sighed to himself. Work-code was a lot easier. "Should I know about this?" he asked. *Am I in trouble?*

Another shake of her head. *No. This time, at least, it isn't you.*

"Want to tell me about it?" *Want me to do something about it?*

"Not now. Maybe later," Cathy said into his shoulder. *I'll live, but right now I'm too mad to talk about it.*

Greg relaxed and stroked her hair. Then he remembered his third stop. "Brengle's has got a new flavor out," he told her. "Bittersweet Bonanza. I picked up a pint on the way over." Cathy was inordinately fond of the exceptionally rich brand of ice cream. "Want some?"

"No, thanks."

"OK. Mind if I have some?"

"Sure, go ahead."

Greg slid his shoulder out from under Cathy's head and went into her kitchen. He retrieved the small carton from the freezer and dumped it into a bowl. On his way back to the living room he fished two spoons out of the kitchen drawer.

Greg plopped back down on the couch and set the bowl in his lap. Cathy curled up against him. "It's really good—sure you don't want any?" he asked her after a bite. Cathy didn't say anything.

A minute later Greg felt her reach for the spoon that she knew would be there. When the bowl was empty, he set it on the coffee table. "Night, hon," he said as he kissed her on the forehead. "Gotta be at work early tomorrow."

They both knew the rules: she didn't ask for any additional explanation, and he didn't offer any. If he had, he would have told her that a Keyhole-III spy satellite, code-named Arcturus, was making a 5:00 A.M. pass over the Baltic republics. As Arcturus's senior imaging officer, he had to be there when the data started coming in. But, since they both knew the rules, he kissed her good night instead, told her that he'd call her tomorrow, and left.

Cathy stayed on the couch, staring out at the multicolored lights of Washington. Not until the gray dawn had dimmed and shriveled them did she fall asleep.

Only a slight bump told Anne that the plane had landed. The drop in pitch of the engine noise had awakened her, but a peek out of the window beside her revealed only unrelieved blackness. Anne listened as the plane rolled to a stop. The cabin door opened, and Anne swallowed several times to clear her ears. The foreigner appeared beside her. He motioned curtly for her to precede him down the aisle. Anne stood, regarded him coolly, and did not move.

Annoyance flashed across the man's face. Anne bit back her smile, then her determination faltered. The look he directed at her felt like the back of a hand across her face.

Arrogance, confidence, and the implacable determination that she would submit to his will radiated from him.

Battered by an enveloping, consuming compulsion, Anne felt herself begin to hurry, to rush, down the aisle. Then, from within her, a voice said, *Be still.* Anne found the strength to slow herself to a dignified walk. She ignored the furious man entirely as she left the cabin.

Distant, fog-shrouded lights were all Anne could see as she descended the stairs. She looked down and stopped. At the foot of the stairs was a helicopter surrounded by men. Men, she noted, quite different from her kidnappers in Egypt. These men were quiet and alert. With obvious discipline, they watched both her and the surrounding area, weapons held at the ready. A small shove from behind urged her on, the first time that her captor had touched her.

Anne lurched forward, loathing his touch. She paused at the foot of the stairs, grateful for the respite, shivering as the skin on her back still crawled. The foreigner walked past her, toward the helicopter's cockpit. One of the guards stepped forward and motioned toward the open door in back of the helicopter. The guards closed in around her. To Anne's surprise, one of them offered her his hand to assist her as she climbed up into the passenger bay. Her smile of thanks was not returned.

Anne grabbed the armrests of her seat as the helicopter shot straight up into the darkness. The upward motion transitioned into smooth forward flight, and Anne drifted into a fitful doze.

Sometime later, as the helicopter changed course, the rising sun shone briefly through the windows set into the sides of the passenger bay. The small square of light awoke Anne as it sped across her face. She had been dreaming of Jake, and her waking mind was still filled with the memory of his hands around hers. Heedless of the troops sitting quietly around her,

Anne felt again the desire that the thought of Jake ignited within her. That desire was now heightened and intensified by the shivering disgust that accompanied the memories of Hassan's and the foreigner's hands upon her. Anne trembled as she realized just how much she wanted and needed Jake MacIntyre.

Abruptly, the helicopter landed. The passenger-bay door was thrown open, and Anne blinked as sunlight flooded the interior of the bay. As the troops filed out, all Anne could see was a cloud-laced sky.

The foreigner appeared and beckoned to her. Anne stepped down and looked around. "No," she gasped. "It can't be. It just can't be." Only her grip on the door frame kept her from sinking to the ground.

All hope fled as Anne realized where she was.

# 31

"C'mon, MacIntyre, the warden wants to see you."

Jake looked up as his cell door clanged open. "Why does the warden want to see me?"

"How do I know?" the guard replied without interest. "Maybe it's time for tea. Now move."

Jake preceded the guard down the center of the three-story cell block. Eyes watched him from both sides as he passed: eyes filled with hatred, resignation, or fear.

As they approached the end of the walkway, a guard encased in a bulletproof plexiglass tower pressed a button. The cell block door slid open. As Jake stepped through, he was reminded of the hatches on submarines. *Only those hatches*, he thought, *keep the pressure out. This one keeps the pressure in.* The door closed behind Jake and the guard. Jake hesitated, unsure of which way to turn.

"Well?" the guard rapped. "Move it!" He prodded Jake with his nightstick.

Jake knew better than to turn around. He looked over his shoulder and shrugged. "Never been to the warden's office."

The guard shook his head. "Forgot that you're a new fish."

He motioned with his nightstick. "Left." Directed by the guard, Jake wended his way through the maze of drab, harshly lit corridors. Distant voices were raised in anger, then abruptly silenced. Doors began to appear in the formerly blank walls. Through one marked Infirmary Jake heard a low, wailing moan.

Cathy's kindness had left Jake unprepared for the harsh reality of his situation. His new status had been firmly impressed upon him from the moment the two agents had taken him into their custody. They had taken him to an empty room in an office building. In that room were two chairs, with a small table between them. Jake was not offered one of the chairs. One man started a cassette recorder that sat on the table. The other man took a sheet of paper out of his coat pocket and started asking Jake questions. Initially Jake answered them, but as they became more incriminating, he merely stared at the men.

"No more answers until I talk to an attorney," Jake said flatly.

The man reading the questions paused. The man not interrogating Jake spoke up. "We're workin' on it, bub. It's just that there aren't all that many lawyers here, so it may be awhile before you get a shot at one. OK?"

"Don't you mean," the questioner asked his partner, "that it'll be a while before he gets *another* shot at a lawyer?" Both men laughed. Jake didn't. The questions resumed.

Jake's questioner finished and put the sheet back in his pocket. The other man switched off the tape recorder, then the two stood up and left. Jake's legs trembled with fatigue as he sank to his knees, hard pressed to keep from collapsing completely as he did so.

No sooner had he relaxed than he heard the door open. "Get up, MacIntyre," a voice said. For an instant Jake thought that the two men had returned, then he realized that different faces stuck out of the same gray suits. Jake rose unsteadily. "Where am I?" he asked the new team.

"Didn't they tell you?" one of the men said in feigned astonishment. "You're in bus therapy."

Jake struggled to stay calm. "What's that?"

"It's a special little something," the other man explained, "reserved for hard cases like you. After we're done with you, we'll put you on a bus. Waiting for you when you get off will be some of our friends. When they get sick of you, they'll put you on another bus, and so on." The man smiled. "The law requires us to inform your immediate family of your whereabouts. But since your boyfriend's dead, there's no one to tell. So you'll just disappear."

Enraged, Jake took a step toward the man. He stopped when the man calmly held up his hand and frowned. "Wait a minute, bub, you're just about to ruin my day." The man gestured toward his partner. "If you hit me, then *he's* the one who'll get to blow your brains out."

Jake returned to his place. He watched in disbelief as one of the men started the tape recorder and the other took a sheet of paper out of his pocket and began reading questions. The same questions. Jake's protests were ignored and the questions continued.

Partway through the session, Jake found the floor rushing up to meet him. His shoulder screamed as he slammed into the hard concrete. Jake rolled to his knees, head bowed in pain as he massaged his shoulder. The point of a shoe nudged him. Jake raised his head and found himself staring into the snout of a Colt Python revolver. The hammer was pulled back, and a finger was on the trigger.

"Help us decide," the man on the other end of the gun said quietly.

"Decide what?" Jake asked.

"I want," the agent said, "to kill you now and say that we sent you back to Egypt. But my partner wants to actually send you back. You know why?"

Jake's eyes never left the gun as he shook his head. "Because," the man said maliciously, "over there they do interesting things to punks like you. Fun things. Things like torture." He jerked his head at the other man. "Eddie says that they start with your soft parts. He also said that we could go watch." The agent smiled at the idea. "So do me a favor, and don't get up."

Jake overcame his growing fear and moved his unwavering gaze from the gun to the man. He struggled to his feet.

It was the fourth or fifth time, Jake didn't remember which, that food was brought. Another suit brought in a tray and set it on the table. Jake could smell the soup, see the thick sandwiches, and hear the hiss as the man not reading the questions twisted off the top of one of the frosty bottles of beer.

Jake swallowed several mouthfuls of saliva before he was able to ask, "What do I have to do to get fed around here?"

The man took a pull on his beer bottle. "Easy. Answer the questions."

Hunger and fatigue rampaged through Jake. *Lie,* something inside him whispered. *What difference does it make? Tell them what they want. Get fed. Get some sleep. Give up.* "OK," Jake muttered dully. "What do you want to know?" *Lie to them. Get what you want and need.*

"How many men helped you in the assassinations?"

"Three." *Good. Tell them more. Don't resist.*

"Their names?"

Jake started to speak, then stopped. What felt like a cool stream of clear, cleansing water began to flow over his mind. It renewed him and encouraged him as it washed away the cobwebs of fatigue and fear in which he had been ensnared. In its wake was another voice. Not the voice of the enemy. A voice that was at once both rich and vibrant, and still and small. *No, Jake. Surrender only to me.*

Jake became aware that the men were looking at him expectantly.

"The names of your three accomplices?" his interrogator repeated.

Jake barely smiled. "Groucho, Harpo, and Chico."

The prison guard called him to a halt in front of an unmarked door. With one eye on Jake, he held a brief conversation with a speaker box mounted on the wall. The door clicked and buzzed, and the guard waved Jake through. The warden's receptionist was another guard. He sat facing the door through which they had entered, at a desk situated between the outer and inner doors of the reception area. After a quick glance at Jake, and after the outer door had closed, the sawed-off shotgun that he casually cradled disappeared. "MacIntyre?" he inquired.

Jake's guard nodded.

The receptionist picked up the phone and spoke into it. He hung up, then reached under the desk. The inner door now clicked and buzzed. "In," he said to Jake. "And don't hog all the hors d'ouevres."

What Jake assumed to be the warden's office was spacious, sunny, and well furnished. Most appealing to Jake was that no concrete was visible. Two men and, to Jake's surprise, a woman, all turned to look at him as he entered. "I'm Warden Delaney, MacIntyre," a small, balding man said. "These people want to talk to you. See to it that you answer their questions."

He turned to the man next to him. "I'll be back in an hour. The guard's right outside."

The woman spoke up. "I'm sure that Mr. MacIntyre won't be any trouble." From where she was seated she turned her violet eyes on Jake.

Jake's brow furrowed slightly. That gaze was vaguely familiar, as was the face that directed it at him.

The warden left. The man he had spoken to turned to Jake. "Please be seated, Mr. MacIntyre."

Jake pulled up a chair, and they both sat down. "As Warden Delaney said," he continued, "it would be immensely helpful to us if you'd answer a few questions."

The woman looked at the man. The man glanced at her, then nodded. "I forget myself," he said apologetically. "You don't know who I am. I'm—"

Jake interrupted him with an angry wave of his hand. "Look, I don't care if you're FBI, CIA, or even MI6. I'm through answering questions until I get a decent lawyer."

The woman looked shocked. "You haven't seen an attorney?"

Jake laughed sardonically. "Sure I have, if seeing an attorney fifteen minutes with a court-appointed public defender, who made it very clear that she'd really rather do something else than lose the case of the decade, falls in that category."

"We'll see to it that you're properly represented, Mr. MacIntyre," the man said.

"But," Jake replied with a knowing nod, "only if I answer your questions, right?"

The man shook his head. "Not at all. In fact, you may leave at any time."

Jake smiled at the irony of that.

"Now," the man continued. "Allow me to introduce myself. I'm Joel Dryden, and this is my wife, Pat."

The realization struck Jake a sledgehammer blow. "Then," he said slowly, the shock on his face plain to see, "you're—"

"Anne's parents," Pat said. "Please help us," she continued quietly. "We want our daughter back."

# 32

It took a minute for Jake to overcome his amazement. "Mr. and Mrs. Dryden," he exclaimed, "you must believe me. I had nothing to do with either the killings or Anne's kidnapping."

"If we didn't believe that," Pat said sympathetically, "we wouldn't be here."

"Anne's friend Lee has told us about your first meeting with Anne," Joel explained. "We hope that you'll be able to add to what we already know."

Jake looked at the Drydens as he wondered what they already knew and what they really wanted to know. He noticed that they both had an impressive demeanor about them. *Joel's obviously ex-military*, Jake decided, *and I can see in Pat where Anne gets her class from. No wonder she offered me their help.*

"Let's back up a little bit," Jake suggested. "I'd seen Anne before our first meeting. We didn't exactly meet."

"Was she with anyone?" Joel asked.

Jake shook his head. "Not that I saw."

"You next spotted her in the crowd at the Pyramids."

"That's right," Jake confirmed. "When I lost my camera."

"I find it a little hard to believe," Joel said without rancor, "that a photojournalist of your caliber would just 'lose' his camera."

Jake swallowed his instinctive, angry reaction. "Mr. Dryden," he replied evenly, "cameras are my tools, and I don't normally lose them. But," Jake added with a wry smile, "it's been a few years since I was last shot at, attacked with a knife, and punched in the face all on the same day." Jake shrugged. "I wasn't at my best."

Joel nodded in understanding.

Pat leaned forward. "How was Annie when you met her on the balcony?"

"Lee told you about that?"

Pat nodded. "Did Annie seem worried or nervous?"

"Not really," Jake replied. "She was surprised to see me, but I can understand that."

"But she didn't seem upset."

"No," Jake replied flatly. "She went to her room for a minute, and after she came back we just talked. I got upset when she couldn't tell me the serial number of your Leica, and she let me know in no uncertain terms that I was out of line."

"That's Annie," Pat replied, impressed by Jake's casual reaction to her daughter's wrath.

"She suggested that I come back that afternoon," Jake said. "But, when I tried, the place was swarming with cops." He looked at them bleakly.

Joel nodded. "That agrees with what Lee told us. Thanks very much. You've added some important details."

Jake held up his hand. "I've seen Anne since," he said quietly.

Pat and Joel sat bolt upright. "You have?" Pat said. "Where?"

"My friend Alex Stratton and I were abducted from Alex's hotel room." Jake closed his eyes and, with a visible effort, continued. "When we got to their hideout, I recognized one of the men there as one of the assassins. They dumped me in a room with Anne while they worked Alex over. I guess," Jake speculated, "that they didn't know we had met."

"How was she?" Pat's voice was low, worried, and insistent.

"She—" Jake paused and glanced at Joel.

"Jake," Pat said in a voice that made him look at her, "tell me."

"It's all right," Joel added. "She's a physician."

"I am also," Pat said quietly, "Anne's mother."

Jake leaned forward, aware of their intense attention. "Well," he began, "she was really beat up, but she seemed OK."

Joel saw Pat catch her breath.

"She told me," Jake assured them, "that they hadn't hurt her, if you know what I mean." Jake looked up in time to catch the end of a glance exchanged by the Drydens. They relaxed slightly, and Jake noticed that they were holding hands.

"They kept us there for most of a day," Jake finished. "We talked about church bells, and Scotland, and food. . . . " Jake trailed off helplessly as he realized how inane he sounded.

"Three topics near and dear to her heart." Pat smiled. *I guess Lee wasn't exaggerating about him*, she thought. "Thank you," Pat said seriously, "for taking care of my daughter."

Just then the anteroom door opened. A large, florid man with thinning red hair came in. "Sorry I'm late," he said in a voice that filled the office. "I'm Samuel Webster, the chaplain."

He looked at Jake. "So you're MacIntyre. If I'd known that you were going to have such illustrious guests," he said, encompassing Jake's visitors with a wave, "I'd have made time to read your file. How're you getting along?" he asked kindly.

"OK, I guess," Jake replied with a shrug. "I'm still not used to it."

"That's good to hear," Webster replied. "I'd be worried if you were. Is there anything you need?"

"I'd like my Bible back," Jake replied at once. "They took it away when I checked into this resort." Jake looked at the chaplain earnestly. "It's kind of important to me. My best friend gave it to me, and I enjoy reading it."

Behind Jake, the Drydens exchanged a long look.

"You'll have it back within the hour," Webster promised.

A guard appeared at the door. "Sorry, folks, but the warden needs his office back." The guard's tone chilled. "Let's go, MacIntyre."

# 33

By 10:00 A.M. Cathy had grown tired of sitting at her desk and brooding, so when the phone rang, she for once considered it a welcome interruption. She was surprised and pleased to hear from Vinnie Petigura. "What's up?" Cathy asked.

"Just got back from a raid," Vinnie reported with a non-chalance that belied the operation's risk. "The creep we picked up when we caught MacIntyre tipped us off to the Shams Ahmar safe house, so we went and had a look-see."

"Really? Did he say anything about MacIntyre's involvement?" Cathy asked.

"Nothing. He, uh, died of the severity of his wounds before the interrogation was completed," Vinnie said in an officious voice. "We've got a make on him, though. Bhanizar al Hassan. A small-time operator, apparently. Ignored by the PLO and the other big outfits."

A bullet through the thigh. A simple flesh wound. *The guy made it to the helicopter under his own power,* Cathy thought. *Lots of deaths from that kind of wound. Especially while under interrogation.*

"Right," she replied. "How about the others?"

"No chance on the one who got crisped," Vinnie said. "But the other was Muhammad Akesh. A well-known trouble-maker and all-around bad boy. Suspected in a dozen shootings."

"Shootings?" Cathy asked as she scribbled on a notepad.

"Right. Never had anything solid, however, but we're glad to get him off our list."

"The safe house was full of stuff," Vinnie said happily. "Firepower like you wouldn't believe. Expensive stuff—we need to figure out their funding. And lots of posters and litera-ture. Looks like they were about to go public. All the propa-ganda had that insignia on it. You remember, the one we found on that shot-up house. The logo with 'Puka Inti' on it." Vinnie's tone changed to one of inquiry. "You made any progress on that?"

"Not yet," Cathy replied. So far, all of her sources had come up dry. Greg had offered to nose around in the CIA files but hadn't yet had the opportunity.

Cathy's thoughts turned to Anne. "Anybody in the house when you came a-knocking?"

"No American girls, if that's who you're wondering about," Vinnie responded. "We picked up a few punks, but they were just local muscle. Didn't know a thing." Vinnie paused, then Cathy heard the faint snap of his fingers. "Oh, yeah. One did mention that, the day we bagged MacIntyre, a man and a woman had taken off, too."

"Could that have been the Dryden woman?" Cathy asked, faintly emphasizing the woman.

"Maybe, hard to say," Vinnie said with a shrug. "This creep was too scared of the guy who left to say much. Called him 'the foreigner'; said he was different, didn't speak their language. Then he clammed up."

"Any other lighthearted tidbits?" Cathy asked. She had taken a genuine liking to her Egyptian counterpart.

"Saved the best for last," Vinnie replied. "We fished an expensive camera out of the Nile. A Leica. We were diving near the wreck of the *Queen Nefertiti*, looking for the body of its owner, and we found it hung up on some rigging."

"Is it MacIntyre's?" Cathy asked.

"Yep. Ran the serial number yesterday. Registered to J. C. MacIntyre in August of 1984."

Cathy's initial elation was dampened by the realization that this breakthrough was more curse than blessing. All this meant was that another piece of physical evidence had been found that linked MacIntyre to a second violent crime. A crime related to the one of which he already stood accused. "Any prints?" she asked.

"Yeah," Vinnie said. "MacIntyre's, and at least three others. Most of them are partials, though. Camera was in the water too long."

*Well, that's something*, Cathy consoled herself. "Anyone else over here know about the camera?" Cathy asked.

"No. Should they?" Vinnie replied.

"It'd help if they didn't." Cathy paused. "Look, Vinnie, do me a favor, will you?" she asked. "Lose the camera for a while for me, OK? Paperwork foul-up or your pet camel ate it, something like that. I need some time over here."

"Something wrong?" Vinnie inquired.

Cathy knew that Vinnie was as eager for a conviction as Mahoney. *Time to fib*, she thought. She disliked having to do so. "Just a little dispute over turf," she prevaricated. That particular plight, Cathy knew, would garner the Egyptian's sympathy. Like any junior officer, he'd had big cases snatched away from him as soon as he'd solved them.

"No problem, friend," he answered. "What camera?"

"Thanks."

Cathy was just about to hang up when she remembered. "How's that kitten doing?" she asked Vinnie.

"Still hanging around here," Vinnie replied. "No one's taken it home yet. One of the secretaries feeds it. Why?"

"Just wondered. Thanks about the camera. I'll let you know when I want it found."

# 34

"Wait a minute," Jake protested. "This isn't my cell."

"No kiddin'," the guard replied sardonically. "Sorry, but the honeymoon suite's booked tonight." He gave Jake a shove. "Now move it."

As the cell door slammed behind him, Jake eyed the large man who occupied the other bunk. The man watched him: interested, intelligent eyes looking out from a face like polished ebony. "MacIntyre," the man said laconically.

"How do you know who I am?" Jake asked.

A slow smile appeared on the man's face. "I read the papers." The smile broadened. "So did you do it?"

"Do what?"

"Off them three government honchos."

"No."

Amusement crept into the man's smile. "Of course not. Whatever you say. Don't make much difference, anyhow, considerin' where you's headed."

Jake bristled. "I'll get out of here."

"You sho' will," the man agreed. "We all will, eventually." The man looked away. "I'm gettin' outta here tomorrow night."

Jake brightened. "Then, this is some sort of transition cell block?"

The man shook his head and laughed softly. "Never heard it called that before, but I suppose you's right. You transitions in, but you don't transitions out."

When Jake said nothing, the man looked at him. "Don't you know where you is, boy?"

"No."

"This here is Maximum Security. It's a kinda truck stop for folks like us who's on our way out." He motioned with his head. "Down at the end of the corridor is a door. On the other side is death row."

The warden looked up from a stack of papers. "You wanted to see me, MacIntyre?"

"I'd like to know why I'm being held in Maximum Security," Jake replied. After repeated demands to see the warden, Jake had been granted an appointment.

Stuart Delaney leaned back in his chair. "Orders, MacIntyre."

Jake gestured helplessly. "Whose orders?"

"I, too, have my superiors." Delaney rested his elbows on his desk. "Actually, it's for your own protection. You've been accused of a particularly spectacular and violent crime. You've also been connected with the kidnapping of a young woman." Delaney folded his hands. "Normally, those would be badges of honor around here. But, in your case, the word's gone out that the girl you allegedly abducted was subsequently sold into slavery."

Jake stared at the warden in disbelief.

Delaney's smile was a thin, greasy affair. "Think about it, MacIntyre. Three-quarters of the men in here are black, and every one of them thinks you're a slaver." He paused. "Anything else?"

"I'm sharing a cell with a black man!"

Delaney looked inquiringly at the guard. "Penrose, sir," the guard replied.

The warden nodded, then shrugged. "Sorry, MacIntyre, but we're overcrowded. If Amos grabs you, scream real loud. We'll try to get there in time." Delaney returned his attention to the pile of papers.

Jake raised his arms in protest. "But—"

The guard's truncheon slammed against Jake's ribs and knocked him to the floor. "Take the prisoner back to his cell," Delaney ordered without looking up.

# 35

Even the first fireflies of the season did little to console Lee as she sat at the table on the Dryden's porch. Normally the winking, yellow-green specks of light were a signal event greeted with fond welcome. Tonight, Lee barely noticed them as they floated across the lawn. She had spent the day alone while the Drydens visited Jake and her mother tended to chores at the Parker home. What she had planned as a day of prayer for Anne and Bible reading had instead turned into a day of brooding and worry.

Debby Parker and Pat came back from the kitchen with trays of coffee and sherbet. They set bowls and cups down in front of Joel and Jack, who were deep in conversation at the far end of the table, then served themselves. The two older women sat down on either side of Lee. To Lee's surprise, a bulky envelope appeared in front of her. She looked up from tracing circles in the condensation on the tabletop left from dinner's glasses of iced tea.

"What's this?" Lee asked.

"These are the pictures of you and Annie in Italy," Pat replied. "We were looking at them the day you called," Pat's face clouded at the memory, "and I put them on my writing desk and forgot all about them. Your mother found them just now when she was looking for a pencil."

She picked up the packet and took out the photos. "There's one in here from Venice that Joel and I don't understand." The physician in Pat Dryden had taken note of Lee's anxiety. An evening of telling them all about happier times was her prescription for snapping Lee out of it.

"Something that you don't understand, Uncle Joel?" Lee exclaimed. She arched one eyebrow at Joel, whose wide-ranging knowledge and reasoning abilities were well known.

"It's the circumstances that I don't understand, Lee." Joel rose and came to the other end of the table. Pat handed him the photos. Interested, Jack Parker followed.

"I can understand why the two of you would want your picture taken at the Rialto Bridge," Joel said as he shuffled through the prints, "considering that it's covered with expensive shops." He peered at Lee over his reading glasses. "And, I can understand why you'd want your picture taken with an exceptionally handsome specimen of gondolier."

Lee began to laugh and covered her face with her hands.

"What I don't understand," Joel said as he produced the photo with a flourish, "is why the poor man looks like something the cat dragged in."

The Parkers examined the photo, which showed the trio standing on the end of a pier in the brilliant Venetian noonday sun. On one side of the man, Lee stood beaming. Anne stood on the other side, looking somewhat unsettled. In the middle was the gondolier. He was hatless, dripping, and trying his best to smile.

"What on earth," Lee's mother began, "did the two of you do to that poor man?"

"Honestly," Lee protested. "We didn't do anything."

The Drydens and Parkers settled down to hear this latest in a long string of their daughters' misadventures.

"Annie and I decided to take a cruise on the Grand Canal." She glanced at Joel. "Just like you suggested, Uncle Joel."

Pat Dryden shot her husband a whom-did-you-go-cruising-on-the-Grand-Canal-with look. Joel winked at Pat, assumed his best poker face, and made a great show of paying studious attention to Lee.

"Well," Lee went on, "we picked out Pietro because he was nice, inexpensive—"

"And very good looking," Debby and Pat said together.

"Mother, really," Lee exclaimed in halfhearted protest. "That had hardly anything to do with it!"

"Well, as soon as we're aboard, Pietro immediately falls madly in love with Annie."

Pat and Joel exchanged an amused glance. That young men were enamored of their daughter was nothing new.

"So, as we're floating past the Piazza de San Marco, with a bazillion people on the bank, Pietro starts to sing to Annie. In Italian. *Loud* Italian." Lee laughed. "And everyone—I mean everyone—along the shore starts applauding. Annie was ready to die of embarrassment."

"Don't tell me that she pushed him overboard!" Pat, who was intimately familiar with her daughter's temper, said in horror.

"No," Lee replied. "I think that she actually enjoyed it."

"I'm sure she did," Joel said firmly.

"Anyway," Lee went on as the others ate, "to prove his strength or something, Pietro turns around and starts poling backwards, still singing away at the top of his lungs. Annie kept thanking him and telling him to shush, but he just grinned and kept on singing."

"But how did he fall into the canal?" Jack Parker asked one more time for the group.

"We came around a corner, and there was this bridge. One of the old, stone, really low bridges."

"Oh, no," Joel said, commiserating with the hapless young man.

"You mean neither of you warned him?" Debby asked, shocked.

Lee made a face and shook her head. "I looked at Annie, and she looked at me. But, by the time we decided that we really should warn him, he was trying so hard to duck under the bridge that he tripped on his pole and disappeared over the side."

"Poor Pietro," Pat said. "I hope you tipped him well."

"No," Joel interjected. "They tripped him well."

"I think," Lee concluded to a chorus of groans, "that he was the maddest about losing his hat. But he really was very nice about it."

The five made their way through the rest of the pictures from Italy. Lee regaled them with stories and, for a moment, the porch rang with happy laughter. When they finished, Pat handed Lee another packet.

Lee took the prints out of the envelope. "Oh, here's the one of Annie on that awful camel!"

Joel looked at the picture. He frowned, then fished the negative out of the envelope. "That's odd," he said, holding the film up to the light. "I didn't send any Vericolor Type III along. That's a professional film that needs refrigeration." He looked at Lee. "Did either of you buy any film while you were there?"

"I didn't. I don't think Annie did either."

They looked at the next picture. Two men, lying prone, one aiming a rifle. Joel took the picture from Lee and examined it more closely. "That's a Heckler & Koch sniper rifle. A military weapon." He frowned. "Lee, what were you two doing around soldiers?"

"We weren't, Uncle Joel. There were two soldiers outside the hotel, but they mostly sat on a bench and slept. We didn't see anything like this."

Joel looked at the picture again. "Those men aren't soldiers." Suddenly lost in thought, he looked up at the ceiling. *If Annie didn't take this picture, then who did? If those men aren't soldiers, then who are they?* As the others watched, realization spread across his face. It pushed aside the puzzlement and left worry in its wake.

"Joel, what is it?" Pat asked. His look caused her to take hold of his arm.

"The FBI has determined that it was an H&K that was used to kill Bob Moncrief. H&Ks are uncommon, expensive weapons; there just aren't that many of them around." Joel ticked the points off to himself on his fingers. "I didn't send any professional film along with Annie, and Lee says that Annie didn't buy any. This can't be her film. Those men are in Arab dress, and that's the Fortress of Babylon in the background. The Fortress of Babylon is where the signing ceremony was held.

"Don't you see?" Joel exclaimed. "Don't you remember what Lee told us? About what Annie told her?"

Lee gasped, suddenly understanding.

"Annie said that Jake MacIntyre claimed that she had one of his rolls of film. One that he needed. One that could exonerate him." Joel brandished the picture.

"If the assassins found out," Pat said, "that Annie had the roll of film . . ."

Joel raced for the phone.

# 36

The cell door clanged open, and Sam Webster stepped in.

Jake lifted his head from his hands and looked at the chaplain. "What am I doing in here?"

"Beats me," Webster replied. "This was news to me, too. Warden's orders—"

"I know," Jake interrupted, rubbing his ribs.

The chaplain took note of Jake's grimace and frowned. "I'll see if I can find out."

Webster took something from his pocket. "Here's your Bible," the chaplain said. "I wrote your name in it."

He looked at the stained margin, then at Jake. "I can get you a new one if you like."

Jake shook his head. "No thanks, Chaplain."

"Call me Sam. It's more comfortable. Plus," he added, spreading his arms to encompass the banked rows of cells, "I'm used to it; I shepherd a flock that isn't especially fond of titles."

Jake took the Bible. "Thanks, Sam." He stood up and stretched, then grabbed his still-tender shoulder.

"That happen here?" Sam asked.

"No," Jake replied through gritted teeth. "Egypt."

"Had it looked at?"

"No. It'll be all right."

"We'll let the doctor decide that." Sam turned to the guard. "See that MacIntyre reports for sick call tomorrow morning." The guard nodded. "If I find out why you're in here," he told Jake, "I'll let you know." The chaplain looked across the cell. "Would you like to talk some more tomorrow, Amos?"

"Sounds like a fine idea, Preacher," Jake's cellmate replied. "Seein' as how it's the last chance I'll get."

"Good." Sam turned to go. "'Night Jake, Amos," he said with a wave. The cell door slammed behind him.

Jake sat back down. "What did you mean," he asked Amos, "when you said 'it's the last chance I'll get'?"

Amos frowned and shook his head. "Are you slow or just stupid?" He leaned back against the cell wall. "Come midnight tomorrow, I's gonna 'transition' outta here."

"You mean—," Jake asked, stunned.

"That's right, boy. I's gonna walk in through that green door at the end of death row, but I ain't walkin' out."

Jake looked at the placid face atop a mountain of muscle. "What did you do?"

Amos raised his right hand and folded it into a sledgehammer of a fist. He gazed at it pensively. "Got carried away."

The phone's harsh ring shattered Cathy's exceedingly pleasant dream into small pieces. Filled with the apprehension that accompanies phone calls that rouse one from sleep, she groped for the receiver and mumbled a sleepy hello.

"Cathy Hagura?" asked an unfamiliar voice.

*A sales call?* Cathy peered at her clock radio. The glowing display read 9:33. Normally a night owl, Cathy had retired early this evening. Emotionally and physically exhausted by the events of the last few days, and since Greg was at work, she'd gone to bed. "Yes?" Cathy replied testily, ready to cut the intruder off at the knees.

"Cathy, this is Joel Dryden. Anne's father."

The remnants of sleep vanished from Cathy's mind. "Is she all right?" Cathy blurted.

"I wish I knew," Joel replied, worry evident in his voice. "We haven't heard a thing."

"Neither have we," Cathy said. "Everything possible is being done to locate Anne."

"Pat and I know that, and we thank you. Actually," Joel continued, "I'm calling about the MacIntyre case."

Cathy switched on the bedside light and grabbed a pad and pencil out of the nightstand drawer. She took notes rapidly, trying to keep up with Joel as he told her about the meeting with Jake, his and Pat's confidence in Jake's innocence, and the newly discovered pictures.

"Let me see if I've got this straight," she said, only half-believing this turn of events. "You've got the roll of film that Jake claims he took."

"Yes, we think so," was Joel's simple response. "It was in with rolls of Anne's film, just as Jake claimed it would be."

"Are you willing to testify to that?" Cathy asked.

"Of course."

"That's good, because I think Jake's innocent too."

"I'm glad to hear that," Joel responded.

"And," Cathy went on, "I think that the pictures are what can get him off the hook."

"Then," Joel said, "let me ask you one question before the prosecutors do. How are you going to prove that Jake took the pictures?"

Cathy slumped back against the pillows she had mounded up. *Good question*, she thought. *Too good a question.*

Then she sat up so suddenly that she dropped the phone. Greg was an avid photographer, and something he had once told her had just leaped into her mind. "I think I just got that figured out."

"OK. I need to come to D.C. tomorrow on business. I'll bring the pictures. They'll be on your desk by eleven."

"Great," Cathy replied. "My office is—"

"I know where it is," Joel interrupted. "Tomorrow at eleven."

"OK," Cathy said, mystified at how he knew where her office was in the warren of government office buildings that made up the State Department complex.

As soon as Joel had hung up, Cathy dialed Greg. "Sorry to bother you at work," she apologized when he answered. "It's important."

"No problem," he replied. "Kinda slow just now." In theory, both of them could be disciplined for Cathy calling Greg at work. The CIA guarded its phone numbers as jealously as it did the rest of its secrets. "What's up?" he asked.

Cathy explained about Joel's call and about her subsequent idea. "Might work," Greg replied slowly. "I'd need another roll of film that could be proven to have been exposed in the camera, however. You got the camera?"

"Not yet. But I will. And I'll work on the other roll of film."

"Get those, and I can't see any problem."

"Thanks," Cathy said. "You're a love. 'Night."

Greg looked at the phone. He shook his head, bemused, then turned back to his work.

That night, Cathy lay awake, thinking and planning, until 3:00 A.M. That was 9:00 in the morning, Cairo time, and as she dialed she hoped that Vinnie was punctual.

"Vinnie, I've got to have that camera," she said in a rush as soon as he had answered.

"Wait a minute," Vinnie replied, confused. "I thought that you told me to put it on ice."

"That was yesterday," Cathy said.

Vinnie could hear the impatience in her voice. "Now I need it."

"May I ask why?"

"If it works, I'll tell you."

*Only after Jake's acquitted,* Cathy added mentally. "Vinnie, what kind of shape is the camera in?" *If only it's not too beat up.*

"Pretty good," Vinnie told her. "Kind of wet and muddy, but not too bad."

"Take it to the embassy for me, will you?" Cathy asked, urgency now in her voice. "I need it ASAP. If you get it to a courier now, I can get it tomorrow afternoon."

"Sure," Vinnie replied. "What's the sudden rush?"

"Let's put it this way," Cathy said casually. "I just got bitten by the shutterbug."

"OK, Cathy. I hope you know what you're doing, 'cause I sure don't."

Something had been nagging at Cathy as she talked to Petigura. Just before she hung up, she thought of it.

"Vinnie, wait! One more thing."

"What?"

"Is that kitten still around?"

"Yeah. Why?"

"Send her along, too. OK?"

"*What?*"

"You don't want her, do you?"

"No."

"Then take her to the embassy along with the camera."

"Cathy—"

"It'll be fine. We do this sort of thing all the time. I once had to baby-sit an ambassador's pet python all the way from Washington to Kathmandu."

"Cathy, if anyone here found out that I was doing this . . ."

"Well, just mark her Top Secret or something."

"Whatever you say. But, if you're ever back in Cairo, you owe me."

"Thanks, Vin. You're a sweetheart. 'Bye."

Vinnie stared at the phone, shook his head, and returned to his work.

# 37

"Mornin', Jake," Sam said pleasantly from behind his desk. The prison physician had examined Jake's shoulder and placed him on light duty until it was healed completely. Jake was surprised that the guard had then escorted him directly to the chaplain's office.

Sam grinned at the look on Jake's face. "That's right," he said. "I need some help, and you're it." The chaplain waved at the cluttered office. "Which would you rather do, type or file?"

"File," Jake replied instantly. He was, at best, a slow typist, but years of maintaining his vast collection of negatives had made him an expert filer.

"Have at it," Sam said after explaining to Jake what needed to be done.

Their tasks were interrupted by the lunch bell. Jake stood and stretched. Sam came over. He nodded approvingly at Jake's work. "Had some men that never got that much accomplished."

"You take a lot of pictures, you sort a lot of negatives," Jake replied.

Jake hesitated outside the dining room to which Sam had led him. "This isn't the mess hall."

The chaplain grinned. "I've just appointed you a trusty. That means that you get to work for me, six hours a day, for the princely sum of fifty cents an hour. It also means that you get to eat in the commissary." Sam waved Jake inside. "C'mon. At fifty cents an hour, I can afford to buy you lunch."

Jake looked up from his reading when Amos was brought back to their cell. Sweat from his exercise period glistened on his face, and he mopped at it with his sleeve. He pointed at Jake's Bible. "You read that much?"

"Just started."

"What you think of it?"

"I'm not quite sure, yet," Jake admitted.

Amos settled onto his bunk. "My momma used to read us to sleep with it. Seven kids in one room, so she read us the excitin' parts: Moses, and Elijah, and David and Goliath. She also read us the parts about Jesus in the temple and about his walkin' on the Sea of Galilee." Amos smiled. "Never did learn to swim, myself." He folded his massive arms. "Well, one day when I was twelve, I got the shock o' my life."

"What happened?"

"Our church got a new preacher, 'n' his wife taught the Sunday school. Well, she had a Bible with pictures in it. One Sunday morning she opened it up, 'n' it was then I found out that Jesus was a white man."

"So?"

"So?" Amos said scornfully. "What's the matter with you, fool? It was the white man that killed my daddy. It was the white man's dirty washin' that my momma scrubbed twelve, fourteen hours a day after Daddy died." Amos stared out through the bars of the cell. "I didn't go to church much after that."

"How did you end up in prison?" Jake asked.

"It was fo' killin' a white man that they put me in here,"

Amos replied without rancor. "If'n I'd killed a black man, they wouldn't've sent me to no death row."

Jake nodded. "So what started you thinking about Jesus again?"

"Stir."

"Stir?"

Amos frowned at Jake. "Solitary, man. Lockdown. You come in here with an attitude like mine, you spend a lotta time in stir."

The bunk creaked in protest as Amos shifted his weight. "Big man like me in one o' dem little lockdown cells, he got nuttin' to do but think. So I got to thinkin' about my momma's singing. My momma, she was always singin'. In church, while she was washin' 'n' ironin', even when she was scrubbin' floors. Always singin' about flyin' away, and her father's house, and gettin' carried home." The big man looked past Jake. "Always singin' about Jesus."

A bell rang—ten minutes until lights out.

"So," Amos continued, unaware of Jake, "one day I remembered what my momma had said the day I left home. She asked where I was goin', 'n' I told her that I didn't know. Then my momma looked me right in the eye 'n' said, 'Son, just remember one thing: You may not always know where you is goin', but with Jesus you always know where you is gonna end up.'"

"Sounds like good advice to me ."

"You think so? One day Preacher Sam, he visited me while I was in stir, 'n' I asked him if'n that was true. It was, he said, 'n' he told me that Jesus loves me. How could that be true? I asked him. How could Jesus love a black man who done killed a white man?"

"What did Sam say?"

"He told me that Jesus be color-blind. He don't care what I done; if'n I asks Jesus to forgive me, then he forgives me.

Preacher said that Jesus' father sent him here to love them that no one else loves." The bearded face relaxed; the shrewd, world-wise eyes warmed. "Imagine that," Amos said softly. "Then Preacher told me that my momma was right. That if I love Jesus, I know where I's gonna end up." Amos shook his head. "If'n what Preacher Sam say be true, then Jesus be one righteous dude."

The guard's nightstick clattered against the bars. "Lights out, gentlemen." He grinned nastily at Amos. "Better get your beauty sleep, boy. You're gonna want to look your best when they serve you up as the main course."

Amos shot the man a dark look, but said nothing. The lights went out as the guard moved along. "Preacher Sam be wrong," Amos said into the darkness. "Ain't no way Jesus could love a man like that."

"You afraid?" Jake asked. The darkness seemed to thicken around them as he waited for an answer.

"Yeah, I's afraid," Amos said at last. "Ain't no one 'cept a fool that wouldn' be. That's why I's gonna talk t' the preacher tomorrow." Amos sighed. "Even though I know where I's goin' t' end up, I wanna make real sure I know how t' get there."

The cot groaned in protest as Amos turned over. "You a prayin' man, MacIntyre?"

"Not really."

"But you reads the Bible."

"I'm new at that, too."

"Will you pray for me?"

Jake hesitated. "I'm not very good at that sort of thing."

"That's OK. 'Tween you 'n' the preacher, I'll make out allright." Jake heard Amos take a deep breath. "I want you to pray that I keeps my head up 'n' my eyes open. When my time comes, I want you to pray that I remember where I's bound."

"How will I know when it's time?"

"You'll know. Believe me, brother, you'll know."

# 38

Cathy tapped her pencil on her government-issue, GSA-scheduled desk pad. It was a habit of hers that told everyone else in the office that she was deep in thought and to interrupt her only at their peril. Things weren't adding up, and that annoyed her. Her other cases, mostly involving the extortion and blackmail of diplomats, had been so clean: Talk the blackmailers into believing that the ransom was going to be paid, stake out the designated drop site, and bingo!

Cathy looked at her desk and frowned. She had developed a habit of writing down on sticky notes the aspects of a case she was working on that were still not resolved to her satisfaction. Then she'd stick them to her desk blotter. When the blotter was clean, the case was resolved, and that made her happy. More than once Cathy had been told by her superiors to remove a last sticky note and declare a case closed. She had started putting these unanswered questions in a little notebook. On its cover she had written "I Told You So!" It made her feel better.

Today Cathy's desk was littered with yellow scraps of paper, and that was another signal for the rest of the office to

give her a wide berth. Her eyes swept restlessly over the notes.
Four stood out:

*How was MacIntyre recruited?*

What is the terrorists' motivation?

How are the terrorists financed?

Who/what is Puka Inti?

*OK, Cathy,* she thought as the pencil kept on tapping. *Get
it together. The first two can wait, and Vinnie's working on the
financing. The last one's the one you can do something about.* Cathy
sighed, not looking forward to what she had to do next. *Time,*
she thought with resignation, *to make a visit to the Lair.*

In five years at State, Cathy had never before needed Allison
Kirstoff's expertise, so they had never met. As she wondered
what the inhabitant of the Lair knew about her and thought of
her, Cathy climbed the two flights of stairs. A short walk down
a windowless hall brought her to a door with 602 stenciled on
it. Next to the door was a maroon-and-gray nameplate that read
A. E. Kirstoff.

Cathy knocked.

"Come in," came a muffled reply.

Cathy hesitated, never having been in Kirstoff's office
before. Then she opened the door and stepped into the Lair.

Cathy stopped just inside. The door nudged her hip in its
effort to close automatically. As she looked around, she at once
began to understand why Kirstoff had such an effect on men.
*This place,* she thought wryly, *must drive the Young Turks right out
of their macho minds.*

The decor was an intricate and seemingly random admix-
ture of feminine softness and the hard, clean edges of high tech.
Cathy grew increasingly disconcerted as her eyes traversed the
room. The office seemed to be a battlefield for the two warring
schools of decor, neither of which was going to allow the other

a moment's rest. No sooner had Cathy's eye rested on a print of a delicate, soft-pastel portrait by John Singer Sargent than it was accosted by a calendar featuring the lurid colors of computer-generated, geometric shapes.

Looking elsewhere didn't help. On a table next to Cathy, copies of Donald Knuth's *Fundamental Algorithms* and Annie Dillard's *Teaching a Stone to Talk* were intertwined as they held each other open in an unlikely paperback embrace.

Kirstoff's hand moved a computer mouse in short, sharp motions across a high-tech, glittering pad. Spread beneath it was an Irish lace doily.

"Just a minute," Kirstoff said absently. Her eyes were riveted on the screen of the large CRT that glowed before her. Cathy took advantage of the time to examine, with the gimlet eye of one woman appraising another for the first time, the enigmatic woman who sat in front of her.

Cathy could see at once why Kirstoff was so hotly pursued. She was tall and slender, and the backless computer chair on which she knelt displayed her long legs to advantage. A headful of thick, coppery hair ended just above her waist. Seen in profile, her aquiline nose accented her high cheekbones perfectly. Lips made even redder by the CRT's light were pursed in concentration.

Somewhat timidly, Cathy walked around behind Kirstoff and looked over her shoulder. She shared the conviction common to those unfamiliar with computers that, if she got too close, the machine would either bite her or catch fire. Cathy looked at the screen, and the amused contempt that she had felt for Kirstoff's victims evaporated.

The face of the CRT was littered with rectangular patches in a variety of colors. Inside some of the patches words and numbers stood in blinking array. Others displayed graphs that changed as Cathy watched. Small flicks of the analyst's wrist caused patches to appear and disappear. Some patches shuffled over and under one another. Others vanished entirely. In one patch, larger and more centrally located than the rest, characters appeared as fast as Kirstoff could type.

Then Cathy noticed the background against which the patches lived and died, and she smiled at just how consistent it was with the rest of the inconsistent decor. It was a soft, breathtakingly lifelike picture of an enormous, dew-covered, dusky red rose.

Without looking up, Kirstoff said something that sounded like "Hang on while I update etseeinittab." After a final, apparently triumphant, flourish of the mouse that she had been manipulating, the large patch vanished. Kirstoff swung the chair around on its casters and gazed at Cathy.

Kirstoff had to barely look up to meet Cathy's eyes. *Tall*, Cathy thought. The analyst's eyes were a blue that bordered on violet, and Cathy was very glad that they were turned on her in inquiry rather than scorn. Kirstoff's face was devoid of makeup. *Not that she needs it*, the still-appraising part of Cathy thought enviously. Simple pearl earrings were Kirstoff's only jewelry.

"Cathy, right?" Kirstoff asked. "Consular Ops?"

Cathy nodded.

"Allison Kirstoff."

She offered Cathy a hand. "Call me Allie." The young woman smiled. The incandescence of that look made Cathy wonder if when Allison was finished with a man she just slid him out under the door.

Cathy shook the proffered hand. "Thanks for making time for me." She gestured at the crowded computer screen. "Especially since you're so busy."

Kirstoff smiled a disparaging smile that wrinkled her nose. "That?" she said, dismissing the machine with a wave. "Nah.

Just messing around." With a lithe ease, Allison reached over and opened a small refrigerator. "Pepsi?" she asked.

Cathy accepted. "Thanks."

"What can I do for you, Cathy? Or is it," Allison asked with a grin, "Agent-with-a-capital-*A* Hagura? Most of the men who come in here prefer it that way."

Cathy had no problem grinning back. *You didn't even wait to see this book's cover,* she chided herself. *You judged her by her reviews.* "Cathy will do just fine," she replied. "I need your help on Tourmaline."

# 39

Jake and Sam's midmorning work was interrupted by the arrival of visitors. Joel and a man Jake didn't recognize came into the office. The guard who had escorted them closed the door behind them.

"Sorry to interrupt," Joel apologized. He motioned to the man who stood next to him. "This is Cyril Edwards."

Both men rose and shook hands with the slight, gray-haired man. "Cyril's an old friend of the family," Joel went on. "When I asked him for a recommendation as to counsel for you, he insisted on meeting you."

Cyril smiled at Jake. "I hope to be of assistance, Mr. MacIntyre." He grinned. "Anyone who's a friend of Joel Dryden needs all the help he can get." Cyril looked at Sam. "Is there someplace that Mr. MacIntyre and I can talk in confidence?"

"In a prison?" Sam snorted. "You must be joking." The chaplain pointed to his desk. "Right here is as good a spot as any. Today's my day to make my rounds. The infirmary, solitary, and other garden spots. Will an hour do?"

"That'll be enough time for our initial consultation," Cyril agreed.

"I've got an errand to run," Joel said. "Be back in an hour."

Sam and Joel left, and Cyril sat down in Sam's chair. He opened his briefcase and took out a yellow pad and a formidable array of pencils. "First off, Mr. MacIntyre, do you wish to retain me as your legal counsel?"

"I don't see why not," Jake replied. "The Drydens recommend you, and you already seem a lot more competent than that public defender they tried to foist off on me."

"Being a public defender is the toughest job in law, Mr. MacIntyre." Cyril smiled. "I should know. I am one."

Jake swallowed. "Sorry."

Cyril waved him off. "As it so happens, I know the woman that they assigned to your case. She's quite skilled, really. Her only problem is that she aspires to the district attorney's office."

"And you don't?" Jake asked.

"Not anymore. After three terms as D.A., I found that I enjoy the 'presumed innocent' part far more than the 'until proven guilty' part."

Jake swallowed again.

"Now that we've got that settled, I'm Cyril, and you're Jake. OK?"

Jake nodded.

"But," he warned, "call me Cyr, even once, and I'll have you breaking rocks until you're old and gray. Clear?"

Jake grinned. "Anything you say, *sir*."

"Touché! Jake, I like you." Cyril picked up his pad and one of the pencils. "Rule number one, Jake. You're to trust me only slightly less than you do God himself, clear? Lie to me and you hang both of us."

"You got it," Jake replied.

"Good. Now, did you kill Bob Moncrief?"

*He sounded taller on the phone,* Cathy thought as Joel sat down at her desk. It had taken two excuse me's on Joel's part to break through Cathy's reverie about her meeting with Allison Kirstoff.

"Sorry, Joel. Please, sit down," had been her embarrassed reply.

"First off, let me say how much Pat and I appreciate all you're doing to locate Anne."

"I wish it was more," she replied, awed by his calm authority. "I really do."

"I know," Joel said. "But, as you know, I'm here to deliver something that may have an effect on the MacIntyre case." He took the packet of pictures out of his coat pocket.

Cathy's eyes widened as she saw the first of Jake's pictures. She pointed at one of the men in the photo. "That one, the one holding the rifle? He's the driver that we killed when we caught them out in the desert. The other one, the commander, was captured but later died of his wounds."

"So," Joel speculated, "either Jake MacIntyre was purposely documenting the activities of his fellow terrorists—"

"Or," Cathy finished the sentence, "he's telling the truth."

Joel related to Cathy what Lee had told him, and Cathy in turn told Joel all that she felt she could divulge about the case. After Joel had asked Cathy several questions that were too insightful for the average layman, Cathy looked at him. "Just how do you know so much?" she asked Joel.

Joel smiled. "I read a lot."

*Great,* Cathy thought. *A spook. Just what I need.* She had been to enough parties with Greg's friends to know the intelligence agent's hallmark obscure smile and evasive answer when she saw it. *Wonder if he's CIA or NSA? I'll ask Greg.*

After Joel left, Cathy faxed the photo to Vinnie, with a

request that he make a formal identification of the two men. She had just finished sending the fax when her phone rang.

"Can you come up?" Allison asked. "I've got something to show you, and it's kinda important." She sounded pleased, even a bit giddy.

Cathy stared at the phone. *If any other woman sounded like that*, she thought with amusement, *I'd figure that she wanted to show me her engagement ring or tell me that she was expecting. But,* Cathy decided as she headed toward the stairs, *since it's Allison, she's probably invented time travel or something.*

"Where's Amos?" Jake asked when he was returned to his cell.

"Death row. Transferred to the prep cell." The guard smiled mockingly. "Hope he didn't owe you no money."

Cathy didn't bother to knock on Allison's door, and her entrance was acknowledged by Allison's long arm waving her over to the computer screen. "C'mere! Lookit!" Allison said happily. She jabbed at the screen with her finger.

"What?" Cathy asked, lost in the maze of information on the screen. Allison clicked a button on her mouse, and one of the patches enlarged to fill the screen.

Displayed on the screen in front of Cathy was an article from the *Department of State Bulletin*. Cathy got a copy every month, and most of them she gave to Greg after she had read them. The article was from the office of the ambassador at large for counterterrorism.

"What am I looking at?" Cathy asked.

"See? Right here." Allison jabbed again. It was a fact sheet and chronology entitled "Sendero Luminoso: Peruvian Terrorist Group."

Cathy dimly recalled having scanned the piece. "So?"

"They did it!" Allison said brightly. "At least they helped."

"Helped do what?"

"The killings."

"What killings?"

Allison looked exasperated. "Your killings. Tourmaline. Moncrief and the rest."

Cathy ran her fingers through her hair. "Wait a minute. I'm confused. The assassinations were in Cairo, right?"

Allison nodded.

"And, if I recall that article correctly, Sendero Luminoso is a bunch of very bad boys in Peru, right?"

Another nod.

"You getting enough air in here? Egypt is a long way from Peru."

"I know," Allison beamed. "That's the really interesting part. It seems that—"

She was interrupted by the strident beeping of Cathy's pager. Cathy started to silence it, then glanced at it instead. "Sorry," she apologized to Allison as she got up, "but there's a courier waiting downstairs with another load of fan mail."

"Agent Hagura?" the courier asked. Cathy nodded. *Must be FBI*, she decided. *And must've really ticked somebody off to be doing this grunt work.*

The courier held out a box. "Sign here."

Cathy signed the receipt book and handed it back.

The man started to leave, then he turned and looked at Cathy.

"I know it's none of my business, ma'am," the man said, "but this is the first T.S. box I've ever seen with ventilation holes punched in it. And the box seems to be meowing."

Cathy smiled at the courier. "Yes, it's a very important cat. Has to do with the assassinations."

The courier's eyes opened wide. "Really? Some kind of evidence?"

"Yes," Cathy replied with a straight face. "We think the cat saw everything."

The courier suddenly looked very confused and quickly made his exit.

Cathy tore open the box and pulled out a cardboard carrier. From inside the carrier she retrieved an indignant and extremely hungry Salome. After a quick check to make sure that the kitten had not suffered any ill effects from the flight, Cathy put the protesting Salome back into her box.

*Gotta get her something to eat*, Cathy realized as the now-muffled demands for food continued unabated. *If she keeps that up much longer, someone's going to notice.* Cathy looked around the office for something that a kitten could eat.

The vending machine offered only corn chips, pastries, and candy bars. *Nothing here*, Cathy realized. *Cat's too smart to eat microwave popcorn.* Then she remembered seeing a carton of milk in Allison's refrigerator. She grabbed her telephone and punched in Kirstoff's extension.

"Allie, it's Cathy. Do you still have some milk left in your fridge?"

"I think so. Let me check." Cathy heard the sound of Allison's refrigerator slamming shut. "About a half a cup."

"Perfect. Can I borrow it?"

"Sure. If I bring it down, will you show me what all the fuss was about?"

Cathy tickled Salome's nose through one of the carrier's ventilation holes. "Sure," she said with an anticipatory laugh.

A minute later, Allison waltzed into the office with the carton of milk. She looked around as she set the carton on Cathy's desk. "Seems like an urgent request just for a cup of *cafe au lait.*"

"No, it's not for me."

"Whatever," Allison said. "Want to join me for lunch?"

Cathy shook her head, this time grinning. "Already have a lunch date." She took Salome out of her carrier. The kitten looked up at Allison and mewed peevishly.

"Aww! How cute!" Allison said. "Can I hold it?"

"It's a she," Cathy explained as she handed the kitten to Allison. "Came in the morning mail from Egypt."

Allison ran her finger down Salome's back. "Egypt? Did you buy her there?"

"Not exactly."

Salome smelled the milk and began crying piteously. Cathy fished a styrofoam bowl out of a desk drawer and poured milk into it.

"What's this?" Allison asked, fingering a small metal tag that dangled from a collar around the kitten's neck. She peered at the tag. "Is that Arabic?"

Allison set the kitten down on the desk, next to the bowl.

"Sure is," Cathy replied.

"It says that her name is Salome." Allison frowned. "Salami? What kind of name is that for a cat?"

"It's pronounced 'Sal-OH-may'. I'll tell you all about it while she eats," Cathy offered as Salome began to lap at the milk.

Cathy and Salome finished at the same time. To the surprise of both women, the kitten then ran up Allison's arm. To Kirstoff's delight, Salome sat on her shoulder and batted at her dangling earrings, then clawed her way up through Allison's thick hair, and perched on top of her head.

Just then, Jim Roberts came in. He gave the pair one long, bug-eyed stare and then backed quickly out of the room.

"Ow!" Allison, who was shaking with laughter, exclaimed as the kitten dug her claws into her scalp. She retrieved Salome from her perch, and with a wistful look began to return her to Cathy.

Cathy held up her hands. "She's not mine."

"She isn't? But, then, why did you . . ."

"I like cats, so I just couldn't leave her in that awful jail. But I can't have one in my apartment." Cathy saw Allison's eyes light up with hope.

"Do you think that maybe I could . . ."

Cathy smiled at the sight of the imperious Allison Kirstoff looking as anxious and eager as a toddler on Christmas Eve. "Sure. I hate to see her go, but I'm glad she'll have a good home." Cathy handed the carrier to Allison, who reverently placed the sleepy kitten into the box.

"Thanks, Cath! I'll take good care of her, I really will! C'mon, Salome!"

"But," Cathy protested, "what about this Sendero Luminoso thing?"

"Tell you later!" Allison promised. She gave Cathy a quick hug and dashed out of the office.

*Well, so much for the revelation of the century,* Cathy thought with an amused laugh. *Peru? I gotta get that woman out in the daylight more often.* Cathy returned her attention to the box. *Let's see what else is in here.*

The box also contained a plastic bag. Inside the bag was Jake's camera, its lens misted with condensation. Cathy took the camera out of the bag and set it on her desk, next to the negatives that Joel had provided. *OK,* she thought as the damp camera stained her desk blotter, *I've got two of the three pieces. Time now for a photographic paternity test.*

# 40

*Awful lot of work for a three-inch piece of blank film,* Cathy thought as the Washington-bound shuttle left the runway. Armed with her badge, her ID card, and her best official demeanor, she had spent an exhausting afternoon at the New York headquarters of Global Photo.

Global's director of archives was a small, owlish man who seemed to Cathy just as musty as the treasures he so zealously guarded. Unprepared for any request out of the ordinary, Cathy's desire to be able to actually take a piece of film had left the little man blinking in astonishment and mumbling to himself. As she recalled her conversation with the man, Cathy slouched down in her seat and gratefully sipped her cold soda.

"But it's simply not done, Miss . . ." He blinked rapidly at her. "What did you say your name was?"

"Hagura," Cathy replied patiently. "Special Agent Cathy Hagura of the U.S. State Department."

"Hagura, Cathy Hagura," he mumbled to himself. "Sorry," he then said. "Not done. Simply not done at all."

Cathy took a somewhat larger swig of soda as she remembered the hour of futile entreaties, threats, and demands to talk to the archive director's superior. "Look, I'm working on the MacIntyre case, OK?" she finally blurted out in desperation.

"MacIntyre?" The man looked startled. "Jake MacIntyre?" Cathy nodded.

"Well, why didn't you say so?" The man smiled happily. "Nice young man, MacIntyre. Fine photographer, and he takes good care of his negatives." He gave Cathy a conspiratorial look. "Not like some of those others, you know. Takes good care of them, he does."

Cathy explained that she needed a small piece of film that had been exposed in Jake's Leica. "Come along then, come along," he said with a wave.

The man led Cathy through row after row of ceiling-high file cabinets. Each drawer was labeled only with a number. *Hope he knows where he's going*, Cathy thought. *Actually, what I hope he knows is how to get back.* The dry, cool air made her shiver. *I'd hate to get lost. He might not mind dying down here, but I sure would.*

Eventually he stopped with an abruptness that caused Cathy to almost run into him. He pulled open a file drawer and riffled through it. "Need a piece of film, do you?" He looked at her, distressed. "That means that we must sacrifice an image. Oh dear." He continued to flip through the neatly-labeled rows of negatives. Each time he held one up to the light, he would mutter, "Can't be that one," and replace it. Eventually, he turned to Cathy, his face a study in anguish. "Young lady, are you absolutely sure that you must have one of his images?"

"You mean a negative?"

"Yes. A negative." The man scowled as if he found the term offensive.

Cathy hesitated, then guessed. "I don't think it has to be a negative. Any piece of film should do, as long as it passed through Jake's camera." *Any film is, I hope, better than no film at all.*

The little man clapped his hands. "Delightful! Got lots of that!" He rooted through the back of the drawer and came up with a strip of what appeared to be amber-colored cellophane. "Here you are," he said as he handed it to her reverently.

Cathy turned the strip over in her hands. "Thanks. What is it?"

"What is it?" the director replied indignantly. "Why, it is the trailer to the seventh roll that MacIntyre shot of the last summit meeting."

"How can you tell?" Cathy asked.

"Really!" the man huffed. "It's all right here, you see." He snatched the strip back from Cathy, then showed her the minuscule printing on the outside of the protective cellophane envelope. Listed were the date, subject, roll number, photographer, and camera used.

"Terrific!" Cathy said, vastly relieved. She reached for the strip. "May I have this one?"

The director started to hand the film to her, then snatched it back at the last instant. "One question, first," he said, looking at her suspiciously.

*Now what?* Cathy wondered. She throttled her exasperation, pretending in doing so that she was throttling this insufferable little man, and looked at him. "Yes?" she inquired politely.

"Did he do it?"

"Did who do what?"

"MacIntyre. Did he kill those men?" He shook his head. "Can't have the film if you think he killed them."

Cathy smiled. "Just between the two of us," she said sweetly, "I don't think he did."

"Oh, good," the director replied. He handed Cathy the film, and before he could change his mind again, she tucked it in her jacket. "Didn't think he did."

"Nice young man," he kept repeating on their way back. "Nice young man."

Greg met her at the airport. "You won't believe," she said after a quick kiss, "what I had to do to get this piece of film."

Greg leered at her. "You won't believe what you're going to have to do if I help you get MacIntyre off the hook."

Cathy rolled her eyes and gave him a shove. "Cool it. And give me back that kiss."

The duty officer on guard at the front desk of CIA headquarters was an old friend. He was used to Cathy's coming over to use the agency's laser printers whenever she needed to print out an especially important report.

"State still too cheap to buy you a LaserJet?" he asked her as he handed her a blank, white tag on a chain.

"You know Foggy Bottom," she replied. "Doesn't count unless it's written in blood." Cathy slipped the tag around her neck. "Say hi to Becky for me, will you?" she said, amazed at how calm she was.

"Will do," he promised. "By the way, nice work on the Tourmaline affair." Cathy shrugged. In agency parlance "nice work" meant "nice shooting."

"Cathy Oakley is what they're calling her over at Cons Ops," Greg added, much to Cathy's chagrin.

Cathy's uneasiness at being around so many computers was compounded by the knowledge that she was definitely someplace she wasn't supposed to be. She knew that she was at CIA headquarters. She also knew that this was one of Greg's labs. As she stood in the middle of the cold, white room, she reflected that there wasn't much else she wanted to know about the place.

She watched as Greg, now all business, slipped the film from Global into a holder. He placed it next to the holder that contained a piece of film from the roll Joel had brought her. He flicked a switch, and magnified images of the pieces of film appeared on twin monitors in front of them.

"See anything?" he asked. Greg stared at the monitors, his face pale in their cold, white light.

"Nope," Cathy replied. "Looks like my TV did before you fixed the antenna."

"Watch," Greg told her. With a flourish he pushed a button, and the images changed. On the formerly snowy screens there were now two groups of uneven, brightly colored rectangles. *"Ta-daa!"* Greg said. "My own idea. What do you think?"

"Wonderful!" Cathy responded. *Show-off.*

"Now watch," Greg continued. "This is the good part. Designed the pattern-matching algorithm myself." He sat down at a computer console and typed a command, then turned to her. "This'll take a few minutes," he said with a grin. "Wanna neck?"

Cathy looked at her boyfriend in disbelief. "No, thanks," she replied, "I already have one."

They both smiled at the latest recitation of their old joke.

Cathy settled down into her seat and looked at the rectangles. *Funny*, she thought, reminded of the flowery background to Allison's screen, *how something as cold and impersonal as a computer could create something so lovely.* She leaned toward the screen. "It's really pretty."

Greg winced. "'Pretty' misses the point," Greg replied. "What you're looking at is the fractal representation of the deformation of the acetate backing of those two pieces of film, based on Mandlebrot's concept of self-similarity."

"Fractals?" she asked, wishing she hadn't gotten him started.

"Yeah," Greg replied, "fractals. A new geometry invented

around 1975. They use it a lot to create the landscapes of planets in the Star Trek movies." Greg smiled. "As a matter of fact, it was a scene in *The Search for Spock* that gave me my idea."

Cathy sighed, and closed her eyes. *Why*, she thought tiredly, *couldn't he just watch football and belch like normal men?*

"I scan each piece of film with polarized light," Greg was explaining, "then I use the data generated by the scans to generate Julia sets and their nonconformal variations—"

"Julia?" Cathy interrupted, feigning jealousy. "So who's Julia?"

"I've been meaning to tell you about her."

"Greg, I'm hurt."

"Now seriously, Cathy, this is important."

"I know. Computers are our *friends.*"

Greg ignored her and continued. "The degree of variance between the sets will tell us just how dissimilar the pieces of film are. If all three pieces were wound through the same camera," he told her, "then the variances should be quite low." What he didn't tell her was that, during the day, this computer looked at pictures of an entirely different sort. It compared new satellite photos with older ones, to determine what had changed in the area being observed.

Cathy sighed with relief as Greg's dissertation came to an abrupt halt. The images on the screens had been replaced by rows of ghostly green letters:

**CONTINUITY FACTOR  99.89**
**SIMILARITY RATIO  94.21**
**DENSITY PERSPECTIVE  +.8755**

A moment later there appeared another line:

**MATCH CONFIDENCE  98.99795**

"Now," Greg said, "give me the piece of film that you wound through the camera."

Earlier that day Cathy had run a roll of film through the damp, protesting Leica and then had it developed. She handed a piece to Greg, who replaced one of the strips in the holders with it. He reran the test, creating a new set of rectangles. Then he exchanged the other strip with the strip he had taken out and ran the comparison a third time. Greg had promised Cathy that this would cover all possible combinations of pairs. She took his word for it.

"Yes!" Greg enthused when the final set of figures had appeared. He pumped his fist in the air. "The results of all three tests are well within tolerances."

"And," Cathy asked, "that means . . . ?"

Greg swung around in his swivel chair to face her. "It means that we just spent twenty-seven thousand dollars of the taxpayer's money in computer time to prove that your three pieces of film were all run through the same camera."

Cathy sighed her relief.

"It also means," Greg said as he rose and put his arms around her, "that it's time to pay up."

He pulled her to him.

"OK," Cathy agreed. "I guess you've earned it." She smiled sweetly up at him. "This time," she said as she pushed him away and headed for the door, "*I'll* buy the Bittersweet Bonanza."


The noise woke Jake from his fitful sleep. He jumped out of bed and looked wildly around for the source of the sound. It was a clattering, booming roar that seemed to come from everywhere at once. Jake pressed his face against the bars of his cell and listened. As the tumult increased in volume, Jake realized that it was emanating from the inmates on death row. As they hammered metal and flesh against concrete and steel, Jake could feel the bars vibrate.

The thunder increased until it was a deafening roar. Then, abruptly, silence reigned. The emergency lights in the cell block dimmed once, then again. Jake stared at them, uncomprehending. All at once he realized what they meant: Amos Penrose was dead.

The thought struck like a thunderbolt: *That could be me. That will be me!* Horrified, Jake staggered back from the bars.

Jake thrust clawed fists in front of him, as if to keep the terror at bay. *No!* his innermost being screamed. *No!* He tripped, bloodied a knee on the rough concrete floor, and got back up. *I must get out of here. I must do something. If I don't do something, I'm going to die!* The terror of the eternal unknown consumed Jake MacIntyre.

*When my time comes, I want you to pray that I remember where I's bound.*

"Amos!" Jake shouted. "You're here!" But the other bunk was smooth and empty. "Amos, where are you?"

A small point of light shone forth in the stygian blackness of Jake's mind: *Pray that I remember where I's bound.*

"Amos, come back!"

*Remember where I's bound.*

Jake fell to his knees.

# 41

Despite the urgings of his empty stomach and aching back not to interrupt his homeward journey, Joel pulled off Maine Route 102 and parked in a turnout. He looked southwest across Somes Sound toward Sargent Mountain, now silhouetted against the bright sky of sunset.

Joel needed to think. As the waters of the sound, turned to copper by the setting sun, merged into the evening shadows, he leaned his arms against the steering wheel and rested his chin on his hands.

One of the things that Joel loved most about the inlet was that it was still. Not quiet, which is the absence of noise, but still—the absence of intrusion. There was a clarity, a brilliance about the place that had, since he was a child, helped him to sort out, decide, or make sense of matters. In some ways, Joel realized, his belief that Jake was innocent was both a blessing and a curse. He and Cyril Edwards had talked about it on the shuttle back to Boston.

"Why do you think that MacIntyre's innocent?" Joel asked in response to Cyril's declaration that he'd defend Jake.

"Because he's smart," Cyril replied.

"By 'smart' I assume that you mean he's smart enough to retain you," Joel said with a grin.

"By that," Cyril retorted, "I mean that murder and kidnapping are dumb crimes. High-risk, low-individual-return crimes. Thug crimes. Not the sort of thing that someone with MacIntyre's education and professional ability resorts to. Not, at least, without a real whopper of a motive."

"Conspiracy? Passion? Revenge? Money?" Willing to play the devil's advocate, Joel offered as many motives as seemed to suit the circumstances.

"None of those fit, and none that I can think of do either," Cyril replied. "As soon as MacIntyre appointed me his counsel, I called my friends at the U.S. Attorney's Office." His smile told Joel just how much he had relished taking on his former colleagues. "I demanded full disclosure of all the evidence that they've collected so far." Cyril looked at Joel. "You know what they've got?" he said triumphantly. "Nothing. No motive, no hard evidence. Nothing. Just some people who say they saw Jake in the vicinity before the shooting and a few prints on a rifle barrel. Plus, despite their efforts to do so, no connection whatsoever has been made between the shootings and Annie's disappearance."

Cyril looked sympathetically at Joel as worry swept his face at the thought of Anne.

"But the prints are Jake's," Joel said, perplexed, "and the rifle has been proven to be the murder weapon."

Cyril smiled at his old friend. "I'm having that worked on," he said.

Joel got out of the car. He stretched, pressing his hands into the small of his back, and breathed deeply of the crisp evening air. A bell-like call echoed across the water, announcing that Joel's intrusion had been noticed by the lord and lady of the sound.

From their nest atop a dead tree on a small island in the center of the fjord, a male osprey launched himself into the sky and soared over Joel's head. It didn't take him long to determine that Joel was no threat to his hearth and home, so he banked seaward, off in search of the family dinner.

Joel watched it as it flew away, a muscular bird with a five-foot wingspan and gray feathers shading subtly into black. Joel looked out at the island, his sharp eyes discerning the mother osprey as she sat on her nest with her two charges. They were youngsters at that stage that made them look scrofulous in the extreme, as if recovering from a severe sunburn. Joel thought of Anne at five, with her dirty face and skinned knees, and smiled at just how disreputable children could sometimes look. He wondered if the fledglings' appearance horrified their mother as much as Anne's had at times embarrassed hers. As Joel watched, Daddy arrived, to the chicks' raucous delight, with the family's dinner.

*At least you're able to take care of your family,* Joel thought as he watched the ospreys feed. Inside him rage flared anew. That rage, the fury of a father at those who would endanger his family, had initially focused itself on Jake. Now, however, the man whom Joel thought had abducted his daughter had become a man who seemed to care about her. Torn loose from its first mooring, that anger drifted about inside Joel in search of a new anchorage.

A sense of impotence added itself to the rage that seethed within him, and the two fused into hatred. Joel's eyes hardened as he vowed to find those who had his daughter. When he did, and when he had Annie back, then he'd kill them. Joel Dryden was no stranger to killing, and he smiled grimly at the prospect. In the anticipation of killing, the hatred inside him had found a harbor.

*Be still.* The phrase came unbidden into his mind. *Be still, and know that I am God.* Joel looked up, and his thoughts turned suddenly outward from their murderous introspection. *Think not of destruction, but of creation. My creation.* Joel looked about him. His heartbeat slowed and his clenched fists relaxed as he allowed the Comforter's stillness and peace to wash over him. It drained away his hatred and replaced it with peace. *All this about you is my handiwork*, he was reminded. *As are you, and Anne, and those who have her. Be still. I am in control.*

A point of land jutted into the cold waters of Somes Sound, and as Joel watched, a light winked on at its end. The land was Blanchard's Point, and the light was in the dining room of his home. Pat, Joel realized, would be setting the dinner table. She'd also be looking at the kitchen clock and wondering why he wasn't home yet.

As he walked back to the car, Joel thought of the psalm of which he had been so potently reminded. Besides "still," he remembered, the word in the psalm could also mean "to heal," "to make whole," "to draw toward evening." In the evening light Joel leaned against the car and said a silent prayer of thanks for a Protector who never failed to watch over him.

Again healed and made whole, he started the car and continued south.

Joel muttered under his breath as he struggled to get the mail out of the box at the end of the driveway. With a final tug he wrenched it loose, then glared at the culprit. It was a thick, manila envelope addressed to Patricia S. Dryden, M.D. Joel tossed the mail onto the seat next to him and continued up the drive.

"Shuttle late?" Pat greeted him as he walked into the kitchen. Lee and Debby had gone back to the Parker home to entertain visitors, so Joel and Pat had the house to themselves.

Joel shook his head. "Stopped awhile to sort things out,"

he replied. He put his arms around his wife and held her, grateful for her nearness. Later that night, when they were together in bed, he'd tell her about how very blessed he had just been.

Something in his tone of voice caused Pat to look at her husband. "It didn't go well?" she asked, referring to Cyril's interview with Jake.

"Actually, it went quite well," he responded. "He's agreed to represent Jake."

"That's good," Pat said with a smile. "So Cyril believes him too?"

"Apparently so," Joel said. "But with Cyril you never know."

"Any other news?" Pat asked. Her face clouded.

Joel gave her a hug. "Sorry, love, nothing. I've talked to everyone I know, and no one's heard a thing."

Pat nestled against Joel as they stood in the kitchen. *Time to trust*, she thought. *Why, Lord, is trusting so very, very hard?*

"Any mail?" Pat asked as they finished drying the dishes after dinner. "I'm expecting a new batch of articles that I'm supposed to referee."

"Oops," Joel replied. "Left it out in the car."

In a minute he returned to the kitchen and handed Pat the manila envelope. "The latest in your series of mailbox eaters," he said with a grin.

Joel sorted through the rest of the mail as he made his way toward the kitchen table. Halfway across the kitchen he paused, stopping underneath the light so that he could better inspect the unfamiliar stamp on one of the envelopes. It wasn't a U.S. stamp, and Joel thought that Dave Wilkins might like to have it for his son. Joel fished his knife out of his pocket and slit the envelope open. A single sheet of onionskin paper was the entire contents of the envelope. Joel pulled it out and unfolded it.

"Oh, Good Lord."

Pat put down the pile of articles and walked over to him. "What is it?"

"I know who has Annie," he said without looking at her. "I don't know how, but I know who."

Joel handed Pat the sheet of paper. On it was written a string of digits:

**011 51 14 657 022**

Her hand on his arm, Pat looked up at her husband. "I don't understand."

Taking Pat by the hand, Joel strode into his study. He turned on the speaker and recorder attached to the phone, then punched in what he had recognized as a phone number. A few seconds later they heard a single ring. Then a voice, obviously recorded, came on the line.

"Good day, Dr. Dryden," the voice said in Spanish. "At 2:00 P.M., local time, any day within a week of hearing this, be at the fountain in the Plaza de Armas. Someone will meet you." The voice paused. "We will know when you heard these instructions, Doctor, and so we encourage you to act expeditiously." Another pause, and the voice became faintly sardonic. "As you well know, ours is a hot and humid climate. Remember that after a week in such conditions, soft and delicate flowers such as yours wither, die, and begin to rot."

The line went dead. Joel stared out through the study window into the moonless night.

Perplexed and worried, Pat took the envelope from Joel's hand. She held the envelope under the desk light and was barely able to make out the blurred postmark: Lima, Peru.

# 42

"What happened, Jake?" Sam Webster's large frame almost filled the tiny isolation cell.

Jake looked up dismally. "I had a bad night."

Sam returned Jake's somber gaze. "So did I."

"Somebody pushed me out of the chow line at breakfast this morning. Knocked me down. So I came up swinging." He fingered gingerly the discolored lump beneath his left eye. "No way I could let someone get away with a stunt like that."

The cot groaned in protest as Sam sat down on the other end. "Maybe so, but it means that you get three days here in paradise." The chaplain grimaced. "It also means that I get to do my own filing."

Jake looked worried. "I don't get to work for you anymore?"

Sam smiled. "I think I can work that out. Warden Delaney allows his new guests one fall. But," Sam said seriously, "only one. That's why you've got to remember to use your head, Jake. You're one of the few in here who can."

Sam took Jake's Bible from his shirt pocket and held it out.

"Stopped by and picked this up on my way over to see you. Thought it might come in handy in the next couple of days."

Jake looked at the book but did not take it.

Sam waited, arm outstretched, until Jake spoke. "Fat lot of good what's in there has done for me."

Sam nodded. "Seems like that, doesn't it? Here you are, in prison for a crime you didn't commit, and in solitary for a fight you didn't start."

Misery and loneliness consumed Jake. He thought of the real reason he was so touchy and found himself saying, "I liked Amos, Sam."

"So did I. He was a good man."

Jake hesitated, then asked, "What did you talk about yesterday?"

Sam smiled. "His life, his family, his failures and successes. All the things a man alone, who is about to die, entrusts as a legacy to another."

"Did he ask you how he could make sure he knew how to get where he was going?"

"He sho' did," Sam said in a bayou drawl. The chaplain laughed quietly. "I've been called a lot of things since I came to work here, but only Amos Penrose has ever called me Preacher."

Jake stared at the gray steel wall. "What did you tell him?"

"I told him that the road he wanted to walk was marked by only two signposts—one marked Faith and another marked Trust. And I promised him that if he followed those directions, then he'd find Jesus waiting for him at the end of the road."

"But," Jake asked earnestly, "how do I know that God's really there?"

"That's where faith comes in." Sam opened Jake's Bible. "Faith," he read, "is being sure of what we hope for and certain of what we do not see." Sam smiled at the look on Jake's face. "I know how you feel. For someone as pragmatic as you are the notion of transferring your certainty from the physical to the spiritual, from the tangible to the intangible, is extremely threatening."

Jake stared at the ceiling. "What do I do to be faithful?"

Sam waited until he caught Jake's eye. "Faith is something you have, not something you do. Like it or not, you can't photograph Jesus."

Jake closed his eyes and rubbed his face with his hands.

Sam looked at him steadily. "It's up to you, my friend. The best advice I can give you is what's written on the other signpost."

"Which is?"

"Christ's own words: 'Trust in God; trust also in me.'"

Sam sat quietly and watched, as he had so often before. Whether it was a young man in his cell, an old man on his infirmary deathbed, or a condemned man for whom age had ceased to matter because his next dawn would be his last, the struggle was always the same. *It's such a shame, Lord,* Sam thought as he watched Jake, *that we embrace so eagerly those things that cost us so dearly and struggle so to embrace that which is so freely given.*

"How," Jake said at last, "do I tell Jesus that I believe in him?"

"You're in luck," Sam replied, grinning. "It's something that *you* get to *do.*" The pastor came over and placed his hand on Jake's shoulder. "It's a prayer. A short prayer, a simple prayer. A prayer that's been said many, many times. Say it with me, and know that each word of it causes the stars to sing together and all the angels to shout with joy."

Sometime later, the guard's knock interrupted them. "Lights out, Pastor." The steel door muffled the guard's voice as he opened it.

Sam stood and stretched. He pointed at Jake's Bible. "Changed your mind about keeping that?"

Jake nodded.

"I'll be back tomorrow," Sam told him.

Sam walked to the door and stepped through. Just before the door swung shut he caught Jake's eye. "Good night, brother."

# 43

Cathy plopped down in the overstuffed chair that occupied one corner of the Lair. "So you weren't kidding about this Peru connection?"

"Dead serious," Allison replied as she grabbed the dossier that Cathy had given her and opened it. "The name of the outfit in Egypt was Shams Ahmar, right?" Allison asked. "Well," she went on without bothering to look up, "in Arabic *Shams Ahmar* means 'Red Sun,' which is an unusual sort of name for an allegedly Islamic terrorist group."

"Does sound strange," Cathy concurred. "The names of most Mideast organizations usually have some sort of ideological flavor."

"That's just it," Allison declared with immense self-satisfaction. "This one does too."

Cathy waited. When nothing was immediately forthcoming, she motioned for her friend to continue.

Allison smiled her devastating smile and tossed the dossier onto her desk. "Under the assumption that one or both of the words in the title were ideologically significant, I ran a simultaneous check on them both, using a fuzzy-logic paradigm to cross-associate them with extrapolations from the relevant agencies' hyperfiles."

Cathy, hopelessly lost, got up and headed toward the door. "I'll be back when you get over your fever."

"Get back here," Allison said. "All I really did was a data base search."

Cathy could relate to that. "Which data bases did you search?"

Allison looked at Cathy out of the corner of her eye and gave her head a small shake. "Don't ask."

"Right." Cathy leaned back in her chair. "You know," she remarked, "Greg and I have to have you over for dinner sometime. The two of you would have a great time not telling each other how you find things out."

"He's CIA?"

"Yes, but don't tell him that I told you."

Allison smiled.

"So?" Cathy asked. "What did you find?"

"Well," Allison said with a wave of her hand that dismissed several hundred thousand dollars of computer time, "besides the unlikely idea of a resurgence of belief in the old Egyptian sun god Ra, *Sun* came up empty. But," Allison leaned forward, eager to share her discovery, "with *Red* we hit the jackpot."

"Great!" Cathy said facetiously. "What did we find?"

Allison looked pained. "What we found—actually what the HP9000 Series 90/300 found—was an NSA report about an increased Maoist presence among the Arab terrorist organizations."

"You mean Maoist, as in Mao Tse-tung?"

"Yep, same guy," Allison replied. "Good old Chairman Mao himself." It was getting dark, so Allison leaned over and flicked on her desk lamp. "It seems," she told Cathy, "that during the heyday of the Cultural Revolution, Mao and his

284

group invited some of the best and brightest of the young Arab malcontents to come study with them. This," Allison went on, clearly enjoying herself, "from the Chinese point of view, had several benefits. First, it kept their friends the Soviets busy wondering what they were up to. Second, it gained them a foothold in the Middle East. Last, and most important to that charming little band of ideologues, it allowed them to inculcate some smart young hotheads with their own warped form of communism and then export it by shipping them home."

"Knowing full well," Cathy said to Allison's approving nod, "just what would happen when the atheism of Maoism and the religious fanaticism of Islam butted ideological heads."

"But," Allison finished, "the whole thing fell apart during the power struggle that followed Mao's death. The infant Arab Maoist groups were abandoned by Deng Xiaoping's regime and left to their own devices. One by one, the groups either fell apart or disappeared. Eventually, both the domestic and foreign agencies keeping tabs on them lost interest."

"OK," Cathy said. "I'm with you so far. But how does all this tie into our gang of punks?"

"In those dead-letter data bases that I rummaged through were names," Allison replied. "A quick cross-match with your information revealed that one of Mao's guests was . . ." Allison paused dramatically. "Bhanizar al Hassan."

"The Shams Ahmar commander. And Vinnie and I thought that he was a small-time operator." Cathy shook her head.

"Going to try and get more out of him now?" Allison asked, her eyes bright.

"Probably not, since he died during the initial interrogation."

"Oh, well," Allison replied offhandedly. "Saves the time and expense of a trial, doesn't it?"

Taken aback by this flash of cold-bloodedness, Cathy glanced beyond Allison. *Whew*, she thought as she noticed Allison's framed undergraduate diploma. *Never realized that Radcliffe girls were so cold-blooded.*

"Well, this is just wonderful," Cathy said, sarcastically. "Now we've got a bunch of Arab Maoists. I still don't see what that has to do with the Sendero Luminoso in Peru."

Allison smiled. "It was that logo that gave it away. You remember," she said in response to Cathy's puzzled look. "The one spray-painted on that Egyptian's house."

Cathy nodded, recalling the insignia emblazoned on the front of Mort Steinmetz's house. She wondered idly what Steinmetz, an Orthodox Jew, would think of being called an Egyptian.

"Well," Allison went on, "since that symbol was our only piece of hard evidence, and since no reference to the entire symbol existed, I started searching the data bases again, this time for references to any part of it."

"Such as?" Cathy asked, trying again to keep up.

"You know," Allison continued, "the star, the snake, that sort of thing. But, none of those panned out." The young woman leaned forward and rested her chin on her fists. "Eventually, I did find it, though. You know what finally did it?" Allison asked in a self-satisfied tone.

Cathy shrugged helplessly. "Haven't a clue."

"The name on the symbol."

"What name?"

"Puka Inti."

"That's a name?" Now it was Cathy's turn to be exasperated.

"Sure is," Allison replied. "Quechua. Peruvian Indian. But," she added in a crestfallen tone, "I'm so sorry. I really blew it."

"How?"

PART II

"When I typed in 'Puka,' I used a *c* instead of a *k*." Allison rolled her eyes in disgust. "Can you believe it? I'm such an idiot. Of course nothing turned up. I could've had it for you hours ago, but because of that I had to expand the search to include the derivative nth-order tuples, and that—"

"*Hold it!*" Cathy shouted.

Cathy reached over and snagged two sodas out of Allison's refrigerator. She handed one to Allison and opened the other. "I'm sure that the Nobel Prize committee is waiting with bated breath to hear how you figured this out." She took a swig of soda and smiled at her friend. "But, can you humor this uneducated peasant and go back to the 'Puka Inti' part?"

"OK," Allison said tolerantly. "It's like this. Sendero Luminoso, or Shining Path, the outfit mentioned in the briefing article, is a terrorist organization dedicated to the violent overthrow of the Peruvian government. They are brutal, nasty, and highly disciplined. Mass murder is their idea of a good time." Allison sounded deadly serious. "Know what Sendero's initiation rite is?"

Cathy shook her head. "Do I want to know?"

"To join up, you cut the throat of a soldier or policeman." Allison paused. "And all of his family's throats, too."

Cathy grimaced. "Guess I didn't."

"No kidding," Allison agreed. "These guys are nuts. That's where Puka Inti comes in."

"How so?" Cathy asked. Allison looked at Cathy. "Most groups call their leader 'Colonel' or 'Commandante,' or something like that, right? Something that confers a militarylike status of commander."

"Right," Cathy agreed.

"Well, Puka Inti is a Peruvian Indian phrase meaning 'Red Sun.' It's the title that Sendero Luminoso gives to its leader."

"It's also the name of the Arab outfit," Cathy noted.

Allison's face became sober. "It's also the title that the Inca gave to their emperor when they deified him. He became the living incarnation of their sun god here on earth to rule his people, divine and omnipotent in their eyes." The young analyst examined the screen of her computer. "Puka Inti's followers, Peruvian or Arab, aren't mere troops. They're disciples."

The setting sun, filtered through the blinds, painted scarlet bands on the far wall of the office. *Looks like blood*, Cathy thought somberly.

Allison settled herself more comfortably. "I used to work over in Counterterrorism," she continued, "and we kept a close eye on this bunch of nasties. Until now they've been strictly a Peruvian headache. They are so bad that, for a long time, the rest of the international terrorist community would have nothing to do with them. CT has always wondered when they'd feel their oats enough to go big time, and it appears that's just what they've done."

"But how," Cathy wondered, "if they're shunned by their fellows?"

"I think I've got that figured out, too," Allison replied. "There's this delightful little organization in England called the International Revolutionary Movement. They sort of act as a worldwide terrorist lonely-hearts club." She tucked her legs beneath her and continued. "If you can believe it, this charming bunch of matchmakers actually stages terrorist conventions."

"Huh?" Cathy said in disbelief.

"Oh, yeah," Allison assured her. "Last one we know of was a few years ago in Italy. Black September, the IRA, Islamic Jihad, all the biggies were there. Also present were a few observers, several of whom have since been identified as belonging to Sendero Luminoso." Allison held up her hands. "Looks like they found a match. My guess is that Sendero found this forlorn, isolated little band of fellow Maoists who were also furious at Deng and took them under their wing."

"A match," Cathy replied, "definitely not made in heaven."

# 44

Cathy came downstairs just in time to hear her phone ring. It was after five, so she trotted across the deserted office to grab it. Figuring that no one but Greg would call her at that hour, she picked up the receiver and said, "Hi, hon. What's up?"

"Thanks, but it's Joel Dryden."

"Oops. Sorry." Cathy blushed as she sat in her desk chair.

"No problem. What's up," Joel went on, "is that we've heard from Anne's kidnappers. Pat and I received a ransom note in today's mail."

"What's it say?"

"That I'm to meet them, within a week, in Lima, Peru."

Cathy sat up suddenly, banging her knees against the underside of her desk. "Did you say *Peru?*" she asked.

"That's right." Cathy heard concern creep into Joel's voice. "I know who's got Anne."

"Sendero Luminoso," Cathy interjected.

Joel paused. "Just how," Joel asked slowly, "did you know that?"

"The department's analyst and I established a link today between them and the assassinations."

"I've got to talk to both you and this analyst," Joel said intently. Cathy heard the rustling of paper. "First shuttle out of Portland tomorrow will put me in your office at eleven, OK?"

"No problem. The analyst's name is Allison Kirstoff. I'll be here, and I'll make sure that she is, too."

Joel hung up. Cathy punched in Allison's extension. "Am I glad you're still there," she said when Allison answered. "Can you be at my desk at eleven tomorrow?"

"What's up?"

"Remember that woman who was kidnapped off that little boat out on the Nile?"

"Anne Dryden?"

"Right. Well, her father wants to come talk to us tomorrow. It seems that our Sendero Luminoso bad boys are the ones who've kidnapped his daughter."

Cathy heard Allison's exclamation of surprise.

"His name is Joel Dryden, and—"

"*What?*" Allison almost screamed.

"His name's Joel Dryden," Cathy repeated. *What is it*, she wondered, *about the name "Dryden" that makes everybody crazy?*

Cathy heard the sound of Allison's fist slamming against the arm of her chair. "Kirstoff, you moron! You should've made the connection instantly!" Allison's voice became silky. "Oh, boy. Cathy dear, you have really got yourself into it this time."

"Into what?"

Allison hesitated. "Not here, OK?" As a matter of pride, every State Department employee was convinced that their phone was bugged. "Let me print off some stuff, and I'll meet you at your place in half an hour."

"OK," Cathy replied. "I'll call Fiorello's."

"Great! I'm starved. But, please, no anchovies."

"I can't believe that you've never heard of Joel Dryden," Allison said from her perch at the opposite end of Cathy's sofa. "He worked for the Company for more than twenty years and is something of a legend over in Counterterrorism." She grabbed a pizza-laden paper plate. "But," she asked Cathy, "while you've been at State you've specialized in the Mideast, haven't you?"

Cathy nodded as she gobbled up a string of cheese that dangled enticingly from her slice of Fiorello's pizza.

"That explains it, as he was mostly active in South America. Listen to this." Allison dragged a sheaf of paper out of her briefcase. "Joel M. Dryden, Ph.D., J.D. Doctorates from Harvard, in international relations, and Stanford, in macroeconomics. Got his law degree from Boalt Hall at UC Berkeley." She shook her head in amazement. "In his spare time, I guess." Allison paused and delicately blotted a dollop of tomato sauce from the page she was reading. "Major, USMC, retired. Served as military attaché to several U.S. embassies in South America before leaving the marines to join the CIA." She looked at Cathy. "There's always been some question as to just exactly when that transfer actually took place."

Cathy recalled tagging Joel as a spy at their first meeting, and nodded to herself in satisfaction. "You mean," she asked, "that Joel might've been working for the Company while he was still in uniform?"

"Sure," Allison replied with a shrug. "Happens all the time. You and I both know that most of the so-called attachés in any country's embassy are actually spooks. The uniform, or lack thereof, doesn't matter."

Allison grabbed another slice of pizza out of the box and resumed reading. "Last posting was to the U.S. embassy in Lima as the economic attaché."

"That means," Cathy reasoned aloud, "that he was the CIA station chief."

Allison nodded agreement. "Ostensibly, his job was to

coordinate and oversee American-Peruvian trade agreements. Supervising the export of llama-fur slippers in exchange for boom boxes is not what Joel Dryden was there for." She kicked off her shoes.

"Remember," Allison said between bites, "a couple of years ago, when the Peruvian president was here on a state visit, and we announced that big new economic aid agreement with Peru?"

Cathy nodded. She recalled doing guard duty at the reception that had followed the signing of the agreement by the two presidents.

"Well, the scuttlebutt at CT has it that Dryden was the actual author of the agreement. He thought it up and sold both the ambassador and the Peruvian president on it." Allison set her plate aside. "The plan's intent was to weaken Sendero Luminoso's appeal by improving the overall economy, and it's worked. The economic reforms that Dryden suggested have really hurt the Senderistas. Soon after the reforms were in place Dryden and his family left Peru, and soon after that, he allegedly retired." Allison looked skeptical. "Ever since then, both Dryden and his former ambassador have been high on the Senderista's hit list." She looked at Cathy. "Remember who the ambassador to Peru was when Dryden was there?"

Cathy frowned as she tried to recall who it had been. Outside, a car horn sounded a long, protesting honk. Then the name came to her, and Cathy's head swung up in surprise. "Robert Moncrief."

# 45

The courthouse hallway exploded with light as Jake was led in. Jake ran the gauntlet of shouted questions and probing lenses as he had before, making sure that his colleagues got what they needed before the phalanx of U.S. marshals around him hustled him into the courtroom.

Cyril frowned as Jake approached. "Where's your suit? You look like an extra in a Cagney movie."

"What suit? They hauled me out of my cell, slapped these manacles on me, and brought me here."

Cyril glanced over at the table where Jim Roberts was unpacking his briefcase. "OK. We'll play it their way, then. You'll have a suit of clothes tomorrow if I have to bring you one of my own."

Jake smiled down at the small, sticklike lawyer before him. "Thanks for the offer, but I don't think we should add 'indecent exposure' to the list of charges."

Cyril chuckled. "Never mind. I'll take care of it. Now, our first job is to get you out of those chains."

"All rise."

The crowd packed into the courtroom came to its feet as the judge strode to his place behind the bench. From the other side of the spectator's rail, Cathy had winked and nodded encouragingly to Jake as the marshals had led him in and to his place beside Cyril. Now, she gripped the rail nervously as the judge took his seat. *This had better work.*

"U.S. District Court, docket number 85-09924, *MacIntyre vs. U.S.* The Honorable Jacob R. Mausbacher presiding. Be seated," the bailiff intoned.

Cathy took her seat just behind Jake and Cyril.

"Mr. Edwards," Mausbacher asked, "is it clear that this is not an arraignment, but is rather a court sitting in *nisi prius?*"

"It is, Your Honor," Cyril told the bench.

"Is what?" Jake whispered.

Cyril smiled. "Is not a trial where your guilt will be determined, but rather a preliminary hearing, the purpose of which is to decide if the evidence presented is sufficient to warrant an indictment."

"You mean I don't get to plead not guilty?" Jake asked.

"No. And, if I do my job, you won't have to."

Cyril came smoothly to his feet. "Point of procedure, Your Honor. I request that my client's manacles be removed."

Mausbacher nodded, then looked at Jim Roberts. "Any objection, Counselor?"

Roberts rose. "The prosecution does object, Your Honor, on two grounds: the violent and heinous nature of the crime for which the defendant stands accused, and the fact that the defendant is currently in solitary confinement for assaulting another inmate."

A rustle of whispers swept the courtroom.

Without looking up from his notepad, Cyril asked, "Is that true?"

"Yeah. I couldn't just let him knock me down, could I?" Jake asked defensively.

"Dumb move, Jake. And you should have told me. While the stunt you pulled is not material evidence, you can bet that every courtroom artist over there is going back and adding manacles to their sketches of you."

Cyril looked at him grimly. "You get portrayed as unstable and violent, and Roberts draws first blood."

Jake, staring straight ahead, tried to fold his arms and found he couldn't.

The case against Jake grew as Roberts, playing to the balcony, smoothly presented his evidence. Jake listened as old friends pointed him out and testified that they had seen him on the roof from which the fatal shots had been fired. An FBI forensics expert testified that it was indeed Jake's fingerprints that had been found on the barrel of the rifle, and a Bureau ballistics man linked the weapon with the bullets that had killed the diplomats. Cathy grew increasingly depressed as the evidence she had helped collect was arrayed against her friend.

"Lastly, Your Honor, the prosecution wishes to submit into evidence this certified photocopy of the defendant's passport. Let the record show that, less than three weeks ago, the defendant spent three days in Syria, a country known to sponsor terrorism."

Cyril jumped to his feet. "Objection, Your Honor. This evidence is both indirect and inculpatory. The prosecution can only presume as to my client's reason for visiting Syria, and any relation between that visit and the matter before this court cannot be proved."

"Objection sustained."

"Then," Roberts continued smoothly, "the prosecution requests that the document be admitted as corroborative evidence that further demonstrates the defendant's connections with known terrorist entities."

"Objection! The country of Syria in and of itself is not a terrorist entity."

"Overruled," Mausbacher ordered. "Given Syria's official policy of harboring and abetting terrorists, the evidence is sufficiently relevant to stand as corroborative."

Another wave of whispers drifted across the courtroom.

Roberts began his summation. "The prosecution, Your Honor, believes the evidence presented demonstrates irrefutably the defendant's competence and intent to voluntarily perform a criminal act. It is our belief that this intention and subsequent action, without justification or authorization, constitute general, and hence criminal, intent."

Cyril was on his feet instantly. "Objection!" He glared at Roberts. "Both the wording of the indictment against my client and the manner in which the evidence has been presented are flagrant attempts to further politicize this already volatile case." Cyril looked at Mausbacher. "Your Honor, such politicization is inevitable, given the nature of the crime for which my client stands accused. It is the prosecution's own attempt to elevate this from an everyday domestic crime to the world theater, which renders the concept of general intent both specious and inapplicable."

Cyril pointed at Jake. "This man is not indicted for murder! Indeed, the complaint against him reads, 'For the wanton and willful assassination of three duly appointed public officials in the performance of their duties.'

"Assassination!" Those in the courtroom jumped as Cyril barked the word. He made sure every eye was upon him, then continued. "Not mere murder, but assassination! Not one man killing another for reasons of greed or lust or any of the rest of our petty failings, but the deliberate, preconceived killing of a public official for a specific purpose. Not an act of blind rage by one individual against another, but the ultimate referendum on a government, a people, or a way of life."

One hand in his pocket, Cyril gestured theatrically with the other. "Assassination, while a passionate crime, is not a crime of passion. It is always performed with the intent of furthering or hindering a specific cause. Assassination is always accompanied by a determinable, demonstrable, specific intent."

Cyril looked up at the bench. "Your Honor, the defense moves that the crime in this case be deemed an act accompanied by a specific intent, that the existence before the fact of that intent be deemed an essential element of the case, and that criminal intent may not be presumed from the commission of the act but must indeed be proved."

"Objection sustained," Mausbacher ruled. "Specific intent will be added to the weight of evidence necessary to overcome reasonable doubt."

Roberts nodded. "The prosecution rests, Your Honor." He sat down and started whispering to Mahoney.

Mausbacher banged his gavel. "This court stands in recess until 2:00 P.M., at which time the defense will present its evidence."

Cyril mopped the sweat from his face with his handkerchief. "Score one for our side," he whispered. Cyril looked at Jake. "It's all tied up at the half."

# 46

"Sorry I'm late, ladies," Joel said as he walked up to Cathy's desk. "We were delayed getting out of Portland."

"Your timing is perfect," Cathy told him. "Jake's arraignment just adjourned for lunch, and I just got back from the courthouse."

"How's it going?" Joel asked.

Cathy nodded encouragingly. "Cyril just managed to get the court to agree to specific intent."

"So the prosecution will have to prove premeditation?"

"Exactly."

"Good for Cyril!" Joel grinned. "That's why the Hispanics he does pro bono work for call him El Zorro Viejo."

"What's that?" Cathy asked.

Joel arched his eyebrows. "The Old Fox."

"What did you get so jazzed about, Cathy?" Allison asked after they had been seated at the streetside café. "You were all excited about specific something or other."

"What a relief!" Cathy exclaimed. "At last, I'm talking about something that she doesn't understand!"

Allison and Joel listened intently as Cathy explained the morning's events.

"Now," Joel said after a bite of his pastrami with Russian dressing, "why the fast shuffle out of the office?"

Cathy turned to Allison. "Doesn't miss much, does he?"

"Of course not," Allison replied. "Once a spook, always a spook."

Cathy glared at Allison, then buried her head in her hands. "Sorry, Joel. This is a perfect example of why we hardly ever unchain her from her computer."

"And why, Miss Kirstoff," Joel asked quietly, "do you imagine me to be a ghost?"

"No, sir, it's not that at all," Allison began. "It's just that, well, over at CT they say . . . " She met Joel's eyes, and her explanation faltered.

*Wow*, Cathy thought as she watched the exchange. She'd never seen Allison wilt before, but she could understand why as she watched Joel's cool, probing, cautionary stare.

"No matter," Joel finally said, softening. "Digging up stuff like that is what we hire bright ones like you for. I'm just very glad that you don't work for the other side." He smiled, letting Allison off the hook, then turned to include Cathy in the conversation. "Now, tell me why you two brought me here. Other than," he added with a grin, "to blow my mild-mannered-retired-civil-servant cover story."

Allison explained how she had combined the evidence Cathy had provided with the information she had unearthed to make the Egypt-Peru connection.

Joel listened, nodding occasionally or asking a question.

"What surprises me," Allison said in conclusion, "is that nobody noticed this before."

"Doesn't surprise me," Joel replied. "Only the U.S. has the resources to notice something like this going on in the Mideast, but we just sort of packed up and pulled out of Egypt after the Carter treaty was signed."

"Is that how you ended up in South America?" Cathy asked.

Joel's brows beetled. "No comment."

Allison looked at her watch and stood up. "Gotta go. I'm already late. Nice meeting you, Joel."

"My pleasure, Allison. Nice job of analysis."

"Thanks. Glad I could help." Allison gave Joel one of her best smiles and hurried off.

"Boyfriend?" Joel asked Cathy.

"Hardly," Cathy replied. "Actually she's going to a sale, I think."

"Shoes?"

"Disk drives, more likely."

"So tell me," Joel asked, "why are we really here?"

"First," Cathy replied, "what are you going to do about Anne? If you don't mind telling me, that is."

"I'm going to go get her." His voice was quietly threatening, and Cathy suddenly felt very sorry for those who held his daughter captive.

"Remember," she said, "how I told you that there might be a way to prove that Jake took those pictures?"

Joel nodded.

"Well," Cathy went on, "with some help from a friend, I have."

"So," Joel asked. "What's the hitch?"

"Hitches, actually," Cathy replied. "First, the proof was acquired in a rather unorthodox manner—"

"Meaning that you have unauthorized access to classified information," Joel interrupted.

Cathy nodded glumly.

"You've worked in this town long enough to know that the

simple fact that it's secret is the least of our worries," Joel said dismissively. "What's next?"

"What's next," Cathy replied seriously, "is that the people I work for want Jake convicted. No matter what."

"Do they know what you've told me?" Joel asked.

"No, and I don't dare tell them."

Joel leaned forward, his elbows resting on the table. "Why not?"

"Because both the evidence and I would disappear if I did."

Joel didn't act surprised. "Tell me why."

Cathy recounted to Joel her run-in with Mahoney and Roberts. "It's not sour grapes," she concluded. "I've been taken off cases before. Some ambassador's son gets a girl in trouble, and the family would rather pay off the blackmailers than face the publicity of a trial." She shrugged. "That sort of thing I can live with. But this is different. Jake is innocent, and they've suspected it all along."

"Then why are they out to get him?"

"Pressure," Cathy replied. "External and internal pressure. The president is chewing out his chief of staff, so O'Brian is crawling up Mahoney's back. I don't feel sorry for them about that part of it; getting raked over the coals comes with the territory. It's the internal pressure," she said quietly, "that's got me worried."

Joel didn't respond.

"I've never seen either of them like this before," Cathy went on. "They're irrational. Mahoney's obsessed with avenging the murder of his best friend, and Roberts sees this as his big chance."

"If Jake is exonerated, how does it change things?" Joel asked.

"Simple. It takes the whole case out of the spotlight. What was to be a spectacular show trial of a prominent American photojournalist becomes nothing more than a bunch of paperwork with the non-American killers already dead. The public loses interest, and that's that. Mahoney's bloodlust goes unsatiated, and Roberts remains a faceless bureaucrat. But," Cathy added bleakly, "if I present the evidence to them then that's that, too. The photos disappear. . . ."

Joel picked up the cue. "And what happens to Cathy?"

"Cathy gets convicted of something or other and spends a long, long time as a resident of Leavenworth, Kansas." She took a bite of her sandwich. "Where, I understand, the pastrami is crummy."

Joel drummed his fingers on the table. "I think that," he said at last, "with help, we can pull off springing Jake."

"Help?" Cathy said. "We don't have to involve Allison, do we?"

"No," Joel replied. "But do you think you can talk your spook friend into giving us a hand? A perfectly legal one for a change," he added.

"I think Greg would be most willing to help," Cathy said. *If he knows what's good for him.*

Joel gave her a searching look. "And it'll take some nerve on your part."

"Well, I knew the job was dangerous when I took it."

"*Semper Fi*, Marine!" Joel said briskly.

"Thank you, sir!" Cathy replied automatically. *Wait a minute*, she thought. *How did he know that I was in the marines?*

Joel laughed at Cathy's puzzled expression. "First," he asked seriously, "are you willing to tell all this to someone else? Someone that both Jake and I trust implicitly?"

Cathy nodded.

"Good. Then stay put while I make a phone call."

*What else does he know?* Cathy wondered as she watched him head toward the phone.

After the court had reconvened, Cyril reached into his satchel. He pulled out a large plastic bag. "The defense wishes to enter into evidence as people's exhibit number one," he said as he reached into the bag, "this camera." Cyril handed it to Mausbacher, who took the damp and corroded camera reluctantly.

Jake glanced at the camera, then leaned forward suddenly. "My Leica!"

Mausbacher looked up. "You admit to owning this camera, Mr. MacIntyre?"

Jake looked at Cyril.

"Answer the question," Cyril told him.

"Yes, Your Honor, that's my Leica. The one I had stolen from me in Cairo."

"Can you prove that?" Mausbacher asked. Jake told Mausbacher the serial number.

"Which is," Cyril added, "corroborated by this copy of the defendant's registration certificate. It was faxed to me from the Leica factory. A copy for you, Counselor," he added innocently, handing one to the glowering Roberts.

"Also attached," Cyril concluded, "is an affidavit from the Cairo Harbor Patrol certifying that they recovered this camera from the bottom of the Nile. It was found near the site where an Egyptian boatman was murdered during the kidnapping of an American woman. The Cairo authorities are convinced that the kidnapping is closely tied to the assassinations and have left that part of the case open. This linking of the crimes," Cyril asserted, "directly refutes the assertion in the indictment against my client that they were separate incidents."

The certificate and affidavit were given to the bailiff to be entered as evidence.

"Oh, yes," Cyril added, acting almost as if it were an afterthought. "One more thing. Another affidavit. This one from the FBI forensics lab, stating that the fingerprints found on the barrel of the murder weapon are those of Jeremiah C. MacIntyre."

Jake looked at Cyril in horror. Roberts's head came up and Mahoney stared at the defense attorney.

"The report," Cyril continued, "also states that the orientation of the fingerprints is that of a man who had grabbed the gun by the barrel—from the front."

Mausbacher gaveled for quiet as a murmur rippled through the spectators.

Cyril turned his attention to the judge. "The defense believes, Your Honor, that this piece of evidence fully corroborates the defendant's sworn testimony and substantiates his innocence beyond reasonable doubt."

"Objection!" Roberts called out as he came to his feet. "As much as my learned colleague may wish it to be so," he said with an elegant gesture toward Cyril, "the so-called evidence just presented is neither conclusive nor satisfactory."

"Objection sustained." Mausbacher looked at Cyril. "Counsel for the defense will refrain from assigning attributes to the evidence submitted. Do you have any additional exhibits, Mr. Edwards?"

"No, Your Honor. The defense rests." Cyril sat down. "Nuts," he whispered to Jake. "I thought we had 'em there."

"Just tell me when it's time to start being nervous," Jake whispered back.

Mausbacher gaveled for silence. "Mr. MacIntyre, as you know this is not a trial, but a hearing for the purpose of determining whether the evidence collected in this case is sufficient to warrant the bringing of an indictment against you and remanding you over for trial."

Jake nodded. *Right now sounds like a great time to start being nervous.*

"Despite the absence of a jury," Mausbacher continued, "these are criminal proceedings and, as such, the legal concept of fair preponderance of evidence shall apply. What this means, Mr. MacIntyre, is that I will weigh the evidence presented and, when we reconvene tomorrow, rule on whether an indictment against you shall be handed down."

The judge rapped his gavel. "Court is adjourned until 9:00 A.M. tomorrow."

Cyril began collecting his notes. "I had hoped that our evidence would be ruled conclusive enough to get you off. But I must admit that Roberts is sharper than he looks."

Jake stood as the marshals arrived. Cyril looked up at him. "This one's going into overtime."

# 47

"Your Honor, the defense moves for summary dismissal of charges."

"Grounds for dismissal?" Mausbacher inquired.

"Newly discovered evidence that irrefutably exonerates the defendant."

Roberts was on his feet instantly. "Objection! The defense has rested!"

Mausbacher looked at Cyril. "Mr. Edwards?"

"It is true that the defense has rested, Your Honor. But this evidence is both material and prima facie."

"Objection overruled," Mausbacher decided. "This case is of sufficient gravity to warrant the consideration of all available material."

Roberts remained standing. "I must object again, Your Honor. This so-called new evidence has not been disclosed to the prosecution."

"Is this true, Mr. Edwards?" Mausbacher asked.

"The evidence was only made available to me late yesterday," Cyril replied calmly. "Furthermore, after reviewing the information, I find that its nature is such that, in the interests of national security, I am required to petition that it be disclosed in camera."

After thirty years on the bench in Washington, D.C., Mausbacher was no stranger to such petitions. "Petition granted," he ordered. He could hear muttering from the press section and banged his gavel. Mausbacher's scowl was, if anything, fiercer than those of the reporters. He was up for reelection and hated what he called "invisible" hearings. "Court will reconvene in my chambers in ten minutes." The gavel banged again.

"C'mon," Cyril said as he rose.

Jake stood and, under the watchful eye of the marshals, made his way with Cyril across the courtroom.

"Behave yourself, now," he whispered. "Old Mossback will be in a vile mood."

"Mossback?" Jake asked.

Cyril smiled and leaned toward him as if conferring. "The judge, Mausbacher. He's fair and learned, but he's been behind the bench so long and is such a sourpuss that several generations of attorneys call him 'Old Mossback.' They say that some senior trial lawyers, old cronies of his, use the name to his face. But never," he finished, "in open court."

Jake was surprised to find that Mausbacher had removed his robes and was seated behind his desk in his shirt sleeves. Jake, Cyril, Roberts, and Mahoney seated themselves in the chairs arranged in front of the desk. A court reporter and a marshal, both with high security clearances, were the only others present.

"OK, Cyril," Mausbacher said. "Let's see what you've got."

Jake started slightly at the informality. Cyril opened his attaché case. "First, Your Honor, the defense presents these photographs, along with sworn affidavits as to how they were found." He handed copies of the photos, as well as affidavits from the Drydens, the Parkers, and Lee, to Mausbacher and Roberts.

"Next," Cyril continued as he handed out another document, "is a copy of the Cairo Police Department blotter, identifying the men in the photos and declaring that said identification, and the subsequent interrogation of one of them, was deemed sufficient evidence for Cairo to mark the assassination portion of the case as closed."

"Why didn't I know this?" Roberts hissed to Mahoney.

Mahoney didn't respond.

Mausbacher looked at Cyril. "While this is all admissible evidence, Counselor, none of it seems a threat to national security." He peered at him over his glasses. "If you've got anything left, Cyril," he said, "it'd better be good."

"Just this, Your Honor." Cyril handed Mausbacher a folder clipped to a sealed envelope. Roberts got just a folder. "This is a report from a senior imaging officer for the Central Intelligence Agency. In his professional opinion, the film that was used to make the prints of the photos of the assassins, the ones that I just submitted as evidence, was exposed in the camera that was submitted yesterday. The camera that has been stipulated to belong to the defendant." Cyril looked at Jake, then back at Mausbacher. "The techniques used to arrive at this conclusion are detailed in that sealed report."

Roberts spoke up. "Objection, Your Honor. Defense is submitting expert testimony without voir dire. The prosecution requests that the evidence be declared incompetent."

"Overruled. Please keep in mind, Mr. Roberts," Mausbacher replied sternly, "that it is the court, not counsel, that determines the competence of a witness to provide expert testimony."

"The agency recognizes the importance of this case," Cyril added, "and is allowing the use of this information. They do, however, ask that because of its sensitive nature it be considered a privileged communication, limited to your eyes only."

"Would I understand it?" Mausbacher asked.

Cyril sidestepped the trap. "I couldn't say," he prevaricated. "The officer in question holds a Ph.D. in optical engineering from Cal Tech, and I'm told that this is very advanced work."

Mausbacher opened the folder. Jake sat very still as the judge read it carefully. "This seems to be a reasonably detailed curriculum vitae of the witness in question." He looked at Roberts. "Do you see any points on which you wish to challenge the qualifications or competency of this witness?"

"No, Your Honor." *Leave it to Edwards to get the spooks involved*, Roberts thought bitterly.

"What?" Mahoney whispered. "You're not even going to challenge it?"

Roberts looked at his boss in disbelief. "You may want to take on the Company," he said scornfully, "but I don't."

Mausbacher set the folder down on his desk. "Anything else, Cyril?"

"The defense is now fully disclosed, Your Honor."

The judge turned to Mahoney and Roberts. "Does the prosecution desire a recess to examine the evidence?"

"We do not, Your Honor," Roberts replied. He didn't look at Mahoney.

"Then, in light of this evidence, I find that reasonable doubt exists."

Mausbacher looked at Jake and smiled. "Congratulations, Mr. MacIntyre. You're a free man."

Cyril applauded.

"Order in the court, Cyril," Mausbacher chided.

"Calm down, Mossback," Cyril replied. He smiled at his old friend and pinochle partner. "Thanks."

As they neared the door that led from the prison to the outside world, Sam Webster put a hand on Jake's shoulder. "Few men leave here under circumstances as joyful as yours," Sam said quietly. "Fewer still take with them the great, living gift that you've been given."

The two men paused in front of the door.

"Now," Sam said, "it's up to you to care for that gift; to see that it is nurtured and fed. To see that it thrives and grows."

Jake nodded.

"Fortunately," Sam said with a grin as he opened the door, "you'll have help."

Jake turned to the sound of applause.

Joel, Pat, Cathy, and Cyril were waiting for him in the sunlit room. Sam gently pushed the dumbfounded Jake through the door, then stepped in after him. Joel shook Jake's hand, and Pat gave him a quick hug.

"Thanks for all your help, Cyril," Jake said. "I have just one question. Why didn't you tell me ahead of time about my camera?"

Cyril smiled. "We couldn't afford to have it look too set up," he said. "Plus, I love a little courtroom drama, and the look on your face when you saw your camera was priceless!"

Jake looked pained. "My poor camera!"

"That," Cyril exclaimed, "is exactly the look I'm talking about."

Jake looked at Cathy. "Thanks for sticking with me," he said. "Thanks for getting together with Cyril. Thanks for covering my," Jake caught himself just in time, "flank."

"No problem, soldier. I helped get you into this, so it was the least I could do to help get you out."

Jake grinned. "I never thought I'd say this to a jarhead marine, but you're a mate."

"So what now, Jake?" Joel asked.

"Now," Pat added, "that you're free."

"Because of all of you," Jake said with a gesture that included the four standing in front of him, "I can walk out that door." Jake pointed at the other door in the room. "But," he added quietly, "it's because of Sam that I'm truly free."

"It wasn't me, Jake," Sam said. "You made the decision. You reached out and gathered the gift in." Sam's watch chimed. "Looks like I've got to go. Jake, come back sometime." Sam smiled. "As a visitor, of course!"

Jake laughed. "I promise."

"You've got my prayers, brother," Sam said. He walked back into the prison.

Jake turned back to the others. "What now, you asked?" he said, his face grim. "I've been thinking about that a lot. I honestly feel I need to help find Anne. I got her into this. But I don't know what I can do."

Joel and Pat exchanged a glance. Their decision had already been made; Jake's determination now reinforced it. "We've heard from her kidnappers," Joel said quietly.

"What?"

"We know where Annie is."

"Where?"

Joel returned Jake's gaze with equal intensity, but he didn't immediately answer Jake's question. Like all fathers, he was still struggling with the unsettling realization that there was another man in his daughter's life. "You could help us, but it might be dangerous."

"Count me in," Jake said.

"I haven't told you where we're going yet."

"It doesn't matter."

"Jake," Pat asked, "is there anything, or anyone, that you need to take care of first?"

"Stopping by my apartment in New York would be a good

idea." He was wearing the clothes he was captured in, washed and repaired by the prison laundry, and he looked at them distastefully. "I could use some new clothes." Jake's face suddenly fell. "And I should call Alex's parents."

"I'll tell you what we know when you get to Trenton," Joel said. "And then, I'll—" Joel sighed and shook his head. "*We'll* make plans to go get Anne."

# 48

"Get out of my office, Hagura," Mahoney said without looking up from his desk. "You've got nothing to say that I want to hear."

"Justice was served today," Cathy said quietly. "But you don't want to hear that, do you?"

Mahoney raised his eyes to meet hers. "I'd prosecute you, but Edwards just called. He told me that he had appointed you a member of the defense team, so that anything you told him is privileged information. He also explained ever so politely that he had obtained a search warrant for the camera, which is how you managed to get the Egyptians to so easily give it up. Imagine that!" Mahoney snorted. "And the warrant even had the camera's serial number on it! And then there's this."

Mahoney held up a sheet of paper. "The report of the expert witness. Let's see . . . what was that expert's name?" He made a show of studying the paper. "Ah, yes. Gregory R. Miahara."

With a sudden movement, Mahoney crumpled the paper and flung it across the office. "How very cozy," he said, putting into the words an insinuation that infuriated Cathy. "The bunch of you had this all figured out."

Pain lined Mahoney's face. "Cathy," he said quietly. "We looked like idiots in there."

"You didn't have to," she finished. "You could've listened."

Mahoney stared past her. "Go away," he said at last. "Just go away until I figure out what to do with you."

"Fine with me," Cathy replied. "I could use a vacation."

Cathy turned on her heel and left Mahoney's office.

When she reached her desk, she called Allison. There was no answer, so she left a message for Allison to call her at home. Cathy hesitated, then took a paper bag out of a drawer. As she stuffed her personal possessions into it, she came across her *I Told You So!* notebook. Cathy stopped and looked around. She spotted what she wanted sticking out of a coworker's trash can. Cathy grabbed the newspaper out of the trash can and cut out the headline article announcing Jake's exoneration. She taped it to the cover of the notebook, then placed the notebook precisely in the center of her now-empty desk. After a final look around, she left the office. This time there were no tears.

Jake replaced the telephone handset in its cradle and smoothed back his hair with his hands. *Man, do I need a drink.*

He had returned to his Greenwich Village apartment to find the floor beneath his mail slot littered with bills, junk mail, and dubious offers to ghostwrite his autobiography. His answering machine was crammed with calls from old friends, complete strangers, and a prominent morning talk-show host who wanted to know if he'd do her the favor of appearing on her show. In connection with this favor, the TV personality offhandedly mentioned a substantial sum of money.

A quick trip down to his garage had revealed that his beloved 1965 MGB-GT was dusty, had a flat tire, and was unwilling to start. A day spent polishing and repairing the car had resulted in a gleaming, purring vehicle. It also resulted in skinned knuckles and a sore shoulder.

That shoulder twinged as Jake pushed himself up out of his easy chair, and he winced. Poor Ian and Mary. He winced again as he thought of Alex's parents, their pride in their only child's success, and of the grand times he'd had with them when passing through England. Now the joy in their voices had been replaced with utter desolation. *And I didn't even get to be there for the funeral.* Jake wandered into his kitchen. *I gotta have a drink.* When a quick search of his liquor cabinet uncovered only a bottle of Amaretto and a box of corn flakes, Jake pulled on a jacket and headed out.

"Jake! Where've you been keeping yourself?" Bill Donnelly asked from behind the bar of the establishment that bore his name.

"What do you mean, where've I been keeping myself?" Jake asked with a derisive grin. "Who's been on vacation; you, or the person who reads the newspapers to you?"

Donnelly laughed. "It's good to see that your stay in prison didn't affect your sense of humor." He reached under the bar and pulled out a bottle. Jake's eyes widened in appreciation at the sight of a bottle of twenty-five-year-old Macallan, a single-malt Scotch of which Jake was extremely fond.

"As I suspected," Donnelly said with a smile at Jake's reaction. "The only good your incarceration did you was to increase your thirst." Three fingers of amber fluid appeared in a glass. "First one's on me, laddie buck. A toast to your hard-won freedom 'n' all."

Jake took his drink and found a table in a corner.

He had taken only a few sips when the bar fell silent. "Mary, mother o' God . . ." Donnelly's brogue-laden whisper could be heard clearly in the resulting hush. "The angels have come t' take me home." Jake looked up from his introspective study of the bottom of his glass and found himself in complete agreement.

The doorway framed two blondes and a redhead tall enough to almost reach the lintel and slender enough not to crowd the jambs. Jake joined in the unanimous, appreciative perusal as the trio found a table. Then, with an amused shake of his head, Jake returned his attention to his glass. After a moment's thought, he frowned.

Jake's head came back up just as one of the three called his name. He and the most striking of the blondes rose at the same time. Every eye in the bar again followed her, this time as she rushed over and wrapped herself around Jake.

"How'd he manage that?" a man at the bar asked Donnelly. "He didn't even say a word to her."

"He didn't need to," Donnelly replied in a wise, conspiratorial tone. "She could tell from clear across the room that he's a man who drinks the right kind of whiskey."

Jake hugged the woman, then held her at arm's length. "Birgitta! I thought it was you!"

"My Lufthansa flight," she replied with a smile, "got in from Düsseldorf this afternoon."

He looked her over again. "You're looking mighty fine, Fräulein."

"Danke schön, mein Herr," Birgitta said, laughing. "So do I get to sit down, or must I drink standing up?"

"Wait a minute," Jake said after the barmaid had left. "I called you Fräulein, but didn't you get married last year?"

"That I did," Birgitta admitted. "However," she added with a dismissive gesture, "I talked that fool Gunther into marrying me in Holland instead of Germany. So when he displeased me, I divorced him during a layover in Amsterdam."

She took a sip of her drink. "I see in the papers that you've been a naughty boy, Jake."

"The past couple of weeks *have* been a little busy."

"And I saw in the papers those pictures you took."

She leaned closer, the edge of the table disappearing beneath her as she did so. "That was a very brave thing to do."

"Very stupid is more like it."

"Not at all," Birgitta replied with a toss of her head. "It's what I'd expect from a man like you. But," she admitted with another smile, "I was surprised to see that you still worked for Global."

"Why?"

"Because, after Cannes, I was sure they would fire you."

"They'd go broke if they did," Jake told her. He laughed and shook his head. "Mort did read me one of the all-time great riot acts. I thought he was going to burst a blood vessel when I came back with the film festival pictures a week late."

Birgitta looked coy. "Was it worth it?"

"Was letting you talk me into spending a week with you on the Côte d'Azur worth getting chewed out by Steinmetz?" Jake smiled a long, slow smile. "No contest."

Birgitta slowly wound a curl of her butter-blonde hair around a forefinger, delighting in the way Jake was looking at her. "You spoiled Monte Carlo for me, you know," she told him when he had returned his eyes to hers. "I haven't been there with a man since you." Birgitta brought her face close to Jake's, her eyes large and soft in the dim light. "I still remember our night on the beach below the Chateau D'If. . . ." She waited until Jake's face revealed that he, too, remembered. Then she sat back, took a long pastel cigarette out of her purse, and lit it.

"What was the name of that funny little friend of yours?" Birgitta asked through a shroud of smoke. "Alan? Albert? You remember, the one you were with when we met at that little bistro in Cannes."

"Alex," Jake replied after a swallow of whiskey. "Alex Stratton."

"That's right!" Birgitta exclaimed, smoke curling from between her lips. "Odd one, wasn't he?" She shook her head disbelievingly. "I can still remember how outraged Margo was when he refused to spend the weekend with her." Birgitta threw back her head and laughed. "Imagine turning down an offer like that from someone like Margo van Valkenberg! What," she asked after another puff, "ever became of him?"

"Alex," Jake said slowly, "was killed when they captured the terrorists that kidnapped us." The smoke was beginning to sting his eyes.

"Really?" she replied in pretended astonishment. "Pity. Now I'll never get to find out just how often he regretted being so incredibly foolish." Birgitta stubbed out her cigarette. "I've never seen anything like it. He just said 'No, thanks,' turned his back, and walked away." She blew a long stream of smoke toward the rafters—as if, it seemed to Jake, to forever dismiss Alex from her mind. Jake watched the plume as it dissipated into nothingness.

Birgitta reached out and gently combed Jake's hair with her long, scarlet fingernails. "I don't leave until Monday afternoon," she told him softly. "We'll have all weekend. It'll be just like it was in Monte Carlo."

"Don't think it will be," he countered, warmed by her touch.

"No? Why not?"

"Because I've been practicing since then, and it sounds like you have, too."

The sip Jake took of his drink served only to inflame him further. "Anyway, in Monte Carlo we had a week."

Birgitta wet her lips. "We could fit a week into a weekend if we tried." She toyed with the stem of her glass. "After all, they do say that practice makes perfect."

Jake nodded his grinning agreement.

"Why don't we," she whispered as she reached for Jake's hand, "find out. . . ."

Jake lifted his glass, unconsciously avoiding her touch, and looked at her over its rim. Birgitta, smiling at the implied assent, finished her drink. She unfolded her long legs. "I'll be right back." As Birgitta passed the table where her friends sat, there was an exchange of German interspersed with laughter. The two friends rose from their table and followed Birgitta, looking over their shoulders at Jake as they did so.

Jake watched them until they disappeared, then slid his glass idly around the slick tabletop. He could feel the roomful of envious eyes, and he smiled in satisfaction at what he considered their tough luck. Jake considered draining the glass, then decided against it. *You gotta be sharp for what you're about to do*, he told himself. *That fräulein won't put up with anything but your best.*

A cloud of smoke from another table drifted past, and Jake waved it away from his face. *Poor Brit*, Jake thought sadly, reminded by the smoke of Birgitta's banishment of his friend. *I remember how very much you wanted a girl of your own. It must've been tough for you to walk away from what Margo was offering.* Jake rubbed his chin. *At least now I understand why you did.*

Jake smiled as the image of Birgitta walking toward him filled his mind. He heard her delighted laughter when she had caught sight of him, then he frowned as that laughter soured into the mocking judgment that she had handed down upon Alex. Jake waved the smoke away from his eyes again. *It must've been even tougher on you, Alex, to take the high road when we all laughed at you.*

Jake realized what he was thinking about and sat up suddenly. *The high road. Alex took it! He did the right thing!* Jake snorted with surprise as something occurred to him. *Wait a minute. Now, I really do understand why he did what he did.* Jake took a deep breath as the rest of the realization presented itself.

*You've gotta be kidding!* he thought incredulously. *Pass up a weekend like this?* Jake rested his head in his hand. No way. Absolutely no way. Birgitta laughed again in his mind. *The laugh she gave you, Alex, is nothing compared to what I'll get if I don't go through with this. Besides, it's been weeks.* A knot formed in Jake's stomach. His breathing became faster and more shallow as desire battled with faith.

*What's it going to be, Jake?* the enemy asked. *Bread or famine? The bread is warm and soft and delicious, and I've got all you can eat and more. It's yours, just for the asking. Or you can go hungry forever in a world where everyone else is feasting. You name it, Jake. What's it going to be? Your choice.*

The pain Jake felt was real, and he grimaced. He felt as if he was starving, and that now he always would be. All the kingdoms of the world were arrayed before him, about to be his alone for a weekend, and he was supposed to turn his back on them. No way. Absolutely no way. Jake started to come to his feet, to be ready to leave with Birgitta when she got back. Then, unable to decide, he sank back down into his chair.

*Did it hurt this much for you, Alex? Did you go through this while I stood there and made fun of you? If you were here now,* he wondered, *would you laugh at me?*

Jake closed his eyes, his teeth gritted against the fear and pain. A long moment later, his fist slammed against the table-top. *No, you wouldn't,* Jake realized.

A slow smile started to spread across Jake's face. With each breath the pain lessened. *I know what you'd do and say, and I know that you wouldn't laugh.*

"Let's go, mein Schatz." Birgitta tickled the back of Jake's neck with her fingernails. Jake picked up his drink, looked at it, then set it back down. *Adios, old friend. You're not even a close second to what I've got to give up tonight.*

He came to his feet and looked down at Birgitta. "I don't think so," he said with a small, regretful shake of his head.

"'Don't think so' what?" she asked, frowning.

"We're not spending the weekend together, Birgitta," he told her gently.

Anger ignited in her eyes. "But why not?"

"There's someone else in my life now."

Possessive jealousy colored the flames in her eyes. "She can't offer you anything that I can't."

Jake smiled. "It's not a she."

Horror doused the fire. "Jake! You can't be serious!"

"I am," he told her. "It's not what you think. But I hope you get to meet him someday." Jake threw a fifty on the table. "Buy yourself some champagne. You look as if you need it."

"Jake—"

"No, thanks. Auf wiedersehen, Fräulein."

Then, in a scene that was to become part of Donnelly's legend, Jake MacIntyre turned his back and walked away.

Half an hour later his MGB coupe shot across the border into Connecticut, heading north.

# 49

Lee came to an abrupt halt as she entered the Drydens' living room. *Wow,* she thought as she surveyed Jake from the doorway. *I know Annie's hoping to meet someone taller than she is, but he's one big man. . . .*

Jake half-turned, smiled at Lee, then resumed talking to Joel.

*Cute, too,* Lee decided. As Pat turned to see why Lee had stopped, Lee changed her mind. *He was cute twenty years ago. Now he's handsome.*

Pat nudged Lee. "Is he to go, or would you just like to devour him here?" She smiled at the face Lee made at her.

Pat introduced them, and Jake looked down at the slender blonde woman. "Are all of your and Anne's vacations this adventurous?"

*How dare he be flippant!* Lee's hazel eyes darkened as she readied for battle.

"We'll get her back," Jake said with a quiet confidence that dispelled her annoyance. "I miss my best friend, too."

Lee started to say something, then stopped.

"And if you're worried about my camera, don't be. I've got lots."

Lee laughed. *Handsome, charming, and perceptive, too.* She smiled to herself. *Annie, it looks like you've saved the best for last. . . .*

"I hope that you didn't get sick of this in prison," Pat said to Jake as she placed an enormous, steaming lobster in front of him.

Jake looked up at her. "Couldn't have. I spent most of the time in solitary, so I only got to have it twice."

Those gathered around the table for the dinner celebrating Jake's release laughed with him. The Parkers had come to meet Jake, and Chris and Kay Andersen had been invited as well.

Pat seated herself at the opposite end of the table from Joel. Pat and Lee reached for Jake's hand. Startled, he looked around to find hands joined around the table.

"Sorry," he said as he took their hands. "This is not the sort of thing that we did in the prison mess hall."

"Jake," Joel said when the laughter had subsided, "would you say grace?"

Jake swallowed. "Sure, I guess." After a moment's hesitation, Jake self-consciously repeated the simple blessing that he and Sam had said at their meals. He added to it his thanks for all those who had helped free him and asked that Anne be taken care of. When they had said amen, Jake looked at Chris Andersen.

"I'm not used to praying." Jake said.

The pastor shook his head. "You did fine," he said emphatically. "Short, simple, true, and heartfelt—just like you did—is the way to go."

"Then," Joel said, "can we expect a sermon like that this Sunday? Just for a change?"

"Only if," Chris retorted, "I can expect you to stay awake this Sunday? Just for a change?"

Later that evening, after the Parkers and Andersens had left, Jake joined Pat and Joel in clearing the table and washing the dishes. Pat noted how expertly he rinsed and dried the soapy dishes she handed him.

"I'm surprised that a bachelor is so good at this," she remarked.

"It's an occupational hazard of photojournalism," Jake replied. "Like every budding photographer," he went on as he handed a platter to Joel to be put away, "I reached that point in my career where taking pictures was my life and washing dishes was my livelihood." He shook his head at the memory of those lean, exciting years. "Photography students wash a lot of dishes."

"I bet," Pat said with a smile, "that med students wash even more."

Afterwards, they sat at the kitchen table and finished the evening's coffee.

"How do you two do it?" Jake asked.

"Do what?" Joel asked in reply.

"Here you two are, helping someone you don't really know to get out of jail when your daughter's a hostage in Peru." Jake saw Pat take Joel's hand. "What I mean," Jake went on, "is that I don't understand why you're not frantic with worry." He hesitated. "I'm worried, and I'm—" Jake stopped and looked out at the moonlight on Somes Sound. Outside, mosquitoes droned.

Pat took a sip of coffee. "We are worried. We love Annie, and we want nothing more than to have her back. But, we also realize that all of her life, even this horrible part, is in God's hands."

"Sometimes," Joel finished, "we're much better at worrying than we are at trusting, but we try nonetheless. If you truly believe that there is a God-made design to everything that happens, then it helps you cope."

"When I was in jail," Jake mused, "I read about trusting God." He smiled ruefully. "It isn't as easy as I thought it would be."

"No," Joel replied, "it isn't. And I know of no other lesson that we have to relearn more often or at such great cost."

The phone rang. Joel got up and answered it. He was gone for a few minutes, and both Jake and Pat could see the bemused expression on his face as he returned.

"That was Cathy," he said as he sat back down. "It seems that she's on some sort of involuntary vacation. The call was to ask if she could spend it with us." Joel looked at Jake. "In Peru."

"What did you tell her?" Pat asked.

"I told her," Joel replied with a grim smile, "that if she can fetch Jake back to the U.S. intact, then perhaps she'll be able to help us do the same for Anne."

The next morning Pat came out onto the sun porch where Jake was leafing through a family photo album. She set down one of the glasses of lemonade she was carrying and peered over Jake's shoulder.

"That Anne's horse?" he asked. He pointed at a picture of a teenaged Anne astride an enormous roan stallion.

"That's Bolívar," Pat replied. "He was Annie's while we lived in Peru."

"You lived there?" Jake asked.

"Joel was stationed in Lima for three years," Pat said. "Anne went to high school there. We lived outside Lima and kept Bolívar on some acreage behind the house. She loved to ride him." Pat smiled sadly. "It broke her heart to leave him behind when we came home."

Jake heard Pat's tone become quieter and more personal.

"You know, Jake, Annie's not like the other women you've known."

Jake began to protest, but one look into the eyes of this woman who was wife, mother, and physician told him that any pretense of innocence would not be well received.

Instead, Jake nodded. "I know that."

Pat took a sip of her lemonade. "Anne hasn't dated much. Never in high school, living in Peru as we were, and rarely when she went to college." Pat sat back and smoothed her skirt over her knees. "When I'd ask her about it, she'd just say that she'd know him when she saw him.

"Actually I wish she had dated more. But Annie has concentrated on her studies, her music, and now on her teaching." Pat set her glass down on the wicker table beside her. She smiled. "I don't think it's a question of her interest. She seems to be waiting. For the right man. The right man for her."

"Why are you saying this to me?"

Pat looked at him intently. "Jake, I am going to say something that I hope you take the right way."

"I'll try to."

"I don't think waiting for the right woman has been one of your virtues."

Jake felt his temper flare but quickly checked himself. Pat hadn't stated it as an accusation, but as a fact. And she was right. Seizing and conquering had been his life-style. Yet his life was changing. Rapidly. Surprisingly.

"You're right," Jake finally replied. "I think I know what you're getting at. You're saying that I might not be good for Anne."

Pat looked at him, smiled, and shook her head. "No. Quite the opposite. If—when—we find Annie . . ." Pat's voice faltered, and she paused. "Jake, I'm saying that if things should work out, Annie might be very good for you."

# 50

"I'm sorry, honey, but absolutely not," Joel said. The finality in his voice caused Lee to glare at him from across the map table, fists defiantly planted on her hips. "This isn't a vacation tour," he continued in the same quiet tone. "This is a rescue mission."

Jake watched Lee impassively, trying to reinforce Joel's authority; Cathy stared fixedly at the map of downtown Lima that was spread out in front of her.

"Lee," Joel said kindly, "I know that you want to help. We all know, and we appreciate it. Please try to view this as we do; as a military operation. And on such a mission, there is simply no room for noncombatants."

His carefully chosen terms did not have their desired effect. Lee bristled. "But," she protested, "you'll need someone else who speaks Spanish."

"That's true," Joel agreed. "But your value in that capacity would be more than outweighed by the fact that we'd always have to be guarding you."

"Uncle Joel, you make it sound like a war."

"It very well might be. That's why there's no place for you."

Joel's upraised hand quelled Lee's next outburst. With a stifled "Nuts!" she stormed from Joel's den.

*That's odd,* Cathy thought as she watched Lee leave. *I'd have thought that she'd put up more of a fight than that.* Joel shook his head as he watched her leave, then he returned his attention to the city map.

"As you can see," he said with a wave at the map, "like most Peruvian cities, Lima is a collection of squares or plazas connected by streets and alleyways." He pointed at a spot in the northeast corner of the city. "Here's the Plaza de Armas. It's big—several acres in size and reasonably empty. It'll be easy to keep track of me in the plaza and on the main streets, but if they bundle me into a car or hustle me off down an alley we're in trouble."

"What if we do lose you?" Cathy asked.

"Wait a week," Joel said flatly. "If contact hasn't been made by then, you go home."

"What about our weapons, Joel?" Jake asked, wanting to change the subject. "How do we get them through airport security?"

"We don't," Joel replied. "Thanks to Cathy, a courier will meet us at the airport tomorrow morning. Our weapons go into today's diplomatic pouch to Peru and will be waiting for us at the embassy in Lima."

Joel bowed slightly toward Cathy, who grinned and shrugged. "Now," Joel asked, "are there any more questions?"

After a glance at the other two he went on. "Then let's look at the possible exits from the plaza."

Pat walked through her now quiet and darkened home. She had made sure that her houseguests were comfortable in their bedrooms upstairs and had let in Jeeves, their large Manx tabby, for the night. A sliver of light shone from underneath Joel's den door. Pat opened the door and walked quietly across the room. The ship's chronometer on Joel's desk read 11:30. In less than six hours he'd be on his way to Lima.

Oiled metal glistened in the light from the banker's lamp that sat on the desk. She watched as Joel reassembled his Colt .45 service automatic and slid it into its worn leather holster. Then in a single fluid motion she slid into his lap, her arms around his neck, interposing herself between the vibrancy of her husband and the cold metal that dealt death and injury.

"Must you?" she asked after a while. He ran his fingers through her hair, and she was very glad that she had just brushed it.

"Love," he said softly, "you know my answer." Joel kissed his wife's forehead. "Remember how terrified Annie was of spiders when she was five? Remember how she'd come tearing into our room, crying, if one walked across the ceiling of her bedroom?"

Joel felt Pat's nod. "Back then, all this dad needed to conquer the imagined evil was a rolled-up newspaper. Now," Joel went on, "Annie has grown, and so has the evil surrounding her. Different wars, different weapons."

"I know it sounds horrible," Pat said quietly, "but I could make it if Annie didn't—," her voice faltered, "come home. But, without you . . . " Pat turned her face to her husband's.

Joel smiled at her and brushed a wisp of hair out of her eyes.

"I feel so helpless," she confided.

"That's the physician talking, isn't it?" Joel asked.

Pat nodded.

"And the wife, and the mother?"

Another nod.

"All of whom happen to be parts of the woman I love very much."

"So?" Pat asked.

"So, it's not Doctor Dryden that I'm relying on," Joel responded. "Neither is it Mrs. Dryden nor Mommy Dryden." Joel rested his chin on the top of Pat's head. "It's Pat Dryden, a godly woman, who's going to help bring us home."

"How?"

"Remember Proverbs?" Joel asked.

"You must mean the verses about the quarrelsome and nagging wife." Pat laughed and relaxed against him.

"Not this time," Joel said with a smile. "I was thinking of the verse that talks about a wife who is 'clothed with strength and dignity' and who can 'laugh at the days to come.'"

Joel placed his hand on Pat's. "Jake and Cathy and I are just the point of the spear that will be used to defeat evil. We're just the glittering bright metal. You are the spear's shaft. Your prayers will give the spear's point direction and impetus and force. Your prayers will bring us home. The prayers of 'a woman who fears the Lord' are not taken lightly, indeed."

The desk lamp shone softly as Joel pulled his wife close. "Now," he said, "let's pray."

# PART III

# 51

Anne awoke from her doze with a start. Her feet were cold. She scooted backward, trying to bring them into the rectangle of sunlight that streamed down from the window set high in the stone wall. Anne had found that, if she wrapped her arms around her knees, she could just fit into the patch of warmth that inched its way across the floor of her cell.

As she moved backward, her face came into the patch of light. Her head throbbed dully as the sun shone on her injured eye. Anne stood and faced the sunlight, ignoring the pain. She covered her good eye and was rewarded with a dim red glow. Thankful relief stung as she leaned back against the cell wall.

At about the time that the patch would begin its slow crawl up the far wall of her cell, the door would open and a tray of food would be placed on the floor. Anne had soon discovered that if she placed the tray back where it had been deposited, the guard would not enter the cell to retrieve it. This both spared her the guard's verbal abuse and allowed her to maintain a vestige of privacy.

She called that meal "supper" solely because it was dark when she finished it. After the guard had taken the tray, Anne would huddle beneath the filthy blanket that she had found in the cell and try to sleep. Only one of her sandals remained—she didn't know where she had lost the other—and as she slept, she kept it clutched firmly in hand. When the skitterings and scratchings of the rats that infested her cell became too much to bear, she would slap the sandal's heel against the stone floor. The resulting *crack!* served to quiet the vermin for a while.

The night before, an exceptionally large rat had poked his snout into the patch of moonlight that faintly lit the cell. Anne had seen him prowling around before and had named him Legion. The smart rap on the nose that Anne had given Legion had sent him scurrying into the darkness, and Anne had felt quite pleased with herself.

*Have I been here three days, or four?* Anne tried to recall as she massaged her numb toes. Since her one meal was the highlight of her day, Anne measured time in supper trays. She recalled one meal, an avocado heaped with chicken salad, that had been delicious. Another had consisted of a mound of rice and a small animal, roasted whole, with all four legs sticking up into the air.

"What is this?" she had asked the guard in Spanish.

"*Cuy,*" was the guard's muttered reply. He locked the door behind him.

Anne looked at the dish, and two animals came to mind. To her immense relief she remembered that *cuy* wasn't Spanish for rat, but that relief was offset by the fact that *cuy* wasn't Spanish for rabbit, either. Finally, unable to bring herself to dismember the unknown carcass despite her ravenous hunger, she had settled for the rice.

When the guard had returned he had shaken his head in disbelief, first at the untouched *cuy* and then at Anne. He picked up the tray, tore a leg off the *cuy*, and gnawed it as he departed.

As she did daily, Anne looked through the small window. She had found that by reaching up she could just grab the sill with her fingers. By pulling herself up with all her strength and scrabbling with her toes, she could peer out of the window for a few seconds.

Accustomed to the backwoods of coastal Maine, Anne found solace in the sounds that filled the twilight air around her. Chirps, whistles, croaks, crashing passages through treetops, and the far-off bleating grunts of llama and alpaca only intensified the silent peacefulness of the place. Anne also knew that she was near a river. Its incessant boom, usually muted by the thick walls, could be heard clearly through the window.

The westering sun was just disappearing behind a range of mountains. One peak to the east was not yet completely in shadow, and as Anne watched, a spectrum of greens played along its flanks. Every leaf on its summit seemed gilded by the setting sun. Its sides were a heap of emeralds at noon, while its mist-enshrouded base was already the color of a lawn by moonlight.

The silhouettes of the mountains against the evening sky caused Anne to think of her first-grade class back in Rockport. She smiled as she thought of her thirty-two, six- and seven-year-olds. *What a wonderful place to bring them!* the teacher in her imagined. *We'd figure out which mountains were volcanoes and that the ones with pointy tops were young, and that the ones with rounded tops were old.* A twinge of frightened homesickness shot through her. *I don't know how they or Momma and Daddy are. I don't even know if Jake is alive. Nobody knows where I am.* Anne could see the first tendrils of fog already inching their way up the near vertical slopes across the valley. She shivered. Twice so far the mist had poured through the unglazed window, condensing on her blanket and hair and leaving her sodden and miserable.

She dropped to the floor and sat back down in the now-dark cell.

Jake, Cathy, and Joel approached their departure gate at Miami International Airport. As they waited in line to have their flight bags x-rayed, Cathy pointed at a prominently displayed placard:

**TRAVELER'S ADVISORY: The secretary of transportation has determined that Jorge Chavez International Airport, Lima, Peru, does not maintain adequate security measures.**

Jake grinned at Cathy. "So that's why you two marines brought a ranger along, eh?"

"That's right," she told him. "We knew that you wouldn't stand a chance by yourself."

# 52

The sound of her cell door opening startled Anne out of her reverie. It was hours until her supper. Wary, she watched, expecting to be confronted by her captor.

Anne relaxed slightly when the door swung aside to reveal a woman about her own age. Dark eyes gazed at her tentatively from an oval face framed by short black hair. The small, slender woman hesitated in the doorway for a moment. Then, after an apprehensive glance behind her, she stepped into the cell and closed the door. "Perdóname, señorita. Habla usted castellano?"

"Yes," Anne replied. "I speak Spanish."

The woman smiled a small smile. "My English is not as good as it should be." She began to say something else, then stopped abruptly.

"My name is Anne Dryden," Anne said. "I'd offer you a chair, but . . . "

The young woman smiled again, and her eyes lightened. "I am sorry, señorita. I forget myself. My name is Celia. Celia Reyes." She stepped down from the doorway and looked around the cell. "They've given you no mattress? No bedding?" Celia brought her eyes up to meet Anne's. "The pigs!"

Anne smiled down at Celia. The vagaries of men had once again bonded women together. "Please, call me Anne."

Celia's eyes flashed as she nudged Anne's thin blanket with her toe. "This is all they've given you?"

Unsure how to reply, Anne merely nodded.

"Are you not cold?"

Anne smiled bleakly and nodded again.

"I'll be right back," Celia told Anne.

Anne heard her mutter "Pigs!" as Celia closed the door behind her.

Moments later the cell door opened again, and Celia returned. Under one arm was a large bundle, while in her other hand was a bucket of water that steamed enticingly. She set bundle and bucket down, then unfolded the bundle. Wrapped in thick blankets was a fluffy towel and a bar of green soap. Celia held up the soap. "It is made from parsley by nuns in Arequipa. Very good for the complexion."

At the mention of her complexion, Anne touched her battered face self-consciously.

"Did that happen here?" Celia asked.

"No. Before," was all Anne could bring herself to say. Celia held out the soap and towel. She smiled as Anne took them eagerly.

Celia leaned against the cell door as Anne scrubbed her face and arms. "I'm sorry that this is all I can bring you right now," she said. "I can only stay for a minute. I told Hector, your guard, that I wanted to find out why you didn't eat the cuy."

"Cuy?" Anne asked from behind a mask of green lather.

"Your dinner the other night. The small, roasted animal. It was unsatisfactory?"

"Oh, no. It was fine," Anne hastened to reassure her. "I just wasn't hungry." Anne rinsed off and toweled herself dry. She picked up the tortoiseshell hairbrush that Celia had brought, threw her a thank-you smile, then grimaced as she hit the first snarl.

"Then you like whole cuy?" Celia gave Anne a questioning look.

Something about Celia enabled Anne to abandon all pretense. "It looked disgusting," Anne said with a laugh.

"But it is considered a delicacy when served whole," Celia replied, infected by Anne's humor.

"Those legs sticking up in the air . . ."

"The men consider it muy macho to tear the carcass apart with their bare hands."

"Please!"

With a wave, Celia dismissed the notion. "Next time, your cuy will be served sliced."

Anne tried to fluff her hair with her fingers. "By the way, what is cuy?"

"A small mountain pig. It really is quite good," Celia assured Anne, opening the cell door. "I must go, or Hector will get nervous."

Anne gestured at the comforts Celia had provided. "Thank you very much."

Celia smiled shyly. She paused, her hand on the door latch. "I'll come back," she promised. Then her voice again became tentative. "As soon as I can."

Anne reached out with the hairbrush. "Don't forget this," she reminded Celia.

"Keep it, please," Celia said with a smile. "I have another." The door closed behind her.

Anne looked at the door for a long moment and then started arranging her bedding.

# 53

Jake had slept on his shoulder during the long flight from Miami. It ached, and he rubbed it as he stood in line to get his passport stamped. Something was wrong, but he couldn't put his finger on it, and it caused him to look around tensely.

Cathy noticed Jake's discomfort. "What's up?" she asked, raising her voice to be heard above the thumping of the passport stamps. "You look like someone who thinks he left the water running."

A tourist ahead of Jake in line pulled a camera out of a bag slung under his arm. Jake snapped his fingers. "That's it! My camera bag!"

"What camera bag?" Cathy asked. "You didn't bring one along."

Jake smiled sheepishly. "I know. That's just it. This is the first time in years that I've gone anywhere without a camera bag, and I keep thinking that I've lost it."

The immigration officer eyed Jake's passport incuriously. He stamped it and the tourist card that Jake had filled out on the plane, scribbled something on them both, and returned Jake's passport. Jake joined Joel and waited for Cathy. The officer spent considerably more time examining Cathy's passport, then asked her something that they couldn't overhear. Cathy started, frowned, and shook her head vigorously. The officer shrugged, stamped her passport, and waved her on.

"What was that all about?" Joel asked as the still-scowling Cathy joined them.

"I have no idea," Cathy replied. "He wanted to know if I was a Peruvian-born, naturalized American." She shouldered her flight bag. "Me? Do I look Peruvian?"

Joel chuckled. "As a matter of fact, you do. Peru has a large population of native-born citizens, including their president, who are of unmixed Japanese ancestry." Joel pointed to where a group of people, Asian in appearance but speaking voluble Spanish, was just exiting from the resident side of Customs and Immigration. "You'll fit right in."

"Well, I'll be . . . ," Cathy muttered.

# 54

Jake and Cathy huddled in the backseat of the battered Volkswagen taxi as it barreled along the Via Expresa, the freeway that bisected downtown Lima. Joel sat next to the driver who, at irregular intervals, would look around and cross himself. Cathy looked at Jake and rolled her eyes. "Bet you five bucks the wheels come off this thing," she said, straining to be heard over the din of the tinny car radio. "You're on," Jake shouted back. "But you collect only if you live through it."

"Ugh!" Cathy said suddenly. She pointed at the gearshift knob. Jake leaned over and saw that it was an enormous scorpion embedded in a clear plastic ball. The driver, noticing their attention, flashed a gap-toothed smile at them in the rearview mirror and flicked a switch on the dashboard. The knob lit up. Cathy closed her eyes and shook her head.

The taxi ground to a stop on a street in the fashionable Miraflores district of Lima. As he uncoiled his large frame from the taxi's interior, Jake looked over the exterior of the American embassy. While Joel and Cathy were used to the environment around embassies, he wasn't. Four Uzi-carrying guards were spaced evenly along the tall, iron-stake fence that separated the embassy from its frontage on Avenida Grimaldo del Solar. All traffic on the street was watched closely; an elderly woman who paused for a moment across the street was hurried along by a wave of a gun barrel.

"Kind of inhospitable, isn't it?" he asked Joel.

"After Tehran," Joel replied, "we got cautious. And after Beirut, we got downright paranoid."

Jake nodded grimly. He remembered the car bombing that had taken the lives of over two hundred military personnel.

A uniformed guard inspected their passports, then let them through the front gate. A long line of people wound its way through the metal detector, then up a flight of stairs. The line ended up at the desk of the duty officer, who determined the visitors' business. As the three joined the end of the line, the D.O. waved them up to his desk.

"Americans?" he asked. The D.O. was a lean, burly man with a gray crewcut and a jaw sharp enough to shave with.

*There's a retired drill instructor if I ever saw one*, Cathy thought.

"I'm Joel Dryden. We've got a ten o'clock appointment with Wes Pearson."

The D.O. reached for his phone and punched a button. He spoke briefly, then hung up. From a pile on his desk he picked up three cards. On each of them was written "2ND FLOOR" in red felt pen. Joel, Jake, and Cathy each got one. "Show these to the sergeant in the security booth," the D.O. ordered. He hooked a thumb over his shoulder, toward a glass enclosure across the lobby.

As they made their way to the booth, Jake noted the air of quiet watchfulness. People sat on rows of benches, filling out applications. When one of the applicants took a seat behind a pillar, Jake saw a guard walk over and move him back into sight. Dozens of five-gallon jerricans labeled Water were stacked under the stairs. Huge fans, designed to disperse a gas or smoke attack, were set into the walls just below the ceiling. Jake tried to imagine what it would be like to work in such an armed camp. *This isn't an embassy*, he thought. *It's a bunker.*

The only light in the security booth was from the bank of TV monitors in the control panel. Their cool glow bathed the uniformed marine guard who manned the booth. He glanced at their cards, then pressed a button. With an electronic buzz the door ahead of them unlocked. "Up the stairs in front of you, then to the right." The small speaker set into the thick, bullet-proof glass made his voice sound tinny and harsh.

"Nothing more boring than booth duty," Cathy remarked as they walked up the stairs. "I should know."

Wes Pearson was waiting for them at the top of the stairs. A stocky, sandy-haired man with a bristling mustache, his face lit up at the sight of Joel. "Joel!" he said, pumping Joel's hand enthusiastically. "It's been ages!"

Cathy noted that while the man radiated jovial cordiality, his shrewd eyes overlooked nothing about them.

"You back on business or pleasure, Joel?"

"Business. Personal business." Joel gestured toward Cathy. "This is Cathy Hagura. I believe something for her arrived in the overnight mail."

Wes, still all smiles, motioned them toward a door. He produced a key card, similar to Cathy's, that opened the door. Wes waved them through.

The instant the door clicked shut behind them, Wes's demeanor changed abruptly. "Sorry," he said. "Didn't know who your friends were."

Wes looked at Cathy. "Consular Operations, right? You were in on that Moncrief thing."

Cathy nodded, then looked at Joel for guidance.

"And this," Joel said with a slight smile, "is someone else

who was 'in on that Moncrief thing.' Wes Pearson, meet Jake MacIntyre."

Wes's hand stopped halfway to Jake's proffered one. The consular officer's eyes flicked from Jake, to Cathy, to Joel, then back to Jake. "What's going on here?" he asked slowly.

"Let's adjourn to your office," Joel said quietly. "Then I'll explain."

"I don't see how it could be the Senderistas who've got Anne," Wes said as he poured them all a second cup of coffee. After Joel had explained why they were there, Wes had shaken Jake's hand and fished their weapons out of his desk drawer. "Should've known the instant this stuff arrived that Joel Dryden was involved," he had commented.

"Who else besides the Sendero could it be?" Joel asked as Wes sat back down. "No other outfit that I'm aware of has the resources to pull off this kind of stunt."

"That's just it," Wes replied. "I don't think that Sendero has the resources either, thanks in part to the work you did while you were stationed here. Oh, they blew up the Banco Comercial over in Puno the other night, and they continue to make being a small-town mayor a high-risk career. But their much-touted assault on Lima has fizzled completely."

Wes spread his hands. "What started when you were here, Joel, is now even worse. The Sendero has deteriorated to the point of becoming guns for hire: most of their money now comes from acting as the drug lords' security service. Guarding the fields, dragooning the natives to harvest the coca crop, that sort of thing. Hardly what you'd call a savvy, sophisticated international operation."

It was clear to Cathy and Jake that this was not what Joel had expected to hear. They watched as he sat thinking for several minutes, gently rapping a knuckle against his teeth as he did so.

"What about the Puka Inti tie-in?" Joel asked at last. "That logo that they found on the wall in Cairo? That's Sendero all the way."

"There is that," Wes admitted. "But it could be a red herring."

Wes looked at Joel. "You're quite sure that your girl's down here?"

"Positive. Nothing else makes sense. We know that Anne was kidnapped, and we know about the Puka Inti insignia. We also know that, one day after Anne's disappearance, a Saudi AWACS aircraft tracked a private jet whose transponder said that it was enroute from Cairo to Peru."

Cathy took sudden notice. Allison Kirstoff hadn't told her that.

"We've verified," Joel was saying, "that the plane entered Peruvian airspace, and that it's owned by a wealthy Colombian. That and the ransom message are all we've got."

"What was that phone number you called?" Wes asked.

"657 022."

Wes dialed the number and got a "number not in service" message. He punched a button on his intercom. "Mark, trace down 657 022, will you?"

Joel stood. "So tell me, is it still where it used to be?" he asked.

Wes nodded. "Downstairs. Turn right, then third door on the left."

After Joel had left, Wes turned to Cathy and Jake. "You two sure keep fast company, don't you?"

"How so?" Cathy asked.

"You're in operations, Hagura. What do you know about Joel Dryden?"

"Just what I've been told," Cathy said guilelessly. "He's an econ type, did a lot of trade-agreement work while he was down here."

Wes snorted. "That's what his dossier says."

He leaned back in his swivel chair. "Let me tell you about Joel's brand of 'economics.' One of his 'trade agreements' involved a little band of Indians called the Ashaninka. They lived way up in the Andes near Tingo Maria. Made their living by growing edible roots and cocoa. A simple, peaceful people.

"Few years back, the Sendero arrived and began to lean on them. Forced them to switch from growing food to growing coca for cocaine. Took some of their youngsters off to be indoctrinated in the Sendero dogma. The Ashaninka men fought back at first, but it was their blowguns and bows and arrows against the Sendero assault rifles. The Senderistas torched their villages one by one until the Ashaninka were faced with a choice: surrender, or flee over the Andes." Wes paused. "It was winter, and those mountains are four miles high.

"Now, for several years before the Sendero arrived, an American missionary named Sharon McKee had been teaching the Ashaninka Spanish."

"Wait a minute," Jake interrupted. "Don't you mean English?"

Wes shook his head. "Nope. Spanish. Like most native tribes, they spoke only their own dialect. Anyway," Wes continued, "McKee helped the Ashaninka stand up to the Sendero. She was threatened, harassed, and nearly killed when a midnight burst of gunfire tore through her hut.

"After the attack on her, the Ashaninka leaders decided that it would be safer for her if she left. She tried, unsuccessfully, to change their minds. Then she reluctantly came back to Lima and immediately turned to us for help."

"Why the American embassy?" Cathy asked. "Why not the Peruvians?"

"McKee had already tried the locals," Wes replied, his voice ironic. "She had sent a letter describing the situation to the Peruvian Security Police. A few days later a couple of Colombian drug traffickers showed up. They gave McKee two things: the letter she had sent to the security police and a warning not to try it again."

"So what did the embassy do?" Jake wanted to know.

"What you'd expect?" Wes replied. "Told her that it was a local problem, offered to get her out of the country, and then ignored her."

Footsteps sounded in the hall. Wes paused until they had passed his door. "But Joel didn't ignore her. He couldn't. The Sendero and everything they stand for are anathema to his beliefs. He listened, and he did something about it."

Wes glanced at the door. "No time for details, but you know what his 'trade agreement' was?" Wes grinned. "The Sendero leader got to keep his hide intact in exchange for the Ashaninkas. *All* the Ashaninkas. Joel saw to it that they were resettled. And," Wes concluded, "I hear that they're doing quite well."

*Wow*, Cathy thought. *I bet even Allison doesn't know this!*

As Cathy and Jake looked at one another, Joel came back into the room. "I was just telling the youngsters here," Wes said cheerfully, "that I've never worked with another econ officer who thought that two Ph.D.'s were a less important qualification for the job than a fourth-degree black belt."

Joel frowned at Wes. As he sat down, the phone rang. Wes picked it up, listened, and made a few notes. "Thanks, Mark," Wes said, and hung up.

"Not surprisingly," Wes said, "the number was disconnected a few days ago. The telephone company says that the service address was 220 Jiron de la Union."

"That's near the Plaza de Armas, where I'm supposed to be met," Joel said.

Wes nodded agreement.

"Convinced?" Joel asked.

Wes nodded again.

Joel looked at his watch. It was 1:35. Twenty-five minutes until his appointment at the Plaza de Armas. He stood up.

As he reached for his gun, Wes covered the holster with his hand.

Cathy and Jake saw Joel's jaw muscles tighten.

Wes looked up at Joel. "I'll drive backup," he said quietly.

Joel didn't move.

"C'mon," Wes chided. He jerked his head toward Jake. "Neither of us are young anymore, like Tarzan over there. Besides," he continued with a grin, "we just got a new, black Mercedes."

Joel stared at Wes for a long time, then nodded. Wes pulled a snub-nosed .38 out of a drawer as the other three clipped their holsters to their belts. "OK then, Cheetah," Joel said. "Let's go."

# 55

"Won't they notice the Mercedes?" Jake asked as the car made its way up Avenida Belén toward the Plaza de Armas. He and Cathy rode with Wes in the embassy car. They were tailing the taxi carrying Joel as it changed lanes ahead of them.

"Doubt it," Wes replied. "All of the *remisse* taxis, the kind that ferry around the rich tourists, are black. Many of them are Mercedes."

The Mercedes followed the taxi as it jogged northeast onto Jiron de la Union. They were only a few blocks from the plaza.

Cathy shifted restlessly. "Do you have any idea what we can expect?" she asked Wes. "What if they just open fire on him as soon as he's in range?"

"Little chance of that. The government still controls Lima, and the Presidential Palace is just across the street from the plaza. Anyone opening fire around there would never make it out alive." Wes turned his head toward Cathy and Jake to emphasize his point. "Remember that."

The little convoy crossed Huallaga, the street that forms

the southern boundary of the Plaza de Armas. The plaza came into view on their right.

"Pretty flat," Jake observed. "Shouldn't have too much trouble keeping him in sight."

Joel's taxi pulled up to the curb abreast of the bronze fountain that dominated the center of the plaza.

Wes's Mercedes stopped a discreet distance behind it.

*Everything about this place is gray*, Cathy thought as she looked out over the plaza. *The sky, the stone the buildings are made of, even that big church over there. They're all the same dreary noncolor.*

"OK. Just keep an eye on him," Wes said as Cathy and Jake got out of the car. "Joel can take care of himself. We'll circle the plaza. If you lose him, or if he gets into a car, flag us down."

The Mercedes pulled away. Jake and Cathy pushed themselves through the clamoring throng of vendors that lined the periphery of the plaza.

Ahead of them, Joel made his way along one of the paths that led toward the fountain. He walked confidently, seeming to be more relaxed than either Jake or Cathy felt themselves. Joel started to brush past a magazine vendor, then stopped abruptly. He listened for a moment to what the vendor was saying, then accepted the magazine that the vendor was waving at him. The vendor walked hurriedly down another path.

Cathy observed, "Either Joel's been overcome by a burning desire to read the international edition of *Newsweek*—"

"Or," Jake finished, "since he didn't pay the man, the game's afoot."

"The game's a *what?*"

"Never mind. Let's not lose him." The two continued shadowing by discreetly walking along the edge of the plaza.

Joel leafed through the magazine as he approached the center of the plaza. He passed the fountain, then turned onto a

358

path that radiated outward from the center of the plaza. On either side of the pathway, patches of grass were interspersed with a few beds of struggling flowers.

"Looks like he found a message in the magazine," Jake remarked.

Cathy and Jake continued their stroll along the plaza's edge. A man sitting cross-legged on the sidewalk invited them to examine the light bulbs, soaps, and packs of gum that were spread out on a blanket in front of him. They passed by, ignoring him.

Joel had slowed his pace and now was headed toward the northwest corner of the plaza.

"Keep it slow," Cathy said. "We've got to stay behind him."

They watched as Joel, fifty feet in front of them, reached the intersection at the corner of the plaza. He waited a moment, and it seemed to Jake and Cathy that he was trying to make sure they were behind him. Then he headed west across Jirón.

"See Wes anywhere?" Jake asked as they reached the corner.

"Nope," Cathy replied. *I'd feel a lot better if I did*, she thought.

Jake started to forge across the street after Joel but was brought up short by Cathy's sharp, whispered "Wait!"

Jake stopped.

"Let's see where he goes first."

Joel reached the other side of Jirón. When the light changed, he turned and headed north, weaving his way around the ice-cream vendors and their pastel-blue pushcarts.

"Let's stay on this side of the street," Cathy suggested. "We may be able to see him better from across the street than from behind him."

"OK." Jake pointed to the large building on the opposite

corner. "See that sign that reads Correos? That's the post office. We're just a couple of tourists going to mail our postcards home to Aunt Millie."

"Aunt Millie will be so happy."

They paralleled Joel as he passed the weathered bronze, dropping-spattered statue of Francisco Pizarro.

Joel darted across a small side street, then pushed his way past the crowded entrance to the glass-roofed alleyway that housed the black market called Polvos Azules. American rock and roll blasted from a boom-box stand set up near the entrance.

Even from across the street, Jake and Cathy were assaulted by the riot of sounds and colors.

The rest of the block was occupied by a house with a large, varnished wooden door set into its whitewashed facade. The door had a smaller door set into its corner. The smaller door opened. Two men stepped out, blocked the sidewalk in front of Joel, and motioned him inside.

"Here we go," Cathy whispered.

Joel stepped through the small doorway. The two men followed and closed the door after them.

Jake and Cathy looked at each other. *Now what?*

The two strolled past the house. When they reached a side street that ran off to their right, they slipped around the corner. The entrance to a bakery cut diagonally through the building on the corner, and the two watched the house from within the entrance's shadows. Jake watched as an Indian woman, with a squalling baby in a sling on her back, walked past the house and disappeared into Polvos Azules.

"Wonder if she's going in there to sell the kid," Jake observed.

"Don't be revolting," Cathy replied disgustedly. "Anyway, who'd want a kid that cries that loud?"

A delivery truck enveloped them in black diesel smoke as it rattled toward the Plaza de Armas.

Jake shifted, restless at the lack of activity. "What if there's a rear exit?" he whispered.

"Not much we can do about it now if there is," Cathy replied. She looked down the street toward the plaza. "What we need is Wes's car."

Jake surveyed the front of the house. It was two stories high and windowless except for a grille set into the small door. "They can't see us unless we get right in front of the door. Stay here. I'll go back to the end of the block and see if I can spot Wes."

He made his way back past the post office to the corner across the street from the plaza. The black Mercedes was nowhere in sight. In front of the cathedral, Jake could see a religious procession wending its way down the street. As he watched, two police cars, blue lights flashing, blocked the intersection at the far end of the plaza. He could hear the faint, furious honking of horns. *Great,* he thought. *Some stakeout this is turning out to be.* He decided to circle around behind the house on his way back.

"Jake!" Jake was halfway across the street when Cathy's shout caused him to whirl. The larger door to the house had opened, and a car was emerging, slipping narrowly through the door's frame.

"Where's Wes?" Cathy shouted.

"Can't see him!" Jake shouted back.

The car backed into the street and then started forward.

Jake ran straight down the center of the street toward the house.

The car headed toward him, two dark shapes visible behind the windshield.

Jake looked over his shoulder as he ran. No sign of Wes.

The car accelerated past Cathy and headed straight toward Jake. As the car approached, Jake stopped, reached under his safari jacket and jerked his Colt from its holster. *Sorry, Wes,* Jake thought, as he braced himself. *But one hostage is better than two.*

One last glance over his shoulder showed that the end of the street was still empty. Jake looked back at the car just in time to throw himself out of its way. It barreled past him. He hit the road, rolled, and came to his knees. With a muttered "Crud!" Jake fired.

The left rear tire disintegrated, and the car slewed sideways to a halt in front of the market street.

Cathy, pistol drawn, ran up to cover Jake's flank. Two men burst out of the right front door of the car. They fled into the depths of Polvos Azules.

Cathy and Jake ran up to the car just as Joel scrambled out of the back seat.

"Move!" Joel shouted, pointing as he ran. Wes's black Mercedes suddenly appeared at the end of the street.

Jake looked into the hostage car, then disappeared into the front seat for an instant.

"Jake, c'mon!" Cathy screamed as she took off after Joel.

Jake caught up with her just as they reached the Mercedes.

"What the heck were you doing?" she gasped.

"Get in!" Wes shouted from the front seat. Behind them, alarms were going off in the Presidential Palace.

The force of the Mercedes's acceleration slammed the door behind them as the car tore off down Avenida Junín.

"So what happened?" Wes asked.

"Where were you?" Jake demanded.

*"What happened?!"*

Jake fought to be patient. "They took Joel into a house. I went down to the end of the street and looked for you. When a car left the house, to avoid losing them I blew out a tire."

Jake looked to Joel for support. Joel, resting his chin in his hand, just stared out of the window.

"You didn't signal, as we agreed?" Wes asked incredulously. *"You opened fire?"*

"Signal?" Jake snapped. "I did everything except send up a flare! Where were *you?"*

"We were stuck behind a procession celebrating the Festival of Corpus Christi," Wes said defensively.

Jake snorted in derision.

Wes shook his head. "Of all the bonehead, amateur stunts . . . "

"Look!" Cathy barked at Wes. "If you had been where you were supposed to be, this wouldn't have gone down this way. The real bonehead stunt," Cathy said acidly, "is missing a pickup."

Wes stared at the road ahead.

"So why did you jump into the car?" Cathy asked Jake.

"Saw this on the front seat," Jake answered. He pulled Joel's Colt .45 from his belt and handed it over.

Joel accepted it and shoved it into its holster.

The rest of the trip back to the hotel passed in stony silence.

Anne's arms ached as she struggled to prolong her evening's survey of the world outside her cell. She watched, entranced, as two hummingbirds darted and swooped around each other. *They're enormous*, she realized. *They must be three times the size of the ones back home.* The horizontal rays of the setting sun ignited the iridescent greens and reds of the birds' plumage, making them look to Anne like fireworks exploding in the twilight sky.

It was obvious to Anne that one of the birds was trying to catch the other. *I wonder if they're courting?* she thought with a laugh. Anne decided that the bird being chased must be the female, so she began to root for her as the bird, hotly pursued by the male, whirred through the sky in a dazzling display of aerobatics.

Just as the two hummingbirds flickered upward and out of sight, Anne heard the sound of a key in the lock of her cell door. She dropped to the floor and turned to face the doorway. *It's too early for supper.* Anne backed as far away from the entrance as she could get.

The door swung open to reveal a large, broad-shouldered man with an enormous handlebar mustache. When Anne saw the look in his eyes, she tried to press herself farther into the corner. This man had neither the sleepy, avuncular demeanor of Hector nor the profane stupidity of the guard who served Anne her supper. Anne could tell that this man was shrewd, smart, and purposeful.

"You will come with me," he ordered.

Anne didn't move. "Who are you?"

"Joaquin Mejia, the Puka Inti's lieutenant."

"Do you work for the man who brought me here?"

Mejia stepped into the cell. "You will come with me."

When Anne stayed where she was, Mejia started across the cell toward her.

Anne tried to back into a corner, slipped, and fell. Mejia walked over to where she was lying and looked down at Anne for a moment. Then, looming large over her, he reached toward her.

Anne screamed. She thrust her fists out to ward him off. Mejia enveloped both of Anne's hands in one of his and, with a smooth, powerful tug, he pulled her to her feet. "You will come with me." This time, Anne followed him toward the door.

Halfway across the cell Mejia stopped. He bent down and scooped up the sandal that Anne kept by her bedding, then led Anne out of the cell.

# 56

"I thought I might find you here," Joel said as he pulled out the chair across the table from Jake. The last of the twilight filtered down through the stained-glass dome that formed the ceiling of the bar in the Hotel Bolívar.

Joel sat down. "Thanks, by the way, for getting my Colt back."

Jake only shrugged in reply.

Joel looked at the white foam that lined the bottom of the glass in front of Jake. "Who got you started on Pisco Sours?" Joel asked.

"Bartender."

"How many have you had?"

"Just this one."

"How many are you going to have?"

"Don't know."

"Then let me help you decide," Joel suggested.

"Know what's in these?" He picked up Jake's glass. "The Peruvian national beverage; a brandy that'll tear your head off if you have one too many." Joel waved off an approaching waiter. "Did you know that down south in Pisco they don't bury

365

their dead?" Joel waited until Jake looked up. "They mummify them. Rumor has it that they embalm the dearly departed by soaking them in this stuff."

Jake looked pained, folded his arms, and slouched back in his chair.

"So what's eating you?" Joel asked.

Jake looked at him aggrievedly. "What's eating me? Well, for starters, how about a blown operation? We almost lose you, we tick off the bad guys to no end, and," Jake raised worried eyes to Joel's, "we didn't get her back."

"Agreed," Joel said with a nod. "I blew the planning; you, Cathy, and Wes blew the execution. What else?"

"After missing the pickup and almost getting us all killed," Jake groused, "that little jerk Pearson sits on his fat duff all the way back and chews me out!"

"Wes is sensitive about missed pickups." Joel smiled to himself. "Has been ever since Korea. 'That little jerk' was a navy lieutenant. One of his ensigns missed a pickup. Wes went in, under heavy fire, and got the stranded man out. The kid he rescued, a teenaged yeoman, died just as Wes got him aboard ship. Maybe," Joel said offhandedly, "if you ask Wes, he'll show you the Navy Cross he was awarded for that pickup. And maybe, if you ask nicely, he'll show you the glass eye that went along with that Navy Cross." Joel crossed his arms. "What else?"

Jake rubbed his hand across his face. Joel's reasonableness was thwarting Jake's desire to be blamed. "Big help you were when Wes was chewing on me," Jake said sullenly. He knew full well that it was a stupid thing to say.

Joel's voice lost all expression. "So that's it. Jake needed his hand held, and Joel didn't come to the rescue." Joel leaned back in his chair and stared across the table. "Jake," he said, his voice now cold, "I'll listen to you being hard on yourself, and I'll put up with you being hard on others if it's deserved. But—and be very clear about this—I will not tolerate self-pity. Not from a former officer in the rangers, certainly not from someone I'm going to have to trust to guard my back in a fight, and absolutely not from a man of God."

Jake slowly folded and unfolded a cocktail napkin as he listened. "When you prayed that prayer back in prison," Joel continued, "you volunteered, friend. You signed up for the duration. And, so far, everything's been wonderful. Now Jake gets his first taste of combat and loses it completely."

Jake winced at the truth. Then he frowned. "Combat?"

"Combat, man. War! We are at war, and you've enlisted." Joel leaned forward, very serious. "And not just you and me, brother; it's everyone who believes. Pat treats every drug-addicted baby she sees as if it were her very own and cries each time she loses one. Annie spends hours on her knees for her six-year-olds, hoping and praying that in five or ten years they won't become the parents of a baby at all, much less one born addicted. Lee has a way with teenagers, especially the suicidal ones. I can't begin to tell you how many are alive today because of her use of the gifts she's been given. And your friend Sam Webster? He's seen men redeemed as they sat in the chair that was about to kill them. In this war," Joel said quietly, "every-where is the front."

Jake shifted uncomfortably.

"What's the single most important criteria by which your combat unit was measured?" Joel asked abruptly.

Jake was startled by the apparent change of topic. "Readi-ness," he replied automatically.

Joel nodded agreement. "So why should it be different for us?" He looked at Jake sympathetically. "I can understand that the concept of being 'ready for God' might be a little esoteric for you right now." Joel smiled. "So, I'll put it in terms that I know you can understand: Annie. Are you willing to do whatever's necessary to fight for her?"

Jake sat quietly, his attention riveted on Joel. *Fight for Anne?* Jake considered the notion. *Why? I know that I said that I'd help get her back, but it's not like I'm responsible for her or anything. It sounds like he expects me to become responsible for her. I don't get it.* Jake frowned.

"Your choice," Joel continued. "I'm not going to make it for you, and neither is God. You can either discipline yourself through training and sacrifice to be readied for combat or," Joel pointed at Jake's glass, "you can head for the rear echelons. But if you do, then I won't have you with me. I'll leave you behind, and Cathy and I will go find Annie."

Joel looked Jake straight in the eye. "And in answer to the first question that I know Annie will ask, I'll tell her that you chose to stay in Lima and drink."

Jake fell silent. He didn't like what Joel was telling him, but he had to admit that the man had a way of putting life into perspective. Responsibility for other people was a new concept, one that he wasn't sure he liked. But he had to admit he valued it when he saw it in other people—like Alex, Anne, and, yes, Joel.

After a long, silent debate, he decided.

Jake grimaced. "You know what annoys me most?"

"What?"

"This is a perfect time to swear, and I don't even get to do that anymore."

"I know just how you feel," Joel said with a laugh. "Come on. Cathy's probably starving by now."

# 57

Angel Valdivin shivered as he stood in front of the American embassy. It was cold, and he stamped his feet to keep them warm.

Since the street outside the embassy was Peruvian soil, Valdivin and two other members of the Peruvian army were assigned to patrol it. Valdivin shifted his Uzi from one shoulder to another, then rubbed his gloved hands together. He was proud of the Uzi, having received it when he was promoted to the elite detail that protected embassies, and grateful that he no longer had to carry the older and less powerful Ingram Model 6 used by the rest of the army.

Headlights appeared at the end of the street. *"Coche,"* Valdivin called out to his squadmates and to the marine stationed inside the embassy's perimeter fence. He glanced at the auto, then muttered when he saw that the car's dome light wasn't on. *Tonto,* he thought as he walked out into the street to flag the car down, *you must be a fool to drive down this street without your inside light on so we can see who you are.*

Valdivin looked up again. *This one's coming way too fast.* He threw himself out of the way just as the car sped past him. From his back the soldier saw something sail over the embassy fence and into the courtyard. "Bomb!" Valdivin shouted as he hugged the pavement. "Everybody down!"

Valdivin swung the Uzi around and fired prone, but his lack of practice with the Belgian-made weapon caused the burst to go high. The car swerved, skidded around a corner, tires squealing, and disappeared. He could hear the marine guard inside the compound yelling into his radio.

Floodlights suddenly illuminated the courtyard. Valdivin crawled to the fence and cautiously peeked over its foundation. "I see an envelope," he reported.

"Is that all?" the marine said scornfully. He started to get up.

"Careful!" Valdivin warned. "It might be a letter bomb. Wait for the bomb squad."

The marine hit the dirt again.

A van, blue lights flashing, rushed down Avenida Grimaldo del Solar. After checking his radio, the marine, rifle at the ready, opened the gate. Four heavily padded men ran in, carrying a piece of pipe, which they upended and set down over the envelope. One of the men then stood and, staying as far away from the open end of the pipe as he could, reached into the pipe with two long pairs of tongs. Keeping the envelope below the end of the pipe, he grabbed it with one pair of tongs, then tore one end off of it with the other.

Valdivin ducked in anticipation of an explosion. When he heard nothing, he looked up again.

The bomb squad man handed the envelope to the marine. "Letter from home?"

"I am sorry," Celia said. "This is the first chance to come see you. Only this morning did the Puka Inti leave for the day."

Celia smiled. "I gave your guard his lunch, then told him that I'd watch while he took his siesta." She shook her head. "Hector does love his afternoon nap."

The small woman looked up at Anne. "I have lunch for us, too. And," she added with a smile, "after lunch, if you wish, would you like to bathe?"

"A bath?" Anne replied incredulously. "I would love a bath! But—"

"Yes?" Celia asked, worried.

"*Before* lunch? Please?"

Anne emerged from the bathing room swathed in towels. With Celia's assurance that she would keep her from being disturbed, Anne had shed her now-ragged clothes and immersed herself in the blissfully hot water. Soap and shampoo had been set out for her, and a gentle current through the huge stone tub carried away the suds from her repeated latherings. Only when she found herself dozing off did she regretfully pull herself from the water's embrace.

"How can I ever thank you?" Anne asked as she walked across the large bedroom. "That was heavenly! That tub is so big. Where does all that wonderful hot water come from?"

Celia smiled. "The tub was built by the Inca. We are atop a dormant volcano, and they diverted a hot spring to flow through it." Celia handed Anne a comb and hairbrush. "If you wish, we can wash your dress. But, it is cold at night, and these might help keep you warm."

She gestured at the clothes spread out on the bed.

Anne shuddered. "Please, I never want to see that sundress again." She ran her fingers over the clothes Celia had provided: a heavy black skirt trimmed in red and yellow, several soft cotton underskirts, a silken shirt, and a loose alpaca sweater. Anne held up one of the underskirts. "I haven't worn petticoats in years," she laughed.

"Quechua women tend the animals in the fields, so they spend a lot of time sitting," Celia explained. "The many layers keep us warm."

Celia helped Anne into the underskirts, then fastened the overskirt around her. Anne put on the shirt, then pulled the sweater over her head.

Celia stepped back and admired the result. "You look just like a *chola!*"

"A what?" Anne's hands caressed the silky alpaca wool.

"A chola. That's what I am. A chola is a Quechua woman. This is what we wear."

"But, you—" Anne gestured at Celia's designer jeans, soft leather boots, and silk blouse.

Celia looked away. "The Puka Inti insists that I wear this."

"Who is this Puka Inti?" Anne asked. "Somebody named Joaquin mentioned him, too."

Something in Anne's voice caused Celia to look at her intently. The face she turned to Anne's was suddenly very young and very scared. Celia motioned for them to sit. She perched on the edge of the leather couch, hands between her knees. Tears appeared at the corners of her eyes. Celia opened a drawer and fumbled for a tissue. Just as she appeared ready to speak, she stopped.

Celia dabbed at her eyes, then stood. "There is no time to tell you now. We must get you back. Hector will be waking soon."

Anne started to ask about the lunch, which looked delicious, then decided against it. As she rose, she noticed a small book next to the box of tissues.

"May I borrow this?" she asked as she picked the book up.

"My Bible?" Celia replied. "Of course, if you wish." Celia looked at the Bible, then back at Anne. "Do you believe what the Bible tells you?"

"Absolutely."

"And, what does it tell you?"

"Among other things," Anne said softly, "to always hope."

Both women jumped as the door to the apartment burst open with a sound like a rifle shot. A man strode into the room, white with rage.

At the sight of Anne, the man she recognized as her captor stopped short. Celia came to her feet. She looked at him apprehensively. The man walked slowly over to the two women. As he inspected her clothing with passionless eyes, Anne rose and stood beside Celia.

"Puka Inti—," Celia said pleadingly.

Without taking his eyes from Anne, the man slapped Celia full across the face, knocking her back onto the couch. He looked at her for a moment, then reached down. The Puka Inti grabbed a handful of Celia's hair and pulled, turning her face toward him and pulling her chin up. He clenched his fist, then pulled it back to strike again, making sure that Celia could see it as he did so.

The memory of Hassan's blows flooded Anne's mind. The descent of the Puka Inti's clenched fist was checked abruptly as her hands closed around it.

"Stop it!" Anne screamed. She pulled on the fist with a strength that nearly unbalanced him. He staggered, then recovered. Like a snake striking, the hand that had been holding Celia's hair lashed out. The blow caught Anne by surprise and sent her reeling.

When her vision cleared, she saw that he was looking at her. She touched the corner of her mouth, looked at her bloody fingertips, and then back at him. He was smiling.

As he turned back to Celia, three men appeared in the doorway to the apartment.

"Puka Inti—," a fat man in front began.

373

"Yes, Hector?" the Puka Inti said mildly. He gestured at the table with its untouched lunch. "I do not remember ordering a tea party." With a savage shove he flipped the table over, scattering the dishes and food across the floor.

"It was her!" Hector protested. He pointed at Celia. "She—"

The pistol's roar filled the room, and Hector sank to his knees.

Anne hadn't even seen the Puka Inti draw.

Hector toppled forward and lay motionless.

"Take this offal out into the courtyard," the Puka Inti ordered. "Tell his wife to come fetch him."

Anne froze when he pointed the pistol at her, then relaxed as he holstered it. "And take her with you."

Celia's screams began as Anne was taken across the courtyard. As her cell door slammed shut, they were joined in dissonant harmony by the high-pitched mourning wail of Hector's wife. The underskirts Celia had provided cushioned her as Anne collapsed, hands pressed tightly over her ears. The patch of sunlight on the wall of her cell vanished as the sun disappeared below the mountain.

# 58

"I'm getting tired of having to climb up and down these stairs to escort you," Wes said as he met Joel, Jake, and Cathy at the stairs that led to the embassy's second floor. "So, I've had passes issued for you. By the way, a couple of packages have arrived for you." As they made their way upstairs, Wes handed each of them a red and white ID card attached to a clip.

"Here's your first package," Wes said as he opened the door to his office.

Joel, Jake, and Cathy looked into the small room.

"I thought I'd never find you." Lee stood in the center of the room, dressed freshly in a cream-colored shirtdress and matching hat.

"I got in last night and had to stay in the most awful hotel. I came here this morning to see if they knew where you were. Mr. Pearson's been very nice, but he wouldn't let me leave the embassy. I was so afraid that before I caught up with you you'd take off somewhere, and then I wouldn't be able to help you find Annie—" Lee's torrent of words dried up the instant her eyes met Joel's.

Cathy saw the same look that Joel had given Allison Kirstoff, now magnified a thousandfold, and flinched involuntarily.

Joel said nothing. He gazed at Lee steadily. Lee bit her lips and swallowed, fighting back the tears that glittered in the corners of her eyes.

"Did I make it clear that you were to stay with Pat?" Joel asked coolly.

"Uncle Joel, let me explain. I just had to come along."

"You did?"

"Yes. I couldn't bear to wait at home—"

"Emily," Joel ordered in a tone that made it clear he expected to be obeyed, "you will remain here in the embassy until transportation for you back to the States can be arranged."

"But, Uncle Joel—"

Joel's voice hardened even further. "Only the grown woman that you've become prevents me from properly disciplining the irresponsible child that you are."

Stung, Lee looked away. The sudden motion of her head flung the tears from her eyes.

Joel looked at Cathy. "Did you know about this?"

"I did not," Cathy bristled. "It was not a smart thing to do. This is a dangerous place to be, as we've already discovered. But," she continued, turning her attention to Lee, "I can understand why she did it."

Lee shot her a gratitude-filled glance in return.

"Wes," Joel declared, "I want Miss Parker on the next flight to the States."

"OK," Wes replied. "The next available is an American flight to Miami."

He checked a chart on his wall. "It would've left next Wednesday at 12:15 A.M."

"What do you mean, 'would've'?" Joel asked quietly.

Wes smiled. "Right about this time every month the controllers at Chavez don't get paid. So right about this time every month, like this morning, they go on strike. It's a cherished Peruvian ritual." Wes shrugged helplessly. "No commercial flights in or out."

Frustrated, Joel pressed the heel of his hand against his forehead. "How long do these strikes last?"

"Well, let me put it this way: If we have any luck in getting Anne back, then you all will be on the next flight out."

Joel threw up his hands.

Cathy, standing behind him, shoulders shaking with valiantly suppressed laughter, caught Lee's eye. She winked.

"As I was saying," Wes continued, "I've had passes issued for you *four.*"

He looked at Joel in polite inquiry. "Unless there are any more coming along?"

Joel shook his head. "At this rate, we may need to charter our own plane."

"There was another package." Wes picked up an envelope that was lying on his desk and pulled something out of it.

Lee gasped.

"You recognize this?" Wes asked. He was holding a sandal.

"It's mine," Lee said.

"Yours?" Wes said, puzzled. "I don't understand."

"It's one of the pair that Annie borrowed from me the day we went sailing." Lee reached out, took the sandal from Wes, and clutched it tightly.

"What else was in the envelope?" Joel asked. Everyone held their breath as Wes upended the envelope. An audio cassette clattered onto the desk. Wes pulled a cassette player out of the desk drawer. He inserted the cassette and pressed the play button.

**A message for Doctor Joel Dryden.**

It was the same voice that Joel had heard on the phone.

>**Doctor Dryden, what happened today was worse than foolish; it was stupid. You have given us ample reason to expect better of you. Therefore, any future disobedience will have the most dire of consequences. You will be given just one more chance, and we expect our instructions to be followed exactly.**

The voice paused.

>**Since we do not appear to be able to persuade you to listen, perhaps this voice will.**

The several seconds of silence on the tape was echoed in the office.

>**Dad? It's me, Anne. I'm OK.**

Every muscle in Jake's body tensed at the sound of her voice.

>**Do what they say, Dad. They are not lying to you. Trust them, please. I do; I believe in what they tell me. These people are not being deceptive; please listen to their words.**

Anne paused.

>**I love you—**

Anne's voice was replaced by the man's.

**You heard your daughter's own words, Doctor. She trusts us. As you are advised to. If you do not, if you make another mistake, in our next delivery will be the foot to match the sandal.**

The tape ended.

Tears streamed down Lee's cheeks. Cathy looked up from the floor, her face grim.

"But, that's not all," Wes said. "Notice how she was cut off? Well, I had our audio boys lift off what was recorded over her voice. Listen to this." Wes switched cassettes.

**I love you, Daddy. I'm praying for you, and Momma too.**

A flood of guttural Spanish was followed by the sound of something striking flesh. Wes punched the off button. "Sorry, but I thought you would want to hear that, too."

Cathy put her arm around the sobbing Lee. Jake stood staring at the wall.

"Wes, put it on again," Joel said.

"This tape?" Wes asked. He held up the cassette from the audio lab. "No, the first one."

They listened intently to another playing of the tape. Partway through, Joel held up his hand. "Wes, back it up a little bit."

The cassette player's speaker squealed as Wes held down the rewind button.

**. . . what they say, Dad. They are not lying to you. Trust them, please. I do; I believe in what they tell me.**

Joel motioned again, and Wes stopped the tape. "Does that sound like Annie to you?" he asked Lee. "Not her voice; her way of speaking."

"Not really, come to think of it," Lee replied. "But I just figured that she's scared."

"You're right," Joel agreed. Then he frowned. "But there's more to it than that. Wes, play it from the beginning."

As the third playing ended, Lee looked up in surprise. "Uncle Joel, Annie called herself Anne! She never does that. Well, at least not unless she's really upset or doesn't like someone. Last time I heard her call herself Anne was when she introduced herself to this blind date I had set her up with."

Jake barely managed to suppress his snort of laughter.

"I agree with you," Joel said. "Not only does she refer to herself as Anne, but she calls me Dad." Joel rubbed a forefinger along his chin. "Annie only calls me that when she's really upset, the news is really bad, or both."

Joel started to pace. "So, we know that Annie's obviously unhappy with what she's having to say. I think she doesn't mean a word of it."

"Not quite," Wes interjected.

Joel stopped in his tracks. "What do you mean?"

Wes smiled. "I think that there's one part that she means very much."

"Which part is that?"

"This one."

Wes switched tapes.

**I love you, Daddy. I'm praying for you, and Momma too.**

"We'll get them," Wes said in response to the look on Joel's face. "We're gonna nail the scum who've got her."

With a visible effort Joel brought himself back under control. "Jake?" he asked. "What do you make of this?"

Jake shook his head. "It sounded forced; sort of stilted. Her cadence was funny."

"Good point," Joel agreed. "Now that you mention it, I noticed that too."

He picked up a scratch pad from the desk. "Let's see if we can figure out how that fits into what Annie's trying to tell us. Play it again, Wes," Joel asked.

This time Joel took notes. "Wes," he said, breaking into a smile. "I disagree with you. I believe that Annie means every word she's saying!"

"Uncle Joel, how could you?" Lee protested.

"Because," Joel explained, "now I know which words are Annie's. Anyone else notice that Annie stressed certain words? It was Lee's noticing Annie's word choice, combined with Jake's clue about her cadence, that tipped me off."

Joel picked up his notes. "Listen to what she emphasized."

He recited certain words from his transcription of Anne's message, circling them as he went. "Do . . . not . . . trust . . . in . . . deceptive . . . words."

"Interesting," Jake said. "But it doesn't help us much. We weren't trusting them anyway."

"It may help us more than you realize," Joel said.

Lee looked up suddenly. "That's from the Bible!"

"Jeremiah," Joel agreed. "That's the part of her message that I believe." He smiled proudly at them all. "Attagirl, Annie."

# 59

Anne waited until Celia had lowered herself painfully onto Anne's bedding. "Who is he?" she then asked quietly. Celia turned a swollen and battered face to Anne.

"His name is Rafael Cienfuegos," she said through bruised lips. "His men call him the Red Sun, the Puka Inti.

"I met him at the university," she continued, in answer to the question in Anne's eyes. "I was a young girl, fresh from the countryside. My father is a farmer in Huancayo. He has worked hard all his life and has done well." Iridescent blue glittered as a butterfly flew past the cell window behind her.

"I am the eldest of his children and the first to go to Ayacucho University. Rafael was a professor there, in archeology."

She looked up at Anne, her face laden with shame. "I was very naive, and Rafael is very charming and handsome. . . . " Anne nodded her sympathetic understanding. She thought of her college days, and of how many of her friends' lives had been damaged by too much, too soon, too fast.

"He possessed me thoroughly," Celia continued. She toyed with a thread from the blanket's frayed edge, her eyes downcast. "At first I was excited by his courting of me and more than willing to let him have his way." Celia wound the thread around her finger. With a savage tug she pulled it from the blanket. "I was such a pituca."

She looked up. "Do you know what a pituca is?"

"No, I don't." Touched, Anne looked at the embittered young woman. *She's just my age,* Anne thought. *But, she's old inside. There's no laughter, no joy, no love. Lord,* she prayed quietly, *please give me the words to say to her.*

"It is a word we in the country use for those who go to the big city, get rich, and then become obsessed with their possessions," Celia explained bitterly. "I allowed myself to become a pituca, obsessed with Rafael's attentions, and I never even made it to a city bigger than Ayacucho." Celia closed her eyes. "But, that's not the worst of it. Only when it was too late," she finished, "did I find out that he was a high official of the Sendero Luminoso."

Anne gasped.

"You have heard of them?" Celia asked.

"Yes. But I didn't think that they could possibly be active here." Anne gestured at her surroundings.

"They are not," Celia replied. "Rafael is." She looked past Anne as she remembered. "In my third year of college something happened. A dispute between Rafael and his superiors in the Sendero. We fled from Ayacucho and came here. That was two years ago." Celia sighed. "For two years Rafael has been building his own army. He recruits from within the Sendero and stirs up unrest within its ranks. He believes that soon he will be strong enough to strike against them."

"He opposes their philosophy, then?"

"No," Celia replied. "If anything, he embraces it more wholeheartedly than the Sendero leaders do. This is something personal. A vendetta."

"Then you are a member of Sendero Luminoso?" Anne asked warily. Celia's answering smile was devoid of warmth. "Do I seem like one to you? I hope not—my parents would be devastated if I was. You see, they taught me the value of kindness and peace, and to be honest and fair with those about me." She shook her head. "One cannot believe in those things and be a Senderista." Celia looked bleak. Age rimmed her eyes. "For two years I've been the only woman here. Only once a month I am permitted to leave; to go to the market at Pisac to buy necessities."

*On days I don't see Lee*, Anne thought, *I call her on the phone.* She shuddered at the idea of two years with no one to talk to. "What about the Cuzco police?"

"They are men, are they not?" Celia said viciously. "Rafael would get word of it. He would go to them and swagger and bluster and bribe. He would describe to them how he was going to subdue me when he got me home, and they would wink and laugh and hand me over to him."

"Then," Anne asked, "if you're alone here most of the time, why don't you run away?"

"Do you know where we are?"

"Yes. I recognized it when I got off the helicopter."

"Then what would you have me do? Just stroll off into the jungle? To stray from civilization out here is to never be seen again. Even the men here do not willingly leave the compound at night."

"Aguas Calientes isn't far. There are people there."

Celia looked at Anne wonderingly. "You don't understand. Rafael has connections throughout the country. If I did not return, my family would be killed before sunrise."

The silence was broken only by the whir of hummingbird wings. The sweet fragrance of the trumpet-shaped flowers that grew on a liana outside the window drifted into the cell. "Do you love him?" Anne asked at last.

"A girl that I once knew thought she did. Now—" Celia's body rippled with the force of the shudder that passed through her. Her whisper was harsh. "I *loathe* him."

"Then why do you come back from Pisac?"

Celia turned her face away in pain. "I tried that once," she admitted. "Just after we arrived here. I tried to take a bus from Pisac to Cuzco, but the men Rafael sends with me caught me as I got on. Do you know what the Puka Inti did when he found out?"

"Did he beat you?" Anne asked, knowing that it was more than that.

"*That* I could have endured!" Celia whispered savagely. "No, when the Puka Inti found out, he bribed a magistrate in Callao to write a letter saying that I had been arrested for prostitution and had hanged myself in my cell. Then he locked me for a week in a cell like this one, with nothing but the letter." The young woman's face was a haggard, pain-filled mask. "I have no home to go to."

*I never realized, God, that evil such as this man really does exist. It reminds me of that verse in Revelation: "Then the dragon was enraged at the woman and went off to make war against the rest of her offspring." What would you have me say to encourage her?*

Celia spread her hands. "It is hopeless."

"I think you're wrong," Anne said gently. "There is hope for you, and me, and everyone."

"What difference does it make if I'm wrong or right?" Celia replied harshly. "Even if I should escape, where would I go? Back to my family? They think I'm dead. Besides, they would disown me if they knew what I have done."

"Do you really think so?" Anne asked quietly. "Do you really think that a father who loves his children enough to want to send them to college would turn away his firstborn when she came home?" Anne thought of her father's hopes for her and smiled to herself. "I think that he wants to dance at your wedding and dandle his grandchildren on his knee."

"This is Peru," Celia scoffed, "not America. No man will marry me once he finds out that I have been . . ." She hesitated, then spat out the word, "used."

"A man who truly loved you would," Anne replied. She took Celia's hands in hers. "And even if no man will love you, God always will."

"God?" Celia responded incredulously. "Love me? After all the things that Rafael has made me do? Impossible." She shook her head firmly. "If I turn to the God I know, he will look upon me and judge me and find me wanting and consign me to an eternity in hell." Fear blossomed in the young woman's eyes. "He has turned his back on me."

Anne saw that fear and started to cry. "Oh, no," she said earnestly. "It's not like that at all. The God I know would never turn his back on you. Turn to him, and he will give his love to you. He will weep with you and forgive you, and he will heal you. He will gather you into his arms."

Celia looked skeptically at Anne. "He would do all those things for me? After what I have done?"

Anne reached out and smoothed a strand of Celia's hair. "There's a woman in the Bible who was 'used' by far more men than you ever will be. But Jesus did not condemn her. He loved her so much that he did do all those things for her." Anne looked into Celia's eyes. "He also did one thing more."

"What was that?" Celia asked in a small voice, tears beginning to stream down her cheeks.

"Of all the people on earth, he chose her, that woman used and despised by all but him, to go tell his disciples that he had defeated death." Anne smiled. "The God I know consigns his children to an eternity in paradise."

# 60

The mist lifted when the Sikorsky S-70 Black Hawk helicopter carrying the army search and rescue team was an hour out of Cuzco. They had scrambled within minutes after Cuzco Control had lost contact with the AeroPeru 727.

"See anything?" the captain leading the team asked the pilot.

"Nothing yet," the pilot replied over the intercom. "It'll be another five minutes before we're over the location of the aircraft's last radar fix."

The captain swept his men with a glance. Only two of the eight men on his team had experience with plane crashes. *They're about to learn the hard way,* he thought. The flight from Cuzco had been rough, and he smiled reassuringly at those who were swallowing hard to keep from being airsick. "Only a few minutes more," he promised them. All were trained as medical corpsmen as well as being expert mountaineers. Most were Quechua Indians, who had grown up in the Andes.

"Remember your assignments," he cautioned them. "Carlos and Ernesto set up the triage station while the rest make a first pass for survivors." They nodded.

"There it is." The copilot pointed toward a jagged gash in the jungle that covered a mountainside ahead of them. The pilot pivoted the helicopter toward the crash site. Scattered bits of metal glinted in the sunlight. "Notify Cuzco Control," he ordered the copilot.

He switched to the intercom. "Crash site located," he told the team leader.

"How's it look?" the captain asked.

*"Lomo Saltado."*

The captain swore. A bad crash in the jungle was called *Lomo Saltado* in a gruesome comparison to the popular dish of chopped meat and vegetables.

"Let's approach by coming up the valley from below," the copilot suggested. "Then we can land there." He pointed down and to his left. "On that level area at the base of the crash." The pilot agreed and nosed the helicopter downward.

"Prepare for landing," the copilot told the team. Behind him the rescuers tightened their safety harnesses.

"You spotted the site, Miguel," the pilot told his young copilot. "You make the approach."

"I have the controls," the copilot replied. The commander smiled at the serious pride in the young man's voice. The pilot set his hands in his lap, then surreptitiously placed them back on the controls when the copilot was not looking.

*It is not that I don't trust you, Miguel,* he thought. *It's just that I remember my first real approach.*

The helicopter continued to descend as it approached the mouth of the valley.

The helicopter suddenly lurched upward before the pilot even realized that he had yanked back on the controls.

"What?" both the copilot and the captain demanded to know.

"There." The pilot pointed. "See?" he asked the copilot.

"That glinting?" He brought the helicopter to a hover. The valley below them appeared to be laced with strands of light.

"What is it?" the copilot asked.

"Barbed wire. The drug growers string it over their valleys to keep planes away."

"Mother of God," the copilot breathed. "If we had hit that . . . "

"A friend of mine did, once," the pilot replied. "I went in after him. The Sendero had slaughtered him."

Ashen, the copilot mopped his brow with his sleeve.

"Possible drug activity below," the pilot informed the captain. He punched a switch that armed the S-70's twin M60D thirty-caliber machine guns.

The team leader swore again. Where there were drug growers, there would be the Sendero Luminoso. "Load weapons," he ordered.

His men looked at one another as they complied.

"Enrique, Guillermo, take the first guard duty."

Under their breath, so as not to be heard by their captain, Enrique and Guillermo swore.

"We're in luck," Wes said as the four walked into his office. "If," he added soberly, "you can call a plane crash luck."

"What happened?" Joel asked as they sat down. "I haven't seen today's *Lima Times.*"

Wes pushed a copy of the English-language newspaper across his desk.

"An AeroPeru 727 outbound from Cuzco went down just west of Huancavelica. Seems that the pilot thought that the weather wasn't going to be as bad as it turned out to be. The plane iced up over the mountains. No survivors."

"Thanks for the happy news," Jake said. "Now, why are we here?" A night of Anne-filled dreams along with the acid taste of the memory of the dressing-down Wes had handed him had combined to make Jake restless and irritable.

Lee looked at Wes, her face pale. "Annie wasn't—"

Wes shook his head. "No, she wasn't. But this was."

Wes held up a dirty and crumpled envelope. "The search and rescue team that found this got shot up pretty badly."

"Sendero?" Joel asked.

Wes shrugged. "They think so, but those mountains are right in the heart of the cocaine-growing region and are crawling with all sorts of bad guys." Wes pointed to a spot on a map that covered one wall of his office. "As soon as the ground team hit dirt, they heard cries for help coming from the jungle around the crash site. When they approached, the attackers opened fire on them from the cover of the jungle."

Two ex-marines and a former ranger winced.

"The team couldn't return fire and saturate the area for fear of hitting any real survivors."

*Sounds like Nam*, Jake thought. *Not knowing who's the enemy makes it no fun at all.*

"After they beat back the attack, they resumed their search and found this envelope. When they saw that it was addressed to the embassy, they brought it here. If you guessed that it's another tape, you guessed right." He reached into the envelope and pulled out a warped and blackened cassette. "Heat kind of got to it, but the audio boys got most of the recording onto another cartridge."

Wes started the cassette player on his desk.

**Dr. Dryden. This is your final . . . of instructions. . . . You are . . . surrender . . . de Armas . . . this coming . . . weapons . . . the foolishness of last time . . . be tolerated. . . . make very sure . . . are alone . . . follow . . . to the letter. . . .**

"Does he mean the Plaza de Armas?" Lee asked.

"Shh!" Wes said. "There's more."

The scratchy tape wound on for a few more seconds. Then Jake felt his heart tighten again as he heard Anne's voice.

> **Daddy . . . listen to them. . . . mean it this time. . . . Daddy, please help me. . . .**

Anne sounded tired and tense. Joel's fist hit the desk with a frustrated thump.

> **Do what they tell you . . . want to come home. . . . I miss Momma . . . want to . . . my first graders . . . and Lee. . . .**

Lee buried her face in her hands. Jake walked over and rested his hands on her shoulders.

> **see Maine . . . visit . . . friends . . . old Mr. Gerizim . . . his young son Ebal . . . I'm scared, Daddy . . . I want to come home.**

The tape cut off.

"She sounds worse than the first time," Cathy observed.

"I'm afraid I have to agree with you," Joel said. "Even if we discount the damage to the tape, what she said still doesn't make much sense."

"How so?" Wes asked.

"We don't have any friends named Gerizim."

"Think she's trying to tell us something again?" Cathy wondered.

"If so," Joel replied, "this time I haven't a clue what it might be."

They replayed Anne's portion of the tape, to no avail.

"What now?" Wes asked. "Once they find out that their courier's dead," Joel replied, "they'll send another tape. That gives us a day or two before they impose another deadline."

Joel thought for a moment, then looked at Wes. "Where did the flight originate?"

"Cuzco."

"Then, while you wait here for the replacement tape, we go to Cuzco. And while they're waiting for us to come to them, we go hunting."

# 61

Jake's head rested in the crook of Anne's arm as he slept. She could not see him in the darkness, but she could feel the weight of him. He moved slightly.

Undoubtedly, she imagined, roused by adventurous dreams. As he moved, his hair tickled the inside of her elbow. Anne ran her fingertips gently over his head. She smiled as she felt him stir. Stirred as well, Anne reached out to pull Jake to her. She frowned as she felt him pull away. Determined to satisfy the longing kindled within her by his touch, Anne reached out again and placed her hand upon him.

Anne awoke with a shriek as the dry, scaly rat's tail slithered away between her fingers.

It was deep night in the cell, and she was alone. She trembled now with despair instead of desire. Anne sat up, miserable, and wrapped the fog-dampened blankets of her bedding around her shoulders. She reached to where she had left Celia's Bible, but it had been tossed aside when she sat up and her fingers closed on nothing. Rocking slowly back and forth, Anne began to cry.

Jake filled her mind. His smile, his habit of smoothing his

hair with his hands, how his eyes clouded when he was angry with her. Each part of him that she thought of set into resonance something within her until she was aching with her need for him. Anne's breath came in long, ragged gasps as if Jake's absence was a vacuum around her.

"Don't take him away from me," she pleaded. "Please, God, please don't take him away!"

*How can that which has not been given be taken away?* a voice within her asked.

"But he has been given!" Anne said. "He's mine!"

A voice, tolerant, kind, and infinitely patient welled up within her. *No, my child,* the voice said. *He, like you, is mine. And that is where you are mistaken. Because he is mine, he is mine alone to give. And I have not given; you have taken. I have not bestowed; you have possessed. Where there is nothing that has been granted, there is nothing that may be received.*

"Nothing?" Anne demanded. "Nothing? What about love? I've waited all my life to be loved by a man like him, and you say that there is nothing?"

Anne's fingernails cut into her palms with the force of her rage. *Would you take that which has not been given?*

"*Yes!*"

*You would then choose desire, and need, and a clutching in the night to satisfy that desire and placate that need. You would choose that which you call "love."*

Anne shuddered and wrapped herself in the blanket more tightly.

*Do you remember what you read from my Word tonight?* the voice within her asked.

Anne nodded numbly.

*Then you know what you would turn away from. You know what would be denied you. You know what would not be yours, because it must be granted as well as chosen. You would deny yourself righ-*

*teousness, fellowship, harmony, and agreement. You would join your bodies, but not your spirits. You would know satiation, but not love.*

*For if you choose that which I do not give, you choose unrighteousness. And without righteousness there can be no fellowship, no growing and learning and working together. And without fellowship there can be no harmony, no accord and rest and peace. And without harmony there can be no agreement, no unity of faith and purpose and devotion to me.*

*And without devotion to me, there is no love.*

Anne felt herself gathered into the arms of her Father.

*I know that you have long waited to be loved. You know that I loved you long before he ever did.*

Anne's sorrow at having grieved her Comforter overflowed, and she wept anew.

*Do you love me?*

"Yes, Lord."

*Then sleep, my child, sleep. I am fellowship. I am harmony. I am righteousness. I am love.*

# 62

"I can't stand it anymore!" Lee's fork clattered as she flung it into the roaring fireplace in the dining room of the Hotel Urubamba.

Three days had passed since Joel, Cathy, Lee, and Jake had arrived in the Cuzco area. Wes had not called from Lima, and Joel had made no progress on Anne's mysterious message.

The waiter standing across the room looked up, then rushed over to them. "Something is wrong, señorita?" he asked as he set a new fork on the table.

Lee blushed. "No," she assured him. "Everything's fine."

"It's all right, honey," Joel said quietly. "We understand." Joel swallowed the last of his *maté de coca*, the green tea made from the leaves of the coca plant. *What*, he thought, *would be the best thing to take Lee's mind off Anne?* Then he grinned to himself. *But, of course.*

"It's Sunday morning, Lee. Market day here in Pisac. And the market here is the best around." Lee brightened, then her shoulders slumped.

"It wouldn't be any fun without Annie."

"C'mon, Lee," Cathy said, picking up her cue from Joel. "I know that I'd sure like to get outside for a while."

"OK," Lee agreed. "You talked me into it."

"Didn't take much," Joel teased.

"But Uncle Joel," Lee asked, "where's the market?"

"You won't be able to miss it. Trust me."

"Be back in an hour," Lee said. She rose and headed toward the lobby.

Joel winked at Cathy. "Thanks. Keep an eye on her, will you?"

Cathy nodded.

"I understand how Lee feels," Jake said after the two had left. "It is getting to be a bit much." He looked at Joel. "How do you stay so calm while the rest of us are falling apart?"

"Please," Joel replied seriously, "allow me the privilege of falling apart, too." He wiped his mouth with his napkin. "You must admit that of all of us, I'm the one most entitled to be scared."

Joel looked out at the clouds as they lifted from the Urubamba valley. "I've seen their kind before. I know what they're capable of doing, and they've got my little girl."

A burning knot exploded and showered sparks across the hearth. Jake watched the embers scattered across the flagstones wink out one by one as he waited for Joel to continue.

"It's my choice," Joel said at last. "It's our choice. There are only two things you can do with fear: give in to it or give it away." He leaned his elbows on the table. "Despite what you hear, fear can't be conquered or overcome. It can be ignored, or suppressed, or called something that it isn't. But, on our own, it cannot be vanquished."

Jake once more remembered Alex's favorite psalm. "But the Bible tells us to fear no evil."

"So it does," Joel agreed. "And why does David say that he will fear no evil?"

"'Because you are with me,'" Jake quoted.

Joel looked at Jake and nodded. "That's the heart of it. David could give his fear away because he knew who was with him. He knew that he was not alone."

Anne's and Alex's words filled Jake's mind.

"David knew that he could give his fear to the one who had already defeated it. The only one who has defeated it."

The rain-glossed cobblestone street outside shone as the sun broke through the clouds. "Look through the Bible; some people gave in to their fear, and some gave it away. Some people quit, and some persevered."

Jake shook his fists helplessly. "But we're not persevering! We're not doing anything!"

"Ah," Joel said with a smile, "but we are. We're waiting, being still, which is the toughest, most frustrating, and least endurable form of perseverance there is." Joel smiled again at Jake's exasperated grimace. "I share your feeling."

He laid his hand on Jake's arm. "If it's any consolation, I can promise you that when God's ready for us to do something, we'll know it."

"Wow!" Cathy exclaimed as they walked across the Plaza de Armas.

What had been no more than an expanse of gray stone yesterday was now a swirl of rain-brightened colors. Since before dawn the *campesinos*, the Indian peasants who eked out an existence by working the land, had been streaming out of their mountain homes and into the plaza. Tattered, intricately woven blankets had been spread out in uneven rows and heaped with the week's produce. Rickety wooden stands piled high with everything from curios to kitchen utensils had sprung up like mushrooms.

Imploring cries of "Miran, señoritas!" reached Cathy and Lee from the vendors whose stalls lined the plaza. Groups of Quechua women gossiped together and haggled over shining mounds of peppers and onions.

Incongruously, a woman dressed in expensive Western clothes and high leather boots was kneeling on a blanket, sorting through a pile of *granadilla*, the passion fruit that grows in profusion on the upper slopes of the Urubamba valley. The woman glanced at them, then watched intently as Cathy and Lee made their way between two rows of blankets.

Lee and Cathy strolled past a blind, rail-thin beggar who was sprawled on the cathedral steps. Despite the cold, he was dressed in nothing but sandals, ragged shorts, and a dirty sleeveless shirt.

Lee fished a dollar out of her pocket and put it in his cup. "Gracias, señorita!" the old, grizzled man said.

"But, how did you know that I was a señorita?" Lee asked.

The man's smile was wide and toothless. "Ah," he said. "When the good Lord saw fit to take away my sight, he also saw fit to bless my hearing. I can't appreciate the beauty in your face, but I can appreciate the beauty in your walk." He grinned right at the embarrassed Lee. "And only señoritas walk the way you do."

Lee's cheeks burned as they walked away. The beggar's cheerful laugh trailed after them.

"So what's wrong with *my* walk?" Cathy asked.

"Nothing," Lee replied gently, "much."

"What? Like what am I doing wrong?"

"Well," Lee teased, "maybe all your military training has interfered with your proper development."

"Oh, great," Cathy said.

"Let me show you. Just watch." Lee walked ten yards and turned back to Cathy. "Like this."

Lee continued her demonstration, not watching where she was going. Suddenly a stream of water showered down upon her head.

Lee screamed.

Cathy couldn't help but laugh as Lee jumped out from under the cold shower. A small girl, holding a long pole, stood innocently. Her little eyes grew wide at the sight of the tall, blonde woman who loomed over her.

A woman rushed over and swatted the child, who started to cry. "I am very sorry, señorita," the horrified woman said. "It is Rosita's job to poke the awning to keep the rain from collecting." The woman pointed at the baggy, blue tarp sagging from a puddle of rainwater. "I promise you that she will be punished when we return home."

"No. Please don't," Lee replied. She knelt, rummaged around in her knapsack, and pulled out a sucker. Lee looked at Rosita's mother and received a grateful nod of permission. She held the sucker out to the little girl, who edged cautiously toward Lee. Rosita looked at her mother, then took the candy.

The little girl stepped back and stuffed the still-wrapped sucker into her mouth. "Oh, you poor sweetheart," Lee said compassionately. "Here, let me help." Lee reached out for the sucker.

Rosita frowned fearfully, then surrendered the sucker after her mother spoke to her soothingly.

Lee unwrapped the sucker and gave it back.

As Rosita stuck the sucker back into her mouth her face lit up.

Lee stroked Rosita's hair. "Jesús te ama," she told the little girl. The white stick of the sucker bobbed slowly up and down as Rosita nodded solemnly. Lee kissed Rosita on the forehead, then rose and said goodbye to her mother. From a nearby stall, the woman in the high leather boots pretended to sort through a pile of knives as she watched them walk away.

"Señorita, thank you," Rosita's mother said. "I am so sorry."

"All is well," Lee said, and she and Cathy walked on.

"What did you tell that little girl just before we left?" Cathy asked as they watched a farmer unload a sack of canary-yellow potatoes.

"Jesús te ama," Lee replied. She picked up an errant potato and tossed it back to the farmer.

"What's that mean?"

"It means 'Jesus loves you.'"

Cathy frowned skeptically. "Do you think she believes that?"

"I'm sure of it."

"But, how could she believe in God? They have so little!"

"I think," Lee said, "when you're that poor, all you have is Jesus."

# 63

"Greg will love it," Lee promised as she held the sweater up.

Cathy had relented as they walked back to the hotel, and Lee had helped her buy sweaters for Greg and herself. "Isn't it a little, well, loud?" Cathy asked as she looked at the sweater they had picked out for Greg. It was blue, with a bright-yellow Inca design on the front.

Lee shook her head. "Greg sounds like one of those professor types who can use a little waking up. And besides," she added with a smile, "if he doesn't like it, you can always wear it."

Cathy laughed. She had to admit that it would go well with her red skirt.

A small woman approached them as they neared the hotel. She looked around nervously, then walked quickly up to them. "Are you American?" she asked.

Cathy looked the woman over. *Too well dressed*, she decided, *to be a beggar.*

"No change money," Cathy said gruffly, assuming that the woman was one of the moneychangers who thronged the plaza. She started to push past the woman.

"Please," the woman beseeched them. "I must speak to an American." She glanced around again, more nervous than before.

"We're American," Lee replied, ignoring Cathy's disapproving frown.

"We must talk, someplace where we cannot be observed."

"No way," Cathy said firmly. "Absolutely no way. You want to talk, you do it right here."

"Please," the woman begged. "If they see me talking to you."

"If who sees you talking to us?" Cathy wanted to know.

"It is very important, and there is so little time." The woman seemed desperate.

"What about the hotel?" Lee suggested. "Joel and Jake are there, too."

"OK," Cathy replied reluctantly. "But I don't like this." She unzipped her jacket.

"What is this all about?" Lee asked as they walked toward the hotel.

"Not here," the woman replied. "Once we are in the hotel."

They were on the hotel steps when two men came out of a building several doors away. The woman saw them, began to run away, then stopped and turned. She looked at Cathy and Lee, terror in her eyes. "An American woman," she whispered urgently. "Dryden."

Lee gasped.

"They have her at Intipunku." The woman fled into a row of stalls.

"Wait!" both Lee and Cathy called after her.

"Quick!" Cathy said. "Get Joel and Jake. I'll try to find her."

Lee, with the men in tow, burst out through the front door of the hotel. Lee looked around the plaza wildly, but neither Cathy nor the well-dressed woman was in sight. "Calm down, honey," Joel said gently, "and tell us what happened."

Between deep breaths Lee explained to them what had happened on the way back to the hotel.

"You're sure she was talking about Annie?" Joel asked. Lee nodded.

"She said Dryden."

"Did she say who 'they' were?"

"No."

"And you're sure that she said Intipunku?"

"That's what it sounded like."

Joel shook his head. "Don't know what that refers to."

Just then Cathy returned, alone and disgusted. "Thought I saw her once," Cathy said, "but she lost me. Obviously she knows these streets better than I do."

"Now what? is becoming the operative question around here," Joel observed glumly. They had gathered in the hotel bar to evaluate their situation. "You're sure," Joel asked, "that she didn't say Inti Raymi?"

Both Lee and Cathy nodded. "It wasn't anything close to that," Cathy said.

"What's an Inti Raymi?" Jake asked.

"It's a festival held around here about this time each year," Joel answered. "Out at the ruined Inca fortress of Sacsayhuaman. Big tourist draw."

"The fortress of what?" Lee exclaimed.

Joel smiled. "Sack-sigh-WHA-man. Not 'sexy woman.'"

"Big tourist attraction doesn't sound like a likely place for them to be keeping Anne," Jake observed.

"I agree," Joel said. "So we're back to square one."

"Joel," Cathy said after the fire had popped and crackled for a while, "if Anne's trying to tell us something in her tape, could Intipunku have something to do with it?" She shrugged. "I mean, *Gerizim* is as crazy a word as *Intipunku.*"

"Maybe," Joel agreed. "But I have no idea how. I've never heard of Intipunku."

"Well, then, let's sic Wes on it," Cathy suggested.

Joel jabbed a finger at her. "Excellent idea! And," he added, "since you both thought of it and were on the scene, why don't you call him?"

It was after eleven that night before Joel got off the phone. A long talk with Wes had been followed by a shorter one with Pat. One had been intellectually draining, the other emotionally. Joel hung up and lay back with a groan of exhaustion.

From where he lay stretched out on his bed, Jake looked at Joel with concern. *Past few days have been hard on him*, Jake thought, *and it doesn't help that Joel's been hard on himself over not being able to unravel that Gerizim puzzle of Annie's.* It seemed to Jake that Joel had aged.

"How's Pat?" Jake asked.

"Hanging together. Worried sick, but doing all right," Joel replied as he massaged his temples. "Women are tough, Jake. When the going gets rough, they keep us from coming apart at the seams."

Joel stopped rubbing his head and looked at his fingertips. "You know, this doesn't feel near as good as when Pat does it."

"Must be her medical degree that makes the difference."

"Undoubtedly."

"You know how I'm reading the whole Bible from start to finish?"

"Big job."

"Well, I just read something that I think you ought to hear."

"If you're going to serenade me with the Song of Solomon, I don't want to hear it."

"I haven't read the Song of Solomon," Jake said seriously. "Should I?"

"For you, Jake," Joel said with a laugh, "I'm not sure that's such a good idea."

"OK, that'll be the next on my list."

"So what's up?"

"I'm reading Deuteronomy, and I got to a place that has some names that sound like the ones that Annie mentioned."

Joel quickly sat up.

"Where?"

"Chapter twenty-seven, starting at verse twelve."

# 64

"Anything from Wes?" Joel asked as they assembled for breakfast the next morning.

"Not yet," Cathy replied. "But he promised that he'd have the cultural affairs folks on it first thing this morning."

Their breakfast arrived, and they joined hands for grace. Afterwards, Cathy was surprised to find that she didn't mind giving thanks nearly as much as she had at first.

"Jake came up with something interesting last night," Joel mumbled through a mouthful of biscuit. "He was reading in Deuteronomy, and he found those names that Annie mentions."

"Deuteronomy. That's in the Bible, right?" Cathy asked.

Lee nodded. "Old Testament. I don't read it much," she added. "Too many laws and curses and things." Lee wrinkled her nose.

"Funny that you should mention curses, Lee," Joel interjected, "because that's just what went on at Gerizim and Ebal. That's where Moses pronounced the blessings and curses. It's real Old Testament stuff," Joel said with a grin. "After he blesses the Israelites, Moses tells them that if they disobey God, 'the

Lord will strike you with wasting disease, with fever and inflammation, with scorching heat and drought, with blight and mildew, which will plague you until you perish.'"

Lee made a face. "See why I don't read the Old Testament much?" she said to Cathy. "All law—no love."

"But," Joel went on with a frown, "try as I might, I don't seem able to figure out what Annie might be trying to tell us by talking about blessings and curses."

"Uncle Joel," Lee said tentatively, "are you sure that's what Annie's talking about?"

"No," Joel said with a shrug. "Got any ideas?"

"Well," Lee began, "I just remembered where I've heard those names before. It was back in VBS, the summer before ninth grade."

"VBS?" Cathy asked.

"Vacation Bible school," Lee told Cathy. "It was so exciting." Lee smiled. "I was madly in love with David Linamen at the time, and Annie and I were in the same class with him—"

"Lee?" Joel interrupted. "Could we get on with the blessings and curses?"

"Sorry."

"It's OK."

"Anyway, one day Dr. and Mrs. Wilkes, the teachers, took us out to a little ravine behind the church. Just like in the Bible, half of us stood on one side of the ravine and pretended that it was Mount Gerizim, and the other half stood on the other side and pretended that it was Mount Ebal. I stood right next to David Linamen."

Joel gave her a look.

"Anyway," Lee quickly continued, "the Wilkeses had us start shouting the blessings and curses at each other. We shouted so loud that the neighbors came out to see what was wrong." Lee smiled at the memory. "There we were, standing on those two 'mountains'—"

"What did you say?"

All heads turned to look at Joel, who was staring at Lee. Lee swallowed, unnerved by Joel's outburst.

"Well, I just was saying that we were shouting blessings and curses at each other from our two mountains, and—"

Silverware fell to the floor as Joel jumped up. "That's it!" Joel looked at Lee. "Emily Parker, you are a genius!"

Astonished, Lee could only stare back at Joel.

"What did she do?" Cathy filled in for the stunned Lee.

Joel sat back down and patted Lee's hand. "I was getting too theological," he explained. "I should have looked at it from Annie's perspective instead of mine. Annie's certainly not an Old Testament scholar, and she basically has no more interest in Deuteronomy than Lee has. OK, maybe a little, but," Joel added excitedly, "she is a teacher. And what would a teacher remember more than a particularly vivid lesson? Something caused Annie to remember a lesson that focused around two mountains."

Joel leaned back in his chair and grinned at them.

"Well?" Cathy demanded.

"When it comes to word puzzles," Joel explained, "Annie's her mother's daughter. This one is a humdinger." Joel leaned forward, and four heads made a conspiratorial circle around the breakfast table.

"Remember that odd reference to 'old Mr. Gerizim and his young son Ebal'?"

Everyone nodded.

"Well, try this: old Mount Gerizim and young Mount Ebal." Now very much the professor, Joel looked at them and waited.

Exasperated, Jake threw up his hands. "So?"

Joel leaned back again. "I know where they've got Annie. There's only one place in Peru," he said, quite serious now, "with an 'old' mountain and a 'young' mountain."

He was rewarded with three blank faces.

"They're Inca names," Joel explained. "'Young Mountain' is the translation of 'Huayna Picchu,' and 'Old Mountain' translates to . . ."

"What?" three voices demanded to know.

"'Machu Picchu.'"

# 65

"Joel, you need to come back to Lima."

"Now, wait a minute, Wes," Joel replied testily. "I'm kind of busy here."

"There's someone here who I think might know where Anne is."

"We do know where she is," Joel replied. "Machu Picchu."

"Huh?" Wes blurted. "How do you figure that?"

Joel explained their joint deciphering of Anne's hidden message.

"Never would've figured that one out myself," Wes admitted. "But it's reassuring to know," he added, "that even the legendary Dr. Dryden needs help occasionally."

"But what Anne's message has to do with Intipunku," Joel admitted, "I simply don't know. She claims to be at Machu Picchu, but Machu Picchu's the busiest tourist site in Peru. Unless they've got her locked up in the tourist hotel there, I have no idea where she might be." Wes heard Joel's exasperated huff.

"So why do I have to come back to Lima?" Joel asked.

"Because there's someone here who knows about Intipunku, but he'll only talk about it to you."

"Someone who knows about Intipunku?" Joel said intently.

"Put him on the line."

"He'll only talk to you in person." Joel thought that Wes sounded even more annoyed than the scratchy connection usually made him sound.

Joel suppressed his anxious frustration. "What's going on?" he asked patiently.

Wes sighed. "First thing this morning, I told the cultural affairs people here about Intipunku. When they came up empty, I called a friend of mine in the anthro department over at the American University. When I asked him about it, he got real funny and said he'd call me back."

"Has he called back?"

"No," Wes said slowly. "But his boss has. The department head. He was practically foaming at the mouth wondering how I knew this secret word. When I told him that someone had whispered it to an American tourist in Cuzco, he came absolutely unglued."

"His name's Ochoa, right?" Joel asked. "Professor Melchior Ochoa?"

"Joel," Wes said, his amazement clear even over the static, "do you know everything?"

"Not hardly," Joel responded. "Still don't know how to keep Pat from buying so many shoes."

"I know what you mean," Wes agreed. "With Kathy, it's hats."

"Anyway," Wes went on, "this Ochoa character calmed down a lot when I mentioned your name. I didn't want to get you involved," he added apologetically, "but when Ochoa kept insisting on knowing just who wanted to know, I got kind of steamed. In any event, he said that he'd explain Intipunku to you, and only you, and only in person."

"Joel! It is so good to see you again!" The portly, middle-aged man came around from behind his desk and embraced Joel warmly. Professor Melchior Ochoa then looked at Wes sharply, as if noticing him for the first time.

Joel followed his glance. "Mel, may I present Mr. Wesley Pearson of the U.S. Foreign Service. I'll vouch for him."

Ochoa's "office" was in the center of what appeared to be an old warehouse. The office had no door or ceiling, and its walls were bookshelves and furniture arranged in a rough rectangle. Through gaps in this perimeter, glowing desk lamps could be seen. Dark and cavernous, with the only light coming from lights set into the high ceiling, the converted building had become a labyrinth of passages that connected these cubbyholes.

At Ochoa's gestured invitation, Joel and Wes sat down.

"As you know, Mel, I need information about Intipunku. What is it?" Joel asked.

Ochoa unlocked one of the ancient oak file cabinets that formed the wall of his office and pulled out a thick folder. The professor took a deep breath, then reached into the folder. "Only for you, my old friend," he said to Joel, "would I do this. Intipunku is the greatest archeological find in Peru's history. An intact, unlooted Inca outpost."

Both men nodded with appreciative surprise.

"But the most amazing thing about it is its location." He spread a map out on his desk. "It is here," he said, pointing to a spot on the map. "Only seven kilometers from Machu Picchu."

Joel tensed. That explained the clue in Annie's message. He stared at the map, then at Ochoa. "Tell me about what's going on there." The director reached into the folder again.

"I don't believe it!" Wes said as he looked at the photos Ochoa had handed to them. "This is incredible!"

"Now, gentlemen," Ochoa replied, "you can see why secrecy is of paramount importance. If word got out that an unlooted Inca site had been found, with all of its gold intact . . . "

"Look at it all!" Wes enthused, still poring over the photographs. He held one up. "What's this?"

"That," Ochoa replied, "is a tumi. The ceremonial wand carried by the Inca himself. It alone is three kilos of solid gold."

Joel, oblivious to the riches spread before him, studied the map. *This isn't making any sense.* "The site isn't more than thirty meters from the Inca Trail," he observed. "How do you keep away all the tourists hiking up to Machu Picchu?" *And how do you hold someone prisoner in a place that's visited as much as a rest stop on the way to Disneyland?*

"We don't try to keep them away," Ochoa replied, smiling. "Dr. Luis Ramirez, the man who first reported the find and is now the dig's director, has come up with a brilliant scheme. The part of the site nearest the trail was excavated, quickly and mostly at night, and the gold removed. So, when tourists show up, they are shown little more than carved stone. Most of them are in a hurry to get to Machu Picchu and don't stay long. The real work continues, undercover and undisturbed."

Joel frowned. *I wonder just what it is that's going on "undercover and undisturbed?"*

"How do you maintain secrecy among the dig personnel?" Wes asked.

"A good question, Mr. Pearson," Ochoa replied. "Again, it is Ramirez's responsibility. He insisted on a free hand in selecting the site personnel, and I agreed completely."

"Tell me about this Ramirez," Joel queried.

"Ramirez is a brilliant man with impeccable credentials." The director smiled slyly. "I consider my luring of him away

from Ayacucho University to be a coup of the first magnitude."
Ochoa rummaged around in the folder. "There is a photo of
him in here somewhere. . . . Ah, here it is."

He handed the glossy print to Wes, who glanced at it and
passed it on to Joel.

"I'll be!"

The other two men watched as all the color drained from
Joel's face.

"What is it?" Ochoa asked.

"Never mind. I'll explain later." Joel came to his feet. "Let's
go," he barked at Wes. "I've got to be on the afternoon flight."

Joel drummed his fingers nervously on the armrest as Wes
fought the afternoon traffic along Avenida Elmer Faucett on
the way to the airport.

"What's up?" Wes asked, his eyes never leaving the snarl
of cars. "What didn't you want to tell Ochoa?" He swore as he
swerved to miss a man pushing a handcart loaded with plumb-
er's helpers.

"I recognized the dig's director," Joel said, his mouth tight.
"His name isn't Ramirez, it's Rafael Cienfuegos. When I last
tangled with him, he was a rising star in the Sendero."

Wes swore again. "That the business you had to leave Peru
over?" he asked.

"The very same." Joel smiled grimly. "Mel's going to have
a stroke when he finds out that his big find is a fake."

"What can I do to help?" Wes asked.

"Find out everything you can about this 'Professor
Ramirez' and stay by the phone. When we need the cavalry,
we'll need it fast."

"You got it," Wes promised.

Joel's face hardened. "I thought he was dead."

"Maybe this time," Wes said quietly, "he will be."

# 66

On the ride back to the hotel, Joel told them what he had found out from Ochoa.

"This was waiting for us when we got back from dropping you off at the airport," Jake told Joel. "I left my Bible in the dining room, and someone stuck this in it."

"It didn't make much sense to us," Cathy added. "But now, combined with what you found out in Lima, it's starting to add up."

Joel looked at the map that Jake handed him. It was titled:

**Intipunku Archeological Site**
**Department of Antiquities**
**American University of Peru**

The map showed the outlines of a dozen buildings. Half were labeled with their apparent purpose, the others were merely marked Work in Progress—No Admittance. One of these was circled.

"Looks like your friend worked up the nerve to come

back," Joel commented. "If 'circle marks the spot,' then Annie's right here." Joel jabbed at the marked building.

They gathered in the hotel lounge. Joel spread out a South American Explorer's Club map of the Inca Trail on a table.

"Here's Intipunku," he began. "It's about an eighteen-mile walk from the trail head. It's steep, rough, and, most important, high. This pass, here, is at fourteen thousand feet. Not much air up there. Now," Joel went on. "Here's what we're going to do. . . ."

Under the pretense of bringing Anne her supper, Celia edged nervously into the cell. "I cannot stay," she whispered. "If the Puka Inti finds out that I'm here . . . "

Anne nodded her understanding. At the sight of the yellowed bruises that mottled Celia's face Anne's detestation of the man flared anew. Celia set down the tray.

"I have told others that you are here," she whispered.

"Who?" Anne asked eagerly.

"Two women," Celia answered.

"They were shopping in the Pisac market yesterday. One was tall and obviously norteamericano, but the other . . . " Celia's eyes clouded with worry. "Her friend said that she was American, but she might have been a Japanese Peruvian. If I have told the wrong people . . . "

"What did they say?" Anne demanded, heedless of Celia's concern.

"I had to leave before I could give them more than your name," Celia confessed bleakly. "My guards came out of the cantina. But later, when I paid for some purchases, I found in my purse a copy of the map that they give to the tourists who pass by on the Inca Trail."

Anne nodded encouragingly.

"I told my guards that I was going to use the bathroom in

the hotel. Then I went into the dining room, but did not see the women." Celia gestured helplessly. "On one of the tables was a Bible with a man's name written inside. An American name. All I had time to do was slip the map into the Bible." Celia looked away. "I am sorry Anne. I tried."

Anne took Celia's hand in hers. "Thanks for trying," she said gently. "I appreciate it very much."

Celia shrugged. "He will probably just throw it away. The paper will mean nothing to this Mr. Jake."

Anne's hand tightened on hers.

Worried, Celia asked, "What is the matter?"

Anne's eyes widened in excited relief. *They're looking for me! They got this far!* Anne shouted to herself. *But how does Jake know that I'm here? Does that mean that Daddy's here, too,* she wondered, *or is Jake here by himself?* Uncertainty mingled with the anticipation in her eyes. *He said that he'd come back for me.* She pressed her hands to her cheeks and looked up out the cell window. Within her, need and hope fused. *It must mean that he cares for me. And, if he has a Bible . . .*

"You know this man?" Celia asked hopefully.

Anne's eyes met hers, and Celia recognized what she saw in them.

# 67

Jake paused and used his sleeve to wipe the sweat from his face. "Hey, point," he called out to Cathy. "You sure you know where we are?"

Cathy looked back at Jake. For the last twenty minutes of hiking she had been in the lead, acting as the "point."

The Inca Trail was well marked, so no pathfinding was really necessary. Nonetheless they had quickly fallen back into the habit, ingrained in them during their years in the military, of taking turns at the dangerous position of first in line.

Cathy sauntered back to where Jake was standing. "The army's lost," she sighed in mock resignation. "As usual."

They shed their packs and sat on them as Cathy spread out Joel's map on her knees.

"OK, soldier, one more time. We got off the morning train to Machu Picchu here, at Aguas Calientes. Joel's friends in the electric company brought us across the company's land over to the trail here, near the Huinay Huayna ruins. We're working our way due north toward Intipunku. Once there, we act like typical, nosy, gringo tourists while we reconnoiter."

"Check," Jake replied. He picked up where Cathy had left

off. "After we disembarked, Joel stayed on the train and got off at Machu Picchu. He's going to work his way down to Intipunku from the other end of the trail. He'll do the overall surveillance while we check out the details."

Jake looked at his watch. "If we're going to hit Intipunku by three, we'd better hustle." They shouldered their packs.

Unlike the other hikers they had waved to on the trail, their packs were loaded not with tents and sleeping bags, but with the fruit of a long discussion between Joel and Wes. A box for them had arrived air express, and from it they had filled their packs with binoculars, night-vision goggles, and tiny headset radios.

"Where'd Wes get all this stuff?" Jake had asked as they unloaded the box.

"From the marines at the embassy," Cathy had replied. "This is nothing," she added. "You should see what they've got in the basement in Tel Aviv. They told me that they'd had a tank down there once, but they had to give it back."

Two hours later Jake and Cathy lay in the shade on a hill overlooking Intipunku. The site was rectangular, with three sides lined with buildings and the fourth formed by the Urubamba River. The buildings along the far side of the compound had been restored, while those that ran down to the river at each end were, with one exception, still roofless and covered with vines.

"I'd hate to have to assault this place," Cathy whispered.

"No kidding," Jake agreed. "You've got all that open territory in the compound to cross, and if they cut you off, your only fallback is into the river." Jake looked over at Cathy, his eyes filled with the need for action.

Cathy had seen him pull Celia's map out of his pack and note the building that held Anne. "Calm down, soldier," she cautioned. "We're not going to blow 'em up, we're going to follow Joel's plan and outsmart 'em." She grinned at Jake's expression. "You still want in?"

"What?" Jake exclaimed. "You think that I'm going to stay behind and miss the chance to see a plan thought up by a marine fool anyone except another jarhead? Not on your life."

They swept the site with their binoculars.

"Not much to look at," Cathy said. "Two guys taking a siesta is about it."

Jake looked at his watch. It was just three. He fished his radio out from his pack. It slipped onto his head like earphones. "Aaron to Moses, Aaron to Moses," he said softly into the voice-activated microphone. "How do you read?"

Joel was "Moses," Jake was "Aaron," and Cathy was "Miriam."

Cathy didn't understand the call signs but figured that she didn't need to. She attributed Joel's and Jake's chuckling delight at having come up with them to the simple fact that it was the sort of thing that really amused men.

"Moses to Aaron," Joel replied. "Read you five-by-five. Where are you?"

"On a hill a hundred meters northwest of the objective."

"How's it look?" Joel asked.

"Almost deserted. We've only seen two hostiles so far, and they're asleep."

"Not surprising. Remember that the festival of Inti Raymi is going on at Sacsayhuaman. It's sort of the Peruvian equivalent of Mardi Gras, and I doubt that even Cienfuegos could keep his men away from the fleshpots of Cuzco while it's in full swing."

"Where are you?" Jake asked.

"Still about three klicks away. Had to wait for a bus up from the train station to Machu Picchu. Inti Raymi has made the place a little crowded."

"OK," Jake replied. "We'll do our tourist bit and report first chance we get."

"Roger. I'll be in position by then. Out."

Jake took off the radio and stowed it in his pack. "Joel got a late start," he told the wondering Cathy. "He's still about two miles away. We're going to do our tourist routine while he gets into position." Jake stood and hoisted his pack onto his shoulders. He looked at Cathy. "OK, buddy, it's showtime."

The sleeping guards roused themselves quickly as Cathy and Jake walked into the compound. "Vaya!" the guards shouted. "No pueden acampar aqui!"

Jake continued to walk toward them, a big smile on his face. "Hi, amigos!" he said amiably. "What's going on around here?"

"Go!" one of the men replied. "No camp here!"

"No camp," Jake agreed. "Look around? Inca buildings?"

"No. Leave now."

"Look, amigos," Jake said with a jerk of his head toward Cathy, "the muchacha is tired. We rest a minute, OK?"

Cathy tried to look suitably fatigued and slipped her hand into Jake's to complete the ruse. Jake shuddered inwardly at the thought of what Cathy would do to him if she knew that he had just called her a girl.

He leaned toward them and winked. "I got Pisco," he lied.

As the pair argued in whispers among themselves, Jake wondered if God would be willing to turn the water in the bottle in his pack into Pisco. After all, Jake reasoned, Pisco was a kind of brandy, and brandy was made from wine. . . .

Their argument was interrupted by the approach of another man. He was well dressed, slim, and walked with confident authority.

"Excuse me, señor," Jake called out. "But do you speak English?"

"As a matter of fact, I do," the man replied. "How may I be of service?"

"Well," Jake said with a grin, "I was just trying to explain to these guys here that we'd like to rest and look around for a minute, but they think that we want to camp out or something."

The man smiled. "You must forgive them. They are only guards, just doing their job. This is an archaeological site, and we have to be careful. There are so many thieves these days."

"We understand completely. If we could perhaps get some bottled water, we'll be on our way."

*C'mon, God . . .* , Jake prayed.

He looked them over. "You are American?"

Jake shook his head. "Australian." He stuck out his hand. "I'm Jeremiah Melbourne, and this is my friend Molly O'Toole." *Sure hope that he doesn't notice the complete absence of an Aussie accent.*

"We do not often get visitors from so far away," the man said. "I would consider it a pleasure to show you around." He spoke to the guards. They left, clearly disappointed at having missed out on the promised Pisco. The men shook hands. "I am Dr. Luis Ramirez, director of this site."

Cathy felt Jake tense as he realized that he was face to face with Rafael Cienfuegos. She tugged gently downward on his hand as a warning to relax. Cienfuegos's eyes wandered over her. "How nice it must be," he said to Jake, "to have a traveling . . . companion."

Now it was Jake's turn to tug on Cathy's hand.

"Come," Cienfuegos said. "Let us begin our tour at the administration building."

As they started after Cienfuegos, Jake felt Cathy let go of

his hand. A few steps later she grabbed it again, tightly. Jake looked at her. Cathy was staring past him, into the compound.

"What's up?" Jake whispered. He was careful not to follow Cathy's gaze.

"See the person walking between buildings over there?" Cathy asked.

Jake shot a glance in the direction that Cathy was looking, then nodded.

"That's her! The woman at Pisac!"

"You sure?"

"Almost positive. I recognize the boots."

Without breaking stride, the woman gave them a long, measuring look. Then she disappeared into a building.

"She see you?" Jake asked.

"I think so. It looked like," Cathy added, "she was glad to see us."

"That makes sense," Jake replied. "Depending on what side she's on, she's looking forward to watching us either rescue Anne or get fed to the fire ants."

"Fire ants?" Cathy asked.

# 68

"Molly O'Toole, indeed!" Cathy snorted as they followed the trail away from Intipunku. "Do I look like an O'Toole?"

Jake shrugged. "It was all I could think of. If we'd confessed to being Americans, he probably would've shot us on the spot."

They rounded a bend in the trail that put them out of sight of the camp. Jake held up his hand and signaled Cathy to stop. After carefully looking and listening for any pursuers, he reached into his pack and took out the radio. Jake put the radio on and covered it with his bush hat.

"Aaron to Moses," he said softly as they resumed walking.

"Moses here," Joel replied instantly. "It's late. What happened?"

"We were treated to a lecture by your friend Cienfuegos on the rape of Peruvian antiquities by 'greedy foreign plutocrats.'" Jake's tone changed. "He's a nut case."

"So he is," Joel replied. "He's also brilliant, vicious, and incredibly dangerous."

"Where are you?" Jake asked.

"About fifty meters to your right."

"How do you know where we are?" Jake asked.

"I've been watching you since you left Intipunku," Joel replied. "I saw the friendly send-off that Cienfuegos gave you." Joel remembered how he'd had to forcibly quash his desire for a good sniper rifle.

"But, if you can see us—," Jake began.

"Don't worry," Joel assured him. "No one followed you. See the big rock just ahead of you? The one in the middle of the river?"

"Got it."

"Turn into the jungle when you get to it. I'm at the top of the hill."

Jake signed off and repeated to Cathy what Joel had told him.

"Fine couple of scouts we are," she muttered.

The need to be quiet made the climb up the hill to Joel's position all the more difficult. The slope was so steep that Jake's feet were level with Cathy's eyes, and the thick carpet of leaf mold caused their feet to slide out from under them. At one point they both froze as something large and noisy crashed away through the treetops.

Jake slipped. His foot shot backwards, caught Cathy neatly in the forehead, and knocked her down. "Be careful!" she whispered irritably as she wiped sweat and rotten leaves from her face.

"Sorry," Jake apologized. "It's been awhile since I've done this sort of thing." He switched on the headset. "Moses, where are you?"

"Look up," Joel replied. Cathy followed Jake's startled glance up the hill. Twenty meters above them stood Joel, concealed by the undergrowth. "Come up and join me," he told Jake. "That is, if you two water buffaloes are through wallowing around down there."

Jake rose and resumed the climb, glad that Cathy wasn't wearing her radio.

Celia closed the door to the building she had been walking toward. Once it was safely shut behind her, she slumped against it and pressed her hand to her racing heart. Terror and hope had welled up equally within her at the sight of the small, dark-haired woman from the market at Pisac. *She must be American,* Celia reasoned. *She said she was, and she's in the company of a man so clearly norteamericano. But, he could be an American drug dealer and she the Peruvian plaything given to him by the local growers.*

Doubt flooded her anew. It cascaded into panic as she realized that the norteamericano might be trying to curry favor with the Puka Inti by delivering her map to him.

As the desire to flee threatened to consume her, Celia opened the door and began to run. Cienfuegos caught her by the arm before she had descended the steps that led up to the building. He swung her around to face him.

Knowing that she was dead, Celia returned his gaze unwaveringly. His ravenous eyes bored into her for a long moment, and she felt her resolve weaken. "Be ready for me at nine," he said. Then he let go of her arms and walked away. Celia almost staggered with relief. *He doesn't know,* she thought. *Or perhaps he does and, tonight, he will toy with me first. He will use me, then he will kill me and Anne.*

She suddenly thought of something Anne had read to her. Celia had asked, "How is it that you're so calm?"

Anne had smiled and reached for Celia's Bible. "I'm calm," she said, "because I know who is on my side." Anne looked out of the cell window. "When I was a little girl, and there was so much thunder and lightning that I was too scared to even get out of bed and rush into my parents' room, I always tried hard to remember a verse from the Psalms that my mother taught me."

Anne had opened the Bible and read, "'The Lord is with me; I will not be afraid.' It's the same now. The more I take that verse to heart," Anne assured her, "the calmer I become." Anne squeezed Celia's hand. "But there's more. The next verse says, 'What can man do to me?'"

Anne closed the Bible and set it in her lap. She looked at Celia. "What can they do to us?" she asked. "Kill us?" Anne shook her head. "They can't even do that; not really. All they can do is send us home to be with our God."

As Celia watched Cienfuegos walk arrogantly away, the newfound love within her challenged her fear, conquered it, and cast it out. Fear's void was filled with resolve. *No, Rafael,* she thought. *No longer will I serve myself up to you like a plate of sliced cuy. Not tonight. Never again. And since you may not have me, you most certainly cannot have Anne.* Celia turned and strode back toward Anne's cell.

# 69

They waited restlessly until the quarter moon had risen. Its light, when combined with the brilliant, high-altitude starlight, gave their night-vision goggles enough illumination to make the compound look like something out of a cheap video game.

A ghostly green rectangle, the window of a heated building, floated in front of Jake's eyes.

"I have two heat sources," Joel reported.

Jake turned his head slightly and another rectangle appeared, bright against the pale green background.

"Copy," Cathy replied.

She consulted Celia's map. Her goggles caused the lines on the coarsely drawn map to stand out clearly. "Neither source corresponds to either the administration building or to the location marked on the map."

Jake realized that that meant that Anne was being held in an unheated building. The night was already chilly, and Jake vowed that someone would pay for mistreating her.

"OK," Joel said. "Then we've probably got two sleeping areas: one for Cienfuegos, and one for everyone else. Here's what we'll do. Jake, you—" Joel paused, and the two figures stretched out on the hillside on either side of him turned their heads toward him. "Go get Annie," he continued. "Cathy and I will take care of Cienfuegos." *Annie lass,* Joel thought with a trace of sadness, *you're not mine anymore.*

"Which building do we hit, Skipper?" Cathy asked Joel, unconsciously conferring upon him the title given to a respected commanding officer.

"Your call. You were down there."

Cathy tried to remember anything she had seen that might provide a clue as to the location of Cienfuegos's residence. When nothing came to mind, she picked the smaller of the two heated buildings. The larger, she reasoned, was more likely to be a barracks. *Great,* she thought as she pointed out the building to Joel and Jake. *Six years in the marines, and I end up flipping a mental coin.*

"I show five seconds to twenty-one forty-five," Joel was saying. Cathy looked at her watch. The amplified light from the tritium-coated hands glowed brightly.

"Mark!" all three said at the stroke of nine forty-five.

"Any final questions?" Joel asked. Jake and Cathy shook their heads.

*Once a C.O., always a C.O.,* Jake thought with a smile.

"Then, there's one more thing to do." Six hands formed a circle in the dark night of the Andes.

A moment later, Joel clapped Jake on the shoulder. "Move out."

*Never had a C.O. in Nam that prayed,* Jake thought as he crept cautiously down the hillside toward the compound. *Wish I had.*

"Sure moves quietly for an army man," Cathy whispered after Jake had disappeared.

Joel covered the mike of his radio with his hand. "Rangers

are right up there with the very best," he told her. "Go read up sometime about the ranger assault on the cliffs of La Pointe du Hoc on D-day."

The plan called for Jake to take ten minutes to work his way around to the Inca Trail and then down the trail to a point just opposite the circled building. Five minutes after Jake had left, Cathy and Joel would creep down the hillside to the edge of the compound.

Cathy jumped as she felt something crawl onto the back of her hand. She looked down and saw a large black beetle, which stopped and waved its antennae at her. Cathy grimaced and flicked the beetle into the bushes. *There's gonna be enough creepie-crawlies down there*, she thought. *Sure don't need to bring them with us.* Joel touched her arm and jerked his head toward the compound. They moved out.

"Jericho." Jake's signal that he was in position came over their headsets just as they reached the bottom of the hill.

"See anything?" Joel asked.

"Negative," Jake replied. "No sign of anyone moving around."

"Isn't that kind of strange?" Cathy asked. "Wouldn't they have posted sentries or something?"

"It's not all that strange," Joel responded. "This is, after all, supposed to be a scientific party, and guns and eggheads don't mix too well."

*Except in your case*, Cathy thought.

"Also," he continued, "they probably think that it's too dangerous in these mountains at night to risk posting a sentry."

*Great*, Cathy thought. *Now he tells us.* A glint caught the corner of her eye. She turned and saw that Joel had drawn his Colt. Cathy took her Browning Hi-Power out of its holster.

"Go," Joel whispered.

Cathy snapped off the Browning's safety as she rose.

In response to Joel's command, Jake hurried across the compound and into the shadow of an outbuilding. He had found to his annoyance that the goggles did funny things to his depth perception. This caused him to misjudge the distance, and he slammed his bad shoulder into the building wall.

"What's wrong?" Joel asked in response to Jake's stifled curse. "You OK?"

"I'm fine," Jake replied. "Just gotta stop playing the bank shots."

Jake knelt and peeked around the corner of the building. No one in sight. He checked his mental copy of the map. It told him that the circled building was just across the small open space at the far end of the building in whose shadow he now hid. Jake crept along the length of the building and stopped just in front of the small courtyard. The building ahead of him was long and narrow, with a series of doors. *Looks like a jail*, Jake thought. If the map was accurate, Jake figured that Anne was behind the third of those doors.

"Ready," he whispered into the radio.

Joel and Cathy emerged from the cover of the jungle and angled across the compound toward the back of the camp. Both dove to the ground as a bright light appeared in their field of view. Cathy pushed her goggles up onto her forehead and looked toward the light. Off to their right, a shuttered window had been opened. As they watched, a man emptied a washbasin out of the window, then he grabbed the shutter and slammed it behind him.

Their target lay directly ahead of them. It seemed dark to Cathy until she put the goggles back on. Once her vision had readjusted, she could see the outlines of light that marked the closed door and curtained windows. Joel motioned her forward, and they crawled on elbows and knees toward the door.

When they were crouched on either side of the steps that led up to the door, Joel keyed his radio. "Ready," he told Jake.

At Joel's *ready*, Jake ran across the courtyard to the other building.

The doors were patches of blackness in the building's deep shadow. He trailed his hand along the wall as he ran, counting the doors.

At the third door he stopped. Jake cautiously tried the handle. It was locked. He took off the night-vision goggles and put them in his pocket. Then Jake reached into another pocket and took out a small but powerful flashlight. He positioned himself in front of the door, the flashlight in his right hand and his Colt .45 in his left.

"Set," he told Joel and Cathy.

Joel put his lips next to Cathy's ear. "Go low, I'll go high," he whispered.

Cathy nodded.

She crept up the steps and crouched in front of the door.

Joel stood behind her, his Colt at the ready. With her free hand, Cathy tried the doorknob. It turned.

"Set," Joel told Jake. "We go on three." Jake snapped off the Colt's safety. "One . . . two . . ."

Joel's shouted "Three!" was lost in the splintering crash as Jake's booted foot slammed against the door in front of him. Before the door hit the wall behind it, Jake was into the cell. He crouched and spun around, shining the light on all four walls. Then he stood and looked around more slowly.

Except for a heap of bedding in one corner, the cell was empty.

On *Three!* Cathy threw open the door and flung herself flat on the floor of the hut. She could feel Joel crouched behind her and could just see the snout of his Colt over her head. She could also see a pair of scuffed boots in front of her. Cathy looked up to see the owner of the boots staring down at her. He was holding a bowl and ladling something from a rusty iron kettle into it. Behind him was a table full of men. They were all looking at her too.

Cathy didn't need to hear Joel's sharp *Out!* As she scrambled rapidly out the door, she heard the bowl hit the floor. Shouts and the sound of booted feet running reached her before she hit the bottom step. Lights came on in other buildings as Joel and Cathy raced across the compound.

# 70

"Jezebel!"

The danger signal interrupted Jake's search of the cell. Convinced that it was indeed empty, Jake shoved his goggles back down over his eyes, then raced toward Joel and Cathy's objective. He heard gunshots and angled toward the compound. Jake threw himself down behind a low wall that bordered the open area. *Great*, he thought as he reconnoitered. *We're back to "Now what?"*

Two figures came into view, running toward the river. Assuming that they were Cathy and Joel, Jake snapped off a few rounds at the group that was chasing them. This unexpected assault from their flank caused the pursuers to dive to the ground. Jake watched as Joel and Cathy ran across the trail and disappeared into the jungle by the river.

"The marines advance to the rear once again," Jake commented.

"You've got her?" Joel panted.

"No. The cell was empty." Jake heard Joel mutter something.

"Can you meet up with us?" Joel asked. "We'll regroup and try the other building."

"No way," Jake responded immediately. A line of flashlights was bobbing its way across the compound toward him. "The posse just figured out where those shots came from. They're headed this way. I'm going to go back to try the rest of those doors. Maybe I got the wrong one."

"Inadvisable," Cathy cautioned.

"Gotta run," Jake said hurriedly. "Will keep in touch."

"Creep," Cathy muttered as she lay in the thorny darkness near the river. She was furious at herself for having picked the wrong building. She was also furious at Jake for having so casually ignored her advice.

"Jake didn't ignore you," Joel whispered in response to Cathy's imprecation. "He's doing what you and I are going to have to do."

"What's that?"

"Improvise."

Jake ran back toward the jail building. As he rounded a corner, he slammed into someone. The impact knocked them down. Jake threw himself onto the prostrate form and landed astride his prisoner's stomach.

"Look at me," he said gruffly. The face turned toward him, a fuzzy green blob in his goggles. Jake pushed his goggles up onto his forehead. A glance told Jake that he had captured the woman that he and Cathy had seen earlier that day. *Terrific*, he thought. *The cleaning lady.*

"I'm looking for someone," he said in flawless Spanish, "and you're going to help me find her." To emphasize his point he brought his Colt into view.

The woman didn't even glance at the gun. "You are Jake,"

she said coolly, looking Jake right in the eyes. "And I am Celia Reyes. Now, if you'll let me up, I'll take you to Anne."

Jake didn't move. Her response had surprised him, and now he was wary. "Why should I go with you?"

Celia glared up at him.

"How do you know who I am? And how do you know Anne?"

"I know who you are," Celia explained impatiently, "because after I saw you today, I described you to Anne." Celia looked amused. "She's told me about you."

Jake shook his head as he got up and helped Celia to her feet. *They sure never mentioned anything like this in officer's training school,* he thought as he surveyed the petite woman in front of him.

"We must hurry," Celia urged. Jake pulled the goggles back down over his eyes and followed her. *If she's lying,* he reasoned, *I can shoot my way out of anything she can get me into . . . I hope.*

Celia led Jake through a twisting maze of narrow corridors. They stopped, then ducked behind a wall as a group of men rushed past.

"Where now?" Jake asked.

"Anne is over there." Celia pointed to a large hut that stood alone. "It is the guest house."

"Then the map was wrong?" Jake asked. Celia shook her head.

"No, it was correct. I had to move Anne today for her safety. I am sorry that I spoiled your plan."

"Maybe that won't be a problem." Jake spoke into his radio, "Joel, I ran into the woman who gave us the map. She's pointed out Anne's location for me. Where are you?"

"Still by the river, working on our leech collection."

*Oh, Lord,* Cathy thought, *not leeches!*

"Can you get Annie and rendezvous with us?"

"Can Anne and I get to the river?" Jake asked Celia.

"Impossible," Celia replied. "The compound will be full of men by now."

"No way," Jake told Joel. "We've stirred up a nest of fire ants here. We'll just have to hole up and wait for daylight."

"Sounds like the best you can do."

Celia tugged on Jake's sleeve. "There is another way out."

"Hang on," he said. "Tinkerbell here seems to have found another way out of never-never land."

"Just behind the guest house is a tunnel carved by the same people who built this place. It leads through the hill and joins up with the Inca Trail. From there you can get to Machu Picchu. It is covered with a locked grate," Celia replied. "The Puka Inti had it secured against intruders."

"And," Jake asked dryly, "you have the key?"

Celia produced it triumphantly.

*Why not?* Jake thought. *Next come the little green men.*

"I stole it the morning he was gone," Celia explained. "I was going to use it tonight to get away from here with Anne."

"Joel," Jake reported, "Celia does have another way out." He told Joel about the tunnel. "So I'm going to send her to you. I'm also going to give her my headset so that you can vector her in."

"That means that you'll be unable to reach us if you need help," Joel noted. "Sure that's wise?"

"Hey, who wants eavesdroppers if Anne and I are going to stroll along this Inca rendition of Lover's Lane?"

Jake heard a chuckle, but he couldn't tell whose. "Blessings," Jake finished. "Out."

"Blessings," came the reply. "Out."

"Here," Jake said to Celia. "Put this on."

Celia donned the headset. "Now say something." Celia spoke, then smiled at the reply.

"You do what Joel tells you to, OK?"

"As long as he does what I tell him to, as well," Celia replied. "This is my jungle."

She and Jake swapped smiles. "I'll pray for you—and Anne," she told him. "Now go."

*The whole thing could be a setup, Mac,* Jake reminded himself as he trotted down the narrow alleyway that ran toward the guest house. *Either it'll be Annie behind that guest house door, or some large hairy type with an AK-47. Lady or the tiger?* He was halfway down the alleyway, high Inca walls on either side, when he heard footsteps behind him.

Suddenly an arm was around his neck. He struggled frantically for air as the choke hold tightened.

Another man appeared in front of him and grabbed his gun arm.

Jake drove his free elbow into the solar plexus of the man behind him. The arm around his neck fell away. His vision cleared and air filled his lungs. Jake pulled hard on his gun arm, and the man who had grabbed him tripped forward. Jake drove the knuckles of his free fist savagely into the man's upper lip. Something crunched, and the man went limp.

The last of three assailants rushed toward Jake. A knife blade glittered menacingly in the moonlight.

Jake sidestepped the charge and caught his attacker a wicked blow in the ribs as he rushed past. The man whirled, grimacing, his face a mask of hatred and pain. The two circled each other, hemmed in by the high walls.

Jake, arms outstretched like a wrestler's, kept his eyes fixed on the center of the man's body. The terrorist, trying to distract Jake, waved the knife in front of him like a venomous fang.

The man charged. Jake was ready. When the point of the knife was inches from his stomach, Jake grabbed the man's wrist, fell backward, planting his feet in the man's solar plexus as he did so. A powerful shove from Jake's legs sent his attacker sailing over him. The man slammed into the hard stone wall behind Jake with a satisfying thud.

Jake came to his knees, wincing as he did so. The impact with the stony ground had strained his shoulder.

Jake looked at the form lying motionless on the ground, then massaged his sore shoulder as he rose unsteadily to his feet. He backed slowly away, keeping his eyes on the man. As Jake began to turn away, he saw a movement out of the corner of his eye. He spun around to see one of the men spring up and race toward him. Jake raised his Colt, then stopped. *The sound of a shot will bring all the rest of them down on me.*

Mouth open, eyes wide, the man charged toward Jake.

Jake waited, his breath now coming in painful gasps, then he pivoted suddenly. He caught the man under the chin with the sole of his boot. The attacker dropped at Jake's feet.

*Hope that's all of them*, Jake thought as he pocketed the man's knife and started toward the guest house. *I'm just about out of impressive karate moves.*

Jake finally reached the guest house. *Celia better have given me the straight stuff,* Jake thought. *I've about had it with surprises for tonight.* He tried the door, which was locked. *At least that's no surprise.* Jake risked a single bullet, which shattered the lock. He kicked the door open, jumped through the doorway, and darted to one side. With his automatic at the ready, Jake played his flashlight over the room.

Anne was backed into a corner, with her arms crossed protectively over herself and defiance in her eyes.

Jake held the light on her, savoring the sight of her and rejoicing that she was unharmed.

"What do you want?" she asked, making it as much of a threat as possible.

"You," Jake replied, with a smile that he knew she couldn't see.

# 71

Celia dashed across the road and into the jungle.

Cathy waited until Celia was almost beside her before she reached up and pulled her down into their cover.

Celia gasped and started to struggle.

"It's all right," Joel assured her over the radio. "We're who you're looking for."

Celia relaxed and sat down.

"Is Anne all right?" Joel asked urgently.

"She is unharmed," Celia replied. "She is very brave."

Joel sighed with relief. *Hallelujah.* "You can take off the radio. You won't need it now that you're with us."

Cathy and Joel took theirs off and stuck them in a jacket pocket. Celia did so as well.

"Now what?" Celia asked. "I want to help."

"You already have," Joel replied. "But we can use you. Without radio contact we've almost no chance of locating Jake and Anne. That doesn't mean, however," he said with a smile, "that we can't help them escape. Here's what we're going to do. . . . "

"Are you sure about this plan of yours, Señor Dryden?" Celia asked when Joel had finished explaining. "It sounds very dangerous."

*And about half-crazy,* Cathy added silently.

"It's the best I can think of," Joel admitted. "Any improvements?"

"How about a hot shower followed by a big bowl of Bittersweet Bonanza?" Cathy suggested.

"Maybe tomorrow," Joel replied, "you can have gallons of it."

He showed Celia his automatic. "Ever use one of these?"

Wide-eyed, Celia shook her head.

Joel removed the ammunition clip from the Colt and dropped it into his pocket. "We'll just have to hope that they don't notice that it's not loaded." He handed the gun to Celia, then took off his goggles. "Better stash these, too," he told Cathy. "The longer we can appear to be harmless, the better. Let's move out."

Never taking his eyes from the doorway, Jake held Anne in his arms. He knew they could afford only a few moments before making their escape.

"I was wondering if you'd find me," Anne said softly.

"I promised you that I would, lady," Jake said. "Are you all right?"

She nodded. "I'm OK."

Jake said a quick prayer of thanks. "I prayed that you would be."

"Celia said that she found a Bible with your name on it." Anne searched Jake's eyes in the dimness for what she prayed she'd find there.

Jake smiled and nodded. After a silence more intimate than any words he could have uttered, he took Anne's fingertips and pressed them to his lips. "That's why I'm here to take you home."

"This is nuts," Cathy hissed as they marched across the compound. "We'll never get away with this."

"Maybe not," Joel admitted. "Frankly, your hot shower idea got my vote, too. But, in any event, we're just about to find out."

Cathy followed Joel's glance.

Three men, rifles leveled, were rushing across the compound toward them.

"Let's hope," Joel whispered, "that they don't shoot first and not bother to ask questions later."

"Who's there?" one of them called as he ran. "Stop, or we shoot."

"Shoot me, Joaquin," Celia answered nonchalantly as she stepped out from behind Joel and Cathy, "and I'm sure that the Puka Inti will have something to say about it."

Joel noted with relief that she remembered to keep his empty Colt pointed at her captives.

The men halted in front of them. Celia regarded them coolly. "After all," she told Joaquin contemptuously, "I know which of us he values more."

"Who are these people?" Joaquin asked, struggling to suppress his anger at being so insulted in front of his men.

"They are my prisoners," Celia replied. "I am taking them to the Puka Inti."

"But, señorita," Joaquin protested. "They are dangerous. We will take them to the Puka Inti for you." The lieutenant reached toward them.

Joel tensed, ready to break the first arm that touched any of them.

"They are my prisoners," Celia sneered, "and I will take

them to the Puka Inti. I want him to know just who has been doing guard duty for him tonight." She gestured imperiously with Joel's Colt. "Now out of my way."

Joaquin saw the automatic for the first time. His face darkened with anger, but he and his men moved aside.

Celia, Joel, and Cathy all sighed with relief when they had managed to proceed safely past the guards.

"You sure didn't make any friends just now," Cathy whispered.

"They are all lecherous pigs," Celia replied ferociously. "They deserve far worse than that."

They crept across the darkened compound, toward one of the buildings that had shown up as heated during their initial reconnaissance. All three jumped as, off to their right, a single shot was fired. As Cathy and Joel exchanged worried looks, Cathy's Browning appeared in her hand.

They waited in the shadows while Celia went inside the building. After a moment she appeared in the doorway and waved. Cathy and Joel ran up the stairs and into the building. "In here," Celia said.

They followed her into an interior room.

"Now," Joel said grimly, "we wait."

He retrieved his gun from Celia. With a swift, savage motion he slammed the ammunition clip back into it.

Gun in one hand and Anne's hand in the other, Jake crept cautiously along the back edge of the compound. They were working their way along behind the last row of buildings toward the tunnel when a rustling in the bushes made them freeze. Jake dropped into a crouch and pulled Anne down beside him. He looked around, but saw nothing.

Anne lost her balance and leaned against Jake. To steady himself, Jake knelt. As his knee touched the ground, something beneath him squealed. Jake and Anne shot to their feet. Jake looked down and found his Colt aimed at a small rodent.

"What is it?" Anne whispered.

"A cuy," Jake replied. "Very good with mustard sauce. C'mon. We need to keep moving."

"Wait," Anne said. "You ate one?"

"Sure. The other night, at the hotel."

"Did you eat it whole?"

"No," Jake replied. "I tore it apart first."

"Jake MacIntyre, you are disgusting!" Anne spoke too loud. Startled, the cuy scurried off into the undergrowth.

Jake shook his head. *I don't even want to know*, he thought. He took Anne's hand. "Let's go."

They crept along a narrow lane formed by the backs of Inca buildings and the base of the mountain called Machu Picchu.

"Should be right around here somewhere," Jake told Anne. He swept the embankment with the flashlight. A glint caught his eye. "There!" he exclaimed, pointing with the light.

The grate was set between the ruins of two Inca walls. Jake reached into his pocket, then fought off a moment of panic when his groping fingers failed to find the keys. *You put them in your right-hand pocket*, he chided himself, *because when Celia gave them to you, your left hand was full of .45 automatic.*

Jake took out the keys and stuck one of them into the lock. *This had better work.* The first key didn't even slide into the lock. The second fit, but didn't turn. "It's always the last one you try," Jake muttered.

With the third key the lock clicked, and Jake pulled the grate open.

Cathy jumped as the outer door to the building banged open.

"Where have you been, Rafael?" Celia called out. "I've been waiting for you."

She was answered by loud footsteps and a torrent of angry, vulgar Spanish. The inner door crashed open. "I've been dealing with intruders," Cienfuegos shouted as he barged into the darkened room. "I haven't had time for you, you little—"

"Hello, Puka Inti. I hear that you've promoted yourself from professor to Red Sun."

Cienfuegos froze as he heard the voice of Joel Dryden. He slowly held up the lantern he was carrying.

Joel stood casually, his gun pointed straight at Cienfuegos's chest. "Nice place you have here."


Jake pointed the flashlight into the mouth of the tunnel and waved Anne in. "Ladies first."

Anne waited for him at the bottom of the steps that led down from the entrance.

Jake closed the grate behind him and made sure that it was locked. Then he jumped down beside Anne. "Ever been spelunking?" he asked her. "Come on. We need to get to where we can't be seen from outside."

They had just rounded a bend when Anne yelled. Jake looked up. She was holding one foot and grimacing with pain. "Sharp rock," she explained.

"Sorry," Jake said apologetically. "I didn't notice that you were barefoot."

He sat down on a boulder. "Here," he said when he had finished taking off his boots.

"But, what about your feet?" Anne protested.

"Got feet like leather," Jake replied. "Use the soles all the time to patch tires." He pulled Anne into his lap. "Put them on, and lace 'em up tight." Feeling that they were safe for the moment, Jake relaxed slightly and enjoyed the warmth of

Anne's nearness. When she was finished, he pushed her to her feet and stood up behind her.

"Better take your weight off that foot," he told her.

"And just how am I supposed to manage that?"

Jake put his arms around Anne's waist and turned her around. "Like this." He straightened up, holding her against him and lifting her feet off the ground.

"How's that?"

"I'm feeling better already."

# 72

"Search him," Joel ordered.

Cathy's efficient frisking produced only the snub-nosed revolver in Cienfuegos's holster. Careful to keep his hands in sight, the Puka Inti settled himself on the corner of a nightstand. Seemingly unruffled by the turn of events, he smiled sardonically at Joel.

*Cocky little sod*, Cathy thought. *You gotta grant him that.*

"I did not think that you would set foot on Peruvian soil again, Dr. Dryden," Cienfuegos remarked.

"I didn't think that I'd have to hunt you down again," Joel replied.

"I can understand that," Cienfuegos agreed. "Considering that the circumstances of our last parting would have given you ample cause to think me dead." He smiled at Joel. "That God of yours must be watching over me."

Joel nodded. "He must be. The good Lord watches over drunks and fools," he replied, noting with satisfaction Cienfuegos's scowl. "Or, so the old saying goes."

Cathy saw the men in the doorway behind Cienfuegos first. Even as she screamed "Down!" she bracketed the doorway with rounds from her Browning. A bullet knocked one of the men out of the doorway, making it easier for the others to return fire.

"Kill them!" Cienfuegos shouted as he threw himself on the floor.

Joel had relaxed a bit too much during his banter with the Puka Inti, and the first shot from the doorway caught him in the arm and spun him around.

Just as Cathy took out another of the men, a hand grabbed her hand.

Celia wrenched the Browning from Cathy's hand.

Cathy looked up, surprised. Then her expression turned to a scowl. "I never should've trusted you."

Celia waved the gun at her. "On the floor. With him."

Joel groaned as he inadvertently put weight on his wound. Cathy sat down next to him. "Let me see the wound," she said.

His hand was clamped over his upper arm. Blood seeped from between his fingers. Cathy pulled his hand away and examined the wound. "Not deep," she said. "But I bet it hurts." *It'll hurt a lot more*, she thought, *if you bleed to death from a severed brachial artery.*

"I'm glad to hear that," Cienfuegos said from where he stood over Joel. "I'm glad to hear that it's causing you pain, but not so much pain that you die before I'm finished with you."

Cienfuegos resumed his seat on the nightstand. "I remember your lecture at the university. All that nonsense about 'peaceful solutions to Peru's problems.' What has that peace that you always preached gained you?" The Puka Inti's smile was a glittering, evil thing. "Now I have a solution for the problem that you represent. An exceedingly violent one. I also have one for your daughter. Quite different than yours, but equally permanent. So bleed, Dr. Dryden. But not so copiously that Anne cannot watch you die, or so that you cannot watch her grow up very quickly at the hands of myself and all of my men."

Cathy kept her hand pressed tightly over Joel's wound. Once, in the desert, a cobra had reared up and looked at her. Now, she felt the same way.

"As for you," Cienfuegos said to Cathy, "I think I'll sell you to the tribe of natives who lives nearby." He smiled, and the cobra spread its hood. "If you're lucky, they'll use you for target practice. That way you'll be dead before they eat you."

He turned to his men. "Is that one dead?" he asked, nudging the inert form with his toe.

"No, Puka Inti," one man replied.

"Take him outside," Cienfuegos ordered. "Then bring me the woman prisoner."

He looked at Celia, long and hard. "Why should I trust you?"

"Why not?" she replied. "I've delivered them to you."

"Very well," Cienfuegos said. "Now leave. I'll talk with you later."

The men picked up their fellow guard and carried him off. Celia followed.

"See, Dryden," Cienfuegos remarked. "Violence wins again. It has won this time, and it will win in the end."

Joel looked up at his nemesis. "It cannot win what it has already lost, Rafael. The battle has already been fought, and peace has triumphed."

Cienfuegos made no reply. The tense silence grew taut as the minutes wore on.

"Leave Domingo with me," Celia told the men after they had reached one of the barracks. "I will tend to his wound. Go get the woman."

*I am sorry for disarming you, Cathy,* Celia silently apologized. *I did not want you to die needlessly.*

Domingo was still unconscious.Celia examined Domingo's wound, determining that it was not serious.

Celia went outside, to a shadowed area near one edge of the compound. She took Jake's radio out of her pocket. Celia examined it by the light of the lantern she carried and found a small dial. *Perhaps,* she thought, *this is like the other radios that I have used.*

As she put on the headset, she looked up into a winter night ablaze with stars. Just over her head, it seemed, shone the Southern Cross. Celia looked at it and remembered that her mother had always called God "El Padre de los Luces," the Father of Lights.

*Father of Lights,* she prayed as she looked up at the brilliant constellation, *help us now. You've taken your Son's cross up into the heavens for all to see.* Celia paused. *Please help us now.*

"Hello? Is anyone there?" she said as she began to turn the dial slowly.

"The woman is gone!" the men reported back to Cienfuegos.

"Idiots!" Cienfuegos snarled. "Find her! Only Celia would have moved her. Find Celia as well, and bring her to me."

The men raced out of the room.

"A reprieve, at best, Joel," Cienfuegos remarked. "The longer you make me wait to kill you, the longer it will take you to die."

# 73

Jake and Anne pushed their way through the screen of vines that hid the tunnel's mouth and stepped out onto the Inca Trail. Once out in the open, Jake snapped off the flashlight.

"Which way?" Anne asked. Jake put on the night-vision goggles and looked around. "The map Celia gave us showed Machu Picchu to the northwest of where you were. That means that the Southern Cross should be right about there." Jake turned and pointed to the constellation. "So," he told Anne, "we go to the right."

Jake grabbed Anne's arm as she took a step forward. "Mind the edge," he cautioned. Jake switched on the flashlight just long enough for Anne to see that the trail disappeared in front of her feet. Far below, the Urubamba crashed over the rocks in its bed.

"Didn't want to go swimming without me, did you?" Jake asked as Anne pressed back against him. "Let's go. Stay right behind me and step where I step."

Celia repeated her message into the radio. She didn't know even if it was working. She'd heard static and a funny whine coming from the speaker, but the voices she had hoped to hear never responded.

In the distance from the other side of the compound Celia heard the sound of Cienfuegos's men. They were shouting and running, coming closer.

Celia grabbed the radio equipment and melted deeper into the shadows at the edge of the compound. She found some leafy cover, and knelt down, holding her breath as the men rushed past her.

"Sorry," Jake sympathized as he helped Anne up. He let go of her hand, then noticed that his fingers were sticky.

"Which fall did you cut your hand on?" he asked. Despite Jake's careful guidance, Anne, hampered by the oversize boots and the darkness, had already slipped twice on loose rocks.

"The one before this one," Anne told him.

Jake pulled out his handkerchief and wrapped it around her hand. They went on.

Cathy didn't remember when Cienfuegos had begun his rambling monologue about the evils of capitalist imperialism, nor did she remember when she had stopped listening. She was concentrating on the large, menacing man with the luxurious handlebar mustache who stood behind the chair from which the Puka Inti was lecturing. The man never took his eyes off her, and the muzzle of his FAL automatic rifle never wavered.

The radio clipped to Cienfuegos's belt crackled into life. "Puka Inti," a voice reported. "Neither woman is in the compound, and the key to the tunnel grate is missing."

Cienfuegos looked at Joel. "How quaint," he said maliciously. "Our two heroines are helping one another across the cordillera as the hounds snap at their heels."

The look in his eyes made Cathy shudder.

"They shall soon find out that these hounds bite with far more than teeth."

Cienfuegos unclipped the radio and spoke into it. "Very well. Get the extra key out of my desk, then follow them through the tunnel. See to it that you catch them before they reach Machu Picchu."

Cathy glanced at Joel, who now had his hand clamped over his wound. The bloodstain on his sleeve had spread almost down to the cuff, and his face was an unhealthy shade of gray. Cathy had seen that color before, and she didn't like what it meant.

Jake tried to ignore the pain from a bruised knee as he helped Anne down a steep flight of Inca-built stairs. They were almost to the bottom when the heel of Anne's boot slipped and she sat down hard.

"You OK?" He could see Anne try to respond. "Get the wind knocked out of you?" he asked when she said nothing. Anne nodded.

Jake sat beside her. "We'll rest here a minute."

"I'm all right," Anne told him when she had regained her breath.

"You're doing fine," he assured her. "We should be almost there." *That's not really a lie, God,* Jake reasoned. *Since I have no idea where we are, we may actually be almost there.* He looked back along the trail. "I think that we're out of sight of the compound by now. Let's try the flashlight for a while."

The flashlight created a brilliant hot spot whenever he looked in its direction, so Jake took the goggles off. Suddenly, he realized just how dark it really was. Anne's face was no more than a pale oval in the starlight. "Sorry. I should've remembered how dark it is in the jungle at night." He pointed the light down the trail. "Let's go."

As the guards emerged from the tunnel, one of them pointed.

"Is that a light?"

"Where?" the leader asked. "Up there. On the trail, up ahead." The leader watched for a moment. Then he smiled, his teeth white in the starlight. "We have them. Report in."

Joel did not react visibly to the report that "the two women" had been sighted, and Cathy tried not to. Instead, she tried to think of how she could turn Cienfuegos's misconception about who was on the trail into a fatal error.

Cienfuegos walked over and nudged Joel with his toe.

Joel slowly opened one eye and looked at the Puka Inti.

"You present me with a dilemma, Joel," Cienfuegos remarked. "You appear to be trying to cheat me out of the privilege of killing you myself." He gestured with his revolver. "So the question is, Do I kill you now, or hope that you can last until they return with your daughter?"

The guards crested the Hill of the Sun Gate, the guardhouse that had protected Machu Picchu in Inca times. The trail ran downhill straight away from them, and they could see Jake's flashlight clearly in the darkness ahead. One of the three knelt and unslung his rifle, a Weatherby .460 Magnum that he had bought while big-game hunting in Montana. It annihilated whatever it hit, and he was very proud of it. He looked through the powerful scope and moved the rifle until the bobbing flashlight came into view. *Sight slightly to the left of the flashlight,* he reminded himself, *to hit the center of the torso.*

The man held his breath, then squeezed off the shot.

The bullet caromed off the rock next to Jake with a sharp *whee.* Jake grabbed Anne's hand and pulled. "C'mon!" he barked. He opened the flashlight up to its widest beam. They raced off down the trail.

"You idiot!" the leader of the guards roared. He clubbed the kneeling man on the side of the head with his pistol. "They are unarmed and don't know that we're here. We have orders to bring them back, and you shoot?" The leader started down the trail. "After them!"

The Puka Inti looked up sharply as the sound of the shot echoed through the valley. *Rats*, Cathy thought. *If only the guard had flinched, too.*

"If those fools kill them . . . " Cienfuegos muttered darkly. He reached for his radio.

The trail widened slightly. Jake and Anne ran beside each other. They rounded a slight curve and nearly slammed into the first of a series of short pillars set into the trail.

"Down!" Jake ordered. He pushed Anne down behind the second of the pillars. Then he turned around and crouched behind the first. Jake drew his automatic and used the top of the pillar to brace the weapon. He sighted along his outstretched arms. "Come on," he breathed. "Come to Papa. . . . "

Three points of lights appeared as the guards crested a hill above Jake and Anne. Jake aimed at the middle of the three and slowly pulled the trigger. He waited just long enough to see one of the flashlights go spinning up and out over the edge of the cliff before he grabbed Anne's hand and pulled her to her feet.

The man with the rifle looked up at his leader. Blood from the wound in his thigh began to form a puddle on the ground. "They are unarmed, you said?" he gasped from between gritted teeth.

At the sound of the second shot, the Puka Inti rose. "It would appear that those fools are going to disobey me after all," Cienfuegos remarked. "Well, I shall deal with them after they have brought back the bodies."

The Puka Inti stood over Joel, drew his pistol, and aimed it at Joel's forehead. Joel stared back at him, his face expressionless.

"A pity that it ends this way," Cienfuegos said. "There will be so little pain, so little terror." He placed his thumb on the hammer and pulled it slowly back.

Cathy closed her eyes, unable to bring herself to watch Joel's life end.

# 74

Anne stumbled. She fell against Jake, almost knocking him over. They stopped and sat down in the shelter of a large rock.

"We're nearly there," he encouraged her. He pointed as they fought for breath.

Anne looked up and gasped.

Jumbled, roofless buildings lined both sides of the valley that stretched away before them to the northwest. The lightless interiors of the ruined structures, surrounded by stone walls silvery in the moonlight, made it look to Anne as if the valley walls were littered with inkwells.

Terraces, edged with the same glistening stone, stair-stepped their way down to a rectangular central plaza. On a squared-off hill a large building and its courtyard shone white. The leaves of a tree rustled in the wind, and somewhere water trickled and splashed.

The bowl of the valley was echoed by the dome of the night sky. At the far end of the ravine, the throat of a dead volcano was an upthrust fist that blocked out part of the Milky Way's view of the ancient city of Machu Picchu.

"We'll head for that big open area," Jake told Anne.

"But," Anne protested, "they'll see us out in the open."

"That's the idea," he assured her. "I'm hoping that some-one—a guard or caretaker or night watchman—will see us first."

Anne leaned against him. "I can't go much farther."

"You won't have to. Feel behind you." Anne reached behind her. Her hands felt the smooth texture of Inca stone-work.

Running footsteps sounded on the trail above them. Hand in hand, Jake and Anne began the long, downhill run to the lost city of the Incas.

An explosion of sound filled Cathy's ears.

For an instant she thought that Cienfuegos had pulled the trigger. But a thunderous noise was coming from outside the hut. Cathy opened her eyes and caught the tail end of a brilliant flash of light, now dimming. Cathy looked at Cienfuegos and the guard.

The Puka Inti had his face buried in the crook of his arm, and the eyes of the guard with the mustache were tightly shut.

As Cathy sprang, she noticed that it seemed to be daylight outside. She hit the guard and sent him sprawling. He came to his knees. Cathy grabbed his rifle out of his hands and cracked its butt across his jaw.

*Just like they taught me in boot camp*, she thought as he slumped over.

Cathy heard a scuffle break out behind her. She spun around, ready to shoot the Puka Inti. Instead, she found Joel on his feet. Joel had Cienfuegos's revolver pressed against the Puka Inti's temple. The hammer was still cocked.

Very slowly, it seemed to Cathy, the light and sound coalesced into something landing in the courtyard of the com-pound. *Either that's a helicopter coming in*, she thought, *or all the*

PART III

*things the tabloids say about Machu Picchu being a spaceport for UFOs are true.*

A low growl from Joel distracted her. He stared at Cienfuegos, his face a mask of hatred. One of his arms hung uselessly, but Cathy could see the trigger finger on the other begin to tighten. *I'm not going to turn away this time,* she told herself. *I'm not going to miss seeing this one die.* She heard men running across the compound toward the hut. *Hurry up, Joel. Shoot!*

"Leave room for God's wrath." Cathy spoke before she realized what she had said. Suddenly her mind was filled with words. "Remember?" she told Joel.

"You said that to Jake the night he found out what Hassan had done to Anne. Jake was furious at himself for not having personally killed Hassan. You shook your head and told him, '"It is mine to avenge; I will repay," says the Lord.'" Cathy hardened her tone. "So how come that doesn't apply to you?"

Joel didn't move. His gun hand trembled and sweat beaded his forehead.

Booted feet raced toward them through the outer room of the hut. Cathy had to relinquish the decision to Joel. She whirled to face the door.

A man burst through, his revolver out and ready.

It was Wes.

Jake pulled his head back as a bullet slammed into the turf in front of him.

"You're right," he whispered. "We are lost." Jake's plan for rescue had fallen apart. Machu Picchu was deserted, and they had quickly gotten turned around in the maze of passages that honeycombed the southern side of the Inca ruin. Now they lay on one of the grassy terraces that surrounded the city's central courtyard.

469

"Were you ever a Girl Scout?" he whispered.

Anne stared at him, then nodded.

"Good," Jake finished. "Then *you* can get us out of here."

Anne looked around. "Let's keep working this way," she suggested. Anne pointed southward, toward the hill outside the ruins where the lights of the Hotel Turistas shone so tantalizingly.

Jake started away, then stopped when he realized that Anne was not behind him. He turned and found her sitting on the grass. "Hurt?" he asked when he had raced back to her.

"No," she replied. "But now that we're on grass I want to take off these horrid boots."

They ran through the ruined homes of Machu Picchu, toward the beckoning lights.

Jake snapped off a shot at a ghostly figure that appeared at the end of an alleyway. The figure shot back wildly, then disappeared. Jake and Anne rounded a bend in the path they were following.

Anne pointed. At the end of the path was a gate, the exit from Machu Picchu. Jake tried the handle on the gate. It was locked.

"*Open up!*" Jake bellowed as he pounded on the gate.

Anne screamed.

Jake whirled around. The path that led to the gate opened onto the main plaza of the Inca city, and as they watched, two figures ran across the plaza.

At Anne's scream the figures turned and ran straight at them. Jake shoved Anne behind him. *If they're going to get Anne,* he told himself, *they'll have to go through me.* He felt Anne's hands on his shoulders as he took his Colt in both hands and aimed it at their pursuers.

Four heads looked to the southeast as the plaza was flooded with light. With a clattering roar a helicopter rose out of the valley and hung suspended in the sky over the ruins. The two men in the plaza turned and fired at the helicopter. Sparks appeared on both sides of the gunship as it fired a burst from its machine guns. Turf exploded around the men. The two threw themselves out of the helicopter's spotlights and disappeared into the darkness.

The helicopter pivoted, turning its lights on Jake and Anne. Jake pumped two bullets into the lock, then threw his shoulder against the gate. The lock fell apart as the heavy gate swung slowly open. Just in front of them a lighted path curved around a bend in the mountain. They sprinted through the gate. The hotel was no more than a hundred yards away.

The downdraft from the helicopter's rotors beat against them as the gunship passed over their heads. It swung around to face them and fired. One of the pathway lights exploded in a shower of sparks as a bullet tore through it. Through her bare feet, Anne could feel the bullets slam into the asphalt ahead of them. The helicopter edged forward, herding Jake and Anne back through the gate and into the central plaza of the Inca city.

The gunship drifted slowly across the plaza. It settled to the ground across the plaza from Anne and Jake. Jake kept his Colt trained on it. *If nothing else, God*, he prayed, *let it be quick.* The helicopter sank into the grass as it landed. With a whine the jet turbines slowed. The hatch on the side of the fuselage facing them opened. "Come and get us!" Jake roared defiantly.

"Why?" Cathy's amplified voice responded from inside the helicopter's cabin. "The marines always rescue the army. So does that mean that we have to carry you, too?"

# 75

"Jake," Joel said after the pandemonium had died down, "meet Captain Gustavo Akimoto of the Peruvian Air Force. He's the pilot of this flying machine gun." A tall, thin man stepped out of the helicopter and walked over to them.

"I can't thank you enough, Captain," Jake began.

Akimoto gestured dismissively. "It is my pleasure. I was the pilot on that search and rescue mission to the downed 727. The Puka Inti's men ambushed the ground team after we landed." Hatred flared in the pilot's eyes. "I could do nothing to assist them," he said helplessly. "So when Señorita Reyes's call came in and Wes asked me for transportation, it was a chance to avenge my butchered friends."

"Pretty clever of Celia to call in the cavalry," Jake said approvingly. He grinned and winked at Celia, who smiled shyly.

"You sure you're all right, Daddy?" Anne asked as she finished dressing her father's wounded arm.

"He's all right," Cathy assured Anne. "He even faked me out about how bad off he was." She grinned. "Never seen anyone so near death move so fast."

Joel inspected his daughter's handiwork. "Nice job, Angel." He put his good arm around his daughter and held her close. "Thanks."

"What happened to Cienfuegos?" Jake asked.

Cathy and Joel exchanged a long look. "He's in custody back at his encampment. Captain Akimoto will see that he's taken care of." His eyes met Jake's, and a bond of hatred overcome was forged between them.

Cathy turned to Wes. "I thought we left you in Lima."

"You did," Wes explained. "The second copy of the tape arrived, and I called your hotel in Cuzco. But when they told me that you had all checked out, I decided to come up and have a look-see for myself. I just happened to run into Gus as he was trying to figure out who Celia was and why she was talking on a military frequency."

"But," Jake asked, "why didn't they hear you coming? Gunships like this aren't exactly quiet."

"That," Wes replied, "was Aki's doing. It's a trick used during raids on coca-processing labs out in the jungle." Wes pointed into the starry blackness. "We came up the valley we're in now, the one that leads up to Machu Picchu. The ridge between this valley and the one where Cienfuegos was based absorbed the sound. At the last moment, Aki zoomed up over the ridge and into the camp. We hit the spots to blind them, then went on in."

"How did you manage to avoid being blinded?" Cathy asked Joel.

Joel smiled. "I've got good ears."

"Wes, I guess I underestimated you," Jake said.

Wes smiled. "In Joel's and my line of work, being underestimated is the best thing that can happen to us. Anyway," he said as Anne came over, "you don't think that I risked my neck for you, do you?" Wes strolled off to join Akimoto.

A moment later Joel snapped his fingers. "I forgot to tell

you, Annie, but there's someone here who's rather annoyed at you."

"What on earth are you talking about, Daddy?" Anne asked.

Joel pointed toward the helicopter.

Lee stepped out into the searchlight's glare. She held a bundle under one arm. Her hands were on her hips, and she looked mad.

"Wes ran into her as he was leaving the embassy to go to Cuzco," Joel explained. "When she found out where he was going, she made it very clear that this time there was no way that she was going to be left behind."

Lee glared at Anne. Anne's colorful Quechua clothes glowed in the brilliant light, she was barefoot, and her shaggy hair was tousled by the evening breeze.

"How dare you, Annie Laurel Dryden!" Lee stamped her foot. "Here I come all the way from America to bring you new clothes, and just look at you!" Lee started to cry. "You look won—" She dropped the bundle. Lee ran toward Anne, sobbing. Crying just as hard as Lee, Anne dashed across the grass and threw her arms around her friend.

Finding himself alone, Jake wandered back into the moonlight. Standing on the edge of a terrace, he looked across the home of a lost warrior race. *How many battles have been fought here?* he wondered. *And in those battles, how many times did good overcome evil like it did tonight?*

Jake looked up. Poised in the midnight sky was the Southern Cross. *It's not how many times evil has triumphed that matters*, he realized. *It's the fact that, in the end, righteousness will.*

A sound caused Jake to turn his head. Anne was standing beside him. "I don't know how to begin to thank you," she told him quietly.

Jake smiled. "I do."

Softly, gently, lingeringly, Jake kissed Anne. *That one's for you, Brit.*

He swept her into his arms. *And this one's for me. . . .*